A TIME FOR DEFIANCE

Books by James D. Shipman

TASK FORCE BAUM

IRENA'S WAR

BEYOND THE WIRE

BEFORE THE STORM

A TIME FOR DEFIANCE

Published by Kensington Publishing Corp.

A TIME FOR DEFIANCE

JAMES D. SHIPMAN

KENSINGTON
PUBLISHING CORP.

kensingtonbooks.com

This book is dedicated to the members of the Dutch Resistance, who bravely fought the tyranny of the Nazis, often giving everything, to keep the flame of freedom alive in the Netherlands.

Chapter 1

Oorlog

War. The radio vomited the threat, screeching of tanks and troops menacing the border. "What do you think now?" Aafke Cruyssen asked her father, as she flipped an egg crackling in the pan. She crossed herself, saying a quick prayer for her country and her family. The impending invasion was all the talk that morning when she'd attended her morning mass at Sint Catharinakerk.

"It's a load of dung," he said, shaking his head. "We've heard it all before. The Germans passed us by in the last war and they'll do so again. We don't have anything they want." He switched the radio off in disgust. Her father reached for a pot, pouring a steaming cup of coffee. He lifted the drink toward his lips and then hesitated. Glancing at his daughter, beneath thick peppered eyebrows, he set the mug down and reached up to the cupboard, extracting a bottle. He twisted the top off and poured some amber liquid into the coffee.

"It's not yet seven," Aafke protested.

"Bah. It's just a drop for warmth."

"It's May, Father."

He pushed past her and shuffled toward a cluttered table. "There's still a chill in the air. Now to business. Arno is expected at eight. You'll help him unload while I do the inventory. Understood?"

She nodded. Taking down two plates, she placed some fried ham and eggs on each, and brought them to the table. Her father dug into the food, his eyes scanning the morning paper. "All these fools can talk about are the Germans," he said. "As if we didn't have enough problems already. Worked themselves into a right panic they have. Now they've gone and taken my boy to the front for no reason, half my children, and the better half at that."

"Father!"

He looked up. "Don't pay me any mind," he said. "You do the best you can. But a skinnier little mouse I've never seen. I don't know why I bother feeding you, none of it ever reaches your bones." He took a deep drink of his coffee. "Bring the pot over, won't you? And the bottle."

She hadn't taken a bite yet, but she complied with his request. She thought about leaving the spirits behind, but she knew there was no point. "I wonder where Christiaan is?"

"At the front!" he snapped, finishing his first cup, and pouring a second. This one was equal parts coffee and brandy. "Those bastard Germans better not come."

They ate in silence, his face buried behind the news. After a while he crumpled the paper and pushed back his chair, draining his cup with the same motion. "Well, I've got to get ready for the delivery," he announced. "Attend to those dishes but do it quickly, mind you. I need you downstairs when Arno arrives."

Aafke rinsed the plates and scrubbed the pans, her thoughts on her brother. Christiaan was a year younger than she, just turned eighteen. He'd had a bare few weeks of training before his unit was rushed to the front. There hadn't even been time for a leave home, just a few hastily scribbled letters. *What good would it do?* she wondered. The rumors of what the Germans had done in Poland haunted her. Tanks rolling through the country, crushing everything in their wake, while airplanes streaked out of the sky, bombing and burning. What chance did her peaceful little country have against all of that? Mustn't think about it right now. Perhaps her father was right. Maybe the Germans would leave the Netherlands alone like they did in the last war?

"Aafke!" Her father's piercing shout rang up the stairs. "Haven't you finished yet? Get yourself down here!"   ·

She set the towel aside, glancing at the half-finished chores. She would have to attend to the rest of it at the end of the day. Aafke peered out the window. The sky-streaked blue, dotted with a few cotton clouds. It would be a beautiful day. And a warm one.

"I said get your behind moving!"

Hurrying down the narrow staircase, she opened the door at the bottom and entered their little store. Her father was at the counter, scribbling notes in a dusty ledger. "It's about time. Arno will be here in the next half hour. We've got to make room for the delivery. With all these war rumors, we should do a right brisk business," he said, rubbing his hands together. "With any luck, we can catch up on the rent and get that bastard landlord Beek off our backs."

Scrambling around the narrow room, Aafke combed the cluttered counters, straightening cans and stacking produce. She tried to weed out some of the overripe fruit, but her father shook his head. "It's still edible. Put the ripest at the top and turn it to its best side." She followed his instructions, but when he wasn't looking, she tossed a few of the worst specimens into the trash.

Aafke could hear the street outside already bustling, cars

rumbling by, drowning out the chirping and chatter of pedestrians hurrying to work or on some errand or another. Today Aafke could smell something different though. An urgency. An escalated pitch to the bustle. She was about to comment on this to her father when the front door of their store banged and rattled as if someone was trying to force their way through. It couldn't be Arno, that wasn't how he knocked and, in any event, he wasn't due here yet. Whoever it was started banging violently on the glass. With the blinds closed Aafke couldn't be sure who they were or what they wanted.

"For God's sakes girl, find out who is making that infernal racket," her father ordered. She stepped over to the door, turning the blinds before breathing a sigh of relief. It was only Mrs. Smit, their neighbor across the way. Aafke glared down through the window at her, a ruffled dump of ill-fitting clothes topped off with a mop of iron-gray hair. There was little Mrs. Smit didn't know about the neighborhood, and less she wouldn't share.

"Open the door, you foolish girl!" she demanded. "I need to speak to your father."

Aafke looked back at Maarten. They didn't normally let anyone in before the store was open. He nodded once without looking up. "Do as she says." She reached up to the lock, turning it halfway and beckoning for the woman to enter. Mrs. Smit shoved forward and slammed into the glass.

"It's still locked!"

Smiling to herself, Aafke turned the knob the rest of the way and opened the door. Mrs. Smit waddled past her, glaring and huffing. "Honestly, Maarten," the woman said to her father, "is the girl simple?"

"I'm right here."

"And lucky your father has a kind heart to keep you."

A kind heart and free labor, she thought. "What's the news?" Aafke asked, diverting the conversation to Mrs. Smit's favorite topic: neighborhood gossip of any kind.

The woman's lips curled around her ears. "Do you know the Jansens?"

"From over on Bergstraat?" asked Maarten. "I do. The husband's some big shot at Philips, isn't he?"

"The same. But he won't be feeling so fine right now. Their daughter is with child, and no father to claim him."

"Jesus, Joseph, and Mary!" exclaimed her father, clapping his hands. "The little flower couldn't keep her petals to herself, aye? That will knock him out of his tower. Hah! What will the neighbors say?"

"They'll say plenty," said Mrs. Smit. "She'll have to go to Amsterdam or the country to have it. Still, the damage is done."

"I'd not be surprised if he loses his post at Philips," said Maarten. "Those prim and proper pricks won't like that, not one little bit."

"You two should stop clucking over there like a couple of chickens," said Aafke, the words slipping out of her mouth before she could stop them.

Mrs. Smit gave her an appraising eye. "You better be careful yourself, girly," she said.

"Now, now," said her father. "Look at her. Skinny as a broom and pale as skim milk. There are no boys lined up outside this store, I can assure you that."

"Father!" The words seared her, and she saw Mrs. Smit's eyes dance and dart.

"You've hit home there, Maarten, I fancy."

Aafke wanted to retort but she was distracted by the commotion outside. Voices were rising and shouts could be heard.

"What's all the barking about?" asked her father.

Mrs. Smit turned and cocked her ear for a second. "I almost forgot. That's the second piece of news. The reason I came here in the first place."

"And what news is that?"

"It's war."

"What?" asked Aafke.

"War. It started a half hour ago. The Germans are coming."

Aafke and her father said nothing for long moments. This only seemed to increase Mrs. Smit's satisfaction, and her sly smirk stretched until it threatened to swallow her face. "I figured you didn't know. Why don't you have your radio on?" She drew herself up as if she'd finished a long list of chores. "Well, I must be going. Much to do and much to see." She shuffled back out of the store, leaving them in a stunned silence.

"I can't believe it," said Aafke, finally.

"I knew it would come," her father answered.

"You've said nothing of the kind. With all your talk of them passing us by."

"Keep those lips shut now!" he warned. "Get back to your work. I've got to think."

She tried to busy herself with straightening again, but her mind raced. The Germans were invading her country. They were at war. What would happen next? Would the English and French come and save them? Could their own little army hold back the Nazis until help arrived? Their own army! "My God, Christiaan!" she stammered out loud.

"Is that thought just occurring to your dim little mind?" her father said. "Yes. My boy is in a fight now." He shook his head. "God help him."

"God help all of them," she said, closing her eyes and whispering a silent prayer.

Her father merely grunted. Glancing down at his watch, his forehead furrowed. "Where's that Arno? It's ten past the hour. He should be here by now."

"I don't know," she said. "He's rarely late."

"Well, don't just stand there with your mouth open. Honestly, I don't know what to do with you. You spend half the day in Mass, then you lounge around when there's work to be done. You're as useless as he is. Go out there and find him!"

Outside? Aafke froze. There was a war on now. Was it safe to go out? She felt a flash of shame. Her brother was on the front lines, facing tanks and bullets. Surely, she could find the courage to walk a few blocks in her hometown. The Germans couldn't reach them this quickly, could they?

"Are you still here?"

"Going now." She stepped around the counter and reached up to retrieve a coat off the handle. It was still early and there might be a chill after all. She turned to her father, but he was deep in his ledger, scribbling notes while he sipped another cup of coffee, probably laced with more brandy. She hurried away and out the store on to Julianastraat.

She was surprised to see the sun still shining and the sky as blue as ever. So strange that nature could ignore the end of the world. Pedestrians hurried this way and that, some she even recognized. But there were no friendly greetings this morning. Faces everywhere were set in a granite grimace, the color drained out like so many corpses. Everything had changed in an instant, Aafke realized, and she wondered if it would ever be the same again.

Striding down the street as quickly as she could, she passed Mauritsstraat and 't Vonderke streets, finally reaching Nassaustraat. Arno's flat was on the opposite end of the street. She moved on and soon found herself at his garage. The double doors had been painted blue at one point but were so chipped and scratched that one had to search to find specks of the original color. A rusted chain held the two sides together, an uneven crack an inch or more wide gaping between them. She stepped up and pressed her face into the chasm, straining to see. After a few moments her eyes adjusted, and she could just make out that the truck was gone.

Arno wasn't here. Had she just missed him? How would

that even be possible? His route to the store would have followed the same streets she just walked. Surely, she would have seen him driving by. But she had been thinking about the war. Was it possible he'd passed her, and she hadn't noticed? No, she was sure she hadn't seen him. But what did that mean? She decided she would wait a few minutes for him before she returned to the store. Maybe he had another delivery before theirs this morning and the war news had delayed him? Yes, that made some sense.

The street here was deserted and the buildings blocked out the sun. Aafke slipped to the other side of the street where she could at least feel the warmth on her face while she waited. Minutes ticked by with no sign of Arno. She didn't have a watch and now she wasn't sure what to do. What if he had taken a different route and was already at their store? Her father would be furious.

She decided she should start back. She twisted that direction and had taken a few steps when she heard the noise. A buzzing off in the distance. She peered up and could see little black dots in the sky. Frozen, she watched in horror as they grew closer, emerging like little silver eagles out of the azure background. They were heading right for her. The rumbling grew until it was a deafening roar. There were two of them, and they were flying so low she feared they would crash into the buildings above her. They roared past like thunder, a few feet over the rooftops. The wind nearly blew her off her feet. Her eyes caught a flicker of black crosses. They were German planes, fighters it seemed to her eye. Her heart shuddered and thumped. She fell to her knees, her breath coming in rapid gasps. The planes shrunk away in moments, until they were little specks again, the sound fading with them. Her eyes were clamped shut, knees skinned beneath her dress from the pavement. She knelt there, shaking, unable to move. *God help us!*

A hand touched her back. She flinched, trying to jerk away.

"Aafke, it's all right," came a familiar voice. She opened her eyes to see Arno leaning over her, eyes searching hers, concern creasing his face. She took a deep breath as he extended a hand and pulled her firmly to her feet. She was surprised at the strength beneath the wiry frame. For a moment she could only look at him, eyes nearly even. He was a decade older than her but a hard life had ground and chiseled his features. "Are you all right?" he asked.

She pulled her hand away, taking a deep breath. "It's nothing," she said. "I was startled by the airplanes."

"I saw them," he said. "The bastards are already flying over us. And where is our air force? Our Queen has been too busy giving butter to the rich, and now we'll all pay for it."

"Where have you been?" she asked. "We were expecting you hours ago."

He grunted. "Her Majesty's government apparently didn't have time to invest in transport either. Some police showed up an hour ago and confiscated my truck. They told me I would be compensated . . . later."

"How awful," she said. She looked more closely and saw a deep bruise on his right cheek. "Did they beat you?"

Arno's lips twisted in a wry grin. "You know me, Aafke. I never liked the police much. I argued with them a bit. Several of those bastards got worse than this, I can tell you that."

"And they didn't arrest you?"

He shrugged. "Too busy with the war, I guess."

"How can we get our delivery now?" she said, almost to herself.

"No point trying," he said. "I doubt the wholesaler would even release the goods. Everything's changed with the invasion. But that's not what you should be worrying about."

"What do you mean?"

"If things go badly, like they did in Poland, the Germans are going to take this city, and take it fast. What do you think all those hungry soldiers are going to do with your store? They'll snatch everything up in a day, and you'll have nothing for yourselves, nothing to trade. The food and other goods you have at your store right now are going to be scarce soon. You need to find a place to hide as much as you can. All the canned goods and items that will last. If the Germans do take over, you'll need everything you can save in the coming months to survive."

She hadn't thought of that. He seemed to see the world, to see through things, to see through her. "What are we going to do? We don't have any place to hide things, and nothing to use to move it."

Arno thought for a second. "I might be able to get another vehicle from somewhere. And we could store the goods in my garage. It doesn't have much use at this point anyway, and I doubt those government swine will return my truck or pay for it, whether we win or lose."

"Could you do that Arno? Could you help us?"

"I'll see what I can do." He looked at her. "But you need to get back to the store. Close it up right now until I can get there. With the war, people will be stocking up, trying to buy as much as they can carry. They'll pick you clean maybe, before the Germans even get here. Don't let them. Lock the doors and wait for me."

"I can't do that. They're our neighbors, our friends."

"To hell with them. It's every man for himself now."

"Why are you helping us, then?" she asked. A flicker of emotion crossed his face for just an instant before it was gone, replaced by that set grin that could mean anything or nothing.

"It's my storage space," he said. "I figure I'll have access to some of it, as a renter's fee." He laughed. "Sorry to deflate your opinion of me. I'm not as selfless as all that."

"You've always been good to my father and our family," she said.

He nodded. "Get yourself home as quickly as you can. Tell your father what I said to you. Get the shop closed and wait for me. I'll be there by early afternoon."

Aafke hurried back toward her home. There were more people on the street now, some staring up at the sky, others with suitcases in their hands, heading God knew where. She wondered why anyone would be fleeing and then it struck her. They must be Jews trying to escape the city. There were rumors about the Germans and their treatment of the Jews. Terrible stories that couldn't be true . . .

She wondered if Arno was right. Would the Germans occupy the city soon? If so, would they try to take everything they owned? He was correct about one thing for certain: if it came to that, having some items in hiding to sell later might be the difference between surviving or not. She hurried her step. She had to get to her father and close the store. Two blocks left and then one. Her breath was coming in ragged spurts as she moved as quickly as she could. She turned the last bend, and their corner came into view. She gasped and froze in place, staring. What were they going to do? In front of her was their store, the door open. And winding out of the entrance and down several blocks was a line of people, queued up to purchase everything they owned. The future was gone.

Chapter 2
Bliksem Oorlog

Friday, May 10, 1940
7:28 a.m.
Dutch Border, Netherlands

They stood bunched up on the near side of the bridge like so many runners waiting for the starting gun. The squad stuck together, jammed into the middle of the throng so tightly they could barely move their arms, although they managed to pass a thermos of tea back and forth for a swig or two. The captain didn't know it was laced with schnapps. That was strictly against the rules. But what the hell, they were heading into combat.

"What can you see, Otto?" one of the men inquired. He peered out over the mass of gray and green, squinting toward the far shore.

"Sheep," he said. "White ones and a cute little black one."

"Are they armed?" joked Lieutenant Fritz Geier, their platoon leader, cracking a crooked grin.

"I don't think so," said Otto. "But the black one keeps glancing this way. He could be a scout."

Fritz laughed. "What could they report at this point, Corporal? We've been sitting here for three days."

Otto grunted and, extending a limb, snatched the container of tea away from a private mid-drink and drew it back, smacking against the head of another man in the process. "Watch it!" the private protested. Otto tipped the metal sphere to his lips and drained it in a gulp.

"That's supposed to be for everyone," said Fritz.

"It can't be. It's empty. Besides, look up, we're crossing now."

The roar of engines mixed with a rising crescendo of voices as the soldiers and vehicles streamed forward, surging onto the bridge. Scattered shots rang out, clanging against the armor of their panzers, but Otto didn't see anyone hit. The defenders, such as they were, must have been few, and were skittish at that. After the first few retorts, they heard nothing else as they shuffled across the span and into Holland.

He waited for fear to hit him. The terror of combat all the veterans of the Polish war talked about—if you could get them to talk about anything. But he felt nothing. Well, that wasn't quite true. In reality he was elated—like he was back on the pitch waiting for a match to start, standing like a mountain in front of the goalie. Fritz had been there too, a skinny little forward rushing to and fro. But this wasn't a game anymore. You could die here. He was surprised he didn't feel the fear. He could smell it around him, taste it in the wooden movements of his squad mates. He grunted, burping up a little schnapps. He would worry later.

They scrambled down a ditch to their right as they hobbled off the bridge, fanning out, rifles at the ready. The ground sloped upward, away from the river through a field of thick grass, toward a farmhouse at the crest of a gentle hill. Fritz motioned for them to halt while he scanned the ridgeline, looking for enemies. "Nothing," he said, finally. "Not a one."

"We should take a prisoner for questioning," said Otto, nodding toward the sheep.

"Questioning?"

"Well, dinner."

Fritz laughed. "Good idea." He fished a length of rope out of his pack and gestured to a couple of the men. "Go capture one of our little friends over there and we'll bring it along for a victory feast."

"Not the black one," said Otto.

"What difference does it make?" asked one of the privates.

"Not the black one."

The soldier looked as if he was going to say something else, but he broke off instead and headed toward the flock to secure their evening meal.

Fritz approached Otto. "Have you seen the captain?" he asked, looking around.

Otto scoffed. "He's probably still on the other side of the river, soiling himself from those sniper shots."

The lieutenant laughed. "We're better off without him. When we've secured the sheep, take two men and let's move up to that farmhouse. It's too close to the road to leave unattended. We'll cover you from here."

Otto nodded. Selecting Schmidt and Abel, two of his best men. He started up the hillside, gesturing for the privates to keep low and fan out. He unslung his Karabiner 98k and cranked the bolt, locking a round in the chamber. Glancing up, he scanned the farmhouse windows, searching for faces, but the glass was empty and dark. He gauged the distance, less than a hundred yards. He picked his way onward. The grass was knee high and the ground uneven.

Halfway up, Schmidt stumbled and fell. Otto turned to chastise him when a sharp crack of thunder pierced his ears. The private hadn't tripped after all. He was hit. Otto dropped into the grass, shouting at Abel to do the same. Rolling a few times to his left, he reached Schmidt. His legs were facing Otto and the ankles danced and shivered. He could hear a gurgling from the private's throat as the soldier thrashed about. "It's all right," whispered Otto. "You'll be all right. Fritz is right behind us with the rest of the platoon. We'll send the medic."

Another shot rang out and Otto was washed in hot liquid. He closed his eyes, his ears ringing, the taste and smell of metal filling him. He wiped his eyes with his sleeve and blinked several times. Schmidt wasn't moving anymore. Scenes flashed in his mind. The hours of training with this man. He remembered meeting his young wife when she visited the barracks one weekend. Schmidt who never stopped smiling, even at the end of a twenty-mile run. All of that was over now. He shook his head. He couldn't think about that.

Otto could feel his heart pulsing now with an intoxicating mix of anger and excitement. He'd seen the flash of the second shot from the farmhouse. He knew where the sniper was. He inched forward, dragging his rifle. A third shot rang out. Abel was hit this time, and the body shuddered for a moment, then was still. Otto reached the private, resting his head directly below the bottom of his boots. Abel was new to the unit. Arriving just a month ago. He'd quickly established himself as one of the top men in the platoon. Athletic, quiet, humble.

A fourth shot. He heard the bullet skip in the ground a few inches from his head. The sniper was persistent. Glancing down at his weapon he took a deep breath. Otto rolled to his right, coming to his knees and raising his rifle. A fifth shot rang out, missing to his left. He took aim and fired. His bullet ripped through the upper right-hand window of the farmhouse, shattering the glass. There was no sixth shot. Rising, he waved the platoon forward.

"Otto, get down, you idiot!" shouted Fritz. He'd hurried up with the rest of the men, weapons at the ready.

"He's dead."

"You don't know—"

"He's dead."

Otto turned and marched up toward the building. Reaching the back door, he kicked it open and rushed in, moving his rifle rapidly through the rooms. Not waiting for the rest to catch up, he stomped up the stairs, arriving on the second floor. He swept down to the last room on the right. It was a bedroom, a nursery with a crib and little stuffed animals covered in blood. A Dutch soldier lay flat on his back, a bullet hole in the middle of his forehead, eyes staring blankly at the ceiling, his face registering a vague surprise.

Otto stared at the soldier for a few moments, then nodded once and stepped back out of the room just as Fritz reached the top of the stairs. "Don't run ahead like that!" he said. "You could have been killed."

"He's dead," said Otto, stepping past the lieutenant and moving back down the landing. He searched around the first floor until he found the kitchen. Opening the covers, he found some bread in a brown paper wrapper. He took the loaf down and sniffed it. It was fresh. This would go nicely with the sheep. He stuffed the bread into the pack and stepped back outside, closing his eyes and letting the sun warm his face. He'd killed a man. His first. He'd seen two comrades die. What did he feel? He had to keep moving. He would think about Schmidt and Abel later. About the Dutchman, the nursery, and the blood.

A half hour later, they were rumbling along the highway in the open back of a two-ton truck, moving farther into Holland. The squad was tightly packed on benches, facing each other as the vehicle rumbled and rattled over potholes. Otto craned his neck, watching the farms and fields on the horizon. The men were quiet, eyes down, a few of them smoking. Only the sheep had anything to say, bleating loudly here and there out of fear or loneliness.

Otto glanced down at the back of the truck. Privates Abel and Schmidt were there, bodies covered by a blanket. Their first casualties. Otto looked away, taking a deep breath.

"What's next?" he asked Fritz. The lieutenant was seated to his right, puffing on a cigarette dangling from his lips while he ran his fingers along a map he was trying to study through the jostling ride.

"We're supposed to take this town," he said, pointing a finger at the paper. "There's a factory there the big chiefs want to collect."

"How far?"

Fritz glanced back down again. "Maybe thirty miles. They want us there today if we can make it."

"Thirty miles! The lines didn't move that far in the last war in four years."

Fritz smiled. "A different war, a different time. And they didn't have us back then. They didn't have the SS."

"Or the Führer."

Fritz nodded. "No, they had that *dummkopf* Kaiser Wilhelm. He's here, you know?"

"Here?"

"In Holland. He holed up here after we lost the last war, and the socialists tossed him out."

"Are we bringing him back to Germany?"

Fritz snorted. "I doubt it. I don't think our Führer wants any competition for the head job. No, Old Wilhelm is a useless museum piece now."

"And Hitler knows best, I suppose."

The lieutenant looked sharply at him. "Without question, Corporal."

Otto grunted. "How long until we get to the town?"

Fritz shrugged. "If the Dutch army doesn't show up, I'd say an hour or two."

"Time for a nap, then," said Otto.

"How could you sleep—after *that*?"

"I'm tired." Otto closed his eyes and, in a few moments, despite the bumping and rumbling, he was snoring away.

Thunder rattled him awake. A boom of artillery crackled through the air. Otto blinked and yawned, checking his watch. It was three in the afternoon. He turned to Fritz, who was smoking another cigarette. "Shouldn't we make camp soon?" he asked. "We've got a sheep to cook and that will take some time."

The lieutenant shook his head. "Do you hear that?"

Otto nodded.

"That's not ours. That's somewhere in front of us and command will want it silenced." He took another deep breath of smoke, closing his eyes for a moment. "Besides, there is a town to take."

"Towns have kitchens," said Otto. "Good for us, bad for the sheep. Why this town?"

"There is a Philips factory there. The boss wants it intact for after the war."

"Are we close?"

Fritz craned his neck. "Look there."

Otto shifted, slamming into Fritz's knees as he did so. Ignoring the protest from his friend, he glanced past the front of the truck and toward the horizon. There were houses in the distance, and a spire or two. "Doesn't look like much."

"There's more past that. A hundred thousand people live here."

"Lots of kitchens."

The column they were in slowed to a halt. Their company commander hopped out of the vehicle in front of them. He was as pale and blond as Otto, but could scarcely weigh half as much. He looked like a lanky strawman who could bend himself in half if he tried. He waved at the truck.

"Stay with the men," said Fritz, rolling his eyes. "I'll see what our *wunderkind* wants."

The lieutenant hopped out of the truck and strolled over to the captain. The booming of artillery was louder now that the convoy had stopped. It sounded like it might be coming from the town. Even as Otto watched, he saw a flash from the horizon and the whistle of a shell. The truck directly behind them exploded, the metal twisting and the vehicle bouncing ten feet in the air before it crashed back down into a ditch. Arms and legs, still with bits of uniform attached, tumbled in all directions. A charcoal cloud, mixed with fire, belched out of the vehicle. Wretched voices tore through the blackness, wailing for help.

Otto stared at the wreckage for long moments. His ears rang and he flinched from the heat of the fire. Fritz was sprinting toward him, motioning frantically for the men to flee the truck. Otto gestured to his men and, grabbing his rifle with one hand, hopped out of the back, landing hard on the gravel. He turned and helped the privates climb out, one after another, shoving them toward the field to their right where Fritz was organizing everyone.

He helped the last man out and started to move away when he realized that the bodies were still there. He reached in and lifted the stiff figure of Abel into his arms. Glancing up, he saw the sheep was still there. With a grunt, Otto set Abel down on the ground and pulled the animal into his arms.

Otto blinked, stunned. He felt the cold earth at his back. The blue sky was above him, the ringing in his ears threatening to crush him. He started to rise but a wave of dizzying nausea tore through him, forcing him back to the ground. A face appeared above his. It was Fritz, full of concern, mouthing something to him he couldn't understand. He closed his eyes for a few seconds, taking some deep breaths, and then pulled himself up to a sitting position. He was about ten yards from the road. Otto glanced over to their truck. It was in flames. He'd been blown away by a blast, he realized.

"Where's the sheep?" he asked.

Fritz's mask of concern shifted to a grin. "You lucky bastard. I thought you were dead!" The words were barely audible through the screeching ring in his ears, but Otto nodded. He looked around and the men were spread out, lying in the tall grass of the field, rifles ready. The body of Abel was a few feet from him, blown clear from the truck. The sheep was there too, grazing at a green stalk of grass, seemingly unfazed by the chaos around it. Otto glanced down at his uniform. There was blood everywhere, so he started patting his body, looking for wounds.

"It's from Abel," said Fritz. "His body took a bunch of the shell fragments. You're lucky to be alive."

"And Schmidt?"

Fritz shook his head, nodding back toward the wreckage. "Still in there."

Even as he said that another truck in the stalled convoy erupted in flames. Otto turned his attention to the fighting. The whole platoon was in the field, he realized, along with some men he didn't know as well from other parts of his company. A mortar team was in the process of setting up a dozen yards to his right, preparing to pour shells into those houses. Nobody seemed to be directing them. "Where's the captain?" he asked at last.

"He's gone," said Fritz. "The whole truck and everyone in it."

Otto thought about that. "Doesn't that put you in charge?"

Fritz nodded.

"You should be moving the men up toward the town and not worrying about me," said Otto.

The lieutenant smiled. "Right again. I just wanted to make sure you were still breathing. Can you move?"

Otto tested his limbs and moved his head to the left and right. The ringing wasn't getting any better and he felt dizzy, but he thought he would be okay to walk. At the worst he would crawl. "What are we going to do?" he asked.

"I've got Hansen on the radio, looking for a little air support or a panzer. If that's coming, we'll sit tight. If not, I'm going to lay some mortar shells up on the edge of those houses and we'll make our way up until we can find that gun and destroy it."

"Are you sure it's just one gun?"

Fritz nodded. "The shells have been coming in one at a time. I'm guessing it's just one crew, with maybe some infantry support, but no more than one squad, I'd wager. So far, I don't think there's been any rifle fire."

"Any idea where the gun is?"

"Not sure, but I think somewhere between or behind those two houses." The lieutenant jabbed a finger toward the ridge. Otto followed it until he could see where Fritz was pointing. He rolled over to his stomach and then pressed himself up to his knees. "Let's go."

Fritz crawled back to the other men, snapping out orders. Otto removed his canteen and took a drink of water, closing his eyes again to fight off another wave of nausea. He splashed some of the lukewarm liquid on his face. That would have to do. He watched the lieutenant motion to the mortar team. The leader nodded and took a shell with a three-pronged fin and dropped it backward into an angled tube, diving out of the way as he did so. The shell shot out of the cylinder and a moment later exploded a few feet in front of a house. The man reached down and adjusted the angle of the tube and dropped another shell inside. The second shot landed squarely on the roof of a house, exploding it in smoke and fire.

"Let's go!" shouted Fritz, motioning for the platoon. The men, about thirty of them, rose as one and ran toward the houses, their bodies as low as they could get, a soldier pausing now and again to fire his rifle. Otto followed, not bothering to crouch, stumbling along as quickly as he could. He wasn't particularly fast in the best of circumstances and the concussion from the blast made it difficult to move, but he kept going, keeping up with the men. They were two hundred yards away from the first houses, then a hundred.

A private in front of him snapped back, twisting around, and crumpling to the earth. Otto kept going, gripping his rifle tightly. Another soldier fell, and another. He caught a flash of fire ahead and made out a figure at the corner of one of the houses. Pausing to take aim, he waited until the man peered around the corner and then he pulled the trigger. His enemy jerked and fell backward, out of sight. Fritz motioned for them to keep moving as they were fifty yards away now. Otto turned his head back and forth, searching for the artillery piece. He couldn't see it. It had to be back behind some of the houses. A bullet whizzed by his head, and he reached out as if to bat it away. He knew what he had to do.

Chapter 3
Invasie

Friday, May 10, 1940
11:18 a.m.
Eindhoven, Netherlands

Aafke stood in stunned silence for a few moments, staring at the winding line of people, many whom she recognized. Neighbors, acquaintances, friends. Even now, several had seen her and were waving or shouting out a friendly greeting. They were all at her little family store for the same valid reason: War was coming, and they were stocking up for the storm.

But Arno said they would need these goods, that they could mean the difference between life and death in the coming months. If she did nothing, they would be picked clean in a couple of hours. Then what would she do? Trying to ignore the friendly gestures, she put her head down and marched toward the store, whispering a prayer to give her courage. Nodding briefly to nobody in particular, she pushed through the door and into the crowded building. She had to twist and turn to weave her way toward the counter. There was scarcely room to breathe. She glanced around at the shelves and saw with horror that they were already half empty.

"Aafke!" her father shouted, spotting her from the counter. "Can you believe this?" he said, jovially slamming the register shut as he completed another sale. "Come up here and give me a hand!" he ordered.

There were more gleeful shouts from those inside, many of whom held an armful of items and were already queued for the register. She kept pushing forward, trying to get to her father. Her mind reeled. What should she do? These were people who mattered to her. They were only trying to stock up a little in a crisis. She gritted and grinned, trying to fight through her emotions. Finally, she reached the counter and was able to step around. Her father's fingers danced on the register as he rang up the next sale, pausing only to take a deep drink from his coffee cup. She had little doubt what was inside.

"Here's my little broomstick!" he called out, raising his mug to her. "We've done a right brisk business this morning, my dear. I hope Arno's almost here. We'll be sold out by noon without him."

"I need to speak with you for a moment, Father," she said, as quietly as she could.

"I can't leave the customers," he said, turning back to the front as the next customer unloaded an armful of goods on the counter. "Thank God you're back. I need your help. And where is that Arno?"

"This can't wait," she whispered.

"Do you hear this?" her father shouted, turning to the customers, and laughing again. "The best day of business I've had in a year and a day, and my daughter wants me to take a break. Should I listen to her?" he asked.

"No!" the crowd shouted, amidst laughter and cheers.

"Ring me up first," demanded a stout elderly woman at the counter. Aafke didn't recognize her. That was unusual and she wondered if she'd come from another part of the city, perhaps going from store to store to stock up on supplies.

"We will be just a moment," she said, forcing a tight smile.

"Nonsense," said Maarten, his hands already reaching for the register again.

Aafke seized his wrist, pulling it back. Her father whipped around to face her, his features mottled with red splotches. He was angry now. She knew that look very well.

"I told you it can wait," he whispered through gritted teeth. "We have customers here and now."

"We have to talk, Father."

"Do you know what this means for us?"

"Now," she insisted, taking his arm, and tugging at him.

He jerked away from her, his face an angry mask. He turned to the crowd. "My daughter seems to think she's more important than all of you. I'm an indulgent father so I'll excuse myself and chat with her for a moment. But don't you worry, I'll be right back to ring you all up. Now no cutting!" he joked, to the laughter of the crowd. He flipped around and hurried up the stairs, his shoulders stiffening and his boots banging on the wood as he went.

Aafke knew just what awaited her. She steeled herself, hoping it would only be words this time. She closed the door behind her. Her father was already in the cupboard, filling his mug back up. He didn't bother with coffee this time.

"So just what the hell is so important that you are ruining the busiest day we've had in a year?" he demanded.

"Father, Arno said—"

"So, it's 'Arno says' now, is it?" he snapped. "You think he knows better than your own dad?"

"If you'd just listen—"

"No, you listen, my little daughter. We're three months behind on the rent," he said. "That bastard at Philips already threatened to take the store away—to take our flat from us. Did you see the line going down the street? We could make that up in one day. Today." He took a deep drink, smacking his lips as if to say that things were settled. "So just tell Arno to move his ass and bring our supplies. The sooner the better." He was already starting toward the door.

"There aren't any more supplies," she said.

"What do you mean, girl?" he demanded. "I've already paid for them."

"The government took Arno's truck this morning," she said. "And—"

"Well, too bad for Arno. But that's not our problem. We can find another transport."

"That's not all," she said. "Our supplier is refusing to make shipment. Arno said—"

"What does Arno know?" her father shouted. "We've got to have those goods. Did you go to the warehouse yourself?"

"No, Arno said I should come back, and we should hide as much as we can. He said with the war on it will be hard to get anything, and we can sell these things for much more. But later on."

Her father paused, his eyes flashing gold in the light. "Black-market goods, is it?" he mused, absentmindedly rubbing his chin. "There was a healthy trade of it in the last war. Hard-to-get items, extra food. Illegal, of course, but some people grew mighty fat on the profits." He turned back to Aafke. "You're right for once, or should I say Arno is right." He poured another finger of brandy into his cup. "A shrewd one, him. Well, he's right. That's exactly what we need to do."

Aafke drew a deep breath of relief. Only words.

Her father took another drink. "That's settled, then. Be a good girl and shoo those customers out, will you, while I do some figuring."

Aafke was shocked. "I ... I can't do that, Father. They'll never leave. You just told them to stock up and that we'd be right back down. We must at least sell to the people already in the store."

"Nonsense," he said. "They aren't walking out of here with what's ours. Just go down there and order them out. Christiaan would have done it for me. And he wouldn't whine and moan about it. Now get your bony tail down there before I give you something to really sulk about."

She felt the sting of the words, but she'd said as much as she dared. Aafke fled the flat, closing the door quickly behind her. She stood there on the stairway for a few moments, taking deep breaths, her eyes closed. She didn't know what she was going to say to the people below, most of whom she knew well, but better to face them than her father. . . .

She arrived back downstairs to cheers from the crammed mass. The store was hot and stuffy, the stale smell of fear and sticky bodies almost overpowered her. She wedged into the narrow space behind the register. The counter was piled high with goods, mostly canned food and sacks of flour and sugar. Things that would last for the coming uncertain weeks. Aafke glanced up and was surprised to see Mrs. Smit at the front of the line, squinting up at her with a toady smirk.

"I'm first," she asserted, shoving her way to the counter. "And be quick about it, girly, it's roasting in here."

Aafke took a deep breath. "I'm sorry—"

"What do you mean, you're sorry?"

"We have to close for the day." The words came out in a whisper, dodging and darting.

"What do you mean you're closed?" Mrs. Smit demanded. Voices behind her gasped and an angry murmur welled up in the crowd.

"Our deliveries were cancelled," she explained in a shaky voice. "We need to inventory our supplies today before we can reopen."

"Surely you can do that after hours?"

"I'm . . . I'm sorry, but it has to be now."

"And why is that?" she snapped.

"We just . . . we just have to."

Mrs. Smit fixed her with a shrewd gaze. "Hoarding it, are we?" she said. "Keeping it all to yourselves while the rest of us starve? I know that game and you're not going to do it to us!" she shouted, craning her neck toward the crowd. "Is she?"

"No!" came the answer. The crowd was angry now and pressing closer.

"If she won't sell us what we need, we should just take it!" someone shouted.

"Take the goods! Take the goods!" the press of people shouted.

"Father!" Aafke yelled. "Help!" But her father wasn't coming. He either couldn't hear her or didn't care. As Aafke watched in horror, the mob surged forward like so many grim automatons, shoving and pushing, filling their arms with everything they could reach. Mrs. Smit was still at the forefront, an ugly grin curling toward her ears. There was nothing Aafke could do. The shelves were nearly empty now and this gang of thieves, so shortly ago their neighbors, was already scrambling toward the entrance.

There was a rattling at the door, a loud pounding. "Let the others in!" shouted Mrs. Smit.

"No," mumbled Aafke listlessly, tears running down her cheeks, her whole body trembling. They were losing everything and there was nothing she could do.

A man reached the front. Juggling his load of goods, he reached out and flipped the lock. The door tore open instantly. Arno stood at the entrance, a wicked club in his hand.

"Arno!" Aafke shouted, relieved beyond measure to see him. "Help me!"

Without hesitation Arno waded into the crowd, not even bothering to speak. He struck the man who had unlocked the door a violent blow on his head. The gentleman crumbled to the floor, goods flying everywhere. There were gasps. Mrs. Smit's face flooded with fear. She unloaded her goods at the counter as rapidly as her fat fingers would allow, then waddled out of the store without another word. The others did the same, most simply dumping the items on the floor. There was cursing and threats, glass broken, milk and sauces mixed in a soupy mess. But under Arno's stern glare the mob was departing, two of them stooping down to scoop up the unconscious fellow Arno had struck and carry him out the door.

When the last person was gone, Arno flipped the lock again. He glanced down at it. "You'll need something more substantial than this," he said. "I'll bring you a chain later today."

"Oh, Arno!" she said, rushing over and throwing her arms around him. She sobbed into his shoulder. He wrapped his arms around her and held her tightly. She stayed there for long moments, absorbing his strength, calming herself. "They were going to take everything," she was finally able to say. "There was nothing I could do to stop them."

"Things are getting ugly quickly," he said, "and they will get worse. Where is Maarten?"

She hesitated, pulling away from him. "He's upstairs."

"No, I'm not," her father's voice wafted through the store. He was at the landing, mug still in his hand.

"Where have you been?" asked Aafke. "Didn't you hear me shout for you?"

"I had things to do," he said. "And I thought you'd be able to handle a simple task in my absence."

"Father, I—"

"It doesn't matter," he said. "Arno's here now." He turned away from her and toward Arno. "So, I hear you've hatched a plan to go into the black-market business with our goods? And you'll be wanting something for yourself from the bargain to be sure."

"I know conflict," said Arno. "I know what's coming." He glanced at Aafke. "I just want to help."

"By hiding our goods at your garage? That won't be for free."

"Nothing is free," said Arno. "Do you want my help or not?"

"What do you have in mind?"

"I've got a line on a horse and wagon. If I can get it, we'll load up as much as we can and take it to my garage. You keep enough here to do a little business."

"And then?"

"We wait. Prices will rise. Then we start selling, a little at a time."

"What's your take?" Maarten asked.

"Thirty percent."

"Ten."

"Twenty."

"Done," said her father.

Arno nodded and turned to Aafke. "It's settled, then."

"What do we do when the goods run out?" Maarten asked.

Arno shrugged. "One day at a time. But I've got contacts. Depending on what happens, I can help with that. But for anything I bring in, that I pay for, the percentages reverse."

"Agreed."

Arno glanced at his watch. "It's getting late. I've got to secure the wagon." He turned to Aafke. "Will you be all right until I return?"

"We've gone our whole lives without your help," snapped Maarten. "We can manage a few hours. Be on your way."

"Thank you," said Aafke.

Arno inclined his head and gave her a wink. "Don't worry yourself. I'll be back soon, and we'll get everything together. In the meantime," he said, glancing at the store, "you might want to clean up a bit."

She bristled a little at the suggestion. This was her house, her store. She was starting to answer when she heard a distant booming. Her blood froze.

"Thunder and lightning," observed Maarten, taking another sip from his mug. "A storm is coming."

"A storm indeed," answered Arno. "But not that kind. The sky is blue outside and the sun shines. That's artillery you hear."

"You'd best be on your way then, boy," said her father. "No time to waste if the Germans are coming. And Aafke, Arno is right, clean up this mess." Draining the rest of his cup, he turned and shuffled back up the stairs.

"Won't he help you?" Arno asked.

"You don't know my father very well."

He hesitated a moment, then took a deep breath. "Well, I'd stay, but you need that wagon more than you need my broom right now. Try to get everything together so we can take it to the garage. Canned food, flour, sugar, spices, oil, anything that won't spoil."

"When will you be back?" she asked. The booming in the background was growing by the moment. She was terrified. Looking around her, she would be alone. The big store windows, always a point of pride, could shatter into infinite bits of shrapnel if a bomb or shell landed too close. She shook her head, driving the fear around the corner.

Arno checked his watch. "An hour, two at the most. Will you be ready?"

She nodded. "I'll have everything together by then."

He grinned, the distant explosions seeming to have no hold on him. "The world is about to fall apart, but we'll do all right. The fat cats will suffer, but to hell with them. Us rats always survive." With that, he unlocked the door and hurried out.

Aafke was left with the mess, her fear rising up to keep her company while she scrubbed and swept. Things looked worse than they were. A half hour later, the store looked like nothing had ever happened. She located some wooden crates in the back and lugged them out onto the front counter. Aafke started unloading the shelves, beginning with canned vegetables and tins of fish. Next came the heavy bags of flour and sugar. She thought about butter, but it wouldn't stay, so instead she loaded up as much lard and oil as she could fit. The work was laborious and took nearly three more hours, but finally she was done. Aafke had ten crates of goods and still enough left on the shelves to do a trickle of business until the time came to sell.

What would it be like if the Germans reached here? she wondered. She'd heard rumors about the last war, the way they treated the Belgian and French citizens trapped behind enemy lines for years. Would they do the same here? She thought of Christiaan, out there on the front lines. Was he safe? What if he was dead already, or badly wounded? She mustn't think about such things. She had to be brave, for her brother, for herself. She checked her watch; it was half past four. Where was Arno?

As if in answer, there was a banging at the door. She took a deep breath of relief and hurried to the door. She started to unlock it and then realized she should check the window. Peeking through the curtains she was glad she had. It wasn't Arno but a neighbor, who was peering back at her. He tapped his watch, as if to announce to her that the store should still be open.

"I'm sorry," she said, loud enough to reach his ears beyond the glass. "We're closed for the day!"

The man frowned. "I just need a few things!" he shouted back. "Please, can't you help me?"

Aafke felt a tug. She didn't like disappointing people. Her hand was halfway toward the lock when she heard another boom. This one was the loudest she'd heard. The war was still out there, closing in. Steeling herself, she shook her head. "I'm sorry," she said. "But we'll be open first thing in the morning." *Was that even true?* she wondered. *Would they be alive tomorrow?* It was so strange to go from peace, life, and their trivial routine to war. She shook her head again, hoping he would just go away.

Fortunately, the man seemed satisfied with her answer and scrambled off, flinching once at the sound of an explosion in the distance. Aafke returned to her work, combing the shelves to see if there was anything else she should load before Arno arrived.

In the street she heard a truck screeching to a stop. Arno must have secured a vehicle after all. How wonderful, that would be even better. She looked around, thinking she should perhaps find a few more boxes. There would be more room in a truck. She started toward the back but there was a loud banging at the door. That was all right. Arno could help her load up the last few things. She hurried over and flipped the lock. Aafke gasped, nearly passing out from the surprise.

Arno wasn't there after all. At the door were three soldiers, towering over her in gray uniforms with thick steel helmets. The lead man, barely older than her, had a black submachine gun hanging from his shoulder. He was aiming the barrel casually at her stomach. She thought for a moment they were Dutch, but then the first one spoke, demanding in German that they be granted entrance. Aafke could see more trucks arriving, and soldiers fanning out, knocking on doors, their rifles at the ready. There was no time to hide things now, no place to hide them. The enemy was here.

Chapter 4
Zich Overgeven

Friday, May 10, 1940
3:20 p.m.
Eindhoven, Netherlands

Otto pressed his face against the side of the house. The stones of the wall, facing away from the sun, were cool, and he relished the feel of them against his cheek. That damned gun still blazed away. They were closer now, although he still hadn't caught a glimpse of it. If they were going to get into the city, they had to neutralize that artillery piece and the men protecting it. Lieutenant Fritz was with him, along with a half dozen men.

"So, what's next?" Otto asked his friend.

"We take out that gun."

"Thanks. Anything more specific?"

Fritz grinned. "Well, it would be helpful if we knew where the hell the thing was."

"I'll go find it."

The lieutenant glanced at him. "You're not exactly the scouting type. Maybe we should send someone a bit smaller?"

"Fine," said Otto, reaching into his pack to retrieve some rations. "But whoever you send needs to hurry. We'll need time to cook the sheep after we take the city."

Fritz directed one of the privates to scout the gun position. Otto leaned back into the wall. The texture of the bricks was comforting, and he breathed deeply, closing his eyes. It was cool here. He'd never loved the sun—always too hot and too bright. Sometimes during matches, he'd have to come out and get under the shade for a time to avoid passing out. The cold was his comrade—a brittle, crusty friend. Rain and snow, frost and freeze.

"He's back," said Fritz, nudging his shoulder. Otto opened his eyes and stepped over to the lieutenant, as they all listened to the private's tale. The artillery piece was a '75, a WWI vintage weapon of French design. The gun was two houses back, in a little courtyard. There was a platoon of Dutch soldiers protecting it. Forty-five men at least. And they had less than thirty.

"Should we call back for reinforcements?" one of the men asked Fritz. The lieutenant shook his head. "The rest of the company is busy. We need to take this out on our own."

"That's impossible," the same soldier said. "They'll mow us down before we can get halfway there. Can't we at least bring the mortar crew up?"

"I sent them with the rest of the company," said Fritz. "Perhaps we should wait a while and see if I can scrounge up some more men."

"*Nein*," said Otto. "We can take them. Here's what we have to do." Otto explained his plan in detail.

The lieutenant nodded. "It's worth a try. When do you want to advance?"

"Now."

Fritz nodded. "Good luck."

Otto took a deep breath, and, rotating to his right, thundered toward the next house. Bullets kicked up dirt at his boots, but he kept on moving. In moments he'd made it, unhit.

He pressed up against the wall, catching his breath. He checked his rifle, working the bolt back and adding two rounds to make sure he had a full load. He tiptoed forward until he reached the far corner of the house. Taking another breath, he peeked cautiously around the corner, ready to pull back. Nothing. There were no bullets waiting for him, or if there were, his enemy was waiting for him to expose his whole body. He moved to his right again, crouched down and rushed between houses. He waited for the crack, for the tearing pain ripping through his body, but it didn't come. He could hear firing behind him. His squad had laid down covering fire, keeping the Dutch busy—at least he hoped.

He reached the next house and passed its far wall. Thunder behind him. The gun had discharged again. He had to hurry. Turning to the left this time, he moved, staying low and hurrying along the edge of the structure, his rifle at the ready. He sprinted between houses again, but this time moving into Eindhoven. He rushed past another house, and another. The gun fired again, but this time he was past it. He moved carefully on until he was sure he was behind the artillery piece.

Now was the difficult part. Setting his rifle down, he reached into his satchel and removed two grenades. They were gray cylindrical metal at the end of wooden handles. He unscrewed the bottom of each Stielhandgranate, careful not to pull on the endcaps, which would arm the grenades. Taking another breath, he turned and sprinted toward the courtyard where he was confident the gun was located. He kept moving, not thinking. He spotted a soldier, an enemy, but he was moving too fast, and the man couldn't react. Lowering his shoulder, Otto rammed him hard in the chest, bowling him over. He passed into the courtyard and there was the gun, smoke wafting out of the barrel. Several men were frantically working to reload it. A couple dozen other soldiers were sitting or standing, some in the midst of what looked like an early dinner.

Otto stormed in among them, shouting now as loud as he could. He could see the wide eyes and the shouts in return, but the men seemed paralyzed by his sudden appearance. Stepping quickly into the middle of the courtyard, he rumbled to a stop just beneath the barrel, and raised his two grenades hard over his head. "*Zich overgeven!*" he commanded, the Dutch words for surrender.

The soldiers still weren't moving. They were stunned. He repeated his order and first one, then another dropped their weapons and raised their hands into the air. "Lieutenant!" he yelled, as loud as he could. "I've got them!"

He waited a few minutes, but nobody came. The Dutch were watching him closely. He was surrounded in every direction, and it was only a matter of time before somebody tried something. He shouted for Fritz again and again. After long minutes he saw gray-green figures rushing in from several houses, rifles at the ready. They were spread apart, moving from position to position, covering each other. "No need for that!" Otto shouted. "I've got them surrounded."

They entered the courtyard, Fritz in the lead. He glanced in alarm at the grenades in Otto's hands, and then his head moved left and right, eyes widening. "Are you mad?" he asked at last.

As the men spread out, Otto lowered the grenades. He took one, then another, and screwed the caps back in, tucking them into his pack. He looked up at the lieutenant. "Where's the sheep?"

"You are mad." Stepping forward, Fritz rapped him hard on both shoulders. "You crazy bastard. You could have been killed fifty times over. Not to mention blowing yourself up in the bargain. What on earth were you thinking?"

"Soldiers don't like grenades. Especially two. Once I was with their gun, it was over. I'm hungry."

"Don't worry yourself, Otto, you'll get the best cut of lamb, and a medal for good measure. But you have to promise me you'll never do anything that stupid again. You can't win this war by yourself. That's what you have squad mates for."

"I've got to retrieve my rifle," he said. Making his way back around the houses, he had a chance to ponder the lieutenant's words. Was he mad? The whole thing had seemed to make so much sense to him. His platoon couldn't take on the Dutch contingent along with their field piece. They would have taken too many casualties storming the position. But the enemy would never expect one, not with grenades in his hand, rushing in before they could react. It was the only way. The only way to make sure he didn't lose more mates today. No, he couldn't promise Fritz he'd never do anything like that again. He would do what needed to be done.

Picking up his rifle, he headed back to the courtyard. His squad had been busy. The enemy were lined up, and his men were moving from soldier to soldier, searching them for pistols and knives, and taking their ration kits to add to the victory feast they would have tonight. Otto heard the bleating of the sheep and saw one of the privates leading the animal around on a leash. He felt a little sorry for the ball of fluff, but dinner was dinner.

Fritz was at the back of the line, chatting with a Dutch lieutenant. He turned to Otto. "Come over here," he said. "I want you to meet this chap. He's from Amsterdam and he used to play a little football."

Otto moved toward them. He glanced at the lieutenant and was shocked to see the soldier to his left drawing something metallic out of his tunic. Otto tried to shout a warning but before he could get the words out the soldier had raised a pistol and fired it into Fritz's back. Blood burst out of his chest in a fountain and his friend stumbled forward, his face marbled with surprise and pain. The soldier fired again, striking Fritz's arm. Otto raised his rifle and fired, hitting the soldier in the chest. The man flew backward, crashing into the cobblestones.

Otto rushed to Fritz's side, turning him over and holding him on his lap. The lieutenant's face was pale. Pink liquid bubbled out of his lips. "We might have played him sometime," he whispered, his eyes fluttering, breath ragged. "Might have played him . . ."

Otto screamed for one of the privates to find a medic. He stayed there, cradling Fritz in his arms, tears running down his cheeks. "You'll be all right. I know you'll be all right."

Chapter 5
Plunderen

Friday, May 10, 1940
3:25 p.m.
Eindhoven, Netherlands

Aafke stepped back into the store as German soldiers rushed in. They were smiling and laughing and moving toward the shelves. One soldier approached her, pulling out a packet of cigarettes. "Have one, pretty girl," he said in broken Dutch. "Have a smoke with me."

She shook her head, unable to speak, frozen with fear. The soldier kept getting closer, shoving the pack in her face. The other men were joking and glancing at her. Finally, a sergeant stepped up and shoved the soldier aside, giving a slight bow to her. "We're here for shopping only," he said in German. He glanced over at the crates. "What's in the boxes?"

"Only some groceries and items," she managed to say. "From . . . from a shipment we received today."

The sergeant turned to one of his men. "Open those up too," he said. "And gather up what you want." He looked down at his watch. "You've only five minutes. Do you have anything to drink?" he asked Aafke. "Something cold?"

She didn't answer—didn't know what to say. She stepped back again, moving away from the German. She finally felt the reassuring stab of the counter behind her, and she moved quickly behind it.

The sergeant blinked. "I'm sorry, Fräulein, have I frightened you? I promise, my men will behave themselves. We're just getting a little food to supplement our rations. Some cigarettes. We'll be gone soon, I promise. Do you have that drink?"

She still couldn't answer. Turning around she reached down and opened an icebox behind the registry. Fishing out a Heineken beer, she turned and handed it to the sergeant.

"Do you have something to open it with?" he asked politely.

She reached for a drawer directly beneath the register and pulled out a bottle opener. She cracked the top off and handed the beer back to the sergeant. He took a deep swig and closed his eyes. Lifting the bottle, he ran the glass against his face. "It's a hot day today," he said at last. "Thank you for this."

She nodded slightly. Her eyes turned to the soldiers; they were stepping up to the counter with loads of goods in their arms. Where on earth was her father? Wasn't there anything they could do to stop this? The first soldier set an enormous pile of goods on the counter. Not knowing what else to do, she rang him up and gave him the total. He paid in German currency, but she was shocked to see he counted out only a tenth of what he should have.

"Sergeant," she said, calling their commander over.

"Yes, Fräulein?"

"I'm sorry," she said, but we do have German visitors sometimes." She looked down at the notes. "The exchange rate, it's wrong."

"I'm sorry, miss," he said, shaking his head. "This is the new exchange rate announced by the government. This is the right amount."

She was horrified. She couldn't let the soldier take the goods for so little money. What would her father say? Surely there was a mistake.

"You will leave us with nothing."

She saw a flicker of regret on the man's face, but it faded to granite. "Orders are orders. There's nothing I can do."

Aafke realized she would have to sell to them. There were many of them and they were armed. Not that they needed to be. If her father came down it wouldn't change things even a little. The Germans would take what they wanted. She thought of the soldier with the cigarettes and, realizing just how helpless she truly was, was grateful the sergeant was there after all.

They conducted themselves respectfully at least, waiting patiently one by one to rob her. She kept hoping Arno would arrive—and do she wasn't sure what. Just having him present would be a comfort. But he didn't come. Neither did her father, who she suspected was sleeping off his "coffee." Finally, the last man dropped his goods on the counter, a few cans of meat and four cartons of cigarettes. When he'd finished paying, the sergeant bowed and led the men out the door.

Only when the door banged closed did she allow herself to let down. She tried to hold back the emotions, but her hands began to shake. Soon her entire body was shivering, and tears welled up in her eyes. What were they going to do now? She looked out at the crates, half empty. All their hard work undone. If Arno was right, it would be difficult to secure shipments. Now, with the Germans here, it might well be impossible. And they'd just made off with much of their reserves.

"What are you doing there, girl?" Her father's voice jolted her. She reached up and dabbed her eyes on her sleeve, not answering.

"Speak up now!"

"The Germans. They're here."

"Yes, yes. I saw them from the windows upstairs. A fair batch of them too. They didn't wait long, did they? Industrious bunch."

"They came into the store. They just left."

"What did they take?"

"They didn't take anything. They . . . they bought some things."

Her father came around behind her. He still had his cup in his hand and now he wore a wry grin. "Did they indeed? Well, I suppose their money spends as well during war as it does in peace." He glanced over at the crates, whistling. "They bought a fair amount. I'll never love the bastards but if they like our store . . . well, it pays the bills. How much did we make?"

She didn't answer. She stared out at the crates again, closing her eyes for a moment. She could feel the tremors returning.

"Cat got your tongue, does it? Well, out of the way, then." He jostled her aside and punched some of the long metal keys on the register. The cash drawer flew out and he eyed the deutsche marks, picking them up and thumbing through the notes.

"What in the hell is going on here?" he demanded. "This isn't a fifth of what we should have."

"It's a tenth," she said. "The sergeant in charge told me. Their government set a new rate of exchange for the invasion."

"What do you mean 'a new rate'? An exchange is an exchange. You can't change it with a wave of your hand." His face mottled and he took a step toward her. "You foolish girl. They lied to you. They robbed you after all. And all the hard work we did will come to nothing. We're going to starve and it's all your fault!"

"What was I supposed to do?" she demanded. "Arno left and you were upstairs sleeping off your—"

"Sleeping off my what?" he asked, taking another step toward her. His cheeks were scarlet now and his hands balled into fists. "I was upstairs doing the books, trying to figure out how we could pay the rent. How we could survive. And you were down here without a thought in your head, flirting and failing." He raised his hands and she flinched. "Bah! What's the point? The damage is done. You should have been cleaning upstairs while I was down here carrying on a man's business. God knows our flat could use it. Honestly, what do you do during the day?"

"I did what I could, Father. There was a half dozen of them. They had rifles and—"

"You're not a soldier. They wouldn't have done a thing to you. All you had to do was demand what was due to us, and we'd have a pretty sum of money for the rent, and half our goods to hide. Instead, you've ruined us, on the first day of this damned war!" He waved toward the staircase. "I can't look at you right now. Go clean the flat. Make yourself useful for something while I try to sort this out."

The door flung open again. Aafke gasped, turning toward the entrance. With deep relief, she realized it was Arno. She rushed over and threw herself into his arms, sobbing into his chest.

"What's wrong?" he asked, holding her tightly. He smelled of tobacco and stale sweat, but his strong arms were comforting to her.

"Your friend there just gave away half our goods," Maarten said.

"What do you mean?"

"A couple Germans came in here and walked off with half the store. They told her a story about exchange rates and she swallowed it whole."

"It's no story," said Arno. "It's the truth. They're paying a tenth of the old rate. Wartime orders. Their soldiers are waltzing through every store in town like this is a shopping spree, buying up everything they can get their hands on." He patted Aafke on the back. "So, you see, your daughter didn't give anything away."

Aafke was grateful for Arno's words. She took a deep breath, collecting herself. Letting go, she turned to her father, who was eyeing her, cup in hand. He took a deep drink and then nodded. "Fair enough, Arno. But what do we do now? I've a handful of German notes and not much else."

"We need to get the rest of the goods out of here now."

"Did you bring the wagon?"

"No. The man wouldn't part with it. Not with the Germans here."

"Then what can we do?"

"We could hide it upstairs," said Aafke. "They wouldn't search our flat, would they?"

"That's not a bad idea," said Arno. "Do you have room?"

"The way she keeps house? Less room than you'd hope. But aye, we've a nook and cranny here and there."

"Let's hurry, then," said Arno, moving toward the crates. He glanced down, looking at the half-full containers. "We can consolidate them." He kneeled and began rapidly moving items from one crate to another. Aafke joined him, and soon they had a box full again with goods. "Let's take this one up."

Maarten turned away, filling up his mug again with something out of a bottle.

"I'll take it," Aafke said. Grabbing the crate with both hands, she lifted the box up to her chest. The weight was staggering but she was used to these burdens. She readjusted the container and started toward the stairs.

"You're strong," said Arno quietly, with words just for her. "Stronger than he thinks."

The words filled her, and she smiled at him, turning to labor across the store and up the stairs. The weight was almost unbearable, but she made it to the top. She thought about finding a spot now but realized haste was critical. She set the box down on their rickety kitchen table and then hurried back down the stairs to the store.

Arno already had another crate full. She took a second box up. Elation filled her, as every moment they were saving their future. She paused in the flat for a few seconds, catching her breath. By the time she returned a second time to the store, Arno had another crate full. Their last one except for what was still on the shelves.

"I'll take this one," he said.

"Thank you."

He grinned at her, giving her a wink. He took a step toward the stairs when a banging jolted them all. Aafke turned in horror to see the front door was flung open and a soldier was standing there, rifle aimed at her heart.

"Halt!" the soldier screamed.

She raised her hands. Arno set the box down and turned slowly, his arms in the air as well. Soldiers streamed in, fanning out around the store, weapons at the ready. A lieutenant strolled in behind them, his eyes darting around the shelves. At last, he focused on the crate Arno had just set down.

"By order of the German military authority I'm confiscating these goods for the war effort," the man said.

"You'll pay full price for them," she heard her father say, as if he was talking to an unruly customer.

"We'll not pay a dime," the lieutenant said, grinning. He looked at his men. "Load everything in the truck and check upstairs." He pointed at the crate. "They're trying to hide things."

The officer marched out of the store and left them. Aafke stood in the middle of the store, stunned, while around her, the soldiers descended like locusts, consuming their future.

Chapter 6
Ontmoeten

Friday, May 10, 1940
4:25 p.m.
Eindhoven, Netherlands

Otto kneeled close by while the medic worked on Lieutenant Geier. Blood still bubbled out of the wound, but Fritz was quiet, his eyes closed, a shot of morphine coursing through his system.

"Will he make it?" Otto asked.

"Too early to tell," the medic muttered, not looking up.

"What about his arm?" Otto asked, glancing at the jagged hole in his upper sleeve.

"That's not critical, the chest wound is what I have to concentrate on. Now leave me alone. No time to talk. Give me a little space."

Otto rose and backed away a few steps. The courtyard was a hive of activity. The Dutch soldiers were standing against the wall, listless, some of them smoking, seemingly disinterested in their surroundings. But what was left of Otto's platoon was moving about, gathering up the captured equipment, picking through the rations and other souvenirs. An hour passed as the medic worked on Geier. Otto glanced over frequently, but he couldn't tell how the treatment was progressing.

Two soldiers arrived in the courtyard, wearing armbands with crosses, carrying a stretcher, and stepping as rapidly as they could toward the wounded officer. They placed the stretcher on the ground and moved the lieutenant over as gingerly as they could onto the canvas fabric. With an audible grunt, the men lifted Fritz up, balancing for a moment and adjusting the weight, before they started to move off. But Otto called out to them. "What are you going to do with him?"

The medic turned. "There's a field hospital set up near the border. We'll get him there in the next hour or so."

"Is he going to make it?"

The medic shrugged. "I can't tell you that for sure, but I think so. He's lost a lot of blood, but the bullet missed his heart. If he doesn't die before we get there and if he avoids infection in recovery, I think he'll recover."

Otto reached out to shake the medic's hand. "How long will it take before I can visit him?" he asked.

"The operation, assuming they can get to him right away— it's going to take many hours. He'll be out for quite a while after that. I'd say tomorrow night at the earliest. Assuming you could somehow get leave, which I can't imagine."

"Let me do the imagining," said Otto.

The medic shrugged again and turned, directing the stretcher-bearers out of the courtyard. Even as they passed, a new group of German soldiers arrived. At their head was a lieutenant he didn't recognize. This officer looked around at the prisoners and the men. He stepped over toward Otto, sizing the corporal up as he approached. "Corporal?"

"Berg," Otto responded with a nod.

"I'm Lieutenant Wagner. What happened here?"

Otto gestured at the 75-millimeter artillery gun. "The enemy had this gun and was firing out into the valley at our convoy. It was defended by about a platoon of Dutch. We sustained some casualties on the road and then filed out into the field. We approached the houses until we were able to surround and neutralize the gun."

The lieutenant glanced at Otto. "Messy. Your platoon is in shambles. You should have waited for the rest of the company before you implemented an attack. You will do well to be more careful in the future. The Dutch have hardly resisted. If you had waited for reinforcements, you could have taken this position without the loss of any life. Do you understand me?"

Otto nodded, not deeming to answer out loud.

"*Gut.* Have your men get those prisoners behind the lines and then get them back here quick. We don't have any time to waste. We must take that Philips factory before the end of the day."

Wagner barked out orders, and the platoon quickly regrouped, weaving through the houses until they returned to the main road where a truck waited. Otto climbed into the back, helping his squad mates into position.

As they rumbled through the suburbs of the city, Otto stared at the darkening horizon, his thoughts consumed by the wounded Fritz and the new lieutenant's harsh words. Would he ever be able to prove himself as a capable leader, or would he always be seen as a reckless risk-taker?

The truck rumbled on until it reached the industrial district of Eindhoven, screeching to a halt in front of a looming industrial complex with rows of tall windows and smokestacks piercing the sky.

"This is the Philips factory!" shouted Lieutenant Wagner. "There shouldn't be any resistance, but fan out and be careful. Now move!" The men sprang into action, spreading out as they approached the factory gates.

"Remember, this is still enemy territory," Otto whispered to his squad, his blue eyes filled with determination. "Stay sharp."

Sudden gunfire erupted from the gatehouse, but Otto's men were ready. They returned fire with deadly precision, killing two guards before they could inflict any casualties on the platoon. With a nod from Wagner, they stormed the factory, securing it within minutes without losing a single man.

"Job well done, men," Wagner said grudgingly, though he avoided looking directly at Otto. "You've earned a short leave. Go explore the city, have some dinner and grab some souvenirs, but be back in two hours."

"Thank you, sir," Otto replied, his throat tight with a mix of frustration and relief. He knew that he'd done more than just prove himself on the battlefield; he'd saved lives, perhaps even changed the course of the battle. And yet, he couldn't shake the feeling that this lieutenant saw him as a liability. For now that didn't matter, as he had his men to attend to.

"Let's go, boys," Otto said to his squad, forcing a smile onto his weary face. "Let's see what Eindhoven has to offer."

Otto took his men into the center of the city. There were German soldiers everywhere, walking in and out of stores, bundles of goods in their hands. The men were smiling, snapping photos, relaxing as if on holiday. Otto found a corner restaurant with some outside seating and took a large table for his men. They were served bread and cheese with some sausage, and three bottles of wine. They were soon feasting, laughing, and chatting, talking about Otto's exploits and wondering where their precious sheep had gone to. When the check came, Otto paid the bill, glancing at his watch. They still had an hour. The squad decided to do some shopping. Waltzing down the street, they entered a corner grocery store.

Otto could tell immediately that something was amiss. The shelves were nearly bare. Crates stood in the middle of the small space, several on their side with groceries spilled out on the floor. A group of German soldiers from the Wehrmacht were moving among the crates, filling bags and boxes, and snatching items off the shelves.

Otto's eyes were drawn to a young woman who stood behind the counter, her blue eyes shining with unshed tears. Her slender frame trembled ever so slightly as she helplessly watched while the soldiers went about their work. "Excuse me," Otto said, approaching the young woman. "What's going on here?"

The woman's voice was barely audible over the cacophony of looting. "They're taking everything, and they won't pay for any of it."

Otto clenched his fists, his muscles rippling beneath his uniform. He couldn't stand idly by while this innocent woman's life was torn apart. "Leave that to me," he said.

"Halt!" Otto barked, striding toward one of the Wehrmacht soldiers who was just about to leave the store with a crate full of goods. "What do you think you're doing?"

The soldier sneered. "None of your business, SS man."

"Put that crate back," Otto ordered, glowering at the insolent soldier. "No one takes anything without paying for it."

"Make me," the soldier snarled, attempting to shove past Otto.

"Wrong answer," Otto growled. In a swift, fluid motion, he hoisted both the soldier and the crate into the air, holding them above his head as if they weighed no more than a sack of potatoes.

"Put it back!" Otto roared, his voice echoing through the store, causing the other looters to pause and stare. He released the man and the soldier crumpled to the ground, landing hard. The crate crashed to the floor and shattered, goods flying everywhere.

A harsh voice barked from the doorway. "What's going on here?!" A Wehrmacht lieutenant, flanked by several soldiers, strode into the store with an air of authority. His eyes flicked between the cowed looters and the defiant SS corporal.

"Corporal, stand down," the lieutenant commanded, leveling a stern gaze at Otto.

"Sir, these men are looting this store without paying. It's not right," Otto replied firmly, standing his ground.

"Those goods are being confiscated for the war effort," the lieutenant retorted. "Now step aside."

"I can't do that, sir," Otto said, his voice steady with resolve. He positioned himself squarely in front of the entrance, blocking any further attempts to remove items from the store.

"Are you refusing an order, Corporal?" The lieutenant's voice was cold with anger, and Otto could sense the tension in the room rising. He glanced briefly at the young Dutch woman, who was frozen with fear.

"Apologies, sir, but this isn't right. We should be protecting these people, not stealing from them," Otto insisted, meeting the lieutenant's eyes unflinchingly.

"Your name, Corporal," the officer demanded, his voice tight with barely contained rage.

"Otto Berg, sir," he replied, knowing full well the risk he was taking.

"Very well, Corporal Berg. I don't have time to sit and argue with you. But I'll be turning in a report to the authorities. This isn't the last you'll hear of this." With a final glare, the lieutenant signaled for his men to depart, leaving the store empty save for Otto and his men.

"Thank you," the young woman said softly, her eyes shining with gratitude. "You didn't have to do that."

"Are you okay?" Otto asked, his concern for her momentarily overriding any thoughts of the repercussions he might face.

"I am now, thanks to you," she replied, smiling tremulously.

As they spoke, a thin man in his thirties entered the store, his brow furrowed in concern. He paused when he saw Otto, his expression turning to one of suspicion and distrust. One of Otto's privates pointed a rifle at the man, who raised his hands into the air.

"It's all right," said the woman. "He's a friend."

Otto turned back to the woman. "What's your name?" he asked.

"Aafke. Aafke Cruyssen."

"I'm Otto Berg. Is there anything else I can do for you, miss?" he asked.

Aafke glanced at the Dutchman, who was scowling like a thundercloud. "No. No, thank you."

"Well, goodbye then," he said, turning to his men.

"Aren't we going to do some shopping?" one of the privates asked.

"*Nein*," said Otto. "Not here. Let's go down the street a ways and see if we can find another store." Otto gestured and his men left. At the door, he turned one last time to look at Aafke. "I'll check on you again sometime," he said, surprised at his own words. He was a combat soldier and there was little reason to think he'd ever be back in Eindhoven.

"Thank you," she said, glancing again at the other man. "That really is not necessary."

"We won't need that," said her friend, his eyes burning a hole through Otto. "Goodbye."

"Goodbye, Aafke," said Otto, turning to leave. As he strode out of the store and rejoined his mates, he couldn't help thinking about the fragile, frail young woman he'd just encountered. He didn't know anything about her, anything at all, and yet he felt like he'd been struck by lightning. He shook his head. There was a war on and his squad to attend to. He would think about this Aafke later. Slapping one of the privates on the back, he pressed on down the streets of Eindhoven, trying to force down the images still running through his mind.

Chapter 7
Strijd

Wednesday, May 15, 1940
5:58 p.m.
Eindhoven, Netherlands

Aafke stared at the near empty shelves of their store as another German soldier approached the counter. He had two dented cans of beans and a coil of rope in his hands. Looking at her somewhat sheepishly, he placed a paltry number of Reichsmarks on the counter, paying for virtually the last items they possessed in the store.

The last few days were difficult to remember. After those first terrible hours, when they had lost so much of their goods, they had managed to hide a few supplies in their flat, but altogether the items added up to nothing more than half a box, a far cry from the twelve crates they had originally intended to secure for their future.

Except for that one incident of looting, all of the Germans who came in had faithfully paid for what they purchased. However, they continued to do so under the absurd exchange rate the German military had set and Aafke knew this placed them in the worst possible situation. They would have little money to buy anything to replace what was gone—even if they could find those groceries.

Arno was trying to help. He'd checked in a few times with her as he investigated, through his contacts, whether there might be more goods available. He had found a few sources in the country who were able to deliver some fresh produce and meat, but the price they were demanding was exorbitant, many times what they would've paid in peacetime. This was a doubly compounded problem because she had so much less to pay with.

Her father was no aid at all. After scolding her, despite her explanation, for selling so much of their goods to the Germans at this new price, he had retreated into his mug, scarcely leaving his bedroom, and never coming back down to the store. She was on her own to try to manage this crisis.

The war news was even worse. The Germans streamed through Holland almost unopposed. Their forces were rapidly approaching Amsterdam, Rotterdam, and other cities on the channel coast. The war couldn't last much longer, and it looked like the Germans were here to stay, at least until the English and French dislodged them, if that was even possible. There were dark rumors that the French lines had been broken by columns of German tanks and were in a frantic retreat into the interior of France.

Aafke thought of her brother. She had hoped there might be some word from Christiaan, but there was nothing. This didn't mean anything, of course. But rumor had it that there were many casualties in the Dutch army, and she lived with the constant apprehension that her brother was wounded or dead.

So she had spent the last few days alone, afraid, with her only company the near-constant stream of German soldiers buying up their future.

And now virtually everything was gone. She had a handful

of Reichsmarks, no goods to buy, and no idea what the future held. If there was any bright point, it was the Germans themselves. So far, except for that one incident, all of the soldiers had been polite and treated her correctly. Perhaps more than correctly. Several of the men seemed quite interested in her company. One young fellow, a sergeant, even asked her to dinner. She declined the invitation, but he was quite persistent, and she worried he wouldn't take no for an answer.

Only one German had shown true courage. That giant of a man, an SS corporal, who had stood up to the looting of a platoon of German soldiers. He had spoken to her briefly, and then gathered his men and left. She could picture his mountain of a build, his blond hair and rugged features. She shook her head. What was she thinking? No matter what he had done, he was an enemy, a man she could never interact with.

Try as she might, though, she could not drive him from her mind. At the oddest hours, his kind act would pop into her head and she would be forced to grapple with the image, reminding herself again and again he had done nothing more than what he should've done, and if the Germans weren't there in the first place and had respected their property, he would not need to have bothered.

There was the thought again. She shook her head, checking her watch. It was nearly six—time to close the store. She laughed at herself. What was the point? She could leave the doors wide open now. There was nothing more to take. As she was heading toward the door, the handle jiggled, and it opened. Arno was there, carrying two brown bags in his arms.

"Quick! Close the door," he whispered, his eyes darting around the store. "Are we alone? Are we safe?"

"Yes," she said. "What do you have?"

"I managed to scrounge up a few things."

"What is it?"

Arno stepped over to the counter, setting the bags down.

Aafke hurried over to him and began rummaging through them. There were canned items, meats, vegetables, and fruit. She was elated.

"However did you come across this?"

Arno shook his head. "Don't ask," he said. "What matters is I have it."

"Should we store this at your garage?" she asked, thinking about what had happened here before.

He shook his head. "It's not safe there anymore."

"What do you mean?"

"It doesn't matter." Arno glanced at the bags. "You need to hide this in the flat. Not all together. In different places in case there's a search. Put some of it in the cupboard so that it appears to be your own food supply."

She laughed. "It might be. The store isn't the only thing running low."

"That's about to change," he said. "They're issuing ration cards tomorrow. It won't be enough, but it will be something." He glanced at the canned items. "You can use a little of this for food but the rest we need to sell."

"How do we do that?" she asked.

"Don't worry about that. I've got some ideas on how to set things up."

"That's so kind of you, Arno. What do I owe you for this? I have a little money. It's the German kind but at least it's something."

"You'll need what you have. I told you I would share what I could find. And I need a place to hide it."

"I still don't understand what you mean," she said. "Why is your garage not safe anymore?"

"How is your father?"

"I've hardly seen him. He stays up in his room all day drinking out of that mug. I'm concerned about him."

"You won't have long to worry. There's no alcohol to be

had anywhere. He'll run out soon enough and then he'll have to find something to do. Just be patient."

"And what do I do about the store?" she asked.

"What can you do? The Germans can't expect you to make something out of nothing. But even they need to eat. They'll make some official arrangements to provide your shipments. Wait and see. They'll need distribution points to feed the population—even if they intend to half-starve us."

He started to rise.

"Oh, Arno, please don't go," she said, placing a hand on his arm."

He turned to her, his eyes searching her face. "I'm sorry, Aafke, but I must. I have things to do, and they cannot wait."

"Can't you stay just a little longer?" she asked. "I could make us some dinner." She **was so** tired of being alone. She needed a little company and **Arno** had been so kind to her. She wanted to show some appreciation.

He looked at her and then took her hand. "Perhaps another time," he said. "But don't worry. Things are starting to settle down here behind the lines. Remember to hide those goods. That ration system will start tomorrow. I'll bet you you'll have a German official in by midday. He'll want to inventory any goods you have so this must be hidden. I'll be back after hours tomorrow to pick up some of this to sell." He smiled at her. "If you had dinner ready then, I wouldn't object." With that Arno turned and walked swiftly from the store.

Aafke stepped back to the door and locked it, pressing her head against the window for a moment. She took a deep breath. For the first time since the war started, she felt a glimmer of hope. If the Germans arranged for them to have merchandise as part of a ration system, that would take care of one of her major fears. Perhaps it would not matter about the new exchange rate if the Germans provided the goods for them to distribute. Not only that, but Arno seemed to have his own resources to secure items that might be sold on the black market. She didn't know what she would do without Arno. With her father absent and her brother gone, perhaps forever, he was her only source of comfort.

She hurried the items upstairs. She placed some of the goods in the cupboard as Arno had instructed, then shoved other items in the cushions of the sofa, behind her boots and shoes in the dark of her closet, and even some in the bathtub.

When Aafke was finished she knocked on her father's door, wanting to tell him about the new goods, and about what Arno had said. But Maarten refused to come to the door or answer her. She finally gave up and moved into the kitchen. Turning the gas on, she left a little fire under the burner and pulled out an old, beaten steel pot, then took down a can of beans from the cupboard. She opened the top and poured them into the pot, slowly heating them as she thought about the future. She ate by herself alone in a dim light and read a book—one of her favorites set in the late 1800s, before the first war, before the industrial age with machinery, machine guns, artillery, and the tanks that had changed the world forever.

It was cooling down outside. She hated the humid heat, but the cold would bring new problems. She had no coal for the furnace and no idea how to secure more. She couldn't imagine what winter would bring. Would the Germans supply them when they needed to stay fed and warm or take everything back to their home country? She wondered about the Jews in Eindhoven. She knew there were hundreds of them. What would the Nazi attitude be toward the Dutch Jews? Would they respect Dutch law and treat them as equal citizens? As the darkness fell, she said a prayer for all the Jews of Eindhoven. She prayed for her brother, her father, and for her poor country and the uncertain future in front of them.

The next morning, Maarten materialized out of his bedroom for practically the first time since the invasion. His eyes were puffy and bloodshot, the color drained from his cheeks. He shuffled past Aafke, who was making herself some breakfast, and grabbed the sack of coffee grounds. He shook it and opened the top, staring into the wrinkled sack. "It's near gone," he mumbled.

She didn't answer. All the loneliness and fear from the past four days whipped through her. She had to hold herself back from screaming at him. Taking two plates down from the cupboard, she loaded a little breakfast on each one, and moved them to the table, slumping down into one of the seats. Maarten prepared his coffee and, when the pot was plugged in and beginning to heat, took the seat next to her.

"Have you heard any news?" he asked. "They've stopped printing the damned paper. Radio's silent too, for the most part."

"Just rumors," she said.

"Rumors from who?"

"The soldiers sometimes tell me things—when they're in the store."

He looked up. "You're fraternizing with the enemy?"

"I don't have a choice, Father," she said, her voice rising. "I was ordered to keep the store open and they're the only ones who've come in over the past few days. Not that they should have bothered. There's nothing left to buy or to take."

Maarten grunted. "And what did your *new friends* tell you?"

"That the Germans are almost to Amsterdam. That they dropped paratroopers in behind enemy lines and bombed Rotterdam to dust. That the war for us is almost over."

"Lies," said Maarten. "Wars aren't over in a week." The pot was hissing and coughing now, and her father rose to attend to it. She was surprised when he poured a full cup without adding anything to it. "I wonder where my boy is?" he said.

"I haven't heard anything from him."

Maarten grunted. "Well, next time you're playing the giggle game with our new hosts, why don't you do something useful and find out what's happened to Christiaan."

"I'll . . . I'll try. But I'm not flirting with them."

"It's just an expression," he said, waving his hand. He sat back down hard. "Nothing left downstairs, you say?" He took a sip of coffee and closed his eyes. "Well, I guess that's that. That bastard from Philips will be along soon enough, demanding the rent. We're already well behind and when we can't pay him this month and he sees we've nothing to sell, we'll be out on our asses in the street. And then what's to come of me?"

"Maybe not, Father."

"What do you mean?"

"Arno came in yesterday. He brought a bag of goods."

"Goods, aye? How many goods?"

"Just a little."

"Bah, why bother me with that?"

"It's something we can sell Father. And that's not all," said Aafke. "He said the Germans are issuing ration cards."

"Let them. How does that help us? We can't eat paper or sell it, for that matter!"

"Father, if there are ration cards there must be something to ration. Arno said the Germans are going to stock the stores in Eindhoven, so the people have something to eat."

"The Nazis are going to be our new suppliers?" Her father tipped his head back and laughed. "Jesus, Joseph, and Mary. Now there's a tale for you. Arno's just trying to butter you up, as he's wont to do."

"No, it's true."

"Why, because Arno says it is?" he asked, his eyes boring into her.

"He's the only one who's helped me the last few days."

"So you blame me for everything, do you? What did you expect me to do? They've taken everything from me, everything I spent my life building. They seized my goods—they've taken my boy."

"I'm still here."

"Bah. Are you? Between those German soldiers and Arno, it sounds like you've had plenty of company the last few days."

"Father!"

"Never mind. It doesn't matter." He took another sip, then stood and moved to the cupboard, removing a bottle of brandy that was almost empty. He poured a finger into his cup.

"I thought maybe you'd stopped."

"What?" he said, then glanced down at the mug. "Ah, this is just a little splash to get the muscles moving. You don't know what it's like to get older, my little scarecrow. It's no day in the sun, I'll tell you. So when are these Germans arriving with our goods?"

"I don't know, Father. I haven't heard from them. I'm just going off what Arno told me. But if the ration cards are issued today, I hope we'd get something right away."

"Make sure they bring us some brandy. I'm almost out."

"I will, Father," she said making a note to most certainly *not* order any alcohol, if she had any choice in the matter.

"And find out about Christiaan."

"How would they know about him?" she asked. "And why would they tell me anything?"

"Do I have to explain everything to you? If I have to put up with your flirting, at least use it for some good."

"Father, I haven't done any such thing."

"Just get the information and get me some brandy." He checked his watch. "You're going to be late."

"Aren't you coming down with me?"

"The Germans aren't coming to our store to see me. Get yourself up, and put on some new clothes. You look like a rumpled ragdoll in that thing."

Aafke rose and stepped into her bedroom, closing the door behind her. She looked down at her dress. There was nothing wrinkled about it. She glanced at the mirror. Was there something wrong with how she looked? She was skinny, too much so according to her father. But plenty of girls were thin. She mustn't let his words get to her, she told herself as she always did. But that other part inside her knew the words were like water, seeping around and through her to settle in the tiny spaces of her soul. She took a deep breath. There was no use arguing. She put on a new dress, her only other one, a pretty white flower pattern, although the brightness was fading. She stepped back out into the kitchen.

"That's my girl," he said. "Any German worth their salt will give you everything we need. Now, get on down there."

"You should join me."

"I've the books to do."

"You've had four days as it is. How many books do you have?"

"Watch your tongue now, missy, before I give you something to talk about. Hurry along now. The Germans will be waiting."

She doubted that. This was probably an enormous waste of time. But she did as she was told, hurrying down the stairs. To her surprise, there was knocking at the door. She sprang over and opened it. To her greater shock, her father had been right. The Germans were here, a group of them. They were in uniform, all of them except the leader, an overweight man in his midfifties, bulging out of a worn gray wool suit. He was smiling at her under furrows of pepper gray eyebrows.

"Pardon us, Fräulein. . . ?"

"Cruyssen," she said. "Aafke Cruyssen."

"Ah, thank you. My name is Herr Schultz. Are you the owner of this store?"

"No," she said.

"Your father and mother perhaps?"

"My father only runs the store." She blushed uncomfortably. "It used to be ours, before the bad times."

"Ah yes," he said with some sympathy in his voice. "We had

them in Germany too. Except more so—with all the money the English and French were taking out of our poor country."

She nodded, not sure what to say.

He stared at the ceiling for a while as if remembering, then seemed to catch himself. "I'm sorry. On to business. Do you and your father make the orders and sell the goods here?"

"Yes," she said.

"Excellent. As I'm sure you are aware, a new ration system was put into place today. This is to assure that there is enough food for everyone, and that nobody hoards food or tries to sell it for higher prices on the black market."

She nodded again, battling to keep her face a mask. Did he know? Would they search the upstairs and find her meager stash of goods? What would happen if they did?

"I'm here to make sure none of that nonsense happens. I will be your point of contact. I'll visit the store weekly, check your inventories, and supply the goods you need." He looked around. "It looks like you need a lot, this place is picked clean." His smile turned to a frown. "You're not hiding food now, I hope?"

"No . . . no, sir," she said, stammering the answer. "It was the soldiers. They came and bought everything."

The man laughed. "I suppose they did. Hungry young men with money to spare have a way of doing that very thing. Well, you don't need to worry much about that now, Fräulein. The soldiers have all gone now—except for a few just to keep the peace."

"That's a relief," she said, then realized her mistake. "I didn't mean, I don't—"

"Don't want German soldiers here? Of course you don't! But I'm afraid we're here to stay. But you'll soon grow used to us. Look at what we're doing for you now. Your store is empty, and we'll fill it. Have trouble with theft, we'll run the perpetrators to justice. You can rely on us for your needs and your security. Now, let's make a list of what we need, then I'll show you the ration cards and how they work. I almost forgot," he said, reaching into his pocket. "Here are booklets for you and your father."

She took the ration cards, thumbing through them absentmindedly as he led her through their tiny store, asking questions and writing down the answers. When he was finished, he patted her arm and smiled a toothy grin. "That's that, then," he said. "We'll be back tomorrow with a load of goods. If anyone comes today, just turn them away."

"Thank you," she found herself saying. She didn't want to, wasn't sure it was proper, but she was relieved. They would have food again, something to sell, and ration cards for their own needs.

Schultz reached out and took her chin in his hands. "Such a pretty young woman," he said. He started toward the door and then paused. "Oh, I forgot one thing."

"What's that?" she asked.

"The bill. Where do I send it?"

"The what?"

He laughed again. "The bill, you silly thing. We can't give these groceries away. But don't worry, I'm sure you have plenty of money from the sale. After all," he said, gesturing at the store, "you sold everything."

"How much will it be?" she asked.

"Not too bad. Perhaps a little more than before. But there's a war on, of course!"

Her heart sank. How would they come up with the money, especially after the exchange rate? She couldn't think about that now. Arno would know what to do. They had some goods to sell. They could make it happen. As Schultz turned again she remembered something.

"Sir?"

"Yes?"

"I have a brother. Christiaan. He's a soldier."

"And?"

"Is there any way you could find what happened to him?"

Schultz laughed again, this time a deep belly laugh with his head back. "Oh you're a coy one indeed! I'm a grocer. Do you think they'd trust me with that kind of information?"

"I'm sorry," she said, looking down.

"Now don't you worry about your brother, Fräulein. He's safe now."

"What do you mean?"

"Haven't you heard?"

"Heard what?"

"The Dutch surrendered. It's all over except mopping up a few troops here and there. Our boys are already on into France, to finish off the frogs and their foolish English allies. Your brother will be home to you in no time, don't you worry."

Chapter 8

Moord

Friday, May 24, 1940
3:17 p.m.
Dunkirk, Belgium

Otto and the remaining members of his squad stood among the smoking tanks and field pieces of the British army. Corpses were strewn across the ground at the crest of the ridge, some missing arms, or even a head.

In the distance, over the rolling sand and scrub brush, Otto could see the beach and the English Channel beyond it. The sand near the water was empty, but Otto knew the English were out there somewhere between them and the water, dug in and ready for the next attack.

His squad was with him—down to three men now. Over the last eleven days, they had seen hard fighting from the British soldiers. So different from what they'd been taught in their training—that the English were weak, decrepit, worn down by too many years of empire. Unwilling to fight.

Otto and his men had learned the opposite. The British ordinary soldier matched their own men in fighting spirit and determination. He did not hate or fear them, rather he respected them for their courage. The English soldier fought them well, but in every other way, their enemy was woefully unprepared to face the might of the German army. The Germans outnumbered the British many times over in men. They also had many more tanks, in concentrated divisions.

Moreover, the Royal Air Force had hardly appeared in the skies over northern France. Here or there they might spy a Hurricane dodging in and out of the clouds on some sort of reconnaissance patrol, but the German Luftwaffe dominated the sky with scores of planes, almost constantly overhead, providing close support to the infantry and the panzers.

The British had fought bravely, but they were doomed. Otto and his men simply waited for the last order to move forward. There would be one last fight, a bright flare of flame before the cream of the British Empire was extinguished on those beaches just ahead.

Even as he considered this, Lieutenant Wagner appeared over the crest of the hill, flanked on each side by two soldiers. The men carried MP38 submachine guns slung over their shoulders. Otto smiled to himself, realizing the lieutenant thought a lot of himself to need such an escort.

"Making your final preparations I hope, Corporal Berg?" asked the lieutenant.

Otto saluted in response.

"What's the situation?"

"All quiet," said Otto. "You can't see anything but grass and ocean. But they're out there, waiting for us. They'll make a good fight of it, but we've got them."

"You think too much of these English."

"They've fought well."

The lieutenant scoffed. "Not well enough. We've driven them back like scared children."

Otto chose to ignore this. "When are we going in?" he asked.

The lieutenant checked his watch. "Within the hour."

"How many panzers in support?"

"None."

He was surprised by that. There was no shortage of tanks. Looking behind him, he could see a row of Panzer IIIs lined up less than a half mile away. "Why no armor?" he asked.

"Orders from above."

"But why? We've got them right where we want them."

"The country is not suited for tanks. Besides, we don't need them. One more attack and the British will break. We'll capture the lot of them or drive them into the sea."

Otto didn't like the sound of that, but he learned in the last two weeks that the lieutenant was nobody to argue with, whether he had logic on his side or not. "Any chance of replacements before we go in?"

The lieutenant shook his head. "You'll be fine, though," he said. "We're hitting them with multiple divisions and we'll have plenty of Bf 109s and Me 210s in close support."

"Where is the rest of the platoon?"

"I'm holding them in reserve. I've got some prisoners to manage behind the lines."

Otto was amazed. The lieutenant was sending four men out of a platoon that should've been close to fifty. He wanted to say something, but he knew there was no point. The lieutenant had made up his mind. He just hoped the man was correct about the other units available for the attack and about the air cover.

Otto turned to his squad mates. "Do you have enough ammunition?" he asked.

"Forty rounds apiece," said one of the privates.

"When the attack comes, don't get ahead of me," said Otto. "I want to spread out and will move from point to point. I'll take the lead. I want one man providing cover, and I'll move up to the next little hill. When I get there, then you move up, one after another, then we'll repeat this maneuver to the next hill. Do you understand?"

The men nodded.

"We should try to eat something," he said, checking his watch. "We have forty-five minutes until the attack starts."

"We've got ammunition, but nothing to eat," the private said.

Otto reached into his pack and drew out a couple of stale biscuits he had grabbed off a breakfast table in a little house in a French village nearby. He'd been saving them for himself, but that didn't matter. He broke the biscuits in half, and then shared them out to the men, keeping the smallest portion for himself.

"Did I hear the lieutenant right? No tanks?"

"Don't worry about that," said Otto, not believing himself. "You heard Wagner. The British are almost finished. We'll have air support and plenty of men in on the attack. But don't do anything stupid," he lectured. "Remember, a wounded animal is most dangerous when it's cornered."

The men ate in silence. Otto felt the hollow spot in his stomach he experienced whenever combat was coming, and a gnawing worry. Not fear for himself, but concern for what might happen to his remaining men.

Abruptly, the attack commenced. Otto heard first one artillery piece, then another, then a crescendo of thunder from behind them as explosions erupted on the horizon covering the sandy ground toward the beach. He strained his eyes, looking for the enemy. He wasn't sure if the Germans were firing at points they had pinpointed or just guessing where the English might be holed up. They would find out soon enough.

A new roar erupted, much closer now. From the left and the right, gray shadows streamed forward in the twilight, storming toward the beaches. "Let's go!" shouted Otto, sprinting toward a little hill less than forty yards ahead. He saw flashes less than a mile away. The British were responding. His heart was in his throat now, and he waited for the bullet or the shell to strike him. He slammed into the sand of the knoll, clinging to the grass while he caught his breath. Waiting a moment, he drew his rifle over the top of the mound and took aim, firing off a few rounds in rapid succession toward the flashes in the distance.

A private slammed into the sand next to him, and then another. He yelled, and all three of them opened fire, pouring round after round at the enemy. The last private crashed hard among them. Otto turned to chastise the man, but he stopped. The private's face was a bloody mass. His body convulsed in fits and shivers before coming to a deathly calm. Otto took hold of the private's uniform for a few moments, clenching it in his fingers, before pulling him off and shoving him down below them.

"Good God!" one of the men shouted, staring back at their comrade.

"No time for that," said Otto, refusing to think about it. "On to the next hill!" He pulled himself to his feet and rushed forward, as much to get away from what he'd just witnessed as to advance on the enemy.

He repeated this maneuver three more times, taking no additional casualties. The flashes were growing nearer. But something was wrong. The lieutenant had promised massive air cover, but Otto had seen nothing. He scanned the sky, searching for the silver-and-gray dots, but there was only open sky with no sign of German fighters.

They were less than five hundred yards now from the beaches. Otto could see Germans near him on both sides. They all seemed to pause here, catching their breath, perhaps steeling their nerves for the final push. Otto removed a handkerchief from his tunic, wiping blood and brains from his face. He threw the cloth into the brush, not looking at the contents.

The thunder behind them increased as shell after shell landed among the English. There was another roar from the men as the Germans streamed onward. Otto rose again, sprinting forward, not looking for cover anymore as he advanced in one surge with the rest. They were less than two hundred yards from the British line, and he could make out individual soldiers now, rising to fire.

And then he saw them. Little brown dots in the distance in the sky. Even as he ran, he watched in amazement as the objects grew closer, materializing into the form of fighter planes out of the clouds and toward the ground. A thrilling jolt passed through him. They were Spitfires, the new British fighter. He'd never seen them before. They were beautiful, like eagles stalking their prey. His men were close behind him and he screamed at them to hit the ground, but the planes were already closing. The Spitfires opened fire barely a quarter mile away, the bullets ripping through the sand. A hot fire lanced along his left arm. He spun around and hit the ground hard. He blinked, his ears ringing, eyes watering, sand in his mouth. He lay there for long seconds, the fire burning up his arm to his shoulder. Reaching with his other hand, he again retrieved a cloth out of his tunic, wiping his eyes. Gritting his teeth, he looked over at his men. He didn't even have to check them. Their bodies were riddled with bullets. They were gone.

Up and down the line he could see mangled German bodies and now a new sound thundered in. It was the artillery, saved apparently for this last desperate moment. The British were firing, their guns giving the Germans everything they had. The German wave had broken. First one man, then more, rose and turned, shuffling back toward the safety of the German lines. Otto looked around, judging the circumstances. There was no point in staying here, he realized. Clutching his wound as tightly as he could, he turned and shambled back toward the German guns. He fought the dizziness as he stumbled away, knowing if he passed out, he would be captured or killed. He turned and fired his pistol from time to time, attempting to cover the general retreat. Soldier after soldier around him dropped as the murderous fire fell in among them but Otto was miraculously spared.

For twenty minutes, a lifetime, he fought this way, death all around him. Finally, impossibly, he reached the ridge where they had started. Otto collapsed into the sand, exhausted. After a while he rolled over onto his stomach to glance out toward the sea. An hour ago, the landscape before him had been serene, a picture painting. But now smoke billowed everywhere. Men lay in crumpled heaps here and there among the grass and sand. Hundreds of them were dead, perhaps thousands. Some men were crawling feebly back toward the lines, most not moving at all. In the distance, the Spitfires dove and darted, chasing his comrades away.

He'd seen enough. Pulling himself to his feet, he checked his wound. His makeshift bandage was an angry scarlet, but it seemed to have stemmed the flow of blood. He knew he should probably wait for a medic, now that he was out of harm's way, but he wanted to report to the lieutenant what had just happened. He was angry now. If they'd had the full platoon, perhaps they could have continued the advance. No, he knew that wasn't true. With all the men present there would have only been more targets. It wasn't the lieutenant who had failed him. It was the vaunted Luftwaffe, their air force.

He stumbled down the ridge, laboring through the deep sand. He made it to the bottom and then a few hundred yards to the rear, reaching the command post a few minutes later, a small stone house, squat and sad, nestled in the lee of the ridge.

As he grew closer, he was shocked to see a jumble of bodies crumpled against the near wall of the home. The mass was brown and green. British colors. He hurried forward and stared down at the men. They were dead, blood splashed on their clothing and against the wall. The stone contained circular pits, flecked with powder. The men had been gunned down.

Otto looked them over and saw they were unarmed. In shock, he turned to a private standing guard at the entrance of the house.

"What happened here?" he asked.

The private didn't answer.

"Tell me," he ordered.

"The . . . the lieutenant ordered these men killed," he said.

"Why? Did they attack us? Did they try to escape?"

The private shook his head.

"Then how can we shoot them?"

"Orders."

Otto took a step forward and the private gripped his rifle hard, bracing as if Otto was a tsunami about to wash over him.

"We don't kill prisoners, Private."

Otto stared at the crumpled bodies for long minutes, his mind reeling. This wasn't war, it was murder. When those fellows were on the other side, rifles in hand, with a chance to shoot him, then it was fair play—not much different from a football match really, except for the deadly part. But this—this was something else.

"Where is the lieutenant?" he demanded.

"Inside," said the private. "But he doesn't want to be disturbed."

Otto started toward the door, but the private blocked him. "I'm sorry, Corporal. Lieutenant's orders."

Otto reached out and pulled the steel helmet from the private's head, rotating it upside down and crashing it on the soldier. The private crumpled to the ground. Otto moved the man away from the door and laid him out flat. He removed a blanket from the man's pack, folded it neatly into a square, and placed it under the soldier's head. Standing back up, he squared his shoulders and marched into the cottage.

Lieutenant Wagner was inside, hunched over a rickety table in the center of the one-room structure, eyes scanning a wrinkled map. He heard Otto's footsteps, but must have assumed it was his orderly.

"Do you have a message for me?" The lieutenant looked up and his face registered surprise to see Otto. "What are you doing here? Did the attack succeed?"

"The attack failed," said Otto. "I lost the rest of my squad." He felt his anger rising. "While the rest of the platoon sat back here for God-knows-what reason, I lost all of my men."

"Are you questioning my orders?" asked the lieutenant. "You'd better not be. I've already warned you, Corporal."

"Time enough to talk about that later, Lieutenant. What about those prisoners of war outside? Let's talk about what you did to them."

The lieutenant laughed, waving his arm toward the door dismissively. "What of them? They were trying to escape. This is wartime, Corporal, not a birthday party. Things happen."

"Not in the German army they don't," said Otto. "We have honor. We play by the rules. You've brought shame on us, on the SS."

The lieutenant's eyes flared. "You don't know much about the SS if you believe that. But listen, Corporal, I was probably too harsh on you just now. You've lost your whole unit. I heard from headquarters a little while ago. They're bringing up reinforcements, but they won't be ready in the next few hours. Find your platoon, resupply your ammunition, and get some food. You're a good man, Otto. I'll forget about earlier. Just go get a little rest." The lieutenant returned to his work.

"It's not going to be as easy as all that," said Otto, taking another step forward.

The lieutenant raised his head, his eyes alarmed now. "What do you think you're about, Corporal? I ordered you out of here. Now go!"

Otto took another step.

"Corporal, did you hear me? This is your last chance." He reached into his tunic and removed a piece of paper. "Do you know what this is?"

"I don't care what it is."

"You will. It's a message from headquarters. There's a report you were insubordinate in Eindhoven with another officer of the Wehrmacht. That officer has demanded an investigation. He's asking for a court-martial. I've been sitting on this for a week. You're a decent soldier, Otto, and the platoon could use you in the days to come. I was planning on making this all go away, but you need to turn around and walk out that door this moment. There won't be another chance, so what will it be?"

Otto lunged at the lieutenant, grabbing him under his shoulders. He jerked the man out of his chair and into the air until he was over his head. The officer was shaking with fear now, and Otto held him there for long moments, staring into his eyes, saying nothing. "We do not kill prisoners," he whispered.

The lieutenant nodded, his face flushed. Otto lowered him, inch by inch to the ground. He shoved the officer back into his chair and then grabbed the report from the desk, tucking it into his tunic. He stared at the officer. "We do not kill prisoners," he repeated, and then left the cottage.

It was not hard for him to find the rest of the platoon. They were behind the building, less than one hundred yards away. The smell of stew wafted through the air. The remainder of Otto's unit, about fifteen men, making up a third of the prewar unit, were strewn out in the sandy grass, plates in hand, picking at their food.

Someone spotted Otto and they called him over. He grabbed a bowl of the stew, which was thick with potatoes and greasy salted pork, and stepped over, sitting down heavily by himself. A man tried to engage him in conversation, asking about the rest of Otto's squad, about the battle that he just endured, but he did not answer. Instead, he closed his eyes and chewed his food mechanically.

He sat that way for a half hour, his mind blank, not tasting anything. He spoke to no one. A soldier moved among them with boxes of ammunition, making sure each of them had a full supply. Otto took his share without comment. He was preparing himself for another assault.

A car pulled up at the cottage. Otto glanced over at the vehicle, guessing the reason for its arrival. An SS lieutenant climbed out of the vehicle with several soldiers, armed with MP38 submachine guns and following the officer quickly into the cottage. A few minutes later they reappeared, heading toward the platoon.

"Otto Berg!" shouted the lieutenant, scanning the men.

Otto did not answer.

"Corporal Berg!" the officer repeated. "Identify yourself this instant!"

Otto raised his hand, not looking up.

The two soldiers accompanying the lieutenant raised their machine guns, taking aim at Otto. The lieutenant took a few steps toward him, keeping his distance from the corporal.

"Corporal Berg, you are under arrest for striking a superior officer and for disobeying orders. You will accompany me to headquarters where you'll be court-martialed."

Otto could feel the men's eyes on him, the stares of shock and surprise. Taking a breath, he rose gradually to his feet until he towered over the lieutenant. He stared into the man's eyes, and then turned to look at each of the guards. Finally, he accompanied them.

The car ride back to headquarters took several hours. They crossed into Holland and headed into the interior of the country. Otto was wedged between the two guards in the backseat, his massive frame spilling over so that the men were crammed against the doors. He was surprised to see the vehicle passing back into Eindhoven.

"Why here?" he asked.

"We have an administrative headquarters," said the lieutenant. "It's not the closest, but since some of the complaints against you occurred here, it's a natural place to conduct your trial."

The vehicle eventually rambled to a halt in front of a nondescript building. Otto was escorted inside and up the stairs to a windowless room on the second floor. There was a table, two chairs, and little else. One of the guards shoved Otto into a seat, removing his dagger and his pack. He remained in the room, keeping an eye on Otto. Time passed. Nobody spoke to him. He was offered no food, nothing to drink.

The door opened and the lieutenant returned, a file in his hand. He sat down across from Otto, taking a sip of tea from a mug. He flipped open the file and skimmed through it, shaking his head and whistling as he did so. Finally, he looked up at Otto.

"Well, Corporal, you've placed yourself in quite an impressive fix. Insubordination and violence in Eindhoven. Just those actions alone, by the way, could've landed you in prison. Your current commanding officer also writes of your poor military skills, losing your entire squad of men. Then you struck and knocked out a private and attacked your commanding officer. I shiver when I think what they are going to do to you. Do you have anything to say for yourself?"

Otto didn't answer.

"Look, Corporal. You lost your entire squad. You've been in the thick of this thing since the invasion started." The lieutenant's voice was soft, sympathetic even. "Isn't there something you can give me, some defense I can write down that might assist you? Tell me what happened here in Eindhoven."

"Some of our men were looting a store. We had strict orders to pay for all goods. The lieutenant broke the rules."

"He denies that. And even if that was true, you can't take matters into your own hands. You should have reported it to your then-commanding officer."

"He was wounded—maybe he's dead now."

The officer was taking notes. "What about this incident today?"

"My current commander ordered the murder of British soldiers."

"What do you mean?"

Otto explained the scene in front of the cottage, and what happened afterward.

"I'm sure there was an explanation."

"No."

"But—"

"No."

"Well, we'll look into it, Corporal, but I'm sure it will be your word against his."

"You cannot murder prisoners."

"It's war, Corporal. These things happen. Even if they shouldn't. And it's not the place of corporals to interfere with the orders of their lieutenant."

"He's not *my* lieutenant."

"The SS sees it differently." He leaned forward, offering Otto a cigarette. "I don't think you realize the gravity of the situation."

"Court-martial."

"Yes, court-martial. But do you realize what that means here? The thing that happened in Eindhoven, well, it's not the end of the world. They might have jailed you for a month or two, stripped you of your rank. With the fighting on, you might even have gotten lucky with a suspended sentence. But striking your lieutenant on the front lines? In a combat situation? They'll put you in front of a wall for that."

Otto said nothing in return.

"Are you listening to me, Corporal?" the lieutenant asked. "You're facing the death penalty. And soon. This isn't like peacetime. They're already assembling the team to try you. Court will be tomorrow afternoon. If you are found guilty, you'll be shot immediately."

"Is this the Germany we live in now?"

"It's exactly the Germany you live in. This is the SS. We follow orders, for Fatherland and Führer. Those British soldiers don't matter. How many have been killed in the past few weeks? Hell, Corporal, how many have you killed yourself?"

"That's different. They could fight back."

"Like I said, Corporal, it's war. You can tell the panel what happened, but I don't think it's going to make much of an impression. You'll serve as a fine example for the men in the ranks. A corporal shot for disobeying orders in combat—that will stop others from doing the same!" The lieutenant closed the folder and started to rise. "I'm sorry, Corporal, but I don't see any hope for you. Heil Hitler!" He strode out the door, leaving Otto alone with his thoughts.

Chapter 9
Ramp

Friday, May 24, 1940
6:17 p.m.
Eindhoven, Netherlands

Aafke couldn't keep her eyes open after staring at the ledger all afternoon. She closed her eyes, thinking about the past.

She remembered a Sunday morning at Mass. She'd been just a girl then, scarcely ten. A hazy smoke hung over the interior of the cathedral. Far away, it seemed to her, a priest stood, his back to the parishioners. His voice echoed through the chamber as he finished the final invocation: "*In nomine Patris et Filii et Spiritus Sancti.*"

Aafke crossed herself and rose, following her family out of the sanctuary and into the nave. She stood nearby while her mother chatted with some of the other women. Christiaan had run outside with a group of boys. He never could stand still; even during Mass his knees were knocking and his hands patting against his leg. Her father had given up on beating him after. It made no difference.

Aafke never ran off. She was right where she wanted to be, in the Lord's house next to her mother. They were almost the same height already, and her mother could scarcely weigh more than her. Aafke reached out and took her hand. Her mother turned and smiled, giving her fingers a squeeze. "Not much longer now," she whispered.

A few minutes later, they collected Christiaan and their mother took them to a bakery across the street from Sint Catharina-kerk. She examined her purse, counting the coins carefully. Eventually she ordered a coffee and some *peperkoek*. They sat at a table outside and she cut the loaf into thin slices, giving a piece to each of them. Aafke loved the gingerbread. As she ate she reached up and touched her mother's golden hair. They were twins almost.

Christiaan jabbered away with his endless energy, describing a giant truck that had nearly run him and his friends over as they scurried back and forth after church. "You must be more careful!" their mother demanded. But Aafke knew it wouldn't do any good.

Finally, it was time to go home. They walked through the streets of Eindhoven. Aafke's mother greeted several people on the street with warm words and her infectious smile. They arrived at their corner store a few minutes later. It was closed for Sunday. They paused at the door while their mother inspected them carefully, brushing a few crumbs off Christiaan's jacket. She took a deep breath. "All right," she said at last. "Let's go. And quietly now, your father may be sleeping."

They tiptoed through the store and then up the stairs. Aafke grimaced with every creak. They reached the door to their flat and her mother fumbled in her purse, trying to find the key.

"What's that infernal racket?" her father's muffled voice demanded. Her mother managed to open the lock and Christiaan pushed through, running into the apartment.

"Oh, it's my boy!" shouted Maarten. "Ho now! Let me take a look at you!"

Aafke and her mother stepped into the kitchen. Her father was there, at the table, a mug in hand, thumbing through the newspaper. Christiaan had plowed onto his lap and was sitting, legs dangling in the air, a big smile on his face.

"Why didn't you come with us, Father?" he asked.

"Too much to do here," he said. "It's Sunday, there's the books to do. And plenty of other things that haven't been finished," he said, turning his head to their mother.

"But surely you'll still take me to the park," said Christiaan. "You promised."

Maarten chuckled. "That's my boy. Always getting his bargain's worth. Indeed I will. But get yourself into your room and change your clothes. You won't be going in your Sunday best." He reached out and mussed the boy's hair before sending him off. He watched the closed door for a moment, before turning to them. A scowl swallowed the smile and an angry vein appeared in the middle of his forehead. "Now then, what do the two of you have to say for yourselves?"

"What do you mean?" her mother asked.

"Church was over hours ago. Where have you been?"

"Hardly that," she said, her fingers brushing Aafke's shoulders as she walked by and went to the counter, turning toward the morning's dishes.

"Don't turn your back to me!" he shouted. "Look at me this instant! Now where the hell have you been?"

"Watch your language, Maarten. I visited for a bit with my friends, then I took the children for some *peperkoek*." She turned to Aafke. "Why don't you run along, my dear."

"She'll go nowhere!" shouted Maarten. "The two of you have lazed around enough today. And *peperkoek*, is it? Are we made of money now?"

"It was a few coins, Maarten, don't be silly."

"Damn you, to call me silly! We're here on the edge of ruin, and you're pissing our last few guilder away on pastry."

Aafke was frozen. She wanted to run out of the room and hide, but he'd ordered her to stay. She moved closer to her mother, taking the hem of her dress in her hands and gripping tightly.

"We'd have all the guilder we needed if you didn't need a bottle a day!" her mother snapped back. "When we married you promised you would abstain, that we would attend Mass together. Do you remember?"

"Bah, a man chooses his own way. Now close that mouth of yours and you and your daughter can get to work on those dishes."

But she hadn't quieted down, Aafke remembered. Her mother had grown angrier, had stood up to Maarten more than Aafke had ever seen. The beating he then gave her landed her mother in the hospital. That's where they'd found the lump in her mother's breast, and she'd been gone a month after that.

Aafke shook her head, fighting the tears. She musn't think about that right now. She tried to concentrate on the books, her finger moving slowly down the ledger. It was after hours, and the lights in the store were dim, causing her to strain her eyes. It was stuffy inside as well, the heat of the late spring day not yet dissipating. But it was far cooler here than upstairs, and there were other reasons to stay below.

She sighed. No matter how many times she looked over the numbers, the answer was the same: They simply weren't making it. The supply system set up by the Germans ran smoothly enough. However, their occupiers demanded too much money to provide the goods necessary to keep the store running and satisfy the ration cards. And there was still the tricky problem of the exchange rate, because the Germans, who frequented the store, were still paying with Reichsmarks at the disastrous rate of exchange.

The only thing that was keeping them afloat was Arno's smuggled goods. The former delivery driver, who had lost his truck on the first day of the war, managed to bring them supplies several times a week. Sometimes this was no more than a backpack brought in after dark. Other times it might be a partial wagonload. These goods, consisting of produce from the country, canned meats, and sometimes cigarettes, allowed them to sell a bit on the side and keep the store solvent. If only barely.

The black-market trade was conducted after hours, sometimes by Arno, and sometimes by Aafke. Her father stayed out of it. Shortly after the surrender, they had received news that her brother was a prisoner of war and had been sent to a camp back in Germany. This information came in the form of an official notice from the Nazi authorities. They still had heard nothing from Christiaan. Since that time her father had largely remained upstairs, ignoring the store and getting deeper and deeper into his cups. Aafke would've thought he'd long run out of alcohol but he always seemed to have another one handy. She knew he would run out eventually and she both hoped for and dreaded that day.

There was a knock at the door. Two light raps, followed by a pause and a third. This was the signal that somebody wanted to buy black-market goods. Aafke felt her heart racing as it did every time she heard that pattern. Was this the moment that instead of a neighbor or a friend she would open the door to find a German soldier waiting for her, or worse yet, a member of the Gestapo? The knock came again. She took a deep breath and stepped over to the door. Peering out, she relaxed immediately. The shadow on the other side was short and squat.

She opened the door and found Mrs. Smit glaring up at her.

"You took long enough, dearie," the old woman grumbled as she pushed her way through.

"What can I do for you?" Aafke asked as politely as she could muster.

"What's the news?" Mrs. Smit asked, looking this way and that at the goods on the shelves.

"We don't have any news anymore," said Aafke. "Just the rubbish the Germans feed us."

"Do you mean their tales of winning the war? Of crushing the Belgians and the French? Of driving the English to the sea? I don't think that's rubbish at all. From what I've heard, the war is over, and we're stuck in the mud while our queen ran off to England, safe and sound and leaving us in the lurch." Mrs. Smit scowled. "I hope she enjoys herself. The Germans will be there too, soon enough."

"Is there something specific that you would like?" Aafke asked. She didn't want to talk about the war. It was all too depressing. And she wanted Mrs. Smit, whom she found increasingly distasteful, out of her store as soon as possible.

"That depends on what you have."

"Just what you see."

"Nonsense, child," she said, waving her hand. "Where are the black-market items?"

"We don't have much else," said Aafke. "We have some cigarettes and a little fruit."

"Any bread?"

Aafke nodded. "Let me show you," she said, walking around the counter and lifting a basket up.

Mrs. Smit shuffled forward, leering at the basket of goods as she picked through the items with her fat fingers. "There's not much here!" she snapped. "Are you hiding the good stuff for others? Or perhaps you're keeping all of that for yourself," she said with a knowing smile.

"This is all we have."

"Well, how much for the bread and three of the apples?"

Aafke named the price.

"Scandalous," said Mrs. Smit. "Charging honest folks such exorbitant prices."

"We're taking great risks to provide this," said Aafke. "And you're buying these outside your ration card."

"Oh, I know all that. That doesn't mean you're not making a pretty profit. I'm not the only one wondering where all our money is going," she said.

"What do you mean?" Aafke felt her blood freeze.

"You're getting rich, that's what I mean. You and that father of yours and working with the Germans to boot."

"What are you talking about?"

"I'm talking about your collaboration with the Nazis at our expense. We know where you get your goods."

"We're not working with the Germans," said Aafke, horrified that anyone could think that. "They control the supplies. They're the only ones we can buy from."

"Suit yourself," she said. "If that clears your conscience. You can try to explain it to your neighbors, but I'm not sure they'll listen." She snatched the groceries out of Aafke's hands, staring at them and shaking her head. "I'm not sure how much longer the people will take it, though." She snapped her fingers in Aafke's face. "Just remember, dearie, the people are watching." Mrs. Smit waddled to the door and slammed it shut.

It was a moment before Aafke realized she hadn't paid for the goods. *Mrs. Smit must be lying*, she thought. The old bat was always stirring up trouble in the neighborhood, whispering poison into people's ears, setting neighbors against each other, gossiping loudly to anyone that would listen.

But another part of Aafke knew all too well what people, especially desperate ones, could come to believe. This was a new and unexpected worry.

Another knock jolted her. This one was loud and insistent. Her heart galloped and she wasn't sure what to do. Should she run upstairs? But what good would that do? If it was the Gestapo, there was nowhere to run. Taking a deep breath, she stepped back over to the door and opened it. Instead of the secret police, there was the grinning face of Arno.

"Don't do that!" she said. "You scared me half to death!"

Arno stepped in, putting his hands in the air. "I surrender," he said laughing again. "I'm sorry, Aafke, I just couldn't help myself. Gallows humor, I guess. Dark times demand light hearts." He reached out for her hands.

"Keep your comments and your hands to yourself," she said, not feeling mollified. "I just had a terrible scare."

Arno's face shifted to concern. "What happened? Were the Germans here?"

"No, thank God. But something almost worse—Mrs. Smit."

Arno laughed again. "Yes, Mrs. Smit is worse than a truckload of Germans. What did that old viper want?"

"A little of this and that, but she complained loudly about the prices, and she hinted that the neighborhood is talking about the money we're earning and think we are collaborating with the Germans." Aafke didn't bring up that the old woman failed to pay. She was embarrassed she hadn't had the courage to stop her.

"Working with the Germans? Hah! As if we would. Don't listen to all that, she's just stirring up trouble."

"But what if the neighbors are saying that?" she asked.

"They aren't, I promise you. Still, if you're worried about Mrs. Smit, I could always . . ." He made the finger-across-the-throat gesture.

"Don't joke about such things, Arno."

"So touchy tonight," he said. "I have just the thing for that. He pulled his knapsack off and unzipped the top, pulling out a bottle of red wine.

"Where did you find that?" she asked. Even Arno had not been able to secure alcohol since the war started. The only spirits available seemed to be the endless supply her father had somehow stashed in his room.

"I can't reveal all my sources."

"That will fetch quite a price."

"Oh no," he said waving his finger. "I have better plans for this, and they start now." He reached into his pocket, removing a pocketknife, and cut the wrapping off the top. He produced a corkscrew, and twisting the same, quickly removed the plug.

"Do you have glasses?" he asked.

"Arno, I shouldn't. My father is upstairs."

"So what?" said Arno, scoffing. "We're having a friendly drink, and it's not like he isn't indulging himself. Come, let's have a toast and a little celebration. Two weeks into this horrid war and we're still alive."

Aafke assented and turned away, returning a few moments later with a pair of drinking glasses.

"Is that all you can offer?" he asked teasingly. "Those aren't fit for a fine bottle of wine, but I guess they will have to do." He took the glasses, carried them over to the counter, set them down, and filled each one to the brim.

"I can't drink all that," said Aafke. "I won't be able to think or stand."

"That's the idea," he said, giving her a wink.

"Arno!"

"I'm teasing, I'm teasing. Drink what you want, and I'll finish the rest."

He fetched a couple of stools and they sat there in the dim light, quietly sipping away. Aafke relished the tart, bittersweet flavor, letting the alcohol fill her. She felt at peace, something she had not experienced since the war started. It made her understand, at least a little bit, why her father escaped so deeply into the bottle. It gave a temporary retreat from all the fear.

"What are we going to do about Mrs. Smit?" Arno asked finally.

"I told you no teasing."

"I don't mean that. But it's no good letting these neighbors get themselves worked up. I think we need to go into the charity business."

"What do you mean?"

"Well, we have these goods, and we're making good money with them."

"Not good enough," said Aafke. "You should see the books. We're falling further and further behind. Honestly, Arno, I think we're going to lose the store."

"Well, that really settles it, then."

"Settles what?"

"We have to expand."

"Expand?"

"Yes. We need to double our operation. More goods equal more money. That will solve your financial crisis and we can give some of the extra away, just a little here and there to some people in the neighborhood. That should take the wind out of our precious Mrs. Smit."

"That's brilliant, Arno," said Aafke, placing a hand on his forearm and giving it a pat. "But how can we do that?"

"Well, it will involve your help, I'm afraid."

"My help? How?"

"I'll explain. . . ."

The next night, Aafke worked away at the dinner dishes, her hands trembling. Arno would be there any minute and they would move forward with the plan he had outlined the night before. When he'd first explained things, it had seemed so easy, so safe. Maybe it was the wine talking then, but she had readily agreed.

Now, a day later, all the old anxieties crowded her.

"Fine meal," Maarten said, slapping himself on the stomach. "For once you didn't do too bad, my little chicken." He was leaning back on his chair at the table, mug in hand, with a smile of satisfaction on his face.

"Hey! Are you listening to me?" he demanded.

"Yes, Father."

"You're awfully busy over there," he observed. "And in a hurry too, it seems. What are you about?"

"Nothing."

"Nothing is it?" he asked, arching his eyebrows.

"Arno will be here in a few minutes, that's all."

Her father laughed. "Arno, aye? That old commie? Don't tell me you're falling for him? He's a decade older than you if he's a day, and with no prospects."

"It's not like that between us. But if it were, who has prospects these days, Father? If it wasn't for the good graces of our landlord, Mr. Beek, we would already be out on the street."

Her father spat on the ground. "Don't talk to me about that bastard landlord of ours. He's doing us no favors and to be sure. More money than he knows what to do with. If he hadn't taken my store in the first place."

"He didn't take your store, Father. You *had* to sell it."

"Quiet with your mouth! I'll have none of that. You don't know what the years were like after the war. And your mother dead—leaving me with a good boy and with you." He took another deep drink. And waved his hand at her. "Go on, then," he said. "Go to your precious Arno. It's not like there's other suitors lined up, nor likely will there be."

She stormed away, not trusting herself to say more. She'd pushed too far already. Even as she reached the bottom of the stairs, she could hear the light tapping on the window. This time it followed the prearranged code.

She opened the door and found Arno there. He had two large bags in his hands. He stepped in quickly. "Good evening," he said.

"Hello."

He stared at her for a moment. "Second thoughts?"

"No, it's just—"

He nodded. "Don't worry. I've done this a dozen times now." He glanced out the window. "It's dusk. We'll wait a half hour more, then head out."

"Where are we going?"

"You'll see."

Fears flooded Aafke's mind. They could be going anywhere. Anything could happen to them. There was a curfew now, set by the Germans, and they were already past the time. If they were caught, they would be arrested, perhaps worse.

Her thoughts were interrupted by Arno's voice. "It's time."

She nodded, not able to speak.

"Don't worry," he said, putting a hand on her arm. "You'll do just fine."

He led her to the door and carefully opened the latch. Arno peeked his head out the doorframe, looking up and down the street. "It's all clear," he whispered, taking a step out.

She followed him out of the store, trying to mimic his movements. They reached the street corner and he paused, peering around, looking up each of the streets. He finally started again, and she followed. There was no speaking, and they kept a careful pace.

They spotted a German patrol in the semidarkness, but the soldiers were blocks away and didn't seem to see them. Arno led them a different direction. They kept this way for perhaps half an hour as they drew farther and farther away from downtown.

Soon, the houses were starting to spread out and Aafke saw they were leaving Eindhoven. "Where are we going?" she whispered.

He pressed his finger to his lips and then turned, continuing. They left the last row of houses and headed into a field. Going was more difficult now. The ground was uneven, and it was quite dark. The moon was not yet out and Aafke had trouble keeping up. Arno was just a vague shadow ten yards or so in front of her.

They passed first one farm and then another, lights twinkling in the windows. A shadow passed now and again in front of the lights as people went about their lives within.

Time passed on and on, and Aafke wondered how far they might be going. But soon Arno led them onto a narrow roadway, and up a slight incline toward a distant farmhouse. He stopped them about fifty yards before the structure, and he paused for long moments, his head cocked, listening. Finally, he motioned for Aafke to follow him, their feet crunching on the gravel until they arrived at the porch. He turned to her. "You've done well," he said.

Aafke smiled in return. Some of the fear had receded and she was able to breathe again. They had made it to wherever they were going.

Arno stepped onto the porch and knocked. The door opened after a few minutes and a farmer stood at the entrance. Aafke did not recognize him. He was a little shorter than Arno, but nearly twice as large, with a bald head and a dirty apron over his clothing, as if he had been busy at work.

"You're late," the man said, and then turned to Aafke. "And who is this?"

"A friend and a helper. Do you have everything I asked for?"

The farmer eyed her, then turned to Arno. "No apples, but I managed to scrounge up a couple cartons of cigarettes."

"Any coffee?"

The man shook his head. "Plenty of bread, though."

"Well, that will have to do," said Arno. He reached into his coat and pulled out a handful of money, holding it up against the light from the interior of the farmhouse. He counted the notes and then handed them to the farmer.

The man grunted, shoving the money into his pocket, and then lifted two large sacks, setting them on the porch. "Leave the bags behind," he ordered. "And be on your way. The Germans are always about." Without another word he slammed the door shut.

Arno removed the satchels he had brought with him and handed one to Aafke. They quickly loaded up the goods. Aafke was surprised by the quantity. This was truly twice as much as he had ever delivered before. There were canned meats and vegetables, potatoes, two dozen loaves of bread, and precious cigarettes.

"You did as you promised," she said.

"It should get us started, at least."

They soon had everything loaded and Aafke picked up the bag. It was heavy, and she remembered the miles they had traveled to get here. It would be a long night.

He looked at her and must have guessed her thoughts. "Don't worry," he chuckled. "You'll get used to it."

Without another word he started out into the darkness. She followed, struggling even more now. She found herself quickly out of breath and she stumbled several times, trying to keep up. About halfway back she fell, sprawling forward, hitting hard in the dust and dirt.

"Are you all right?" Arno asked. He put his hands out and took hers. His fingers were calloused and strong.

Aafke was embarrassed and pulled herself quickly to her feet. "I'm fine," she said, perhaps a bit too briskly.

Arno grunted. "Let's move along, then." They continued in the darkness, the twinkling lights of Eindhoven growing in intensity and number as they approached the city.

A light flashed out of the darkness, washing over them. "Halt!" a voice commanded in German. Aafke froze, her worst nightmare coming true.

"Run!" shouted Arno, bolting to the right and back into the darkness. Aafke stood frozen for an instant longer, and then took off after him, sprinting through the blackness, the bobbing flashlights reaching out for her.

She could hear the German shouts and she waited for the bullet that would bring her down, but they were making fast progress, and the light no longer chased her. By some miracle the ground was more even here, and there were no more mishaps. Arno kept running for about a hundred more yards and then he fell to the ground, panting in a shallow ditch at the edge of the field.

Aafke crashed down next to him, her breath coming in rapid gasps. It was long moments before she could turn to see the light flickering away in the distance and the shouts of the German patrol already fading away.

She couldn't believe her luck. They'd gotten away. Somehow, they'd survived. "We made it," she managed to whisper between breaths.

"Were not home yet," he said, turning to her and grinning. "But yes, I think we are going to make it." He waited a few minutes more and then rose, pulling her up after him. When she was up, he looked her over in the dim light. "Are you all right?" he asked at last.

"Never better," said Aafke and she meant it. She felt more alive than she had felt in her entire life. This whole night of uncertainty and danger, punctuated by the chase at the end, had been the most terrifying and exhilarating experience. And she had Arno to thank for it. "Thank you."

He looked at her for a moment and then nodded. "Let's go," he said. Arno led them onto the road and back into Eindhoven. They played the same cat and mouse game, moving quietly from block to block until they reached the safety of the store. As they reached the porch, Aafke was surprised to see her hands shaking as she retrieved the keys to open the door. Once inside, she collapsed on the floor, utterly exhausted.

"Well, that was quite an adventure," said Arno.

"Has that ever happened to you before?" she asked.

He nodded. "One other time, and not as close as all that. The Germans are a pesky breed, and they seem to think there's some smuggling going on that they need to monitor. They patrol the fields coming into town, looking for just such people as us."

"Thank you again for bringing me, for showing me how to do this."

She could see the color change in his face even in the dim lights of the store. He turned without responding and glanced down at the goods. "Well, we've got a beginning. These should bring in the money you need and allow you to give a little to our disgruntled neighbors, to keep their tongues from wagging so much." He looked at her again and opened his mouth as if he was going to say something more, but then seemed to change his mind. "Well, it's been a long night. I've got to get some sleep." Arno turned and headed to the door, turning as he was about to leave. "Thank you too, Aafke."

She checked her watch. It was nearly four a.m. She was far too excited to sleep, so she organized the goods, placing them into crates hidden under boxes behind the counter. She made herself some coffee, had a little breakfast, and watched the sun come up from their upstairs flat, thinking about everything she had seen and done the night before.

She opened the store on time. There was already a little line. She smiled, showing them inside and ringing them up as they passed the ration cards. She thought about handing out a few items as goodwill, but she realized she should wait and talk this over with Arno. They had to be careful.

The door banged open, and she glanced up, surprised to see Mr. Beek, their landlord, at the door. He waved congenially, but she felt her blood freeze. "Good morning," he said, stepping up to the counter.

"Good morning, sir. What brings you to this part of town?"

"Business, I'm afraid," he said, reaching into his pocket and retrieving an envelope.

"What is that?"

"Something for you to read in private," he said, glancing at the other customers.

Aafke reached for the envelope.

"I would wait until you're alone."

She ignored him. Opening the unsealed envelope, she drew out the papers. It was an official document from the local court informing the present occupants that Mr. Beek was seizing the store and the flat they lived in for failure to pay their past-due rent. They had twenty-four hours to clear the debt or they were to vacate. She looked up and could see a hint of sadness in the man's face.

"I'm sorry, but there's a war on, and after all, business is business."

Chapter 10
Proces

Sunday, May 26, 1940
11:15 a.m.
Eindhoven, Netherlands

"I did what was right," said Otto, answering the question for the thousandth time.

"And you think you knew better than your superior officer?" the lieutenant asked. The officer had returned to his cell and questioned him overnight. Hours without relenting. Otto had wondered whether he would be tortured, but apparently that was reserved for victims of the SS, not for its members.

"You can't execute prisoners."

"They were trying to escape."

"Against a wall?"

"You admitted yourself you weren't there. That you only came on the scene after."

"Yes, after the execution of unarmed prisoners."

"This is getting nowhere," the lieutenant said, waving a document in his hand. "I will give you one last chance to sign this admission of guilt. If you do, I will advocate for your life. If you don't, I promise you won't live another day."

"I'll take my chances with the court-martial."

The lieutenant shook his head, rising. "Fine," he said. "You're an idiot, Corporal. Your actions have shown that before, and now. Our army doesn't need fools."

"Only thieves and executioners?"

"To accomplish what we must for Fatherland and Führer? Perhaps."

"That's not the Germany I know."

"Careful, Corporal, you're coming very close to treason."

"What if I am? Do I get two bullets instead of one?"

The lieutenant reached across the table and slapped Otto hard across the face. His head didn't move. He stared at the officer, eyes a burning calm. The man held his gaze for some time, then looked away. "I've wasted enough time on you," he said. "There's obviously nothing I can do to help you. Expect your court-martial this afternoon, and your firing squad at first light. Heil Hitler!" With that he rose and stormed out of the interrogation room.

Otto stared down at the plate the guards had brought him. There was a little bread and a couple slices of apple. The slices had browned in the last half hour. He hated that. Why did the man have to go on and on when there was fresh fruit at hand? He grabbed one of the slices and took a bite, closing his eyes. A firing squad tomorrow morning. Well, he'd faced death a dozen times in the past month. But this time it was sure. He looked back down at the apple, frowning at the brown. . . .

An hour later, he was escorted out of the cell and down the hallway to a larger room. There were three SS officers sitting at a table, a single chair facing them. One of them was the lieutenant who had interrogated him. A guard tried to shove him down into the seat, but Otto didn't budge.

"Leave it," commanded the lieutenant. "Corporal, take a seat."

"Please."

"What?"

"You didn't say please."

"Do you see what I was telling you about this man?" the lieutenant asked the others. He shook his head. "Such a waste. Fine, please sit down, Corporal."

Otto took his seat.

"You know why you are here, of course," the lieutenant went on, shuffling some papers in front of him. "You have heard the charges against you?"

"*Ja.*"

"Do you have anything to say for yourself?"

"I was following orders—and they were not."

The lieutenant sighed. "I've been through this with you already, Berg. It's not your place to decide what orders to follow. Not when they come from a superior officer."

"So you said. But looting is against the rules. Shooting prisoners is against the rules."

"Like I said, a waste. I don't think there is anything more to say. You directly disobeyed an order in Eindhoven. In a separate incident, during combat operations, you assaulted your superior officer. Finally, you refused to admit your guilt and accept the mercy of the court. As such, we must make an example of you."

"I don't think so," said a voice at the door.

Otto looked over in surprise to see his friend, Fritz Geier, standing in the doorway. He was dressed in the uniform of an SS captain. Otto was shocked to see that his friend's left arm was missing. The uniform was pinned up at the shoulder to hide his missing limb. Fritz nodded at Otto and then turned back to the three-officer panel.

"What's the meaning of this?" the lieutenant asked.

"The meaning of this is what I just stated," said Fritz. "That I don't think the sentence will be carried out."

"What's going on?" a middle-aged officer inquired. Otto noted he was a major, and he outranked his friend.

"Just that I've come to collect my friend, and I think we've had about enough of this."

"You have no jurisdiction here," said the major. "I order you to leave immediately." The officer turned his head slightly toward the back of the room and gestured at some soldiers waiting there. "Guards, take this captain away and don't let him back into the building until justice has been carried out."

"Do you realize this man is a hero?" said Fritz, pointing at Otto.

"What do you mean?" asked the major.

"He single-handedly stormed and captured a 75-millimeter artillery gun, stopping the gun from slaughtering German troops on the way into Eindhoven."

The lieutenant/prosecutor shrugged. "That's beside the point. Corporal Berg disobeyed direct orders and assaulted a superior officer. It's wartime, Captain. Examples must be made. Now if we may continue—"

"Certainly, that's true," said Fritz. "But not this example."

"I think we've heard enough of this," said the major, turning back toward his guards.

"Oh, it's not just my opinion," said Fritz. "My uncle thinks rather highly of *Sergeant* Berg, who has been promoted and awarded the Iron Cross, by the way." Fritz tapped an envelope he was holding up to his forehead. "Here are the orders."

"That doesn't matter!" snapped the lieutenant, growing angry now. "Actions in battle, and even a promotion, do not override the authority of this court."

"True, true, but still, you should probably take a look at this," said Fritz.

Otto watched the major gesture at a guard, who took the envelope and walked it over to him. The officer removed the documentation, reached into his tunic for some spectacles, and read the papers. Otto noticed the color draining from the man's face. He turned to Fritz.

"Your uncle is Reichsmarshal SS Heinrich Himmler?"

"Yes," said Fritz. "The head of the SS. You may have heard of him." There was heavy sarcasm in his voice, and he now wore a smirk of satisfaction.

"This is an outrage!" shouted the lieutenant, banging his fist on the table. "I don't care who his uncle is, justice must be served!"

"Are you mad, Lieutenant?" the major asked. "Shut your mouth." Shoving the papers at the lieutenant, the officer continued. "This Berg has been personally promoted and cited for bravery by Himmler. Look at the date. These orders were effective yesterday. This is the end of the matter."

"But—"

"That's the end of the discussion, Lieutenant. I suggest you keep your mouth closed before you do yourself further damage. The major turned to Otto. "Well, Corporal, or I guess *Sergeant*, you're exceptionally lucky. It appears you have friends in the highest places."

"Just so," said Fritz, checking his watch. "And if you don't mind, I'd rather collect my friend now. We have an afternoon lunch date I prefer not to miss."

"This isn't the end of this," said the lieutenant, his face an angry scarlet.

"Any time, and any place," said Otto, his voice almost a whisper. Otto rose and marched to the door, grasping his friend's shoulder. "Thank you," he whispered.

Fritz escorted him out of the building. In less than a minute they were on the streets of Eindhoven and Otto was free.

"Let's get moving," Fritz said, stepping quickly away and down the street.

"What's this lunch date?"

"I made that up, although I certainly could eat. We need to get away from here as quickly as possible."

"Why is that?" asked Otto.

"I didn't want to give the major, or the good lieutenant there time to realize that while the promotion and medal came directly from Himmler, there was nothing addressing the charges against you or ordering your release."

"So you think I'm still in danger?"

"I doubt it. We're away now. I'll arrange to transfer you to a different unit. Or if you want, you could join me here."

They found a restaurant and ordered some wine and a little cheese and bread.

"What did you mean I could join you here?" asked Otto after they had settled in.

Fritz looked down at his empty sleeve. "Well, as you can see, my combat days are over. But my uncle transferred me into a local unit here in Holland. I'm stationed in Eindhoven to keep an eye on things."

Otto furrowed his brows. "You don't mean the Gestapo?"

"The same."

"I'm surprised."

"By what, my friend? What would you have me do? Should I become a supply officer, counting paper clips and cigarettes twenty miles behind the lines? Or maybe you would just have me go home, with the cripples and the shirkers? I want to serve the Reich, and I want to serve the SS. This post was available, and I was able to get up to speed while I was still in the hospital. Besides, we are doing important work here."

"Police work."

"Yes, police work. But remember, the future has enemies everywhere. The war is not only fought on the front lines."

"And what does that have to do with me?" Otto asked.

"I could use a good assistant," said Fritz. "You're bright—"

"Bright?" asked Otto, arching an eyebrow.

"Well, bright enough," said Fritz, laughing. "You are strong, protective, and fiercely loyal. You would do me and the Fatherland much good here. That's why I intervened in your trial. Well, that and saving your life."

Otto thought about these words as their food arrived. His friend had always been fiercely loyal to the Führer, and to his uncle. He had learned not even to joke about things like secret arrests and draconian methods. Whatever Otto's concerns about some of the Nazi methods, Fritz could not see it. And now he wanted Otto to join him to serve as just such a secret police officer—to make those very arrests. To place other people in the little rooms across from tables where they might face the same fate Otto had barely avoided.

Otto shook his head. "I'm sorry, my friend, but you know me. I'm not made for a desk. I need a football pitch or a meadow to stomp around in."

"Meadows full of shells and bullets," said Fritz. "That's all you'll get back out there. Think about it, Otto. The French are almost done but we still must fight the English. And I can't imagine the Führer will leave Russia alone forever. There's a lot of war in front of us and you're not immune or immortal. I don't want to have to tell your mother one day that you died on the battlefield in some nameless place when you could have stayed back here, safe and sound, doing equally as important work as you could have done out there. Perhaps more so." Fritz leaned forward. "And think on this: I would have direct control over your promotions here. I could make you a lieutenant, an officer—hell, someday a captain. You'd be your own boss."

"You've always been good to me, Fritz. At the academy in Munich, when everyone else turned their noses down at me because of my upbringing, you were there."

"Ha! They were jealous. You were the best footballer at the school."

"The best footballer at an academy full of aristocrats and industrialists," said Otto. "And me on scholarship—working the tables at meals."

"I never cared about any of that."

"That's why we're friends."

"And now I want us to stay together! Think about it. Imagine how proud your mother would be. Lieutenant Otto Berg! Forget those old washed-up aristocrats from school. You're part of the new ruling class—the SS! You can make a future for your children. Germany is going to rule the world and you can be part of the leadership class."

Otto owed so much to Fritz. He wanted desperately to say yes, but he knew what it meant. Knew what he would have to give up. He shook his head again. "I'm sorry, my friend. It's just not for me."

Fritz lifted his glass and drained the rest of it. "I knew what your answer would be, but I had to ask. Well, I'm good for my word. I'll find you a new unit, probably in a different division, I'll keep you in the field as you desire. Unfortunately, I can't make you a lieutenant in the armed forces. But the way you fight, you'll do well for yourself. Just quit punching officers and you should be fine."

Otto laughed.

"I'm serious. You were very lucky just now. If this trial had occurred in France, you'd already be dead, and there would be nothing I could have done about it."

Otto nodded. "I'll be careful."

"I certainly hope so. Well, it's settled then, but you don't have to go anywhere tonight. Let's celebrate your promotion. There are some beautiful women in this town. Let's see if we can attract a few of them!"

Otto nodded, already knowing he would find some excuse to get out of it. "Let me check into a hotel room first, and there's also something I need to look in on."

Chapter 11
Uitzetting

Sunday, May 26, 1940
Noon
Eindhoven, Netherlands

Aafke sat at the counter, stunned. What was she going to do? *Three months of back rent.* They were barely making ends meet as is and that amount of money was impossible—even with Arno's stepped-up plan to acquire and sell black-market items. She and Maarten were going to lose their store, and, worse yet, their apartment. They would be out on the street and who would take them in? They didn't have an extended family here and her father was not the type to cultivate friendships. Arno might be able to help them for a little while, but his flat was tiny.

Who would they go to? Were there social services still in Eindhoven? And were those run by the Germans? She thought of their reputation in the community already. They could ill afford to go to the enemy for any assistance. Thankfully, they'd been slow so far this Sunday, and she'd had some time to herself.

Just then the front door jingled and she looked up, finding to her vast relief that it was Arno. His eyes were red and forehead creased, as if he hadn't slept since their adventure. He stepped inside, closing the door behind him, and looked at her.

"It looks like you got the same amount of sleep as I did," he said.

"Oh Arno!" she cried running to him. She buried her head in his chest, sobbing.

"What's happened?" he asked.

After a while she calmed down enough to tell him about the eviction. "There's nothing we can do," she said at last.

"Nonsense. There's always something if one only has the will."

She felt a flicker of hope.

"Like what?"

"Well, we already agreed to expand our operation. We just need to do so on a much larger and faster scale."

"That's impossible. How would we do that?"

"I'll track down a wagon we can use today. We collect all of your money and all of mine. I'll cart it out to the countryside and obtain a full wagonload worth of goods. Then I'll bring it back in. In the meantime, you spread the word in the neighborhood that we will have a huge sale after the store closes tonight. With any luck, we will raise enough to pay the back-due rent."

Aafke was horrified for a number of reasons. "You can't do that."

"Why not?"

"For one, you can't bring goods like that in during the day. The Germans are everywhere. They would spot you in an instant, it's madness."

"I think I can do it. I know a few of the Germans around. A carton of cigarettes here, a pound of coffee there, and they'll let me through."

"And what if you encounter the wrong kind of Germans?"

He shrugged. "It could happen. But what else am I supposed

to do? This is my place to hide and sell things. Sure, I might be able to build a little something up out of my location, but that would take months and I'd probably lose my own place in the meantime. My fate is tied to yours. So I'll take the risk."

"Even if that wasn't crazy, you can't put your own money into the enterprise with no hope of repayment. This is our problem, not yours."

"Did you hear what I just said? Your problem is my problem. If we don't make this work, the money I have right now might pay a month or two of rent, then I wouldn't have anything to buy goods with or any way to make more money. Before I know it, I'd be out on the street as well. Like I said, our fates are tied together, Aafke."

She wanted to keep arguing, but she could see his mind was made up. "You've been so good to us," she said, finally, putting a hand on his arm. She could feel his muscles tense underneath his shirt. "I don't know what we would've done without you."

"There's no 'we' about it. I'm not doing this for Maarten. I'm doing it for you."

She stepped forward and threw her arms around him, holding him close for a moment. "Thank you," she said.

He stepped back and looked at her. "Think nothing of it. We will have to take our chances and hope for the best."

"Be careful, please."

He broke into a crooked grin. "You know me, Aafke. I always survive."

Arno departed a few minutes later, leaving specific instructions about what to do in his absence. She kept the store open as usual. However, she pulled select neighbors aside, whispering to them about this evening and asking them to spread the word among trusted friends.

The hours ticked slowly by. Arno had said he should be able to secure the goods and return, perhaps as early as late afternoon. Aafke tried to keep herself as busy as possible, but her eyes flipped over and over to the clock behind the counter. At three o'clock she started to worry. But it wasn't sensible to do so yet, she knew. After all, it would take a while for Arno to have secured the wagon and traveled out into the country. He might also have had to make several stops before he could obtain everything they needed. The afternoon wore relentlessly on. She couldn't remember a day that had lasted longer. She almost wished for her father's company to pass a bit of the time. Almost.

Three o'clock turned to four, and her fear grew by the hour. He should've been back by now; she knew something terrible would happen if Arno were caught. The police would question him, perhaps harshly. She had heard rumors already in the town of neighbors disappearing, returning days later, broken, beaten—if they returned at all.

But perhaps they were just rumors. She wasn't sure if the tales were true. Everyone in the stories was always a friend of a friend, or an uncle across town. But whether accurate or not, the whispers were enough to fill her mind and imagination with terror.

Five o'clock arrived. She was supposed to close the store. Soon after, she expected a rush of friends and neighbors coming to stock up on black-market goods. As of now, she didn't have nearly enough to give them. Besides, the only people coming might be the Gestapo, tipped off by Arno under torture and arriving to arrest her.

She checked her watch again. She couldn't wait any longer. She needed to close the store. She stepped over to the door and reached out toward the handle. It rattled violently, and the door flew open. She gave out a gasp. It was Arno.

His face was covered with sweat and lines of stress.

"What happened?" she asked.

"Don't ask. I was almost caught, but I made it through.

We've got to get everything inside quickly. There's a German policeman only a couple blocks from here, walking this way."

Aafke rushed out with Arno. She was amazed to see the wagon bulging with goods.

"You've done wonderfully."

He nodded. "If we can keep it. We've got to hurry." He grabbed the first sack and handed it to her. They moved with lightning speed. The sacks were heavy and Aafke was soon out of breath. "Faster," said Arno, glancing down the street.

She did not hesitate to comply. They were terribly exposed outside like this, and they were not alone. Pedestrians were walking by, some of them eyeballing the wagon suspiciously. Any one of them could be an informant who would turn them in to the police.

The minutes ticked by. She expected any moment for the policeman to come around the corner and scream for them to stop. But they were down to the last few sacks now and everything was going according to plan. Arno lifted the last bag out and jumped down. Pulling it into the store, he sprinted back to the street. "I'll be back."

"Where are you going? People will be here any time."

"I've got to return the wagon. It would be suspicious if I left it out here."

Aafke scurried around while Arno was gone, opening sacks and trying to take some kind of inventory. She also dragged the goods, bag by bag, over near the counter, to make a little room in the center of the store, and so she could keep an eye on things as customers came in. She checked her watch again as she finished. It was 6:15 now and still no Arno. She'd told her customers to come back at 6:30, but to be careful that no Germans were around before they knocked on the door, and not to cluster outside. She hoped they had listened to her. The risk wasn't over. They were being reckless having people come when it was still light out, and in such large numbers. She just had to hope that their luck lasted as it had so far in this venture.

Arno arrived a few minutes later. She was so relieved he was there. She gave him a hug. He smelled of sweat, straw, and oil. He'd been their savior since the war started and he'd done it again today. "Thank you," she whispered, still holding on to him. "I don't know what I would do without you."

"It's all right," he said, patting her back. "It's going to be all right, Aafke. I'll never let anything happen to you."

She started to say something but was interrupted by a knock-in code at the door. She pulled away. "Our first customer."

"Let's save your store," he said, giving her a wry grin.

The evening passed quickly and without incident. The neighbors were eager to buy and looked with bulging eyes on the piles of goods. There was plenty of bread and fresh produce, but also hard-to-find items like shoe polish, rope, coffee, and cigarettes. The money rolled in until the register was stuffed full and Aafke had to find some empty cans under the counter to store it. There was more money here than she'd ever seen before. She hadn't been able to count it, but she was sure there would be enough to save the store by the time the goods were sold. She felt peace overwhelming her. They were going to make it. Her father, Arno, and her.

The door opened again and Aafke looked up to see who their next customer was. She was shocked to see two German soldiers there. They were SS, a corporal and a captain. They strolled in and headed toward the counter, the taller soldier beaming at her. Aafke's heart fell. Everything was over.

"Do you remember me?" the corporal asked, grinning from ear to ear.

She smiled back, holding back the terror. Behind the Germans, the customers were edging out of the store. Arno stood at the entrance, helpless to aid her. "Excuse me?" she said.

"I said, do you remember me, Fräulein?"

"I'm sorry," she said trying to fight for time, to figure out something to do here. "I don't know what you're talking about."

The corporal frowned. "But surely you do remember me.

The first day of the war? The soldiers were looting your store. I came in and stopped them."

She did remember now. She forced another smile and nodded. "Yes, sir. I do. Thank you again," she said. She glanced at Arno, who pointed to his wrist. Aafke understood immediately. "I'm sorry, gentlemen, we are just closing. Is there anything I can get for you?"

The captain slapped the corporal on the side. "She doesn't seem very happy to see you, Berg. Let's go get a drink."

"One moment," he said. "Are you all right, Fräulein? Have you been safe?"

"We're managing."

"Are the Germans treating you correctly?"

"Yes. As well as could be expected."

"I'm Otto," he said. "Do you remember my name?"

"Yes . . . thank you again, Otto. And I'm so sorry, but I really do have to close now."

"This is my friend, Captain Fritz. He is stationed here in Eindhoven. I won't be here long, but he will. If you need anything, or if anything happens to you, you must reach out to the captain, and he will take care of it."

Captain Fritz nodded. "He speaks the truth, Fräulein. Anything you need, anything at all, just call the SS headquarters here in Eindhoven, or walk yourself down to the building." He turned to Otto. "You were right, by the way, my friend. She is very pretty."

Otto blushed slightly. "That wasn't for her to overhear."

"She doesn't mind, does she? Look at her, she's blushing as much as you are."

Aafke's face was flushed, but not for the reason he thought. "Thank you again, Otto, and thank you, Captain, for your kind offer. Now, I'm so sorry, but we really must close for the night."

Otto nodded at her. "It was good to see you."

"Thank you again for helping us that day."

The door opened behind them. Arno was holding the handle. Aafke willed them to leave.

"Well, our business here is done," said the captain. He turned and started toward the door.

"I will be back to the fighting soon," said Otto. "I won't be here again for a while. Maybe forever."

What did this man want from her? "I hope you are safe," she said.

He smiled again at that. "Thank you, Fräulein. We will take our leave." He turned and followed his friend. They reached the door and Fritz turned to Arno.

"You're coming with us," he said.

"What are you talking about?" asked Aafke.

The captain smiled. "Fräulein, you are very pretty, as I said, but you must also be naïve. I'm not stupid. It's well past your closing time. The floor is strewn with goods you have no business possessing. You and your friend here are smugglers and black marketeers. Out of courtesy for Otto, I'm going to leave you behind, but your friend here is coming with me for questioning.

"Oh, but you can't!" she said, turning to Otto. "Can't you stop him?"

Otto turned to the captain. "Is this necessary?" he said.

"I'm afraid so. We can't have a black market. It takes away from the supply of legitimate goods, and the quota to send to Germany." He turned to Aafke. "But don't worry, we'll return him at some point. Assuming he cooperates." The captain stepped around the counter and opened the register, whistling. "That's quite the haul." He looked up at Aafke. "Touch nothing. My men will be back to collect the money, and the goods."

Aafke looked over at Arno. She thought he might fight, or try to run, but the Germans were blocking the entrance. He turned to look at her, nodding grimly. The captain took him by the arm and escorted him out of the store.

Otto turned back around to face her. "I'm sorry, Fräulein. I didn't know this was going to happen. I would help you if I could."

Tears were streaming down her face now. "Get out!" she said.

"But—"

"Get out!"

The corporal looked as if he would say something more, but then turned and clomped out of the store. She was left there alone. Arno was arrested and would be tortured, perhaps killed. Surely that captain wouldn't leave them alone now. The store would be searched, and everything seized. They would probably be arrested as well. She stood there, at the counter, her body shaking, trying to figure out what she would do. Finally, she collapsed to the ground. Curling up, she lay there on the hard floor, eyes closed, waiting for the soldiers to come.

Chapter 12

De Terugkeer

Friday, June 4, 1943
6:00 p.m.
Eindhoven, Netherlands

The passenger train rattled and sputtered as it approached the station. Otto sat near the window but stared straight ahead, taking an occasional sip out of a worn metal flask. A private next to him cracked a joke in his direction, but the sergeant ignored the man, his mind wandering through the tortured pathways of the past few years since he'd been here.

The train lurched to a stop as they reached the platform. Otto took another deep swig of the fiery liquor, then rose and pulled a worn knapsack from a rack above the seats. He stepped off the train without bidding the private *auf Wiedersehen*. Nobody was there to greet him. There was no reason anyone would be. But he knew where he was going and what he intended to do.

The sun was already setting behind the buildings, although darkness would not come for several hours. The streets were nearly abandoned. The few pedestrians who passed Otto by kept their eyes averted, out of fear or of loathing—perhaps a bit of both. As he stomped toward downtown, he noticed the destruction of a building and damage to a number more. Eindhoven hadn't escaped the war entirely, it seemed. The Americans and British had made sure of that. He wondered if they had intended to hit the Philips factory his men had captured on that first day of the war. If so, they'd missed badly.

After a mile, he reached the place he'd been looking for, a shabby grocery store set on the corner. He paused at the door. He wasn't sure why he was there. He'd barely said a word to the girl inside. She had every right to hate him, after what had happened the last time he saw her, more than three years ago. But something drew him to her. He had to make sure she was okay, and to apologize. She would likely throw him out of her store, if she would even speak to him, but he owed that much to her.

Otto took a deep breath and opened the door, hurrying into the grubby interior. He scanned the space quickly, noting who was in the store. There were a couple patrons who stared in surprise at his figure filling up the doorway. They quickly averted their eyes. Otto nodded to them. The customers weren't a threat. He glanced at the shelves. They were mostly bare. Hard times had come to the city, as they'd come to all of Europe. Still, things could be worse. This wasn't Russia after all. Images flashed in his mind as he thought of that place. He put a hand on one of the shelves, steadying himself a bit, and then grunted, moving toward the front of the store.

There was nobody tending the register. A metal bell sat on the counter, and he tapped it, a *ding* sounding through the space. He heard rapid footsteps shuffling down the stairway. The door opened and a middle-aged man appeared. He flinched when he saw Otto's uniform, but quickly recovered, putting on a grim expression of acceptance. "How can I help you?" he asked.

"Is Aafke here?" Otto asked.

"I don't know any Aafke," the man said, and his face appeared genuinely puzzled by the question.

Otto looked around, wondering for a moment if he was in the right store. But he remembered the corner, the cross streets. "She owns this store, or at least her father does."

"Oh, you must mean the girl who lived here before. I'm sorry, sir, I don't know where she is now."

"What happened?"

"They were evicted not too long after the war started."

"Evicted?"

The man nodded. "Failure to pay their rent. I knew the owner a bit, Maarten Cruyssen. He had a daughter. And I think you're right, her name was Aafke." The man looked at him suspiciously. "But what could that have to do with you?"

"You don't know where she went?"

"No, I don't."

The man's tone told him in no uncertain terms that even if he did know anything, he wasn't about to share the information with a German.

Otto turned toward the patrons, who were standing about as far away from the counter as they possibly could. "How about you?" he asked. "Do you know where Aafke is?"

Neither of them answered him. They stared with fear in their eyes, one of them visibly shaking.

"They don't speak German," said the owner. "I'm sorry, sir, but there's nothing we can do for you."

Otto wanted to ask the man more, but he realized there was no point. He looked back at the patrons for a moment longer, then stepped out of the store. It was getting dark now. The city was blacked out and it was already difficult to see. Fortunately, Otto had memorized the route from the station. But he wasn't going back there right away. He checked his watch; it was half past seven. Thinking about the map of the city in his mind, he turned to his left and hurried on his way. With any luck, he would arrive at his next destination in time.

SS headquarters in Eindhoven was a nondescript building in the center of a city block. Three stories high, there was no sign or anything else to indicate the ominous power of the place. But the structure emanated a sinister feel. As he entered through the front door, a private at a desk, set squarely in a narrow corridor, rose as if to stop him, but glancing at Otto's medals and rank, he seemed to change his mind. "How can I help you, sir? We are closed to the public."

"I want to see Fritz Geier."

"*Major* Fritz Geier is not available for any appointments today. Check back tomorrow, or perhaps the next day."

"Tell him Scharführer Otto Berg is here to see him."

"I told you, he's not available."

Otto stepped closer to the desk, putting a giant fist down on the table. "Call him." He wasn't even sure that his friend would still be here. It was a Friday and after hours. But Fritz had always worked long hours, and under the strain of war, it seemed likely he would have continued his practices.

The private sized up Otto and, swallowing hard, he picked up the phone. Waiting a moment, he cleared his throat. "*Guten Abend,* Sturmbannführer. Sorry to disturb you. There is a sergeant here for you. *Ja,* his name is Otto Berg. What's that sir? Yes, all right, I'll tell him. Heil Hitler!" The private hung up the phone. "I apologize. You should have told me you knew the major. He will see you. He's on the third floor—take a left, last office at the end of the hall."

"*Danke, Sturmann.*" Otto stepped around the private and clomped down the hall and up the stairs. The halls were deserted except for an open office here and there. He reached the third floor and turned down the long hallway. The door at the end of the corridor was open and a warm light filled it. He reached the doorway and looked inside. His friend was sitting at his desk behind a pile of paperwork. Fritz had a large office with several windows looking out onto the street. A fire crackled in the hearth. The walls were paneled in cherry and a portrait of Adolf Hitler was perched on the wall directly behind him.

"Otto, my friend," he said, rising and moving around the desk. He grasped Otto warmly with his one hand. "Why didn't you call ahead? I could have made arrangements for us to have a grand evening."

"I just arrived tonight," he said.

"Well, have a seat. Would you like something to drink?"

"*Ja.*"

Fritz poured them each a full glass of brandy and they settled into their seats. Otto noticed his friend was watching him closely, perhaps wondering about the purpose of his visit.

"I got your last letter," Fritz said at last. "What was it, about three months ago? Although it took some time to get to me. I'm so thankful you weren't at Stalingrad. God bless those poor boys."

"That was badly managed," said Otto.

"Careful with that kind of talk," warned Fritz. "I'm a friend but defeatism is not tolerated, especially since—"

"Since we are being defeated?"

His friend laughed. "You're impossible, Otto. But yes, especially that." He leaned forward. "Is it really as bad as all that? Are we truly losing the war in Russia?"

"It's hard to say," said Otto. "We certainly underestimated them. And we've taken incredible losses. The Soviets seem to have an endless sea of resources. They keep coming at us with more men, more equipment every day. We grow weaker and they grow stronger. It doesn't mean we can't stop them, but something will have to change. My own division is in tatters. We are heading to France to refit and for some rest. There aren't a tenth of us left."

Fritz whistled. "I've heard rumors about the losses. But they are being replaced with fresh recruits by every report."

"Not nearly enough. We've had a trickle for the past six months." Otto hesitated. "That's not all."

His friend's face showed yet more interest. "Tell me everything, Otto. You can trust me."

"Terrible things have happened in the east."

"What things?"

"Murder, rape, whole villages. Sometimes in reprisal for the death of a single German soldier. Sometimes for no reason at all. God save our people if the Russians ever make it back to Germany."

"They won't," said Fritz firmly. "The Führer will save us."

"And does the Führer know about the murders?"

"The Russians are barbarians. Cruel killers all. And this is war, Otto." He took a deep drink from his glass. "Surely you remember we've had this conversation before. I hope you haven't gotten yourself into more trouble?"

Otto shook his head. "I always find a way to avoid the worst things going on around me. But I haven't struck any officers, if that's what you mean."

"Good," said Fritz, laughing. "At least there's that." He refilled his glass and gestured at Otto, who shook his head. "You must remember, my friend, that these things happen in times of conflict. But the war will be over soon enough. We will turn the tide against the Russians and win the conflict in the east. Then we can turn on the Americans and English, and all will be peaceful again."

Otto didn't believe it. He'd seen too much. The Soviets would keep steamrolling through the east. At some point, perhaps years from now, they would reach the Fatherland if the western allies didn't beat them to it. Based on what he'd seen in Russia, his people would have very hard times ahead. But he didn't say these things to Fritz. He just nodded and sipped his drink.

"You don't have to go back, you know," his friend said after a long silence.

"Then they'd shoot me for sure."

"No, I mean it. There's still a spot for you here."

"Police work." Otto spat the words.

"Keeping the peace. We have partisans here now, just like you have in Russia. They stir up the people, sometimes killing their own and blaming us. They burn buildings and kidnap innocent citizens. You don't have to go back to Russia, you could stay here."

Otto shook his head. "It's not for me, Fritz."

"How do you even know? Before, you wanted to serve your country in combat. You've done that, Otto. Years of it. You said a tenth of your division is left? What happens next time? How much longer can you be the only one to survive? Think of your mother. How is she, by the way?"

"She's getting by. She asks about you sometimes."

"Is her English background getting her into trouble like it did during the last war?"

Otto shook his head. "She was a young wife then, too young to know how to react. And also, I don't think the people are as angry at England this time. She does miss me, though, and she worries about me, of course."

"See, my friend? Why leave her to fret? You could be safe here, and still serve the Fatherland."

The words stirred him, particularly about his mother. He was the only thing left in the world for her. "I can't—my comrades."

"How many of them can be left? And what about your friendship with me? You could have new men here to serve with. And to serve under you. I still have the power to make you an officer. I wouldn't even have to make a call. It's a stroke of a pen."

He was right, of course. Almost all the men Otto had led into Russia were long gone. It wasn't truly comrades who held him back, it was a vague distaste for policework and perhaps even more, a guilt of placing himself in a situation of safety when others had to go back to the front. It was one thing for Fritz, who had lost an arm. But Otto was perfectly healthy. Still, he'd fought for over three years now. He'd been wounded multiple times. His mother kept asking in her letters when he would be out of harm's way. He'd responded that they must wait until the end of the war, but was that true? Was there another way?

"You hesitate, I see," said Fritz, wagging a finger. "I know what's going through that thick skull of yours. All the honor and duty. But we have all of that here as well, and a sense of camaraderie every bit as deep as what you've had in the Waffen-SS. I have an idea. We have an operation tonight against a resistance group. Why don't **you tag** along?"

"I have to get back to the train," said Otto, checking his watch. "I only had leave for a few hours."

"Don't worry about that," said Fritz, pulling a sheet of paper out of a drawer. "I'll write you a forty-eight-hour leave."

"Just like that?"

His friend smiled confidently. "Just like that. Another sheet of paper and you're a lieutenant, and permanently assigned to me. But I'll let you decide that after the operation."

Otto considered this. What harm would it do to stay here for another couple of days? He could use a little rest. "Fine, I'll stay."

"Excellent," said Fritz, scribbling furiously on the paper. He finished in less than a minute and then picked up his phone. A few moments later, a corporal entered the room. "This is Rottenführer Hemmel," said his friend, gesturing to a slightly over-weight man in his thirties. "Hemmel, take this to the train station and give it to the division commander. Sergeant Berg here is going to stay with us for a couple days and accompany us on our little operation tonight."

Hemmel looked up at Otto with the eager eyes of a child at

Christmas. "Oh, you won't be disappointed," he said enthusiastically.

Otto nodded noncommittally and turned back to Fritz as the corporal shuffled out of the room on his errand. "So, what is this operation?"

"We've received intelligence of some undesirables hiding in town."

"Resistance members?"

"*Ja*. We are going to ferret them out and bring them in for questioning."

"Where are they?"

"In an apartment only a few blocks away from here. You'll accompany me, along with Hemmel and a couple of young privates we are breaking in." Fritz chuckled. "Hemmel is supposed to be leading the operation, but as you might have seen, he has a little trouble getting up the stairs quickly. I'd like you to lead the group."

"I don't have any experience in this sort of thing."

"It will be easy. You just need to get the men up to the second floor and into the apartment as quickly as you can."

"Will the people we are going after be armed?"

"Will you care?"

Otto grunted. Fritz was correct, he'd faced armed adversaries nearly every day for the past three years. "How many are you expecting?"

"Just two, possibly three. If they have weapons at all, it would be a pistol or two. If you're fast, they won't have any time to prepare."

"Sounds good, but I don't have any weapons myself. I left everything on the train."

Fritz reached into his drawer again, removing a 9mm pistol. "This should do just fine."

Otto took the gun, checking the clip and the safety. "When do we go?"

"As soon as my fat friend gets back from the station. I'd say less than an hour."

It was two hours, as it turned out, before everything was organized. They'd squeezed into a Mercedes with Otto and the two privates in the back. Fritz rode in the front, with Hemmel driving. They took off from the headquarters and rumbled into the darkness, the headlights providing the only light in the blacked-out city.

"I don't usually go in for these smaller operations," said Fritz, chatting away as if they were headed out for a night at the theater. "But I'd like to see you in action, my friend. It's been a long time and I want to see if you still have your polish."

Otto didn't answer that. As they ripped through the streets, he felt a rush of excitement, as he always did when he was heading into combat. Although he faced danger now, he relished these times, when all the doubts and fears melted away. Everything was simple during operations. Just him and his men, working together to achieve a designated purpose. He didn't have to worry about losing the war, about murders or his nagging thoughts about the conduct of the war. He just had to capture these enemies of the state. That was something he could understand, could hold on to.

The car screeched to a halt. Otto tensed in his seat. He was surprised at the emotions coursing through him. He was actually nervous. *Don't be a ninny*, he chastised himself. He'd been in far more dangerous situations nearly every day for the past three years. But something was different about this. It felt more dangerous when it shouldn't. An intoxicating mixture of the unknown and fear. He hadn't looked forward to an operation in a very long time, he realized. Here was something he could sink his teeth into.

"Let's go," he whispered to Hemmel and the two privates. The corporal in the front seat rolled out onto the sidewalk. His cheeks were already flushed, and he was half out of breath, but he gave a confident nod. The man had done this before, it appeared. Otto wondered about the two privates, who looked at best eighteen. "How many of these missions have you been on?" he asked. Neither of them answered. "As I thought. Don't worry about it. Just stay behind me and the corporal. We'll advance first. Keep your weapons ready, but fingers off the trigger. Just back us up, and you'll be fine."

"The major says you're a combat veteran," said Hemmel. "Since the beginning. Is that true?"

"*Ja.*"

The corporal looked impressed. "I was going to serve but I was brought into the security branch." He looked embarrassed by that.

"We all serve the Fatherland," said Otto, not necessarily feeling that it was all equal, but there was no reason to demean these men. Hemmel looked appreciative. "Let's go up and see what we see. What apartment is it again?"

"Two-oh-one," said Hemmel.

"All right," said Otto, retrieving the pistol from his holster. "Follow me."

Chapter 13

De Tweede Terugkeer

Friday, June 4, 1943
6:02 p.m.
Eindhoven, Netherlands

Aafke sat at the sewing machine in the dim light. She worked the needle back and forth on the German uniform. Her fingers were cramped and she was exhausted from the stifling heat of the place. Around her, the thrum of hundreds of other workers buzzed in her ears. She glanced at her watch. The day was almost done. She thought of the half loaf of bread sitting in their cupboard at home along with a little ersatz coffee. She would love to bring an egg or two home for her father, or even a little milk, but they didn't have the ration cards for it.

As she worked, her mind drifted. She remembered the last time she'd seen her brother, over three years ago. He'd come home on a twenty-four-hour pass and surprised her as she was closing up the store.

"Do you have any cigarettes?" he'd asked, trying to disguise his voice.

Aafke had looked up and rushed to him, throwing her arms around his neck. He was half a foot taller than him, wiry but strong as a rail. "Christiaan, it's you!"

He looked her over, frowning. "You've lost weight," he said, furrowing his brow in mock concern. "There's no rationing. Has Father sipped up all the grocery money?"

"Careful," she said, looking around. "He'll hear you."

"I should hope he would."

"Where have you been? How long can you stay?"

"Not long," he said. "Just the night. I've been at the border. You should see the Germans stacking up on us. More every day."

"Oh, but surely they won't bother us!" she'd said, praying it was true.

"It's to be hoped they won't. But nobody is sure. The English and the French want to come in and man the line with us, but the government won't let them."

"What if the Germans do come?"

His face changed, growing serious. "We won't stop them. I don't know if we can slow them down."

"Why did they have to take you?" said Aafke, grabbing his arm. "We need you here. *I* need you."

"No, you don't. You don't need anyone. You can handle anything that comes your way."

"That's not what Father thinks. He thinks I'm useless. He tells me practically every day."

"Don't you pay any attention to him, sister. He couldn't survive without you. He'll realize it someday." His face grew red. "He hasn't been hitting you, I trust? I warned him before I left."

Aafke shook her head, lying a little. Her brother had enough troubles.

"Good. Well, that's something at least. Where is he?"

"Upstairs."

Christiaan squared his shoulders. "Well, I guess I'd better go up. Are you coming with me?"

"I've a little more to do down here. Besides, he'll want you all to himself for a while."

"Don't be too long. And don't worry. We'll ply him with drinks and he'll be asleep in no time. Then we can catch up. Let's stay up all night, Aafke. I don't want to waste a minute's time with you."

"Oh, Christiaan," she said, throwing her arms around him again. "What am I going to do without you? You better stay safe. Promise me!"

"I promise. Now get your chores done down here and hurry up. I love you, sister."

"I love you too."

A shrill whistle screamed through the factory, tearing Aafke out of her daydream. It was quitting time, finally. She rose and stretched, her back on fire from hours of hunching over her labors.

As she filed out of the factory, thoughts of Christiaan still drifting through her mind, she felt a sense of relief wash over her. It was the end of another long day, and she could go home and rest. She strolled through the streets, her head down, avoiding eye contact with the strangers around her. As she walked, she couldn't help but feel a sense of foreboding. Things were changing fast in the city, and not for the better. The Germans had become increasingly aggressive in the past year. Perhaps it was the war. From the smattering of news caught from the BBC on illegal radios, it appeared the war was not going well for their occupiers. The attitude of the soldiers had gone from a pure arrogance to bitterness and anger. There were more raids, families disappearing into the night never to be seen again. The Jewish families in town had disappeared, shipped away or in hiding. The rumors about what happened to those in German custody were too terrifying to dwell on. Certainly they couldn't be true, could they?

When she finally arrived at her apartment building, she climbed the stairs slowly, her legs aching from standing all day. She unlocked the door and stepped inside, the heat within almost overwhelming her. It wouldn't cool down for another couple of hours. By August, it wouldn't cool down at all. Maarten was sitting at the table, reading a newspaper.

"Good evening, Father," she said, taking off her coat.

Maarten grunted in reply.

"That's not much of a greeting."

"Fine. How was work?" he asked mechanically, not looking up.

"It was busy," she said, pouring herself a cup of water. "But at least we're still here."

"No thanks to you," her father snapped.

It was going to be one of *these* kind of nights. She took a deep breath and steeled herself for what was to come. She said a silent prayer it would only be shouting. "I'm not going to go through all of this again."

"So you think I should forget?" he asked, glaring at her now. He took a deep drink from his mug, wiping his chin with a grubby sleeve. "Look at us: store lost, flat lost, starving to death. No word from your brother in a year. I can't take much more of this. And you to blame."

"All of that was three years ago, Father. You'd think you could give me a day without bringing it up. And remember, I did it because I was trying to save your store."

"Save it by foolish smuggling that cost us everything and damned near our lives to boot? I can use less of that kind of help."

"And what help have you been?" she snapped, unable to control herself despite the risk. "You haven't worked in years. All you do is mope around our apartment, drinking your cheap brandy and complaining about how unfair the world has been to you."

Her father rose, his face an angry scarlet mask. "I'd be very careful what comes out of your mouth next, missy."

She'd gone too far and she knew it. Her hand went unconsciously to her cheek, where the last bruise was almost faded. "I'm sorry, Father. You're right. It was my fault."

He sank back into his seat. "That's my little broomstick," he said, closing his eyes and taking a deep drink from his mug. "Now put some dinner on the table."

"There's not much here," she said. "Just a little bread, not much more than a half loaf."

"There's got to be more than that," he said. "What happened to our sugar and flour tickets?"

"Gone," she said. "And we've no more for a week. But we'll have another bread ticket tomorrow. We'll have to make this stretch."

"Can't you go out and trade something for a little more?" he asked.

She laughed. "What would I trade, Father? And besides, weren't you just complaining about the black market getting us in all this trouble in the first place?"

"Ah, but that was then, and this is now, isn't it? It's not like you haven't done it, and recently."

He was right, of course. She managed to smuggle a little bit out of the factory. Some cloth under her dress, a needle or some thread. It wasn't stealing. Well, it *was* stealing, but she was taking from the Germans, and the traitorous Dutch owner who made profit from the war. Whatever she could take from them was fair game. Perhaps it was even helping in the war effort. At least that's what she told herself. She traded these paltry goods for the little extras now and again, mostly butter, eggs, and, of course, her father's brandy. If he didn't drink, they'd have had enough to eat. She thought of saying so now, but decided against it.

"Well?" he asked.

"I'm tired, Father."

"Come on now, we can't live on a half loaf of bread. Surely, you've got something you could trade."

She did. A few needles she'd taken the day before. But she usually waited until she had more before she took the risk. After all, if she were caught she would be arrested and beaten, or perhaps even killed. Ah well, no reason to argue over it. "I'll take what I have and see if I can bring anything back."

"That's a good girl. And remember, brandy first."

"But you just said—"

"Brandy first, girl! And some more bread. Butter too, if you can swing it."

She was exhausted but she willed herself to her feet. Sometimes she would almost pass out from her hunger. But she'd grown used to the feeling. She went into her room and opened the top drawer of her dresser. Retrieving the needles, she headed for the door. "I'll be back in a little while, Father."

He shooed her with his hand. "Remember the brandy."

She hurried down a flight of stairs and out onto the street. It was near twilight. There was a curfew, and she would have to hurry, because if she were caught after it was fully dark, it wouldn't matter if she had black-market goods or not, she'd still end up in a Gestapo cell. She looked in both directions. The street seemed deserted. She headed toward a local market a few blocks away. She arrived just as the last stalls were being pulled down.

She scanned the remaining vendors, not recognizing any of them. Her pulse increased. It would be reckless to approach somebody new. She had dependable sellers. Still, she didn't want to face her angry father. And she could use some more to eat. She saw an older woman, long hair streaked with gray. She was by herself and was struggling to move some of the items out of the stall and over to a waiting wagon. She decided to risk it.

"Excuse me," she said. "Could I help you with that?"

The woman eyed her suspiciously, but after seeing that Aafke was by herself, she seemed to relax. "Actually, that would be a great relief. It's getting late and my husband hasn't arrived to help me load up."

Aafke hurried to the stall and picked up a box that was filled with bread and a slice of cheese. Her mouth watered at the smell, but she didn't touch the food, instead lifting the crate and moving it over to the wagon. She worked with the woman for a few minutes, emptying the stall until there was nothing left.

"Thank you," the woman said. She reached into a box and pulled out an apple, offering it to Aafke.

"Thank you," said Aafke. "Is there anything more I could buy?"

"I'm closed for the day. I'm sorry."

"Surely there's something," Aafke whispered.

"Do you have ration cards?"

Aafke shook her head slightly. It could have meant yes or no.

The woman peered at her again, looking her up and down. She seemed to consider the request and then she looked this way and that. "What do you have?"

"I've sewing needles," she said. "Industrial. Five of them."

"That's worth a loaf of bread," the woman said.

"Come now," said Aafke. "I didn't rob you. Please return the favor. I need two loaves, a bottle of brandy, a stick of butter, and that slice of cheese."

"Preposterous," the woman protested. "Take your apple and go."

"Please," said Aafke. "Please make the deal."

The woman stared at her again. Aafke could barely make out her features in the darkness.

"One loaf, a bottle of brandy, and half a stick of butter."

"Deal," said Aafke, handing over the needles. The woman took a small box and loaded up the items.

"You'd better get home with those," she said. "If you're caught, they'll have questions. And remember, you didn't buy them from me."

"I'll remember. And I'll buy again from you."

"We'll see," said the woman. "Good night."

"Good night." Aafke headed back into the darkness. The wooden box, modest as it was, felt heavy for her in her weakened state, and she was winded as she walked. The darkness was nearly complete now and she knew she was past curfew. She had to hope and pray that she could make it home without being spotted by a German patrol. She made it one street, then a second. On the third, she spotted a flashlight waving in the distance, but it seemed to be turned the other direction, and after a few terrifying moments, she could tell whoever it might be was heading away. She kept moving and reached her street, hurrying to the center of the block where her apartment building was located. She finally arrived in front of the main door. She had made it.

She turned toward the entrance. Violent hands grabbed her arms, pulling her backward. She let out a scream.

"Quiet!" ordered a harsh voice behind her. She was whipped around, and she gasped.

Arno stood before her. Even in the near darkness she recognized his features. He was thinner, his cheeks sunken in, and he looked like he'd aged a decade. But it was him. Without thinking, she threw herself into his arms. He stiffened at her touch, but then seemed to relent and he put his arms around her as well. "Dear God," she said. "You're alive."

"Yes," he said. "And so are you."

"What happened? Where have you been?"

He released her. "That's a long story, and not one we should discuss outside and after curfew."

"Will you come up?"

"Yes."

"Are you in danger?"

"Always now."

"Will they track you here?"

"I don't think so. I've been watching you for days."

"What? Watching me? Why?"

"I'll explain inside."

Confused, but happy to see Arno, she led him inside. Things would change now. No matter what, she would no longer be alone.

"Tell me what happened to you," said Aafke, pouring a glass of brandy for Arno. Her father glared at her as she did so, but she frowned at him. She divided the bread and cheese evenly and brought plates over to the table.

"After that bastard German brought his Gestapo friend to your store and I was arrested, the Germans took me to their headquarters and interrogated me for days. At first it was just questions, but then they started to beat me. They wanted to know who I was working with, who my suppliers were, and how you and your father were involved. I didn't tell the fascist pigs anything," said Arno, spitting on the floor. He must have realized what he had done because he looked up at Aafke.

"Don't worry about it," she said.

"After a while they seemed to forget about me. I languished in a cell there for weeks, maybe months. I don't even know. One morning they dragged me out. I thought they were going to execute me, but they shoved me into the back of a truck with some other men and drove us out of the city. We traveled for hours until we reached a camp somewhere in northwest Germany. The place had barbed wire, towers, everything." He took a deep drink of his brandy as if he needed to steady himself before he continued.

"Conditions there were horrible. We slept on moldy wet straw in drafty barracks the prisoners had built on the site. We were given coffee for breakfast and a little watery soup for lunch and dinner. Every morning before dawn we marched out into the countryside to work all day on local farms. They would bring us back well after dark and then force us to stand for another hour or more while they conducted roll call. Anyone who fell out of line during the marches, or collapsed at work, was shot out of hand."

"Arno, I'm so sorry," said Aafke, taking his hand. "You did that to protect us."

"Nobody protected me," her father muttered, tearing off a crust of bread.

"Nonsense, Father. If Arno had told them about us, we would have been carted off with him."

"Bah."

Aafke ignored him and turned back to Arno. "What happened next?"

"I was growing weaker month by month. I knew at some point I would be the one who would stumble out of line and receive a bullet in the back of the head. I had to do something. A few months ago, we started working at a new location. The German farmer there was different. He brought us bread and dried meat when the guards weren't around. There were only ten of us helping him, so there was enough to go around. I gradually built up some strength.

"One day we were at the farm, eating our lunch in the barn. Our guards were out front, having a smoke. I managed to loosen some of the boards in the back and wiggled my way through them to the outside. I sprinted off into some nearby woods. They must have discovered me missing quickly, because I could hear them yelling, chasing me through the trees. But I kept going, crossing a stream, and making my way west as best as I could. Hours later, I found an abandoned cottage and laid up there overnight. In the morning, I stole some clothing and a little food from another farm I came across and made my way back into Holland. I reached Eindhoven about a month ago."

"That's amazing," said Aafke. "I don't know how you survived."

Arno grunted. "I did what I had to do."

Something occurred to Aafke. "If you arrived in Eindhoven a month ago, why are you just coming to see me now?"

"I had some contacts to make. And I had to make sure you weren't compromised."

"Compromised?"

"I didn't know if the Germans had arrested you as well. You might have sold out to them; you might be working with them."

"Arno! How could you say such a thing?" She was taken off guard that he would see her that way, and she felt unexpected hurt that he would wait this long to see her.

"I've learned to trust no one."

"What made you decide to come now?" she asked, her voice a trifle bristled.

"I've been watching you. With the hours you work and the little black-market sales you've conducted, it became clear to me that you're not collaborating. You're far too thin, for one. Too poor to be working with the enemy. When I saw you break curfew tonight, and overheard your conversation with that vendor, I knew it would be safe to make direct contact."

"How do we know you're not working with the Germans yourself?" she asked. She knew it wasn't true, but her feelings were hurt, and she found herself lashing out at him.

"Don't ever say something like that to me again!" he shouted, banging his glass on the table. "I would never collaborate with those bastards, and if I have my way, I'll kill every last one of them before I'm through."

"There you go poking a hornet's nest, with no more common sense than a mouse," her father said to her, slurring his words. "Look at the man. He's survived. He's been out there doing something, when all you've done is get me kicked out of hearth and home."

"She didn't lose you your store," said Arno, turning on her father. "You lost it yourself with your drinking and your sloth. If you'd run your store properly before the war started, you wouldn't have owed that back money in the first place."

"Jesus, Joseph, and Mary, aren't you the judge and jury," said Maarten, taking another deep drink of brandy. He looked at Aafke. "To hell with the both of you, I'm going to bed." He rose unsteadily and shambled off to his bedroom, slamming the door behind him.

"I'm sorry about him," said Aafke. "He's grown worse with each month that goes by. With no word from Christiaan, and with this horrid war, it's just been too much for him."

"He's a mean-spirited bastard and he always has been," said Arno. "You shouldn't have to put up with him."

"He's my father."

Arno nodded. "So is blood to blood. I'm lucky my folks are long dead—that they aren't having to live with this."

"What are you going to do now?" Aafke asked.

"I have false papers. I made contact with the resistance when I first returned to Eindhoven. They interviewed me for information about the camp. They told me there are places like that all over Germany."

"How terrible."

"That's not the worst of it. They said there are bigger camps out east, places nobody ever returns from. They've sent some of us there, and all the Jews."

"The Jews? Why?"

"You know all the German propaganda about them. We thought it was just baiting, food for the masses to keep them angry at someone other than the Nazis. But it goes beyond that. The resistance thinks they may be liquidating them all."

"Why would they? All that slave labor. Why would they waste it? And with the war in the east going badly!"

"Who knows why those lunatics do what they do. The Jews certainly believe it. They are hidden all over Eindhoven, and in the countryside. But they are being betrayed, sometimes by our own neighbors, sometimes for money, or even just for spite."

Aafke felt tears welling up. "What can we do about it?" she asked. "There must be something."

"There is. You can join us."

"Join you?"

"They've given me command of a little group. Their commander was killed and I was asked to take over." He took her hand. His fingers were calloused and hard but she felt an electric thrill at his touch. She was a little surprised by her own reaction. It had been so long. "Join me? Together we can start bringing justice back to the world—even if just in little ways in our tiny part of Europe."

She didn't hesitate. "I'd love to, Arno. How do we get started?"

"Tomorrow, I'll take you—"

Arno was interrupted by a sharp knock at the door. Aafke felt her blood freeze. The knock was something she'd dreaded for years. It had to be the Gestapo.

Arno's face paled and he looked at her in surprise, his eyebrows furrowing into a glare of betrayal.

"It wasn't me!" she insisted.

The hammering came again, like thunder, nearly tearing the door off the hinges.

Chapter 14

De Achtervolging

Friday, June 4, 1943
9:17 p.m.
Eindhoven, Netherlands

Otto followed Hemmel up the stairs to the second floor of the apartment building. The old combat feeling he possessed was so different from how many of his comrades experienced danger. Otto felt only a rush of excitement, combined with a steely calm that slowed time down. He loved the feeling and he found himself grinning as they made their way up the stairwell.

At the landing, Hemmel checked a piece of paper he had with him, and Otto saw it was a crudely written map. "This way," the corporal said at last, moving toward the far end of the corridor. The lighting in the building was dim, the walls dingy with tired floral wallpaper. Finally, they reached the door. Hemmel pressed a finger to his lips, motioning for the two privates to move to opposite sides of the door. He nodded once at Otto and then rapped his knuckles heavily on the door.

There was silence in response. Hemmel glanced at Otto, a

grim grin forming over his fleshy features. "Nobody ever answers," he whispered. "Do you want to give it a try?"

Otto nodded, moving up to the door. He slammed his heavy fists down a few times. The wood shook and shivered, and a crack formed near the top. Hemmel whistled at Otto's strength.

"Now I know why the major wants you."

There was still no response. Hemmel turned to the door. "Open up!" he ordered. "Gestapo!" He waited a moment longer and then turned back to Otto. "Force it."

Otto looked at the hinges and the lock. He took a step back and then rushed forward, kicking the center of the wood with all his strength. The door shattered, tearing open, the lock ripping through the frame. He was the first one inside. He glanced around quickly, his pistol raised. The apartment was even dingier than the hallway. A few pictures hung on tattered walls. A bookcase with a few trinkets stood against a wall. A metal table sat in the middle of the room, covered by half-eaten plates and a bottle of alcohol. An open door led into a bathroom, and another door opposite him was closed. But what caught Otto's immediate attention was the window. It was open, with flimsy cloth drapes fluttering in a light breeze. Otto rushed to the window and looked out. It led to a fire escape and a courtyard below. He heard a rattle of metal and a loud thud. Straining his eyes, he just caught the shadows of two figures escaping into the darkness.

"They're getting away!" he shouted, turning to thunder back out of the apartment. The privates followed him, close on his heels, the corpulent Hemmel falling far behind. Otto bounded down the stairs and then went out the front door. Fritz was standing there, looking up in surprise.

"What is it?" the major asked.

"They escaped out a back window. They are out on the street."

"Let's go!" shouted Fritz, jumping into his car.

"Hemmel is behind us!" said Fritz.

"No time, leave him behind!"

Otto and the privates jumped into the car, with Otto in the passenger seat. "Go!" he shouted.

"Which way?" Fritz asked.

"Behind the building!" said Otto. "Next block over!"

The car jerked into motion, speeding down the street and turning a corner sharply. Turning again, they sped down the street, headlights blaring. Otto craned his neck this way and that. "There!" he shouted, spotting movement at the end of the street. "They just turned the corner!"

"Hurry, damn it!" shouted Fritz.

The car rumbled down the street, tearing around the corner. "There they are!" shouted Otto, spotting the figures. The car raced after them, gaining ground. But the couple turned sharply to the right, darting into some kind of park. "Stop here!" shouted Otto. He was out of the car before it was fully stopped. Flashlight in one hand, his pistol in another, he thundered into the park, the privates close behind him. His eyes darted this way and that as he ran. The space was pitch black. There was a pathway running through the middle, and park benches set here and there, but there were also dirt paths darting out in several directions. Otto sprinted another hundred yards and then slowed down, both to catch his breath and get his bearings. "Spread out!" he commanded the privates.

He flashed his light ahead of him. He could make out another street in the distance. The park was not large. As he watched, a car pulled up and three men rushed out, also carrying flashlights. Fritz must have radioed in for assistance. Otto smiled, relishing the rush of events. They had them now. They just had to comb the park and they would have their prey. He moved forward toward the flashing and bobbing lights, keeping his eyes averted as much as he could so that his limited night vision was not entirely compromised.

Otto picked a side path and started to make his way down it, flashing his light at bushes and trees as he went. He was starting to get a sense for the size of the garden, which was about two-thirds of a city block. As he went, he kept his ears pricked, waiting for the shout that would signify they had captured the couple. He reached the buildings at the end of the grass without seeing anyone, and started to move along the wall, flashing the light back toward the central path again and again, expecting to find the resistance members. His heart was pumping with the chase, and he was laughing to himself at how much fun he was having. It reminded him of the early days of the war, or the height of his time out on the pitch as a defender.

Another few minutes passed and still nothing. He was surprised they hadn't come across them yet. Then he heard shouts. Finally! The noise was coming from near the second vehicle and he jogged in that direction, pistol at the ready. As he bobbed between the trees the shouting increased and there was a sound of a scuffle and the slamming of car doors. The vehicle's engine turned abruptly on, and it slammed forward, skidding and skirting as it picked up momentum.

"They've taken the car!" a voice cried out in the darkness.

How could that be? Otto sprinted forward and found a Gestapo agent on the pavement, hand to his head, blood dripping down his fingers. He stared at the man for a moment and then shouted back into the darkness. "Get the other car! They are escaping!"

Otto attended to the agent on the ground while he waited for the other vehicle to pull around. He retrieved a handkerchief out of his tunic and applied it to the man's head, holding it firmly in place. It looked like he'd been bashed with something solid, like a hammer or a tire iron. He might have a cracked skull or even brain damage, Otto realized. He gently lowered the policeman until he was lying flat on the pavement. "Hold that in place," he whispered. "They'll be here soon."

After what seemed an eternity Fritz pulled up in the second vehicle, revving up the engine to urge haste. Otto's men emerged from the darkness. He gestured at one of them toward the agent. "Take care of this man," he said. "Don't move him, as he's badly injured." Gesturing to the other private, he grabbed the side door and jumped inside.

"Go!" he yelled, as the policeman piled into the backseat. The car spun around, nearly skidding out on the pavement as Fritz took a sharp corner to head out of the park.

They hurtled through the streets of Eindhoven with their headlights blazing. Otto leaned forward in his seat, peering through every alleyway they passed, searching for any sign of the resistance members they were chasing. But after several minutes they still hadn't caught sight of them, or their stolen car, and he began to worry that they had missed them in all the commotion and confusion of their escape from the park.

Finally, after ten minutes of searching, Fritz had to admit that they were not going to find the vehicle and he slowed the car to a stop. Otto sighed heavily in frustration.

"Let's go back," Fritz said reluctantly. He put the car into reverse and started heading slowly back in the direction of Gestapo headquarters. But as they were turning a corner, something caught Otto's eye—a faint glimmer of metal bouncing off their headlights. Before he could process what he was seeing, Fritz had slammed on his brakes. A vehicle was barreling down on them with headlights turned off.

Otto gasped and grabbed for his pistol as Fritz quickly threw open his door. Before Otto could take aim, the car whizzed by, throwing up dust and leaves in its wake. It careened around a corner at breakneck speed. He jumped back into the car. "After them!" he screamed. Fritz slammed his door and buried his foot on the accelerator, ripping off into the night. He tore around the next corner, just catching a flash of the darkened-out car in front of him as it sped down another street to the left. They careened after, whizzing through turn after turn.

"We're gaining on them!" shouted Otto, as the tail of the car grew gradually closer.

"Shoot at them!" Fritz ordered.

Otto rolled down his window and took aim. It was difficult to target with the car bobbing and spinning, but he concentrated and tried to time the shot. When they straightened out in another block, he fired three quick rounds. One of the bullets hit the back window, exploding the glass. The car in front of them jerked almost in surprise and began fishtailing, whipping back and forth as the driver tried to avoid the bullets.

"Did you hit one of them?" Fritz asked.

"*Nein*," said Otto. "Just the window!"

"Fire again!"

Otto lifted himself up and leaned far out of the window this time, holding on to the door with his left hand. He took aim again, this time at the tires, and fired the rest of his clip in rapid shots, the bullets peppering the pavement and the spinning wheels. The vehicle jerked violently to the left, jumped the sidewalk, and crashed into a building.

"You did it!" shouted Fritz.

Otto was elated. His blood coursed with the thrill of the hunt. Fritz slammed on his brakes, nearly throwing Otto out of the car. They ground to an abrupt halt.

"Get them!" Fritz ordered.

Otto pulled himself out of the window, the private ripping open his door behind him. He reached for his belt and drew out another magazine, unloading the empty one and slamming the bullets into place.

A flash burned his eyes. At the same moment he felt the concussion as a wave of heat and force drove him backward, throwing him to the pavement. His ears roared with a thunderous explosion. For a few moments he couldn't move. But he pulled himself up to a sitting position, his eyes blinking away the stars in front of them. The car they'd chased had exploded, flames licking through the interior. A black bellow of smoke belched out of the interior, wafting up into the darkness.

"Are you all right?" Fritz asked, rushing around from the driver's seat.

Otto nodded. "We were lucky," he said.

"Not all of us," said Fritz.

Otto turned behind him and saw the private was also lying on the pavement, his eyes staring blankly up into the darkness. He had a meter-long piece of metal sticking out of the center of his chest. Blood bubbled and boiled out of the angry wound as his heart tried desperately to function. Otto tried to crawl toward the man, but Fritz stopped him.

"No point, my friend," he said. "He was dead before he hit the ground. It's a miracle you weren't killed as well."

Otto hobbled to his feet and limped over to the car. Even now, the flames were beginning to dwindle. He peered into the front seat and saw the charred bodies of a man and a woman. The man was in the driver's seat, eyes open as if in surprise. The woman was slumped over against the passenger window, her head burned to a crisp except for a tuft of blond hair.

"Good work," said Fritz, clapping his friend on the back.

"We failed," said Otto. "You can't question them."

"It's still a success. They won't be hurting anyone else."

"What do you mean?" Otto asked.

"These two killed a German soldier just a week ago. They shot him in the head while he was eating dinner in a restaurant. He didn't see them coming because he'd had his head down, writing a letter to his wife and his three-year-old daughter."

Otto felt his stomach wrench at that. He stared at the two figures, burned and battered by the fire and the crash. "It served them right."

"Indeed, my friend. Like I told you, we are fighting our own war here, and one just as important as you were engaging in with the Russians."

Otto grunted, not sure what to say. He kept staring at the two of them, imagining them sneaking up on an innocent German soldier who was just trying to write to his family. Perhaps Fritz was right. Perhaps this was noble work after all.

"Will you join us?" he asked. "We need you, Otto. You saw my assistant Hemmel. A good lad, but lazy and out of shape. I need a warrior, a giant like you to chase down our enemies and bring peace to the city."

"For the Occupiers."

"For everyone. This is the new world order, and we are here for the Dutch as well as for ourselves. They are just getting used to things, but for a few bad eggs they are already getting into line."

Otto stared at the figures in the car, not answering. He was so excited by the chase he couldn't seem to calm down. And as he stared at the fire, his mind raced over the image of a young German wife and her child, receiving news from the authorities that their husband and father was never coming home.

Chapter 15

Tegenstand

Friday, June 4, 1943
11:18 p.m.
Eindhoven, Netherlands

Arno and Aafke stared at the shuddering door, frozen by the pounding doom. The sound sent shivers down Aafke's spine, her blue eyes reflecting a mix of terror and determination. She clenched her fists, imagining the worst: the Gestapo here to arrest her for her petty black-market dealings, and Arno caught up accidentally in the storm.

"Arno," she whispered, her voice barely audible, "we must leave. Now."

He nodded, his glasses momentarily slipping down his nose as he glanced at the back window. "What's out there?" he asked.

Aafke followed his glance. "Nothing, a courtyard."

"Is there any way down?"

She nodded. "There's a fire escape."

"Let's go," he ordered.

But before they could move, a muffled voice called out from behind the door. "Arno, it's me, Peter. Open up!"

Arno hesitated for a moment before unlocking the door, revealing Peter, a stout man with unkempt brown hair and piercing green eyes. He was panting, sweat beading on his forehead.

"Peter," Arno breathed, relief washing over him. "How did you know I was here?"

"I didn't," Peter replied, his voice urgent and strained. "I've been looking all over Eindhoven for you. I had almost given up, but I remembered you've been watching this place . . . this girl, so I came here last."

"What do you want?" Arno asked. He seemed annoyed now that the danger had passed.

"I've got terrible news."

"What is it?"

"The Gestapo, they got Gerrit and Christina."

"Where are they?" Arno asked, starting to stand. "Are they at SS headquarters?"

"They're gone," said Peter. "The Gestapo gunned them down."

Arno sunk into his seat. "The bastards," he muttered, clenching his fists so tightly that his knuckles turned white. "Both of them are dead? Are you sure?"

"Positive. One of our contacts saw the whole thing happen. It was a car chase and they ran them down. The car exploded. There's no way anyone could have survived the fire."

"We have to act quickly. The rest of us are potentially in danger."

"Agreed," said Peter. "But first, we need a plan."

"What the hell is going on in here?" asked a voice from the other room. It was her father, staring out bleary-eyed from his bedroom.

"Nothing, Father," said Aafke. "Go back to bed."

"Well, keep it down," he said, eyeballing Peter. "And get these men out of the apartment. What would the neighbors think? My daughter without a chaperone. Jesus, Joseph, and Mary." He stumbled out of the bedroom and grabbed the brandy bottle off the table. "I'll be taking this," he said. "For safekeeping." He shambled back out of the room, leaving the three of them to stare at each other.

Arno turned to Aafke. "I'm sorry our reunion was disturbed," he said with a defeated smile. "I'll come see you again after I've taken care of a few things."

"I'm going with you," she said.

"Nonsense," said Peter. "We don't have time for this."

"I want to join."

Peter's eyes widened. "How does she know — "

"Because I told her," snapped Arno. "I trust this girl and so can you."

Peter looked at her and back to Arno. From his expression, it seemed he wasn't nearly as sure as his leader.

"We'll take her with us."

"Let's go, then," he said finally.

The trio slipped out through the back window, the night's shadows enveloping them as they navigated the mazelike streets of Eindhoven. German patrols prowled some of the intersections, their presence a sinister reminder of the enemy that lurked around every turn. Aafke clung to Arno's arm, her heart pounding in her chest as they narrowly avoided detection time and again.

After what felt like an eternity, they emerged from the city and reached a dilapidated cottage hidden within the dense woods. Vines twisted around its crumbling walls, and moss blanketed the rotting roof. Moonlight filtered through the trees, casting eerie patterns upon the broken windows. It was a place that had long been abandoned by all but the most desperate.

Inside, the air was thick with tension. Aafke was introduced to Peter's sister, Maaike, a woman with long brown hair and a gentle smile that belied the hardships she had un-doubtedly faced. Beside her stood Joelle, a fiery young woman with raven-black hair and an intense gaze that bore straight into Aafke's soul. After the introductions, Arno settled in to discuss what they would do next.

"We have to do something to pay them back," Arno began, his voice low and urgent. "Tomorrow, we'll wait outside a restaurant I know, frequented by German soldiers during lunchtime. We'll find an appropriate target and follow him. When he's a safe distance from the restaurant, we'll assassi-nate him."

Peter nodded. "I've been wanting to try out the sniper rifle we've secured. No better time to use it."

"I want to help," Aafke interjected, her voice unwavering.

"Absolutely not," Arno replied firmly. "Women do not take part in direct operations."

Aafke was surprised by that. "It's just you and Peter, then?"

He shook his head. "There are others. But Peter and I can do this by ourselves tomorrow. Don't worry. There's plenty for you to do."

"What?" snapped Aafke. "Prepare you a victory dinner? Sew you some new clothes? Sweep these dirt floors? Arno, I can't just sit here and do nothing," she insisted, her eyes plead-ing with him to reconsider. "I need to be a part of this."

Silence hung heavily in the air as the others exchanged glances. "She could drive," said Peter, chewing on a pipe.

"Why does *she* get to help?" snapped Joelle, scowling at Aafke. "What, Arno's new girlfriend sets foot in here on her first day and gets to do things we're not allowed to do?"

"I'm not his girlfriend," said Aafke. "I . . . I just know him. And I'm not trying to supplant any of you. But we should all be involved. We should all be a part of this."

Arno stared at the women for a moment. "Fine," he said. "I don't have time to gather any other men tonight anyway. Aafke can drive and Joelle and Maaike can ride along in the back with me. Peter will ride up front, with the rifle. But this doesn't change anything," he warned. "This is a onetime operation. When things are settled again, it will be men only."

Aafke didn't argue. She would take things one step at a time. If they were successful in this, she was sure he wouldn't object when the next operation came along. She was thrilled by the prospect of doing something, anything. After years of squalor, starvation, and pain, she was finally going to strike back at the Nazis. "Shall we go now?" she asked.

"And be shot down like our friends?" Joelle said sarcastically. "You better teach her something about logistics. If we barreled into town tonight, we'd be stopped before we made it three blocks. They'd arrest us or kill us, like our friends. We have to wait until tomorrow."

Arno nodded. He took a bottle down from a shelf and poured a drink for each of them. "Tonight, we honor our dead. Tomorrow, we avenge them."

As the night wore slowly on, tension within the cottage grew palpable as they cleaned their weapons and prepared for the mission ahead. The loss of Gerrit and Christina hung heavily in the air, a stark reminder of the dangers they faced. Maaike worked quietly alongside Aafke, offering occasional smiles of encouragement. But Joelle's coldness was unmistakable, her dark eyes filled with resentment every time they met Aafke's gaze. It was clear she disapproved of Aafke's involvement in the operation.

Aafke tried to ignore Joelle's hostility, focusing instead on the task at hand. She felt a strange sense of camaraderie with these people, bound together by their shared determination to fight back against their oppressors.

As morning broke through the trees outside, the group continued their preparations in silence. Aafke's thoughts raced as she considered the events that would soon unfold. Would they succeed in their mission? Would any of them make it out alive? And at what cost?

The slow morning wore on, until the sun reached its zenith. Arno, glancing at his watch, rose out of his chair.

"Let's go," he said quietly, and the group loaded into the car. As they drove toward the city, the hum of the engine filled the air, accompanied only by the steady drumming of Aafke's heart and the unspoken fears of the resistance members sitting beside her.

The sun hovered high in the sky, casting shadows across the cobblestone streets as Aafke maneuvered the car through the bustling city. Her hands gripped the wheel tightly, knuckles white with tension. There were Germans everywhere, and all of them seemed to be staring at their car. Aafke realized there was almost no civilian traffic on the street. She tried not to think about it, to focus on following Arno's directions, but she couldn't stop her hands from shaking or halt the feeling of dread washing over her.

"Pull over here," said Arno. Aafke eased the car over to the side of the road.

"Look there."

She peered across the street. A large outdoor restaurant rested on the corner of the block. Aafke knew the place but had never eaten there. Before the war it was an expensive place, too costly for her family's limited means. Since the occupation, it was a favorite haunt of the Germans. Even now as she watched, the tables were filled with gray-and-green uniforms accompanied in many instances by Dutch women. The patrons were drinking wine and feasting on all sorts of delicacies as if there was no rationing, was no war.

"Remember, stay calm and focused," Arno whispered to Aafke, his voice strained with anxiety. "We can't afford any mistakes."

Aafke nodded, swallowing hard against the lump that had

formed in her throat. She felt a mix of excitement and dread churning inside her but knew she couldn't let her emotions get the better of her. They were depending on her, and she was determined not to let them down.

Several soldiers left the restaurant over the next few minutes. Aafke expected Arno to order her to follow them, but he was holding back, obviously waiting for something. She noticed a pudgy SS corporal emerging from the sea of tables. He was accompanied by a beautiful blond woman, about her age. She was obviously Dutch. Aafke wondered what kind of woman could betray her own country by dating a German. The corporal was all smiles, laughing as he fished a stack of Reichsmarks from his tunic and paid the bill. A car pulled up and he led the woman to it, getting in behind her. Arno's eyes narrowed as he took in the scene. "That's our target," he said quietly. "Let's move."

Aafke pressed her foot down on the accelerator, following the car as it pulled away from the curb. Her heart pounded in her chest, her fingers clenching and unclenching the wheel as she tried to keep her focus.

"Stay close, but not too close," Peter advised from the backseat. "We don't want to spook him." Peter reached down and lifted the KAR 98 sniper rifle to his knees. He pulled the bolt back and then in again, driving a bullet into the chamber. He looked through the scope for a second and then back up at the car. "When it stops, I want you to take us to within a hundred yards, but not closer. Once you park, don't move again. I'll lean out the window, aim and fire. Once I've hit the target, you need to get us out of there no matter what. If anyone tries to stop us, run them over. If they catch us, you won't want to live through what they'll do next."

Aafke nodded as Peter rolled down his window. She was following about fifty yards behind the car, which fortunately wasn't making any turns. She slowed down somewhat, increasing the distance as Peter had directed.

"I wonder where they are going?" she asked.

"SS headquarters," said Arno.

"How do you know?"

"That's Rottenführer Hemmel," said Arno. "We've been waiting for him for a long time, and today we are going to get him."

Aafke felt her heart rising in her throat. This wasn't just any target; it was a major one. She felt the stakes, the tension in the car.

"You're losing him!" Arno shouted.

"You told me not to get too close."

"Speed up!"

Aafke stepped on the accelerator, and then had to slam on her brakes. To her horror, a cart was moving into the intersection directly in front of them. Their car screeched and shimmied as the brakes strained to stop them. They slammed to a halt a bare yard from the wagon.

"They're getting away!" shouted Arno. Peter peered out of the window, perhaps searching for a shot, but the cart was too bulky, completely obscuring their view. Aafke cursed under her breath as the cart meandered by, the driver seemingly oblivious to the urgency that had taken hold of the resistance members.

"Go, go!" Arno urged her, his voice tense as the target car disappeared around a corner, now several blocks ahead.

Panicked, Aafke gunned the engine, but instead of lurching forward, the vehicle sputtered and died. Her hands shook as she tried to restart it, only to kill the engine again. She could feel the weight of Arno's gaze on her, filled with disappointment and anger.

"Damn it, Aafke!" he shouted, his voice strained with frustration. "This is why I didn't want you involved in this! You're not ready for this kind of operation!"

Aafke bit her lip, struggling to hold back tears of shame and embarrassment. She knew she had let them down but couldn't find the words to apologize or explain herself. Inside, a storm of emotions raged: fear, regret, and an overwhelming sense of failure.

"Arno, ease up," Peter interjected, obviously trying to diffuse the tension. "We've all made mistakes before. Let's just focus on getting out of here before we attract unwanted attention."

But, as if on cue, the uniformed figure of a policeman appeared beside the car, rapping sharply on her window. Peter quickly covered his rifle with a blanket. A cold shiver ran down Aafke's spine as she met the officer's steely gaze.

"Your papers, please," he demanded, his voice gruff and authoritative.

Aafke's mind raced, frantic thoughts weaving through her head like a storm. The last thing they needed now was to be caught by the police, their lives and the resistance hanging in the balance.

"We are in a hurry," she said. "We were following our friends and were caught behind that cart."

"Shut your mouth, you bitch," snapped the officer. "Your papers!"

To her surprise, she heard rustling behind her. Looking back, she saw Arno reach into his pocket and hand the policeman a set of documents. The officer studied them carefully, obviously looking for any sign of forgery. Aafke held her breath, feeling the tension radiating from the other occupants of the car. After what seemed like an eternity, the policeman finally nodded and handed back the papers.

"You can be on your way," he said curtly.

Aafke breathed a sigh of relief. She turned the ignition, and the car started this time. She moved back into the road, trying to remain calm as she drove them through the streets of Eindhoven to safety. But there was a stone-cold silence in the car. She knew she had failed Arno.

After another half hour, they arrived back at the cottage in the woods. Aafke pulled into the bare yard and shut off the engine. The occupants of the vehicle departed in silence, none of them looking at Aafke. Only Arno remained behind. Once they were alone, Arno confronted her, his expression grave and unforgiving.

"Aafke," he said solemnly, "you failed us today. This is exactly why I don't allow women to conduct operations."

"Failed you how?" she demanded. "A cart pulled in front of me! What was I to do? That could have happened to anyone."

"I told you to stay close."

"You told me not to be too close."

"It doesn't matter," he said. "We've missed our opportunity and you've failed in the eyes of everyone inside. This isn't what I wanted for you. I wanted you to grow into your role, to earn their respect."

Aafke was stunned by the words. *A failure.* That's all she'd ever heard. She'd never lived up to her brother in her father's eyes, she'd lost their business and their home, and now she was losing Arno's respect before she'd had a chance to earn it. "Why do you even care?" she whispered, half to herself.

"Because I need you . . . people like you. You can help us." He checked his watch. "It's getting late. You should go home. I'll clean things up with the others. Things should be fine."

"No, I want to come in. To explain."

He shook his head. "Not now, Aafke. They need a little time to get over this. I'll be by in the next few days."

She didn't know what else to say. She felt tears stinging her eyes. She turned to him, but he was already opening the door and marching toward the cabin. She could do nothing except depart and trudge the long walk back into Eindhoven. By the time she reached her apartment building she had recovered herself. She felt more resolve than ever. She would prove to Arno, to all of them, that she was a productive member of the group, that she had what it took. Joelle's words lingered in her mind as she climbed the last steps to the second floor: *your girlfriend.*

She fumbled for the keys, realizing for the first time that she'd skipped a day of work. She'd have to go in early and explain. She also had nothing for dinner. Her father would be furious. More problems. *Well, to hell with all of them*, she thought. She rattled the lock and opened the door. Her father was sitting at the table, his back straight, his face pale. Seated next to him was a German, staring at her with a stern face. She closed the door quietly behind her.

Chapter 16
Besluiten

Saturday, June 5, 1943
2:15 p.m.
Eindhoven, Netherlands

Otto sat in Fritz's office, sipping tea. The major was attending to some documents while the two men visited. After a few minutes, he rang a bell and an attendant entered, taking the materials away. The major poured himself some tea from the china set on his desk and grabbed a cookie before turning to Otto.

"So, my friend, what did you think about last night's operation?"

"Invigorating and final."

Fritz laughed. "I'm glad you enjoyed it, but that's not quite what I meant. Break the operation down for me."

"It was successful."

"You don't have to hesitate, my friend. Pretend you don't know me. Just give me a combat analysis of the operation."

"You needed both cars there at the beginning. The privates should have had submachine guns. One car should have parked in the street behind the building and the men should have been waiting, one on each corner. When entering the apartment, the agent should have kicked in the door without announcing who was there, so there wouldn't be time to react."

Fritz nodded. "And Hemmel?"

"He's a good man, I'm sure."

"But good for what?"

"He's not fit for this kind of operation. He's out of shape. Too slow. He's going to get men killed."

Fritz nodded. "I agree." He looked at Otto. "But he's all I have, unless you join me."

Otto hesitated. "I appreciate the offer. But I'm still struggling with it."

"You don't see this as important work?"

"It's not that. But I don't want to let my men down. And there's still the fight with Russia out there."

"And the same fight here. That couple we brought to justice last night aren't the only ones, Otto. We've had a dozen assassinations this year already."

"I thought you said the people were growing used to the occupation?"

Fritz shrugged. "Most of them have, but there is always a bad element out there. That's what I need your help with, to ferret out the undesirables. With a man like you, with your experience, your strength and intelligence, we can root out the resistance and truly bring Eindhoven to a place of peace and stability. That's all the Führer wants for people everywhere."

"I'm still not sure."

"Listen, my friend. You still have another day. Take it for yourself. Walk the city, eat in the restaurants. Find yourself a pretty Dutch girl to share the evening with. You can come back to me tomorrow and give me your decision."

Otto rose, liking the idea. "Thank you, Major."

"It's Fritz behind closed doors. And remember, Otto, if you

join us, you would be fighting a different kind of battle—one that ensures our soldiers have a stable homeland to return to when the war is over."

As Otto departed the office, he struggled with his conflicting emotions, realizing that the decision before him was not an easy one. Each path held its own dangers and sacrifices, but ultimately, only he could determine where his loyalties truly lay.

Striding through the halls of SS headquarters, the air seemed to grow colder and heavier. The faces of the soldiers and officers he passed were stern and unyielding, their eyes betraying nothing but unwavering loyalty to the cause. Otto couldn't help but wonder if he was the only one plagued by doubt. But there was something he wanted to do before he left the building. At the front desk he asked a question and was directed back to the second floor.

Reaching the records department, he hesitated for a moment before entering. The room was dimly lit, filled with row upon row of wooden filing cabinets. A lone officer sat at a desk near the back, poring over documents.

"Excuse me," Otto said quietly, drawing the officer's attention. "I need to access some information."

"Of course, Sergeant," the officer replied, his words tinged with a hint of curiosity. Otto explained what he was looking for and a few minutes later the officer handed Otto a slip of paper, which he took without comment.

Leaving the records department and the SS headquarters, Otto stepped into the warm, hazy afternoon. The streets of Eindhoven stretched out before him like a maze of decisions yet to be made. And as he walked away from the place, he knew that the choice that lay before him would define not only his future but also the fate of those he cared for most.

Otto's boots clapped against the cobblestone streets as he made his way through Eindhoven. The sun was setting, casting a faint orange glow over the town, and the chill in the air clung to his uniform like an unwelcome companion. He could feel the weight of the slip of paper in his pocket, bearing the address he sought.

As he walked, Otto couldn't help but notice the fear and anger in the eyes of the locals. They were like flickering embers, glowing briefly before being snuffed out by the sight of him. Their expressions belied Fritz's words. These people hated the occupation, hated him. If he stayed, he would not just be fighting a few disgruntled radicals, he would be at war with a nation.

"*Spaar wat kleingeld, meneer,*" a young boy whispered, extending a hand for spare change. Otto hesitated, then reached into his pocket and dropped a few coins into the boy's palm. The child's eyes widened, and he scampered away, disappearing down a narrow alleyway.

"*Wil je dat ook voor ons doen?*" a raspy voice called out from behind him. An old man with a weathered face glared at Otto, his words laden with bitterness. Otto continued walking, trying to ignore the disdain that seemed to follow him like a cloud.

Finally, he arrived at the address on the slip of paper. The modest brick building loomed before him, its windows dark and uninviting. Otto felt a knot tighten in his stomach, though whether it was from nerves or the cold, he could not say. He took a deep breath and marched inside.

Pausing at the door on the second floor, he gave a hard knock, the sound reverberating through the stillness of the dark corridor. After a moment, it creaked open to reveal a haggard-looking man with graying hair and a rough exterior that betrayed a life filled with hardship. Otto guessed this must be Aafke's father.

"*Ja?*" the man asked warily, his eyes narrowing as they took in Otto's uniform.

"*Goedenavond, Meneer Cruyssen,*" Otto began, his voice steady despite the pounding of his heart. "I am Sergeant Otto Berg. Is your daughter Aafke here?"

"She's not here," the man said gruffly.

"Can I wait for her?"

"Please, come in," Maarten said hesitantly, opening the door wider. Otto stepped inside, his boots leaving dirty tracks on the worn wooden floor.

"Thank you, *Meneer Cruyssen*," Otto replied, removing his hat and gloves as he surveyed the small, dimly lit living room. Sparse furnishings adorned the space: a threadbare sofa, a rickety table, and a few framed photographs hanging crooked on the walls. The unmistakable scent of stale alcohol hung heavily in the air.

"Would you care for a drink?" Maarten asked nervously, gesturing to a half-empty bottle of brandy on the table.

"Please," Otto said, accepting the offer with a nod. He watched as Maarten poured two glasses with trembling hands, the clink of glass against glass punctuating the silence that had settled between them.

"What do you want with us?" her father said. "If she's done something wrong, it wasn't my doing. I just live here."

Otto realized the man thought he was here to arrest them. He couldn't stifle a grin. "What's your name?" he asked gruffly.

"Maarten."

"I'm not here to arrest her. I'm here to talk to her."

"But why? What does she have to do with you?"

"Very little. I met her on the first day of the war. There were Germans at the store—your store I take it? They were looting the goods without paying. I confronted the officer and stopped them."

"That was you?" Maarten asked.

"Yes."

"Little good it did us. Your kind drove us out of business nonetheless; we lost hearth and home because of you. Although Aafke didn't help."

Otto took another sip of the cheap alcohol. "Are you ex-pecting her soon?"

"How would I know? The girl comes and goes at all hours, with hardly a care for my well-being." He leaned forward. "Say, do you have any cigarettes, or any food on you?"

Otto fished into his tunic and drew out a pack, handing them over to Maarten. The little Dutchman grabbed eagerly at the container, ripping it open and fishing out a cigarette. Otto reached over with a lighter. Maarten took a couple of deep puffs and then leaned back, closing his eyes.

"That's the stuff," he said. "And real tobacco. I've hardly tasted it since the war started. Forget the food. I'd live off these for a day or two."

"You can have them."

Maarten looked at Otto shrewdly. "You still haven't told me why you're here. What do you want with Aafke? Don't tell me she's working with the Germans!" He crossed himself. "Jesus, Joseph, and Mary, what will she do next to dishonor this family?"

"She's not working with us. I just wanted to see her again. To make sure she's all right."

"Oh, we're fine and dandy," said Maarten, taking another puff. "Look where the Lord has landed us. No food, living in this dingy hellhole. Nazis bossing us around. My son missing. We've never been better!"

"Where's your son?"

"You tell me. Your lot captured him in the first week of the war. He wrote letters for a while but then they just stopped. God knows what happened to him. And all your fault."

"It's not me. It's the war," said Otto.

"The war, is it? Well, the war didn't bring us to you, it brought you to us. So I call it your responsibility."

Otto was about to answer that when there was a rattle at the door. Aafke walked in the doorway. She froze, her eyes widening as she took in the scene before her.

"Come on in, you little nitwit, he's not here to arrest you. This is the fellow who saved your bacon on the first day of the war. He's come calling for you."

Aafke stepped cautiously into the apartment, closing the door behind her. She stared at them for a few moments longer and then spoke. "What can I do for you?"

"I'm Otto. Do you remember me?"

Aafke's eyes flickered with the first glimmers of recognition, her gaze darting between Otto's face and the floor as if to verify the memory that had resurfaced. "Yes, I remember," she admitted, her voice barely more than a whisper. "You saved our store that day."

Otto nodded. "I did."

"But why are you here now?"

"I wanted to check on you, to make sure you're okay."

"We're fine," she said, turning back toward the door. "Thank you for coming." She opened the door again and gestured toward Otto.

"Now don't be rude," said Maarten. "This fellow brought me cigarettes and who knows what else. Sit down, Aafke, and have a drink with the lad."

Aafke hesitated, glancing nervously at the door before finally sitting down and accepting a glass of water. She took a sip before setting it on the table and turning her gaze toward Otto.

"So, how have you been these last three years?" he asked.

Aafke seemed to contemplate his question for a while, as if she had to work up courage to answer it. She ran her hands over her lap before speaking.

"It's been a long war," she said slowly, her voice heavy with emotion. "We've had little food, little coal for heating in winter, and the Nazis constantly breathing down our necks. We've had no news of my brother, and we can't do anything about it."

She shook her head sadly. "But we've managed to make it through somehow."

Otto leaned forward. "What happened to your brother?" he asked, hoping he might be able to help somehow. "What's his name?"

Aafke looked up, clearly surprised by Otto's question. Tears started to well up in her eyes but she quickly blinked them away. "His name is Christiaan," she said softly. "He was taken away from us three years ago and we've heard nothing in the last year or more." She looked down at her hands, wringing them together as if in a silent prayer for Christiaan's safety.

"I may be able to find out where he is," said Otto, his tone gentle but determined. "I have some contacts that might be able to help us locate him."

Aafke looked up, her eyes full of hope. For a moment it seemed as if she was about to say something, but then she glanced over at Maarten and hesitated. "I don't know," she said slowly. "It's too much to ask for."

But Maarten was quick to overrule her. "Nonsense," he said firmly. "The Germans owe us this much. We have no other way of finding out what happened to our Christiaan. This fellow has offered his help and we must take it." He fixed Aafke with a stern gaze and she reluctantly nodded in agreement.

"Very well," she said softly. "If you think you can find him, I'm willing to try anything." She looked back at Otto and gave him a small smile of thanks before turning away again.

"I have something I would like to ask in return," said Otto.

"What is it?"

"I'd like to ask you to have dinner with me tonight."

"I couldn't. . . . It's been a long day. Perhaps some other time."

"This may be the only night I'm in Eindhoven. I'm due back to my unit tomorrow."

"Come on now, dearie. Don't play the shy one. Go out and

have a bite with this boy. He's doing us a favor. You don't say no to the boys usually."

"Father, that's not true. There's never been anyone!" Otto saw her face flush red. "We shouldn't be talking about this right now, in front of our guest."

"Take her to dinner," Maarten said, waving his hand dismissively. "And bring me back something good from the restaurant. Something only Germans can buy. And some brandy too. That's my price for taking her."

"She's not a commodity to be bought and sold," said Otto. "If she doesn't want to go, I won't force her."

"Bah, that's not what I meant," said Maarten, fishing out another cigarette. "But she'll go with you. She owes you for saving the store."

Aafke looked at her father and then back to Otto. She opened her mouth as if to protest, but then stopped. There was a knock on the door that startled them out of their conversation. Aafke glanced between her father and Otto before standing up to answer it. She took a deep breath and opened it. There was a man standing there in civilian clothes. He was in his midthirties. He turned sharply as if he was going to flee.

"Don't worry," Aafke said. "He's not a threat. Arno, this is Otto. He's the one who saved our shop that first day of the war."

Arno turned back, staring at Otto with a fiery hatred in his eyes. "I remember you," he said. "You came back with your Gestapo friend a few weeks later. Your friend arrested me and just about killed me."

"That wasn't my doing," said Otto. "I'm just a soldier."

Arno stared at his uniform. "You're SS," he said, spitting on the floor. "What the hell is he doing here?"

"He came by to check on me," said Aafke. "I haven't seen him since that last time. I promise you." She was obviously trying to explain the situation to this man.

"She's going to dinner with him," said Maarten. "Look, he brought us cigarettes."

"Father, I'm not going to dinner," she insisted. "That was your idea, not mine." She turned to Arno. "I was going to tell him no."

Arno stared at the two of them. "So this is who you are?" he said, anger dripping from the words. "You have dinner dates with Nazis?"

"No, Arno! You don't understand, I don't know this man."

"You called him by name."

"I just met him those two times, I don't know how he found his way here."

"She's speaking the truth," said Otto, starting to rise. "I'm sorry, I didn't mean to—"

"You're lying," said Arno, staring at Aafke. "You won't see me again." He turned toward the door.

"Arno, please, don't go!" She reached for his arm but he shoved her away, making Aafke fall hard against the table.

Otto exploded, rushing forward, and slammed Arno against the door, holding him with both hands. "Don't you ever touch her like that!" he shouted.

"Otto, please! Leave him alone!" Aafke shouted. He turned and saw the tears spilling down her cheeks.

"I won't let him hurt you. I won't let anyone hurt you."

"Please, just go."

Otto hesitated. "But I wanted to talk to you."

"Go."

He released Arno, who whipped open the door and rushed out of the apartment. Otto turned back to Aafke. "I'm sorry," he said. "If you would just—"

"I said go."

"I'm sorry."

"Don't ever come here again."

"Don't say that, Aafke, he's going to find Christiaan," Maarten interjected.

"We don't want your help," she said.

"But I could find—"

"No, just leave us alone."

"Very well. I hope you are safe. If there is ever anything I can do for you, contact Major Geier at SS headquarters. He'll know how to find me."

She turned away and refused to look at him. Hesitating another moment, he turned and departed, quietly closing the door behind him.

Chapter 17
Rehabilitatie

Sunday, June 6, 1943
5:23 a.m.
Eindhoven, Netherlands

Aafke tossed and turned in her small bed, the cold sweat clinging to her body like a second skin. Her thoughts raced, replaying the confrontation she had had with Otto when he showed up uninvited at her apartment. She could still feel Arno's anger and the unspoken accusation in his gaze. What would the others think? They already doubted her, and how could they ever trust her now after seeing her with a German soldier?

"Get a grip, Aafke," she muttered under her breath, her voice hoarse from lack of sleep. "You can fix this."

She stared at the shadows dancing on the ceiling, fueled by the flickering candlelight. The wind howled outside, rattling the windowpanes, and echoing her own inner turmoil. With each gust, her worry grew, fear gnawing at her resolve. But she couldn't let them down. She wouldn't.

As the first light of day crept through the thin curtains,

Aafke reluctantly rose from her restless slumber and dressed in the simple clothes that defined her existence during the Occupation. Every thread felt heavy, weighted down by the burden of what she had to do now to rectify things. She tied her blond hair into a tight braid and slipped out the door, her blue eyes filled with determination and anxiety.

The sewing factory loomed before her, a dark, oppressive monument to the regime she despised. Aafke steeled herself, inhaling the acrid smell of coal and machinery as she entered the building. The din of the machines was deafening, but it couldn't drown out the whispers of suspicion that followed her.

"Fräulein Cruyssen!" a gruff voice barked over the noise, making her jump. The German foreman, a squat man with a cruel sneer, approached her. "Why are you late? And where the hell were you yesterday?"

"Please, Herr Müller, I am not feeling well," Aafke lied, her voice wavering slightly as she clutched her stomach for effect. "I think it is best if I go home."

"Again?" he snarled, his beady eyes narrowing in suspicion. "You better not lie to me, girl. If you are sick one more time after today, you will lose your job. Do you understand?"

Aafke swallowed hard, nodding her head in submission. The threat of termination paled in comparison to the fear of the consequences of her actions with Otto. But she knew that if she was going to regain the trust of her fellow resistance members, she would have to face whatever came her way.

"Thank you, Herr Müller," she whispered, her voice barely audible above the cacophony of machines. As she turned away from him, her heart pounded in her chest and her mind raced with thoughts of what lay ahead. She couldn't shake the feeling that her world was on the brink of shattering, but she refused to let it break her.

Steeling herself, Aafke slipped out of the sewing factory's back entrance and began her journey to the resistance hideout.

Each step felt heavier than the last. She glanced over her shoulder, afraid that she was being watched. Yet, somewhere deep within her, a fire burned, fueled by determination and resolve.

As Aafke reached the outskirts of the city, the familiar sight of the forest loomed ahead. The trees seemed to beckon her, offering sanctuary from the oppressive atmosphere of the city. Breathing deeply, she ventured into their embrace, following a narrow path that wound its way deeper into the woods. The branches overhead interlocked, forming a vaulted canopy that shielded her from prying eyes.

The resistance members had chosen their hideout well. It was a small, unassuming cottage nestled in a clearing, surrounded by dense undergrowth. As Aafke approached, she could hear the animated voices of Peter, Arno, Joelle, and Maaike within.

" . . and then we'll cut the telephone lines." Peter's voice carried through the thin walls of the cottage.

"Good idea," Arno agreed. "That should buy us some time."

"Enough time for what?" Joelle interjected, her tone laced with skepticism. "We still don't have enough information about the target."

"Joelle has a point," Maaike chimed in gently. "We need to gather more intelligence before we proceed."

"Then that's what we'll do," Peter said.

Aafke hesitated at the door, her hand reaching for the handle, but trembling with anxiety. She knew that once she stepped inside, there would be no turning back. Yet, she also understood that if she didn't explain what had happened with Otto, they would never work with her again. Taking a deep breath, she opened the door and stepped into the cottage.

"Who's there?" Arno called out, his voice tense as he moved to block the entrance.

"It's me, Aafke," she replied, her voice barely audible above the pounding of her heart.

The room fell silent as they turned to face her, their expressions a mixture of surprise and suspicion. Aafke knew this was her moment to set things right, or at least try to. She looked each of them in the eye, her determination unwavering.

"What the hell are you doing here?" Arno asked, anger laced in his voice.

"Let me explain, please," she said. The room was thick with tension. She nearly lost her nerve, but she had to try. "Otto showed up at my apartment uninvited," Aafke began, her voice firm but laced with a hint of vulnerability. "I hadn't seen him in three years, and I barely knew him in any event. I didn't even remember his name. He just appeared out of nowhere. I swear to you, I have never worked for the Gestapo or the Nazis."

The room was silent as they absorbed her words, weighing them against their own suspicions. Aafke could see the varying reactions on their faces, each one mirroring the tension and uncertainty that filled the air.

"Uninvited?" Peter asked, his voice betraying a mix of curiosity and concern. "What did he want?"

Aafke hesitated, unsure of how much to reveal. "He just wanted to see if I was all right, I guess? He had helped us on the very first day of the war. That was the only time I'd ever seen him, except one more time when he visited the store."

"We know all about that," said Joelle. "That little visit cost Arno his freedom and almost his life. Strange that the Gestapo wasn't interested in you as well."

"I was saved by Arno. He never talked. Otherwise, they would have arrested me and my father as well."

"Convenient," said Joelle. "Why didn't they take both of you in right away? It's not like the Gestapo to leave any loose ends."

"I don't know why they didn't arrest me."

"That's exactly what someone working with the Nazis would say."

"Enough," said Arno. "I believe her."

"You shouldn't," said Joelle. "She'll betray us all."

"If I was working with the Germans, then why aren't they here with me right now? I could have as easily led them here as come alone. You can trust me."

"Trust is earned," Joelle snapped, her gaze locked on Aafke. "And right now, you haven't done anything to prove yourself."

Aafke met Joelle's stare, her jaw clenched, and her eyes filled with defiance. "I understand your doubts. But I would never betray any of you. Otto's appearance at my apartment was a shock to me too. I don't know what he wants or why he came. I don't know what else I can do or say to you. I want to help. I'm here to be a part of this."

For a moment, no one spoke, the tension in the room palpable. Aafke could feel the weight of their gazes on her, as they each grappled with their own thoughts and fears. She knew she had to convince them, or risk losing everything she held dear.

"Please," she whispered, her voice raw with emotion. "You have to believe me."

Arno stared at her for a long moment, his anger slowly giving way to something else—concern? Understanding? It was hard for Aafke to tell. Finally, he let out a heavy sigh, his expression softening ever so slightly.

"All right," he said. "We'll trust you, Aafke. But we need to be cautious. Joelle is right about one thing—we can't afford any mistakes. For now, we need to proceed with some things we are working on. Please don't come here again uninvited. We will contact you."

Aafke was hurt but she took a deep breath, holding it in. "When?"

"We will let you know. Go back to your home and work. And don't let that German back into your apartment again!"

"Don't worry, I won't."

Arno nodded by way of dismissal. Aafke looked to the others, who would not meet her gaze. After a few moments, she turned and walked out of the cottage and back into the forest. She fought back her tears, knowing they would do her no good. She had to do something. Something to win their trust. And she thought she knew just what that was.

Aafke did not return to the factory that day. Instead, she spent the afternoon on the streets of Eindhoven. She stood on a particular street corner, watching the comings and goings of an establishment across the street. She was cold and hungry, but she didn't move. She was looking for a specific person. She checked her watch as the afternoon turned to early evening. Perhaps he would not even come. But just as she was beginning to lose hope, she spotted the man she was looking for. Waiting another few minutes, she looked around to make sure nobody was watching her, then crossed the street and entered the same restaurant they had targeted the day before.

As she walked past the tables and then entered the inside portion of the establishment, she could feel the familiar hum of adrenaline coursing through her veins. This was her chance to make things right, to show the resistance that she was still one of them. Pushing open the door, she stepped inside and scanned the dimly lit room, looking for her target.

She spotted him at the bar, a disheveled, slovenly figure in a rumpled uniform, tipping back a beer. His posture seemed to communicate a sour mood. With a deep breath, Aafke strode confidently toward the man, her heart pounding with nervous anticipation. She had to play this perfectly, or risk losing everything.

"Is this seat taken?" she asked sweetly, feigning ignorance as she slid onto the stool beside him.

Corporal Hemmel glanced up, his bloodshot eyes narrowing slightly as he studied her face. After a tense moment, he grunted and returned his attention to his drink. "Suit yourself," he mumbled, taking another swig from his glass.

"Thank you," Aafke replied, forcing a smile as she signaled the bartender for a drink of her own. "You seem distressed?"

"Something like that," Hemmel grumbled, his gaze never leaving the amber liquid in front of him.

"Ah," Aafke murmured sympathetically. "I know how that feels." She took a sip of her own drink, watching him from the corner of her eye. "Sometimes, it seems like life just keeps kicking us when we're down, doesn't it?"

Hemmel huffed a bitter laugh, finally turning to face her. "You have no idea." He looked her over as if for the first time and gave her a leering smile. "I've never seen you in here before. What brings you into the lion's den?"

"I live in the country. I don't get into town very often, but I had to come in to deliver some groceries to a local store for my father, and I thought I'd get something to eat before I went home."

"Interesting," said Hemmel. "And you just walked into a bar full of German soldiers? That didn't intimidate you?"

"Should it?" she asked, giving him a smile.

"I guess not," he said, laughing. "Can I buy you a drink?"

She smiled encouragingly. "I'd like that." Inside she felt like throwing up, but she shoved those feelings down. Any mistake now could be fatal. "Why don't you tell me what's wrong," she suggested, her voice soft and inviting. "I'm a good listener."

"All right," he sighed at last, leaning in closer. "Let me tell you about my life." He talked for almost an hour, telling her all about his childhood, his life in Germany during the depression, about his wife and children, and his life in the Gestapo.

"Another round, please," Hemmel slurred, banging his empty glass on the bar. Aafke tried to keep pace with him, feigning intoxication while remaining clearheaded and focused on her mission.

"Thanks," she said, accepting another drink from the bartender. "So you said you were demoted?"

"Damn right I was," Hemmel growled, bitterness seeping

into his voice as he recounted his tale of woe. "This Waffen-SS hotshot sergeant shows up in town, and suddenly I'm yesterday's news. Major Geier wants this Otto to take over for me. Like I'm not good enough or something."

Aafke bit back a gasp as she recognized the name. Otto? Was it possible that he was the one who had caused Hemmel's demotion? She knew she should be careful, but her curiosity got the better of her.

"Otto? What's so special about him?" she asked innocently, taking a sip of her drink.

"Who knows?" Hemmel muttered, downing half his glass in a single gulp. "All I know is that he's some kind of war hero or something. But that doesn't mean he can just swoop in and take my job!"

"Of course not," Aafke agreed, her mind racing as she considered the implications. If Otto was working for the Gestapo now, maybe he had come to her apartment for more reasons than one? It couldn't be. She'd just reconnected with Arno. But she had driven the car in the recent operation. Was there a connection?

"Listen," she murmured, leaning in close to Hemmel and letting her fingers brush against his arm. "It's getting late, and I don't know about you, but I could use some . . . company. What do you say we go somewhere a little more private?"

Hemmel's bleary eyes widened in surprise before a slow grin spread across his face. "You sure know how to make a man feel better, sweetheart," he said, stumbling to his feet. "Lead the way. We'll have to walk because the bastards took my car away today as well."

Aafke took Hemmel's arm, steadying him as they made their way out of the restaurant and into the darkened streets. Her heart pounded in her chest as she led him through a maze of alleyways, hoping against hope that her gamble would pay off.

She led him out of town, and he stopped her. "Where the hell are we going?" he demanded, and she could see suspicion etched on his ruddy features.

"I told you. I live in the country. It's not far now."

He grunted and allowed her to take his arm again. She led him along the road and then cut abruptly into a field. As they moved into the trees, he halted. "Why do we need to go all the way to your house?" he asked. "This looks pretty good to me."

She felt panic rising and she scrambled for an excuse. "No," she insisted, pulling at his arm. "A bed will be better. And you can spend the night."

"You're my kind of girl," he muttered, slurring the words. "Lead on."

"Almost there," she whispered to Hemmel, who was now leaning heavily on her for support. "Just a little farther, and we can have some fun."

"Can't wait," Hemmel mumbled, his breath hot on her neck.

They entered the clearing of the dilapidated cottage. Smoke rose out of the chimney and there were lights on in the windows. Thankfully, the curtains were drawn so Hemmel couldn't see anyone inside.

Aafke threw the door open wide, her chest heaving with a mixture of adrenaline and fear. The dimly lit room revealed Arno, who stood frozen in shock, his eyes darting between her and the intoxicated man she practically dragged into their sanctuary.

"Are you *insane*?" Arno's hands clenched into fists as he took a step toward them. "You brought an enemy soldier here?"

"Trust me, Arno. I had to do something to prove my loyalty. You'll remember Corporal Hemmel. He's ours now, to do with as we wish." Aafke's blue eyes pleaded with him for understanding while Hemmel swayed unsteadily on his feet beside her. The German seemed so intoxicated now that he didn't even see someone else was in the room.

"Where's the bed?" the drunk Hemmel asked, scanning the room.

Arno rushed forward and punched the German in the face. Hemmel's head snapped back, and he slumped to the floor.

"We need to question him!" said Aafke. "Why did you knock him out?"

"I need time to think," said Arno, refusing to look at her. "Let's get him tied up before he wakes up and realizes what's happening."

Together, they dragged the drunken corporal into a small bedroom and tied him securely to the bedframe. As Aafke double-checked the knots, her heart raced with anticipation. This was it; she would finally regain the trust of her friends and comrades.

"Why don't you tell me what the hell you were thinking?" demanded Arno when they were finished.

"I did this for us—for the resistance. You believe me now, don't you?"

But instead of gratitude or relief, she found only anger in his eyes. "Aafke, you jeopardized everything we've worked for by bringing that man here! Our hideout, our plans. What were you thinking?"

"I was thinking that I needed to show you all that I'm not a traitor!" Aafke's voice trembled with hurt and frustration. "I'm sorry if I made a mistake, but I couldn't stand the thought of you doubting me any longer."

"Proving yourself isn't worth risking all our lives," Arno snapped. "You're not trained for this kind of operation. What if he had been armed, or what if he was followed?"

"Arno, please . . ." Aafke's voice broke as she reached out for him, her eyes filling with tears.

"Enough," he growled, brushing her hand away. "We need to deal with the situation at hand. We'll talk about this later."

Aafke clenched her fists at her sides, her voice rising in desperation. "How am I supposed to prove myself if you won't even give me a chance? I've been loyal to this cause from the very beginning, and I would never betray any of you."

"Your loyalty isn't the issue here!" Arno shouted back, his face red with anger. "It's your recklessness! You can't just go charging into situations like this without thinking about the consequences."

"Then tell me what I should have done!" Aafke demanded, tears streaming down her cheeks. "I couldn't bear the thought of losing all of you—of losing you, Arno. So I did what I thought was necessary."

Arno stared at her for a moment, his chest heaving with emotion. Suddenly, unable to contain himself any longer, he reached out and grabbed her arm, pulling her toward him.

"Arno, let go of me," Aafke whispered, her eyes wide with shock.

"No," he said, his voice low and intense. "Not until you understand that you can't keep putting yourself—or the rest of us—in danger like this."

"Arno . . ." Aafke's voice trailed off as she looked up at him, her heart pounding in her chest. She could feel the heat of his grip on her arm, the intensity of his gaze boring into hers.

"Maybe I haven't been clear enough with you," he continued, his voice trembling with barely restrained passion, "but I care about you, Aafke. More than I should. And it scares me how much I'm willing to risk for you."

"Arno, I—" Aafke began, but before she could say anything else, his lips crashed down onto hers, silencing her words.

For a moment, Aafke was too stunned to react. But then, as the heat of Arno's kiss sent shivers down her spine, she found herself melting into his embrace, her anger and fear forgotten amidst the all-consuming desire that threatened to consume them both.

In that moment, Aafke knew that no matter what happened

next—no matter how dangerous or uncertain the future might be—she would never stop fighting for the resistance, or for Arno.

But even as passion overtook them, the reality of their situation loomed large in Aafke's mind. Hemmel was tied up in the bedroom, a testament to the risk she had taken—and the potential consequences that still hung over their heads.

"Arno," she whispered, pulling away from him just enough to look into his eyes. "We need to focus on dealing with Hemmel and ensuring our safety."

He nodded, his expression serious once more. "You're right. We'll handle this crisis together, and we'll continue to fight for our cause. But promise me one thing, Aafke: never take such risks again without discussing it with me first."

"I promise," she vowed, her heart swelling with newfound determination and hope.

Chapter 18

Ontkenning

Monday, June 7, 1943
12:48 p.m.
Eindhoven, Netherlands

The sun peered through the windows of Major Geier's corner office. Otto waited for his friend to return from lunch. He sat rigid as a statue in his chair, preparing for the coming conversation.

"Ah, Otto!" Fritz entered with a grin on his face, the door slamming shut behind him. "I have news. Corporal Hemmel has gone missing. It seems he didn't take his demotion too well." He chuckled as he slumped down into his chair.

"Missing?" Otto furrowed his brow, his eyes narrowing slightly. "That's unfortunate."

"Indeed," Fritz agreed, still smiling. "But don't worry. He'll show up again in a few days, after he's drowned his sorrows in schnapps and Dutch skirt. I'll be understanding, although he is absent without leave."

Otto hesitated as all the promises and opportunities hung

over him still. He had but to reach out and grab them: promotion, security, safety. He thought of Aafke, her blue eyes filled with defiance and resilience, and how she had spurned him. No, he had nothing here now. His unit needed him, and there was no reason to stay in Eindhoven. Taking a deep breath, he made his decision.

"I've thought long and hard about your offer, my friend. I appreciate it, Fritz, but I must decline," Otto said firmly. "My unit needs me, and I cannot abandon them."

The major's smile faltered, his dark eyes narrowing. "Are you sure about this, Otto? Think about what I'm offering you."

"Thank you, but I've given it much thought," Otto responded, his voice unwavering. Inwardly, he wrestled with the emotions that threatened to consume him: loyalty to his comrades, the desire to protect Aafke, and the growing disillusionment with the Nazi regime. He could not bend to the role of oppressor.

"I don't think you understand, Otto," he said, his voice low and intent. "I went out of my way to secure this position for you. You owe me."

Otto shifted uncomfortably, remembering the trial that had nearly cost him his life early in the war. Fritz had been there, using his influence to save him from an unjust fate. He owed him, yes, but at what cost?

"Remember when I saved your life?" Fritz pressed, his gaze unyielding.

Otto's jaw tightened. "I haven't forgotten, Fritz," he said, his voice strained. "But that doesn't mean I can ignore what's happening around us."

Fritz scoffed, waving a dismissive hand. "You're too sensitive, Otto. We're keeping these citizens safe from terrorists"—he leaned in, lowering his voice—"and other undesirable elements."

"Other undesirable elements?" Otto asked, his voice barely above a whisper, as if speaking louder would shatter the fragile balance between them.

Fritz leaned back in his chair, a cruel smile playing on his lips. "Eindhoven is now officially Jew-free, Otto," he said, enunciating each word carefully, as if tasting their bitterness. "We've rounded up all the Jews and sent them to labor camps in the east."

Otto felt a chill run down his spine, his breath catching in his throat. "You can't be serious," he stammered, struggling to keep his composure. "We grew up with Jewish families, we played soccer with them, attended the academy together. . . . How can you simply erase them like that?"

"Have you been hiding under a rock for the past ten years? You know what the Jews have done to us, to our people. They betrayed us in the last war and drove us into another war now. A war that, as you are so quick to point out, we appear to be losing. The Führer wants them out of the way."

"What do you mean by that?"

"I mean that when this war is over, you'll be hard-pressed to find a Jew in Europe."

Otto was stunned by that statement. The man sitting across from him was no longer the friend he had known. This was a monster, a fanatic who reveled in the suffering of others.

"Have you truly become so blinded by power, Fritz?" Otto asked, his voice laced with disgust. "How can you justify such atrocities? These are innocent people!"

"Every Jew is a potential enemy, Otto," Fritz replied coldly. "It's for the greater good. You should know that by now. And they are in hiding. All over Eindhoven. I wanted you to help me find them. They are the true resistance."

"Greater good?" Otto repeated, his mind reeling from the twisted logic. He remembered the laughter of their Jewish friends, the shared victories on the soccer field. How could Fritz have forgotten those times so easily? What had happened to the man he once knew?

"Tell me, Fritz," Otto said, "do you truly believe this is the right thing to do?"

Fritz's eyes narrowed, and for a moment, Otto thought he saw a flicker of doubt in their depths. But then it was gone, replaced by an icy resolve. "Yes," he said simply, his tone leaving no room for argument. "I do."

Otto stared at him, the enormity of their differences crashing down upon him like a tidal wave. This was not just about duty anymore. It was about what kind of men they had chosen to be. And as much as it pained him, Otto knew there could be no reconciliation between them.

"Then I pity you, Fritz," he whispered, his voice barely audible over the sound of the rain. "I pity the man you've become."

The rain continued to pour outside, casting a dreary atmosphere over the dimly lit room. The drops hammered against the windowpanes, echoing the pounding of Otto's heart as he tried to make sense of Fritz's words.

"Otto, you must understand," Fritz began, his voice stern and unyielding despite the flicker of doubt Otto had seen earlier. "Sympathy with the Jews is a treasonable activity. You cannot let your emotions cloud your judgment."

He leaned in closer, his eyes locked onto Otto's. "I've let your defeatism about the war slide, but I cannot allow this. One more word and I will have no choice but to have you arrested."

Despite the suffocating weight of Fritz's words, something stirred within Otto, a fierce determination that refused to be silenced. He rose from his chair, meeting Fritz's gaze with equal intensity.

"Then arrest me, Fritz," Otto snarled, each word dripping with defiance. "But know that if you do, you'll be arresting someone who refuses to fall for foolish propaganda. I won't be a policeman for a tyrant, and I will not serve one second under you."

With that, Otto stormed out of the room, the door slamming shut behind him like the finality of a guillotine. His boots echoed through the empty hallways, each step heavy with the weight of his convictions.

As he walked, Otto's mind raced with the repercussions of what he had just done. He understood turning his back on Fritz meant turning his back on the life he had known, but he could not bring himself to feel regret. Instead, he felt the stirrings of a newfound purpose, a determination to cling to what he knew was right.

The memory of their Jewish friends played in his mind like a haunting melody—their laughter, their camaraderie on the soccer field, the bonds they had shared. How could Fritz have forgotten those times so easily? Had he truly become so blinded by power?

"Forgive me," Otto whispered to the ghosts of his past. "I will make this right."

He had made his choice. Now all that remained was to face the consequences.

The train's rhythmic clatter provided a melancholic soundtrack to Otto's thoughts as he stared out the rain-streaked window. Paris loomed ever closer, yet his heart felt heavy with the weight of his severed friendship and his conscience. As the landscape blurred past him, he found himself drawn once more to the memory of Aafke.

"Sir, would you like something to drink?" a young woman asked, her voice cutting through his reverie.

"No, thank you," Otto replied absently, his eyes never leaving the window. There was something about Aafke that haunted him—her vulnerability, the fierce kindness that shone through even when she tried to push him away. What was it about her that drew him in so irresistibly?

"Very well, sir," the woman said, moving away to attend to other passengers. Otto barely noticed her departure, lost again in his thoughts.

As the train pulled into the station, Otto braced himself for the next chapter of his life. He had chosen his path, and now he must face whatever awaited him. He gathered his belongings and stepped onto the platform, the cold air stinging his face as though to wake him from his internal turmoil.

"Corporal Berg!" a harsh voice barked, jolting him from his thoughts. Before he could react, two members of the SS approached him, their expressions inscrutable beneath the shadows cast by their caps.

"Your presence is required," one of them informed him ominously. "The boss wants a word with you."

"Understood," Otto replied, trying to keep his voice steady despite the sudden surge of adrenaline. He followed them without protest, his mind racing with questions. Why did they want to see him? Was this retribution for his defiance?

As they led him through the bustling station, Otto couldn't help but feel a twinge of fear. He had taken a stand, but at what cost? What would become of him now? And yet, even as these thoughts swirled through his mind, he clung to the image of Aafke—her strength, her resilience, her unwavering spirit.

"Sir, this way," one of the SS men said as he gestured toward a darkened room. Otto hesitated for a moment before stepping inside, steeling himself for whatever lay ahead.

He took a deep breath and faced the darkness, ready to confront whatever challenge awaited him.

Chapter 19

De Eindhovense Dating Club

Tuesday, June 8, 1943
7:30 p.m.
Eindhoven, Netherlands

Aafke stared into the dimly lit room of the cottage. She and Arno were alone, a rare moment of solitude amidst the chaos of war. The flickering candlelight cast shadows against the walls, giving the room an air of intimacy.

"Corporal Hemmel has been handed over to one of our higher-ups," Arno began, his voice low and measured. "Your actions have gained us invaluable information and respect within the resistance."

Aafke's cheeks flushed with pride, though she tried to remain humble. She remembered how angry Arno was when she'd first brought the soldier there. And she remembered what happened after. "I did what I had to do," she murmured.

"Thank you, Aafke." Arno's gaze locked onto hers, his eyes reflecting gratitude and something deeper that made her heart race.

Their lips met, tentatively at first, then with growing passion. Aafke felt as though she was being swept away by a powerful current, her body responding to Arno's touch with an urgency she'd never experienced before. As they kissed, Arno guided her toward the bedroom door, his intentions clear.

"Arno, wait," Aafke whispered, pulling away slightly. She felt the intense conflict between her faith and her desire. "We can't . . . I can't sleep with you before we're married."

For a brief moment, irritation flashed across Arno's face, but he quickly masked it with understanding. "Of course, I'm sorry," he said softly as they reluctantly separated.

Desiring to keep the momentum of their newfound closeness, Aafke launched into her proposal. "I've been thinking about how we could use our unique position to further help the resistance. I came up with the idea for an Eindhoven dating club."

Arno raised an eyebrow. "Go on," he said.

"Maaike, Joelle, and I would take turns repeating the same operation I just pulled off with Hemmel. We would go to bars frequented by Gestapo and other high-ranking Nazis," Aafke explained, her voice filled with determination. "We'd pose as collaborators, luring them out under the guise of sleeping with them. Once we have them alone, resistance members would be waiting to either assassinate or abduct the Nazis."

Aafke stared at Arno, her blue eyes blazing with determination as she awaited his response to the plan. The room seemed to close in on them, the tension palpable. The flickering candlelight cast shadows on the walls, adding an eerie atmosphere to their discussion.

Arno clenched his fists, a muscle ticking in his jaw. "No, Aafke," he said firmly, his voice strained. "I've already told you that women shouldn't be directly involved in operations. And besides, I can't risk you like that. It's too dangerous."

"Arno, we can't just sit back and let others fight our battles for us," Aafke pleaded, her voice shaking with emotion. "I'm strong enough to do this. We must do something more than cooking and cleaning!"

He sighed, rubbing his temples. "There are plenty of ways you can help. You have access to fabric from the factory where you work. You could sew German uniforms for our disguises. That's still making a difference."

"Is that all you think we're good for?" Aafke snapped, feeling her anger rise like a tidal wave. "Sewing and taking care of your meals? We're capable of so much more! This dating club can bring a new and important element to your operations!"

They stood mere inches apart, each refusing to back down. Aafke's heart pounded in her chest, her breaths coming in shallow gasps. "Please, Arno," she implored, her voice cracking. "Don't underestimate us. We can do this."

For a moment, silence hung heavy between them. The candle flickered, casting wavering shadows on Arno's face as his expression softened. His eyes met hers, filled with conflict and an unspoken understanding.

"All right, Aafke," he conceded, his voice barely above a whisper. "We'll try it one more time. But any problem at all, and I'm going to have to shut this down. You don't know the risk I'm taking with this. It's not just the danger to you and the others. I don't know what the other groups will think. Using our women as bait. You must promise me you'll be careful. If anything is amiss, you get yourself out of there."

A surge of relief washed over Aafke, but she couldn't ignore the undercurrent of fear that accompanied it. She knew the risks they were about to take, but she also knew it was necessary.

"I promise, Arno," she whispered, her voice filled with resolve. "We will be careful."

The sun hung low in the sky, casting a warm glow over the wooden table set with a meager meal. Aafke's heart raced as she saw Peter, Joelle, and Maaike approaching the cottage, their footsteps crunching on the gravel path. She knew that the moment of truth was at hand—it was time to present her daring plan to the others.

"Ah, there you are," Arno greeted them as they entered the cozy room. "We were just discussing our next move."

The group gathered around the table, the aroma of freshly baked bread and homemade soup filling the air. As they began eating, Arno cleared his throat and turned to Aafke.

"Go ahead, Aafke. Tell them about your idea."

"Why is she telling us anything?" asked Joelle, scowling. "We didn't even know if we could trust her a few days ago. I'm still not sure we can. Why has she been elevated so swiftly?" Aafke could feel the woman's eyes watching her knowingly.

"True enough," said Arno. "She is new. But she's stumbled onto something that might be of use to us. And it will get all of you females off my back," he said, chuckling a little. "Go ahead and tell them."

Aafke nervously fiddled with the hem of her skirt as she faced her comrades. Her voice trembled slightly as she began outlining the plan, hoping that her determination and conviction would shine through her words.

"We'll take turns going to bars frequented by Gestapo and other prominent Nazis. Posing as collaborators, we will lure men out of the bar under the pretense that we will sleep with them. Once they're away from their comrades, we bring them to a designated location where resistance members will be waiting to either assassinate or abduct them."

Maaike's eyes sparkled with excitement, her gentle smile turning into a fierce grin. "That sounds brilliant, Aafke! It's an unexpected tactic—I'm sure we can catch them off guard."

"Thank you, Maaike," Aafke replied, feeling a surge of confidence from her friend's support.

Joelle, however, was not as enthused. She shifted in her seat, her fingers tapping restlessly on the table as she studied Aafke with narrowed eyes. Aafke tried to ignore the growing tension between them, focusing on the details of the plan.

"Arno and Peter will provide us with backup, ensuring our safety and assisting with the abductions or assassinations when necessary," Aafke continued, her voice gaining strength. "We'll rotate between Maaike, Joelle, and myself as the bait to avoid arousing suspicion."

As she finished speaking, Arno and Peter exchanged glances before nodding in agreement. They rose from the table. "We'll leave the three of you to the details. Peter and I are going to one of our contacts to pick up some supplies. We'll be back in an hour or so." Arno's eyes lingered on Aafke for a moment before he followed Peter outside.

With the men gone, Aafke looked to her companions, her expression resolute. "We can do this. We just need to stay focused and work together."

"Of course, Aafke," Maaike agreed. "We're all in this together."

But Joelle's irritation had reached a boiling point. She slammed her fist onto the table, glaring at Aafke with fire in her eyes.

"Really, Aafke? Why are you the one in charge of this operation? I saw the look you just gave Arno. Are you sleeping with him?"

Aafke recoiled at the accusation, her cheeks flushing red with anger. "No, I'm not. And this has nothing to do with that, Joelle. I came up with the plan, and I'm committed to seeing it through. Our feelings for each other—if there are any—won't interfere with the success of the mission."

Joelle's lips curled into a smile. "So there is something between you. I knew it. What did I tell you, Maaike? Our leader was entirely too interested in tracking you down. I told him it wasn't worth the risk for some woman who had no contacts, no experience. Now this is all too clear."

"That doesn't matter," said Maaike. "She's part of us now. And she's managed to do something that neither of us have. She's getting us into the game."

"With what's between her legs as the bait."

"Enough!" said Aafke. "You don't know me, Joelle! I would never give myself to any man to get what I want. Even if Arno is the one, I wouldn't be with him before I was married."

Joelle tipped her head back and laughed. "How provincial. But you want to lure Germans to hotel rooms. What are you going to do when one of them gets you on the bed and gives you his schnitzel before the rest of us can get to you?"

"That won't happen," said Maaike. "We'll be there for each other."

Joelle looked at both of them. "Fine. Whatever your motives, the plan has merit. But don't think you're our leader, or even part of this group yet. You'll have to prove you're worth more to us than Arno's dessert."

"Fine," Aafke said, her voice unwavering. "I'll prove it. And when we succeed, you'll see that I'm not doing this for Arno or anyone else. I'm doing this for all of us—for our freedom."

"Fine," Joelle spat through gritted teeth. "I'll follow your plan. But don't expect me to trust you completely."

"Trust has to be earned," Aafke replied. "And I'm willing to work for it."

The unspoken truce hung heavy in the air as Arno and Peter returned to the cottage, their arms laden with supplies.

"All right, everyone," Arno said, his voice firm with resolve. "Tonight, we put Aafke's plan into action. We need to be careful, smart, and, above all, ruthless. The enemy won't hesitate to kill us, and we can't afford to hesitate either."

As the sun dipped below the horizon, bathing Eindhoven in a cloak of twilight, Aafke, Maaike, and Joelle ventured into the city. They sought out a different bar from the one where Aafke had lured Corporal Hemmel, keen to avoid any unwanted attention. The three women moved like shadows, the weight of their mission pressing down on them like a physical force.

"All right," Aafke whispered, "I'll head in and—"

"I'm going first," said Joelle.

Aafke turned. "That's not the plan."

"I told you, you're not our leader. The plan is a good one, but I'm going first. Either that or I'm going home, and you can play this game by yourself."

Aafke looked to Maaike for support but she was staring at the pavement. She wasn't going to get involved in this conflict. "Fine," said Aafke. "You're first. Are you sure you're ready for this?"

"More than ready," Joelle replied tersely, her jaw set in determination. She paused for a moment, staring at the entrance to the dimly lit bar.

"Then go," Aafke said. "Remember the plan and stay focused. We'll be right here, waiting for you to come out. I rented a hotel room just two blocks away. Here is the key. When you bring him out, don't look our way. We'll see you and follow. We won't be more than a block behind. When you get him in the room, offer him a drink, go to the bathroom. Anything to delay things. We'll knock on the door and pretend you've ordered up some champagne. We'll rush in and secure the target. Arno and Peter won't be far behind."

Joelle squared her shoulders and took a deep breath. Then she stepped out of the shadows and disappeared into the bar, leaving Aafke and Maaike to battle their own nerves as they waited in the darkness.

Aafke's heart pounded in her chest, each thud echoing the weight of responsibility she bore. Her thoughts raced with images of Joelle, of Arno, of the lives that depended on their success tonight. But through it all, one thought remained constant: They had to win this fight. There was no other option.

The night air was thick with tension as Aafke and Maaike huddled in the shadows, watching the entrance of the bar. Their breaths came out in short, nervous bursts. The dim glow from the bar's windows cast flickering shadows on the cobblestone street, creating an eerie atmosphere.

"Joelle's been in there for over an hour," Maaike whispered, her voice trembling with anxiety. "What if something happened to her?"

Aafke clenched her fists tightly, feeling the cold seep through her gloves. She knew they couldn't afford to panic, but the unknown fate of their comrade weighed heavily on her. "I'm going in to check," she decided, determination lacing her words. "Stay here and be ready to signal Arno and Peter if anything goes wrong."

As Aafke entered the smoky bar, the sound of boisterous laughter and clinking glasses assaulted her ears. Her eyes darted around the room, searching desperately for any sign of Joelle. When she found only unfamiliar faces, a sense of dread crept over her. Where was Joelle?

"Have you seen my friend?" Aafke asked the bartender, her voice steady despite her fear. "Black hair, about this tall?" She held her hand up to indicate Joelle's height.

The bartender shook his head. "She left with a German soldier about fifteen minutes ago. Out the back. Looked like they were heading down the alley."

"Thank you," Aafke mumbled, her heart pounding as she quickly left the bar.

"Maaike!" she called in a hushed tone, rushing over to her friend. "Joelle's gone. She left out the back. We need to find her before it's too late."

Together, they searched the nearby streets and alleys, their lanterns casting eerie shadows on the walls. With each passing minute, Aafke's fear grew heavier, suffocating her like a thick fog. She couldn't help but imagine Joelle lying injured or worse, somewhere in the darkness. They finally backtracked to the hotel and went up to the second-floor room. They knocked but nobody answered.

"Curfew's approaching," Maaike warned, checking her watch. "We have to go back."

Reluctantly, Aafke agreed, and they made their way back to headquarters, their minds racing with worst-case scenarios. They hadn't had time to track down Arno and Peter, and they had to hope that the men had the good sense to leave the city before curfew hit.

As they approached the cottage, Aafke was surprised to see the lights on and figures inside. They approached cautiously now, and she wondered what had happened. She peered through one of the windows and was relieved to see Peter, Arno, and Joelle inside, sitting at the table and clinking glasses together. She rushed through the door.

"Joelle!" Aafke exclaimed, her eyes wide with disbelief. "Thank God you're safe! What happened? We thought you were dead."

"Safe and successful," Joelle replied smugly, her eyes gleaming with triumph. "I managed to conduct the operation entirely by myself."

Aafke's relief quickly turned to anger, but before she could say anything, Arno spoke up, his voice filled with praise. "She did an excellent job, Aafke. You should be proud."

Feeling a mix of frustration and helplessness, Aafke wanted to yell, to berate Joelle for taking such a risk, but she knew there was nothing she could do in that moment.

"Joelle," she said tightly, striving to keep her emotions in check. "Next time, stick to the plan. We need to work together if we want to succeed."

"I had it under control," she said. "And I didn't need your help. I brought us a sergeant. One rank above your precious Corporal Hemmel. I guess that puts me in the lead." She smirked at Aafke, a strange mixture of satisfaction and disdain crossing her face. "I thought the other night when you pulled your little plan off that it was a big deal, but I've proven just how easy it is. These foolish boys are all alike. They see a pretty girl and they are blinded by what's inside their pants."

Aafke was sure the comment was directed at her. She glanced at Arno, but he was already standing, moving to the bedroom where their prisoner was tied to the bed.

"We'll keep him here tonight," said Arno. "Then I'll turn him over in the morning. Good job, Joelle. Our group's reputation is going up and up."

Joelle smiled at him and then glanced sideways at her. Aafke felt a piercing jealousy. She wasn't sure what game Joelle was playing, but she knew now that it involved Arno—and Joelle wasn't someone to cross.

Chapter 20

De Redding

Sunday, September 12, 1943
2:05 p.m.
Gran Sasso, Italy

The glider's interior was a confined space, with barely enough room for the dozen SS soldiers and their equipment. The atmosphere inside was stifling, a mixture of sweat, tension, and the stench of fear. Otto Berg clenched his jaw as he gripped the edge of his seat. He could feel the weight of the other men's gazes on him, each one sizing him up, wondering if he would hold his own in the operation to come.

"Five minutes!" barked Major Skorzeny from the front of the glider. His voice brought Otto back to a few months earlier when they first met, under less-than-favorable circumstances. . . .

Otto had sat handcuffed in the back of a black sedan, flanked by two armed guards. As the car pulled up to a heavily fortified SS headquarters in Paris, Otto's heart raced with dread. He feared after his insubordination to Fritz that he would be executed, never to see his comrades again. He was escorted through the corridors, past cold-faced officers who looked at him as though he were already a dead man.

"Sit," ordered an SS major as they entered his office. Otto complied, his eyes nervously darting around the room, taking in the maps, weapons, and photographs of high-ranking Nazis that adorned the walls.

"Sergeant Otto Berg," the major began, flipping through Otto's file. "Iron Cross, First and Second Class, for bravery. Quite impressive." Otto remained silent, knowing that any attempt to defend himself would be futile.

"However, it seems you also have a history of defying orders that don't sit well with your conscience. A telegram was sent to headquarters by a Major Geier describing you as defeatist and sympathetic to the Jews.

"Tell me, Berg, do you deny these accusations?" the major asked, his eyes boring into Otto's like a drill.

"I do not deny defying orders, but I am no traitor," Otto replied, his voice cracking under the strain. "I serve Germany and my comrades, but I will not follow blindly. If doing what is right makes me a traitor, then so be it."

The major studied him for a moment, his expression inscrutable. Finally, he spoke again. "Your mother was English, correct? And you speak fluent English?"

Otto hesitated before answering. What was this about? Did they think he was working with the enemy? Well, no reason to deny it. It was common knowledge in Munich that his mother was English. "Yes, sir," he responded.

"Very well," said the major, a hint of a smile playing across his lips. "I am Major Skorzeny. You may have heard of me. I requested your services before I received this telegram from Major Geier. Frankly, I don't care about your past. I've read your file. You're brave under fire and you have some language

skills I'm interested in for the future. Consider this your chance
to prove yourself, Sergeant."

Otto agreed, thus avoiding any further investigation into his
comments to Fritz. He was shocked that his closest friend had
turned against him, but that was the world he lived in. Children
turned in parents for perceived disloyalty to the Führer. He
hadn't expected this from Fritz, but perhaps he had been naïve.

The months of training were the hardest he'd had in his life.
Most of it was up and down mountains at high altitude. When
he was done, he was in the best shape of his life. He also enjoyed his comrades. There were no conscripts here. These men
were the elite of the elite. Otto had craved working alongside
such men, and now he was having his chance.

"Two minutes!" Skorzeny's shout snapped Otto back to the
present. The glider shook violently as the pilot airplane released
them, leaving them to glide silently through the crisp air.

"Prepare for a rough landing!" Skorzeny yelled over the
wind and the groans of the aircraft. Otto steeled himself, gripping his weapon tightly as the ground rushed up to meet them.

The glider slammed into the side of the mountain with a
bone-jarring impact, sending Otto, and the other men inside,
tumbling forward in a chaotic mass of limbs and equipment.
Pain shot through Otto's body, but he gritted his teeth and
struggled to regain his footing amidst the wreckage.

"Move!" Skorzeny barked from somewhere behind him, his
voice tense and urgent. Otto could hear the pain in his words—
the crash had not spared anyone. As he climbed out of the mangled fuselage, Otto saw that several men were injured, some
more seriously than others.

"Form up! We're moving out!" Skorzeny ordered, his voice
cutting through the sounds of groans and labored breathing as
the men began to pick themselves up and fall into formation.

Otto took one last look at the crumpled glider before joining his comrades, his heart pounding in his chest. He knew that they were on a dangerous mission, but he hadn't expected it to begin like this. However, there was no turning back now. They had to press forward, or all of their sacrifices would be for nothing.

"Toward the hotel!" Skorzeny commanded, leading the way with an Italian prisoner in a general's uniform firmly in his grasp. Skorzeny had brought the man with him, whom he intended to use as a hostage to win them passage. Otto and the rest of the men followed closely behind, their boots crunching on the rocky ground as they hurried toward their target.

As they approached the hotel, they could see that the gate was defended by Italian troops, their weapons at the ready. Otto felt a surge of adrenaline course through him as he prepared for the impending confrontation. But Skorzeny, always cunning, had a plan in mind.

"Stop!" Skorzeny shouted at the Italian soldiers, his pistol pressed against the general's temple. "Let us pass, or your general dies!"

The Italian troops hesitated, their eyes darting between Skorzeny, the hostage, and each other. Otto could see the fear etched into their faces, and he knew that they understood the gravity of the situation.

"Move!" Skorzeny growled, and the soldiers reluctantly stepped aside, allowing the commandos to rush through the gates and into the hotel.

Otto sprinted alongside his comrades, his heart pounding in his ears as they charged through the corridors. He was well aware that time was of the essence—any moment now, reinforcements could arrive and doom their mission. But he couldn't shake the feeling that there was something more at stake here, something greater than just this particular operation.

Stay focused, he told himself, trying to push away the nagging thoughts that threatened to distract him from the task at hand. *Do your duty, and trust your comrades.*

And with that, Otto threw himself wholeheartedly into the fray, determined to prove that he still belonged among these men, and that he was not the traitor that some believed him to be.

Otto's boots thundered on the polished marble stairs as he ascended, his breath ragged but determined. His heart raced in his chest, an unyielding drumbeat that spurred him forward. He rounded a corner and came face-to-face with three Italian soldiers, their eyes wide with surprise and fear.

"*Non muovere!*" one of them shouted, raising his rifle.

But Otto didn't hesitate. He lunged at the first soldier, grabbing the barrel of the rifle and using his momentum to swing it against the man's head. The soldier crumpled to the floor, unconscious.

"*Diavolo!*" cursed the second soldier, reaching for his sidearm. But Otto was already upon him, gripping the man's wrist with one hand while delivering a powerful punch to his jaw with the other. As the soldier staggered back, Otto wrenched the pistol from his grip and tossed it aside.

"Please," the third soldier gasped, his hands raised in surrender. "I have a family."

Otto hesitated for a moment, torn between duty and compassion. Then, making a decision, he rammed his fist into the soldier's solar plexus, leaving him doubled over and gasping for breath. It wasn't a lethal blow, but it would keep him out of the fight.

"*Sei fortunato,*" Otto muttered, sparing the man a glance before pressing onward. He had no time to waste—every second counted.

Reaching the top of the stairs, Otto scanned the corridor and saw the door to a suite at the end. With a surge of adrenaline, he sprinted toward it, his powerful legs propelling him forward like a locomotive. Without breaking stride, he launched a devastating kick at the door, splintering the wood and sending it flying off its hinges.

"*Chi è là?*" demanded a voice from within—a voice that sent a chill down Otto's spine. It was the unmistakable voice of Benito Mussolini, the man they had come to rescue.

"Signor Mussolini," Otto began, his voice firm yet respectful as he stepped into the room. "I am Sergeant Otto Berg, and I am here to liberate you."

"About time," the dictator grumbled, his eyes narrowing as he assessed Otto. Despite his captivity, he still managed to exude an air of power and authority.

"Come with me," Otto instructed, gesturing for Mussolini to follow him. He could hear the sounds of gunfire echoing through the hotel—the rest of his comrades were still engaged in fierce combat. They needed to move quickly.

As they hurried through the hotel, Otto couldn't help but feel a swell of pride in his chest. This was what he lived for: the camaraderie, the danger, the thrill of battle. For a brief moment, he felt truly alive.

"Excellent work, Sergeant," Skorzeny declared as they reached the hotel's entrance, where the remainder of the commando unit had assembled. Otto could see the flicker of admiration in the major's eyes as he extended his hand. "You've proved yourself invaluable on this mission."

"Thank you, sir," Otto replied, shaking Skorzeny's hand firmly. The praise from such a high-ranking officer filled him with satisfaction. This was the pinnacle of his career so far, and he relished every moment of it.

Yet beneath the pride and excitement, a thread of unease wound its way through Otto's thoughts. He knew that the world around them was changing, and not necessarily for the better. But whatever the future held, he would face it head-on, just as he had faced the Italian soldiers on the stairs.

For now, he would savor this victory and the fleeting sense of belonging it brought him.

Chapter 21

Vangen

Monday, September 13, 1943
3:47 p.m.
Eindhoven, Netherlands

The dimly lit cottage buzzed with intensity as Aafke and Arno sat at a wooden table, poring over their hand-drawn maps. The shadows of the room hid secrets and whispered conspiracies, but in the heart of this clandestine world, Aafke felt alive.

"Another successful abduction, Aafke," Arno said, his voice barely above a whisper, his eyes shining with pride. "We're making a real difference."

Aafke nodded, her face serious despite the joy she felt at their small victories. "It's more dangerous each time."

"Indeed," he agreed solemnly. "But remember that we're fighting for freedom. For our loved ones and our future."

As if to emphasize his point, Arno gently placed his hand on Aafke's. She looked down, feeling the warmth course through her veins. The touch was intimate, but also protective, reminding her of the bond they had forged amidst the devastation of war.

"Arno," she began, her voice wavering slightly, "I want you to know how much I appreciate everything you've done for me—for all of us."

Their eyes met, and for a moment, Aafke could see the depths of emotion hidden behind Arno's stoic facade. He leaned in closer, his breath warm against her cheek.

"Nothing is too great a risk when it comes to your safety, Aafke," he murmured.

Aafke found herself leaning toward him, their lips meeting in a kiss that tasted of desperation, longing, and triumph. Arno's arms encircled her, pulling her closer as the intensity of the kiss grew.

But as Arno's hands began to roam, a sudden clarity pierced the fog of her desire. Aafke gently pushed him away. "Arno," she whispered, regret and determination warring in her voice, "we can't."

Arno pulled back, his breath ragged and his eyes clouded with frustration. "Aafke, do you not see? The world is burning around us, and yet you cling to these old beliefs."

"Arno, please," Aafke said, her hand on his arm, trying to convey the depth of her feelings. "This isn't just about religion or tradition. It's about my heart and my promise to myself. I need to remain true to who I am, even in the midst of all this chaos."

He stared at her for a long moment, the weight of their unspoken desires hanging heavy in the air between them. Then, with a sigh, he nodded his understanding and stepped away, leaving Aafke to grapple with the consequences of her choices and the tenuous hope that they might still find happiness amidst the darkness of war.

"Your beliefs are a relic of the past, Aafke!" Arno snapped, stopping in front of her. "They're holding you back. As socialists, we know that religion is a silly fantasy meant to control the masses. We need to be free from such constraints, especially now, when our very lives depend on it."

Aafke clenched her jaw, unwilling to back down. "I will not change who I am for anyone, Arno, not even you. My beliefs give me strength and purpose, and I will hold onto them no matter what!"

Arno sighed, running a hand through his hair as he looked away. "Fine," he muttered, his voice tight with frustration. "But don't come crying to me when you realize that your precious beliefs have cost you everything."

Aafke's heart ached at the bitterness in his words, but she held her ground. She needed someone to talk to, someone who might understand her struggle. Rising from her seat and heading into the bedroom, she found Joelle and Maaike huddled together near the makeshift radio, their faces tense as they listened to the crackling news reports.

It must have been clear that something was wrong. "Are you all right?" asked Maaike.

"Let me guess," Joelle said with a sardonic smile, not bothering to look away from the radio. "You're still holding onto your precious Catholic beliefs, and he's having trouble seeing past them?"

"Joelle!" Maaike scolded, her eyes wide with disapproval.

Aafke ignored Joelle's sarcasm, determined to make her point. "Yes, that's part of it. But it's more than just my faith. It's about staying true to myself in a world that seems determined to tear us all apart."

"Come off it, Aafke," Joelle scoffed, rolling her eyes. "What good are your values if they keep you from the ones you love? We're fighting for our lives here. Maybe it's time to let go of the things that don't matter and focus on what does."

"Joelle, enough," Maaike interjected gently, placing a hand on Aafke's shoulder. "Aafke will know the right place, the right time."

As Aafke looked into Maaike's kind eyes, she felt a surge of gratitude for her friend's empathy. Yet deep down, she knew that her convictions were as much a part of her as her heartbeat or the blood coursing through her veins. And as the war raged on around them, Aafke would find herself forced to confront the harsh realities of love, loyalty, and sacrifice—even as she fought to preserve the fragile flicker of hope that still burned in her.

The sun dipped low on the horizon, casting a golden glow over the cobblestone streets of the city. Aafke watched as the young German officer approached, his uniform crisp and clean, betraying none of the horrors that had befallen their homeland. She hesitated for a moment, feeling the weight of her own deception pressing down upon her.

"*Entschuldigung*," she said sweetly, batting her blue eyes at him. "*Können Sie mir helfen?*" As the officer turned to face her, Aafke felt a familiar flutter of fear in her stomach, but she pushed it aside, focusing instead on the task at hand.

"Of course," he replied, his voice tinged with a soft accent. "What do you need help with?"

"Can you walk me home?" Aafke asked innocently, feigning a lost and vulnerable demeanor. "I'm afraid I've gotten turned around."

"Sure," he agreed, taking a step closer. "Where do you live?"

"Down this way," she gestured toward a narrow alleyway, her heart pounding in anticipation. This was the plan—lure him away from the prying eyes of the street and into the shadows, where Joelle and Maaike would be waiting. Together, they would neutralize the threat and gather whatever intelligence they could. Their target today was a member of the staff of an important general stationed in Holland. He might have intricate knowledge of troop and gun placements that could be passed on to the English and Americans through the resistance network.

As they walked deeper into the alley, the warm glow of the sun faded, replaced by a damp chill that seemed to seep into Aafke's bones. The walls closed in around them, blotting out the sounds of the city beyond.

"Here we are," Aafke whispered, stopping at a dead end. She glanced around nervously, expecting to see Joelle and Maaike emerge from the shadows at any moment. But they were nowhere to be found.

"Are you sure this is the right place?" the officer asked, his eyes narrowing suspiciously.

"Y-yes," Aafke stammered, her mind racing with panic. Where were they? What would she do now?

"Good." He grinned, stepping toward her and closing the gap between them. "Now we can be alone."

Aafke's heart pounded in her chest as she realized the danger she was now in. She couldn't let this man overpower her—not when so much was at stake.

"Please," she whispered, trying to keep her voice steady. "Just wait a moment."

"Ah, but I don't want to," he replied, his grin widening. As he reached for her, Aafke's hand closed around the hilt of the small knife hidden within her coat. She had never intended to use it, but now it seemed her only chance at survival.

"Get away from me!" she screamed, her fear fueling her fury. In one swift motion, she pulled the knife free and drove it deep into the officer's gut, feeling the resistance give way as it pierced his flesh.

He gasped, his eyes widening in shock before crumpling to

the ground with a heavy thud. Aafke stumbled back, her hands shaking uncontrollably.

"God forgive me," she whispered, tears streaming down her face as she looked upon the lifeless body of the young German officer. What had she done?

Aafke sprinted through the darkening streets, her heart pounding wildly in her chest. She could still feel the warm blood on her hands, the weight of taking a life heavy upon her conscience. The headquarters loomed ahead, and she prayed that Joelle and Maaike were safe inside.

"Arno!" she gasped as she burst through the door, her breath coming in ragged gasps. "Something's gone horribly wrong!"

Arno rushed to her side, his eyes filled with concern. "What happened? Where are Joelle and Maaike?"

"Th-they didn't show up," Aafke stammered, tears streaming down her face. "I was left alone with the officer, and I . . ." She choked back a sob, unable to continue.

"What did you do?" Arno pressed urgently, his grip tightening around Aafke's shoulders.

"I had no choice, Arno!" she cried out desperately. "He tried to take advantage of me, and I . . . I killed him."

"Dear God," Arno whispered, the realization dawning on him. "We've been set up."

"Set up?" Aafke echoed, her voice trembling with fear. "By whom?"

"Let's discuss this later," Joelle interrupted coldly, emerging from the shadows. "Right now, we need to find Maaike."

"Where is she?" Aafke demanded, her blue eyes flashing with anger.

"Captured by the Gestapo," Joelle replied bitterly. "It seems they knew about our plan all along."

"Then we must do something!" Aafke insisted, her voice shaking but resolute. "We can't just leave her in their hands!"

"Agreed," Arno chimed in, his jaw set with determination. "But we must tread carefully. If they know about our operation, it's only a matter of time before they come for us as well."

"Then we strike first," Aafke declared, her eyes burning with defiance. "We'll rescue Maaike and show them that we won't be intimidated."

"Are you insane?" Joelle snapped, her voice dripping with disdain. "You've already killed one of their officers. They'll be out for blood!"

"Enough!" Arno interjected, his voice firm. "We're all on the same side here. We need to stay focused and work together if we want to save Maaike and protect ourselves."

"Arno's right," Aafke agreed, taking a deep breath to steady herself. "We must stay strong, for Maaike's sake and for our own."

"Very well," Joelle conceded reluctantly. "But remember, Aafke, your actions have consequences."

Aafke felt the weight of Joelle's words, but she refused to let them break her spirit. She had made her choice in that dark alley, and now she would face the consequences head-on.

"Let's move quickly," Arno urged. "Time is not on our side."

With Maaike's life hanging in the balance, Aafke knew there was no room for fear or doubt. Despite the danger that lay ahead, she clung to the hope that their small band of rebels could defy the odds and overcome the darkness that threatened to consume them all.

Arno paced the small room, his hands clenched into fists at his sides. The walls, covered in maps and hastily scribbled notes, seemed to close in on him as he struggled to contain his growing panic. Aafke watched him from her spot near the window, her heart racing with a mixture of fear and concern.

"Arno," she began softly, "we can't let our worry for Maaike blind us." She hesitated, then added, "If we lose hope, we've already lost."

He stopped pacing, looking at her with haunted eyes. "You don't understand, Aafke. If they break her . . . if Maaike tells them everything . . ." He trailed off, unable to finish the thought.

"Maaike is strong," Aafke insisted, her voice firm. "She won't betray us. We have to believe in her if we want to survive this."

"Belief isn't enough," Arno snapped, his temper flaring. "We need action, not blind faith!" His words hung in the air between them, heavy with unspoken tension.

Aafke swallowed hard, feeling the sting of his words. She knew that he was right, that their situation called for more than simple trust in their friend. But she also knew that without hope, they would be lost.

"Arno," she said quietly, reaching out to touch his arm. "I know you're scared. I am too. But we have to keep moving forward, together."

He looked down at her hand on his arm, then met her gaze, his eyes softening. "I'm sorry, Aafke. It's just . . . I can't bear the thought of losing you too."

The weight of his confession settled over her like a blanket, heavy and warm. Aafke had known, on some level, that Arno cared for her. But hearing him say it aloud, faced with the very real possibility of losing each other, made the feelings all the more intense.

"Arno," she whispered, her voice trembling. "I care for you too, but . . ." She hesitated, struggling to find the words to express her conflicting emotions. "It's just . . . I can't forget my beliefs. I won't."

"I don't expect you to," he said softly, his hand covering hers on his arm. "But Aafke, we live in a world where our lives are at risk every day. Can't you see that love is something we should cherish, not deny ourselves?"

"Love is not the issue," she replied, her voice thick with emotion. "It's everything that comes with it. My faith is important to me, Arno. It's what has kept me strong through all of this."

"Your faith," he muttered bitterly, pulling away from her touch. "Is it your faith or your fear that's holding you back, Aafke?"

"Arno!" she snapped, stung by his accusation. "You have no right to question my beliefs, just as I have no right to question yours. We may not agree, but we need each other right now. For Maaike, and for ourselves."

Arno stared at her for a long moment, his anger slowly dissipating as the truth of her words sunk in. In the end, they were on the same side, fighting for the same cause. And tearing each other apart would only serve their enemies.

"You're right," he conceded, his voice barely audible. "We need to stay focused. For Maaike."

Aafke nodded, her heart aching with the weight of their unspoken desires. But she knew that their love could not be the focus now. The danger they faced was far too immediate, and the stakes far too high. She only hoped that they could find a way to navigate the treacherous path ahead, together.

The moonlight streamed through the cracks in the boarded-up windows, casting eerie shadows across the room. Aafke paced back and forth, her hands wringing together nervously as she mulled over the disastrous outcome of their recent mission. The smell of damp wood and stale cigarette smoke hung heavy in the air, a constant reminder of so many desperate conversations that had taken place within these walls.

"Maaike could be talking right now," Arno whispered from his spot at the edge of the table, his gaze distant and troubled. "Every minute that passes, we're at greater risk."

"Arno, we can't afford to panic," Aafke said firmly, stopping her pacing to look him in the eye. "We need to think this through rationally. What's our next move?"

"Rational thinking won't save us if they're already onto us," he replied, his voice strained. But he took a deep breath and forced himself to refocus. "All right. Our first priority needs to be our safety. We should relocate our base of operations immediately."

"Agreed." Aafke nodded, the weight of their situation pressing down on her. "But what about Maaike? We can't just leave her to the Gestapo's mercy."

"Of course not," Arno said, his eyes flashing with determination. "We'll do everything we can to find her and get her out. But we need to be careful. If they suspect we're coming, they'll use her as bait to trap more of us."

Aafke's heart clenched at the thought of leaving Maaike behind, but she knew Arno was right. They couldn't let their emotions cloud their judgment.

"All right," she agreed reluctantly. "We'll gather everyone and explain the situation. Then we'll start planning our next move."

As they set to work coordinating with the other members of their resistance cell, Aafke couldn't help but feel the weight of her Catholic faith bearing down on her. The danger they faced was more immediate now than ever before, and she found herself grappling with the conflict between her desire to be close to Arno and her devout beliefs.

"God, please give me strength," she whispered under her breath, her fingers tracing the outline of the cross hanging from her neck. "Help me make the right decisions in these dark times."

"What are you praying for?" Arno asked quietly, his gaze fixed on her as she fidgeted with her cross.

"Strength," Aafke replied simply, her eyes meeting his. "For all of us."

He hesitated for a moment, then reached out and gently squeezed her hand. "We'll need it."

As they stood there, united by their shared pain and determination, Aafke knew that they would face whatever trials lay ahead together. But she also knew that the danger they faced was far from over, and that the path they walked was fraught with peril at every turn.

Chapter 22
Rusten

Tuesday, September 28, 1943
11:55 a.m.
Munich, Germany

The Marienplatz, Munich's bustling public square, was a whirlwind of movement and sound, as people hurried about their daily errands. Otto Berg, his Knight's Cross proudly worn around his neck, walked alongside his mother, Wendy Berg. As they strolled through the plaza, he thought of everything she'd gone through.

His mother was English, originally named Wendy White. She met Otto's father at a soccer match in England when he was playing for the German national team. She'd moved to Munich with him after their marriage. The First World War had been hard on her. She was accused of being a spy, mocked and spit at on the street. But she had held her head high through it all, even the death of her husband during the kaiser's last offensives in 1918.

His death had left her with a baby boy, a meager military

pension, and not much else. The interwar years had been difficult. Wendy cleaned houses and worked late nights as a wait-
ress. She had few friends, most people in the city still angry that
Germany had lost the war and now faced crippling economic
times. Her one great joy had been her little boy, Otto, who as
he grew displayed the same athletic ability his father had possessed.

Otto shone on the pitch, dominating the teams that his local
team played until he was selected to attend a special academy in
Munich. He was sent there on scholarship, playing for the
school's team—still the star. The school was the most presti-
gious in Munich. That was where he had met Fritz Geier, the
nephew of another rising star: Heinrich Himmler. After gradu-
ation, Fritz and Otto played for one of Bayern Munich's devel-
opmental teams, and were on their way to making the club
itself, just like his father had. But then the war clouds gathered
again. Fritz offered Otto a chance to avoid the draft, to avoid
serving as a conscript. Otto joined him in the newly formed
military branch of the SS. And the rest was history.

Now he had just returned from Berlin, receiving the
Knight's Cross for bravery from Hitler himself. As part of the
decoration, he'd been granted a two-week furlough.

"Otto," Wendy said, her voice soft and concerned, "something is on your mind. What is it?"

He hesitated for a moment, watching pigeons pecking at
crumbs on the cobblestones beneath their feet. "It's just . . . I
can't shake this feeling that something is wrong, Mutti. With
the war, with Germany, with everything."

Wendy put a gentle hand on his arm, urging him to slow
down and face her. Her own eyes, the same shade of blue as his,
bore into him with an intensity that seemed to cut through any
pretense he might have considered.

"Talk to me, son. I don't agree with everything that's happening in our country now. I want to help you."

Otto sighed, running a hand through his hair as they leaned against the ancient stone wall of the Rathaus. The building loomed large over the square. The chimes of the nearby glockenspiel echoed through the space, punctuating the quiet laughter of couples strolling arm in arm and the chatter of friends gathered around café tables. Despite the war raging on, Munich's citizens were determined to enjoy the simple pleasures of life.

"Father would have loved to see this," Otto said suddenly, his voice soft with nostalgia. He gazed at the New Town Hall, its Gothic Revival facade a testament to the city's resilience in uncertain times.

"Your father was always so proud of Munich," Wendy replied, her green eyes misting over with memories. "Do you remember the stories about the football matches he played here before the Great War?"

Otto nodded, recalling how he had hung on to every word his mother told him as a child, imagining himself following in his father's footsteps. Football had been more than a game for their family, it was a bond that transcended time and loss. But he had more to say about the war.

"Sometimes I wonder what he would think of me now," Otto mused, his hand absently brushing the Knight's Cross hanging from his uniform. "I'm not sure if he would recognize the Germany we're fighting for."

"Your father was a man of honor, Otto," Wendy said gently, placing her hand on his arm. "He believed in serving his country, and in doing what was right. He would be proud of you, no matter what."

"But I've seen terrible things—things that make me question if I can still call myself a soldier for Hitler's Germany. I don't think these same things happened in the last war."

Wendy glanced up at him, her eyes filled with concern. She tightened her grip on his arm, urging him to continue.

"Russian men, women, children . . . I can't shake the images of them, helpless and terrified. Cut down by our troops simply because of their nationality, or their religion," Otto confessed, his voice barely above a whisper. "How can I serve a country that treats people like this?"

"War is terrible. We don't know everything your father went through. But he found a way to be true to his honor. You can do the same. I know you had a difficult time in Russia. But now you have this new unit. Is Skorzeny's unit consistent with your beliefs?"

Otto's jaw clenched as he mulled over his mother's words. He could see the pride and love for his father in her eyes, making the weight of his decision feel even heavier. He recalled the camaraderie among the men under Skorzeny's command, their willingness to fight and die for each other.

"Yes. So far, at least. I have found honor in serving alongside my brothers-in-arms," Otto admitted.

"Then you've already found the right path," Wendy replied, her voice steady but tinged with sadness. She leaned into him, resting her head on his shoulder as they stood there amidst the chaos of the square. "You have to forget about what you've seen, if you can. This war won't last forever. You're not responsible for what our leader has done."

Otto glanced at the sea of faces, wondering if anyone was listening to them. What his mother had just uttered could easily land her in a Gestapo jail. But everyone seemed to be going about their business without paying them the least bit of attention. He relaxed again, considering her words. There was a mixture of comfort and relief. Still, he was troubled.

"Aren't we all responsible for what happens in this war?" he asked finally.

Wendy looked at him for a moment and then nodded. "You're right. When this is over, if we lose, we will all pay the price."

Otto watched as a group of children played in the Marienplatz, their laughter mixing with the distant rumble of military vehicles. The sun cast long shadows across the cobblestone square, and Otto felt the warmth of its last rays on his face before it dipped below the rooftops. He turned to his mother, her eyes reflecting the fading light.

"Otto, what about Fritz Geier?" Wendy asked, her voice gentle yet probing. "How is your relationship with him these days?"

Otto sighed, rubbing the back of his neck. "We had a falling-out last time we were together. I tried to talk to him about my concerns regarding the treatment of the Jews, but he wouldn't hear it. He called me a traitor for questioning Germany's policies."

Wendy looked at her son with sadness in her eyes. "Fritz was once a good friend of yours. He did a lot for you, when nobody else at the school would give you the time of day. And he saved your life, Otto. Perhaps you can try reaching out to him again. Through friendship and understanding, you might be able to help him see that some of Hitler's policies are immoral."

Otto hesitated before nodding slowly. "I'll try. It won't be easy, but I owe it to our friendship to at least try." His voice trailed off, and he stared at the ground, lost in thought.

"Is something else bothering you, Otto?" Wendy asked, concern etching her features.

He hesitated, his jaw clenched as he wrestled with whether or not to confide in his mother. Finally, Otto looked up at her, vulnerability shining in his eyes. "Mother," Otto began hesitantly, his voice barely audible above the din, "there's something else I haven't told you . . . I met a woman while in the Netherlands, Aafke Cruyssen."

Wendy's eyes narrowed in curiosity. "Go on," she prompted gently.

"From the moment I saw her, I couldn't get her out of my mind," Otto admitted, his cheeks flushing with embarrassment. "She rejected me, of course. How could she not? I feel like a fool. What future could we possibly have?"

Wendy studied her son for a moment, weighing her words carefully. "Otto," she finally said, her voice steady, "if there is one thing I've learned in my life, it's that love seldom follows logic. You must follow your heart and see where it leads you. If this woman has become so important to you, then perhaps there is a reason for it. And don't forget," she said, laughing, "I too was pursued by a German whom I told to leave me alone. But he kept at it, and now look at me."

As they walked through the crowded square, Otto considered his mother's words. Aafke had stirred something inside him that he couldn't quite explain. He knew it was dangerous to entertain such thoughts, but the memory of her fiery spirit and determination lingered in his mind.

"There's something I want to give you," she said at last.

"What's that?"

She reached into her jacket and pulled out a small package, wrapped up with string.

"What is it?" he asked.

"It's your father's watch. I gave it to him on our wedding day. He wore it every day of his life, even the day he was killed." As she said these last words, her eyes filled with tears. "I want you to have it to wear it. I should have given it to you long ago, but I couldn't part with it, and I was afraid . . ."

"Afraid I might be killed in combat too if I was wearing it?"

She nodded. "Stupid, I know. But I can't lose you, Otto. You're all I have in the world . . . unless you and this Dutch girl get together and make babies for me."

"Mother! I barely know her."

"I know, I know. But a mother can hope." She turned serious then. "Promise me something, Otto," Wendy said suddenly, her tone more serious. "Promise me you'll be careful. I can't bear the thought of losing you."

Otto looked into his mother's eyes, seeing the worry etched in their depths. He nodded solemnly. "I promise, Mother. I will do everything in my power to stay safe."

With that vow hanging between them, Otto and Wendy continued through the Marienplatz, each lost in their thoughts as the twilight deepened around them.

Chapter 23

Wachten

Wednesday, September 29, 1943
2:17 p.m.
Eindhoven, Netherlands

Two weeks had passed since Maaike's capture, and each day felt like a leaden weight pressing down on them all. At least those who knew what was going on.

"Hurry it up now!" shouted Maarten, his words slurred. "It's all a man can do to get a meal around here."

Aafke was jolted out of her daze. Staring down, she took a deep breath and finished cutting up the cooked cabbage. She shoved some on a plate and moved to the table, dropping the contents in front of her father.

"It's about time, girly. It's halfway to supper and you've given me nothing."

"There's nothing *to* give!" she snapped.

Maarten's arm snaked out and he grabbed her wrist in an iron vise. He dug his fingers in, the nails biting into her fore-arm. "You just watch your lip, dearie. It's bad enough that you leave our flat like a pigsty. That you forget half my meals. I can forgive that. But I won't forgive your mouth."

She didn't have the strength to even argue. "I've got to go, Father."

"And where do you have to be going at this time of day?"

"How about back to work? So I can bring us something to eat for supper. Or would you prefer I stay home and we have nothing?"

"Go then," he said, dismissing her with a wave. He reached down and took his mug, tipping it back and emptying the contents. "I'm better without you. If only Christiaan was here, he'd take care of things."

Aafke dismissed herself, not even bothering to say goodbye. She had something to do today, but it wasn't work. She hurried through the streets of Eindhoven and then out of town, making her way to the woods where their headquarters was located. She arrived a half hour later and gave their secret knock, waiting for an answer. The door opened and Arno was there. He nodded to her and then they stepped into the main room.

The air was thick with tension and unease, the only light seeping in through the ragged, soiled drapes. Peter and Joelle sat huddled around a rickety wooden table, their eyes heavy with exhaustion and worry.

"Maaike's been gone too long," Arno said hoarsely, adjusting his glasses as he stepped over to the map spread across the table. "We need to do something."

"Like what?" Peter snapped, his voice filled with frustration. "We've done everything we can without being caught by the SS. She's my sister. Don't you think I've done everything I can think of to save her?"

Aafke scanned the map desperately for any clue to Maaike's whereabouts. She couldn't shake the feeling that she should be doing more, fighting harder for her friend. But how? It seemed as if all of Eindhoven had been swallowed up by darkness, its once-beautiful streets now haunted by the specter of the Occupation.

"Maybe there's another way," Aafke suggested hesitantly, her voice barely above a whisper. "What if we could bribe an SS member to help us get her out of there?"

"Are you insane?" Joelle spat, her black hair falling into her face as she looked at Aafke incredulously. "You want us to risk everything we've worked for by trusting one of those monsters?"

"Joelle's right," Arno said solemnly, his brown eyes clouded with concern. "It's far too dangerous, Aafke. We can't afford to expose ourselves like that."

"Then what do you suggest we do?" Aafke demanded, her voice rising as the desperation threatened to consume her. "We can't just sit here and do nothing!"

"Look, I understand how you feel," Arno said, his tone softening as he regarded the young woman with sympathy. "But we have to think about the bigger picture here. We're not just fighting for Maaike; we're fighting for our entire country."

"Exactly," Joelle chimed in, her eyes fixed on Arno as if searching for some sign of agreement. "We have to be smart about this, Aafke. Recklessness will only get us killed."

"I agree with Aafke," said Peter. "We have to do more."

"She's your sister," said Joelle. "Of course you want to do more. But we can't risk all our lives just for hers."

"Do you think they know she's a Jew?" asked Peter.

"I don't see how they would," said Arno. "She's under false papers and, unlike a man, there's no physical way to tell."

"In a way, it might be better if they did know," said Peter. "They might shoot her out of hand, or ship her off to one of those camps out east. Now they are torturing her every day, looking for answers."

"Do you think she'll talk?"

Peter shook his head. "Maaike is tough. Tougher than she looks. It would take a lot for her to betray us."

Aafke saw the cloud pass over Peter's face. She knew he was tortured not only by the fear of what might happen to his sister, but also the realization that she could indeed betray them if enough pressure was put on her. Everyone had a breaking point. "Don't worry, Peter," she said. "We trust you."

"If you hadn't come up with this plan in the first place, she'd be here with us now," said Joelle. "You should be the last person trying to offer comfort here."

"To hell with you!" shouted Aafke, feeling the stab deeply because it was true.

"Joelle, we aren't going to cast blame here. We all went along with this plan, and it's worked well for months. We've been the wonder of the resistance. But we had to be realistic. The Germans were bound to catch on at some point."

"Fine," she conceded bitterly, her voice thick with unshed tears. "But we can't just forget about her. We have to keep looking, keep fighting."

"Of course," Arno agreed. "We'll never give up on Maaike, I promise you that."

As they sat there in the gloom, haunted by the absence of their friend, Aafke couldn't help but wonder if they would ever see Maaike again. And if they did, what horrors would she have faced at the hands of their enemies? The thought sent a shiver down her spine, and she gripped Arno's hand tightly, drawing strength from his steady presence.

"Whatever it takes," she whispered fiercely, her blue eyes shining with determination, "we'll find her, and we'll make them pay."

"Whatever it takes," Arno echoed, his voice low and resolute. Together, they stared at the map, tracing invisible paths through the city streets as they planned their next move.

A loud knock at the door startled them. Nobody knew about

this cottage, as far as Aafke knew. She felt the electric terror course through her body. It had to be the Germans. She looked at Arno, who pressed a finger to his lips. With his other hand he drew a pistol, raising it to the door. He stepped quietly over and aimed the pistol head high at the entrance. "Who is it?" he asked, his voice gruff.

"It's Johannes," came a voice through the door.

Arno relaxed, turning to the others. "It's all right," he said. "Johannes is the leader of another group." Arno opened the door. A man stood there, in his midthirties, with peasant clothes and blond hair spilling out of a woolen cap. He stepped into the cottage and looked over all of them for a second, as if to make sure the space was safe.

"Can I get you something?" Aafke asked.

"Do you have some drink?"

Aafke nodded. She stepped over to a shelf and drew down a half-empty bottle of brandy. Looking at Arno, who nodded in affirmation, she pulled down five glasses and poured them each some. Johannes took the drink and tipped it back, consuming the contents in a moment. His face flinched for an instant and then he slumped down into a chair, looking at each of them again for a moment. "I've grave news," he said at last.

"What is it?" asked Arno.

"They've killed Maaike," said Johannes, turning his head to spit on the dirty floor. "The bastards executed her this morning."

For a moment, there was only the deafening silence of disbelief. And then Peter slammed his fist onto the table, his face contorted with grief and rage.

"Damn it! This is your fault!" he shouted at Aafke, his words like poison-tipped arrows. "Joelle is right. If you hadn't insisted on these missions, Maaike would still be alive!"

Aafke reeled back from the accusation, feeling as if she had been physically struck. She turned to Arno for support, but instead of defending her, he stared stonily at the wall. Finally, he whispered. "There's some truth to it, Aafke, you wanted to get the women involved. I tried to stop you."

She couldn't believe what he'd said. Aafke rose and stormed out of the cottage, tears spilling down her cheeks, unable to bear her friends turning on her. Aafke's thoughts raced with anguish and confusion. How could Arno, the man who had promised to stand by her side through thick and thin, blame her for Maaike's death? And how could Peter, their fearless leader and trusted friend, turn on her in their darkest hour?

"Maaike, I'm so sorry," Aafke whispered into the darkness, tears streaming down her cheeks. "I never meant for any of this to happen."

Her grief-stricken words echoed through the empty forest, a haunting reminder of the price they had paid for their desperate fight against oppression. She walked around for an hour or more, not heading any particular direction, her mind twisting and turning from grief to anger. Eventually she made her way back into Eindhoven, heading toward her apartment. She intended to outdo her father for once in drinking, until she found oblivion for a time. Tomorrow, she would face reality, and try to figure out what she was going to do. As she was approaching her building, a familiar voice called out to her.

"Fräulein Cruyssen? Are you all right?" She looked up to see a German uniform marching toward her. Through her tear-burned eyes she realized it was Otto. Aafke hesitated for a moment, surprised by his sudden appearance but also aware of the opportunity it presented. Her mind raced, formulating a plan. With a shaky breath, she forced a smile onto her lips. "I . . . I'm fine. Just a little upset, that's all."

Otto's eyes softened. "I know I don't really know you, and pardon my boldness, but I don't like seeing you this way. Would you allow me to take you to dinner? Perhaps it will help take your mind off things."

"Thank you," Aafke replied, her voice wavering slightly as she accepted his invitation. In her mind, she steeled herself for the task at hand. "I know I said no before. But this time, I accept."

They walked a few blocks to a nearby restaurant Aafke knew was frequented by the Nazis. Otto was rambling away about the war, and some recent operation he'd been involved with in Italy. She hardly listened. She was tense, a mixture of fear, anger, and determination coursing through her. As they entered the dimly lit restaurant, the scent of rich sauces and roasted meats filled the air, momentarily distracting Aafke from her mission. It had been so long since she had enjoyed a proper meal, and the thought of partaking in such luxuries while her friends suffered and died left her feeling sickened. They were soon seated and Otto ordered some wine. When they each had a glass, he turned back to her, his eyes searching hers intently. Aafke noticed for the first time how intensely blue Otto's eyes were, as if they were piercing through her.

"Tell me about your life during the war," Otto urged gently, his eyes searching Aafke's face as they sat across from each other. "I know it must be difficult."

Aafke hesitated, unsure of how much to reveal, but ultimately decided to share some of her hardships. "We lost our grocery store early on as you are aware," she said, staring down at her untouched food. "I've been working as a seamstress to make ends meet, but finding enough food has been a constant struggle."

Otto nodded sympathetically, his own experiences with the harsh realities of war evident in the lines that creased his forehead. "I've seen many things too," he said quietly, taking a sip of wine before continuing. "The war on the eastern front is something out of the Bible. Death, destruction, atrocities committed on both sides. I wasn't sure how much more of it I could take. But then fortune found me. Recently I've been part of a special operations group. I'm away from the front lines now, and with other men who find the sport in war."

"Sport?" she asked incredulously. "How can you say such a thing?"

"I'm sorry," said Otto. "You must think me heartless. It is rather the opposite. The regular fighting was too much for me. The death, the loss of friends and comrades. The commando operations allow me to get away from all of that. Our leader is Skorzeny."

"Who is this Skorzeny?" Aafke asked, feigning curiosity while her mind raced with questions about Otto's involvement with the notorious SS officer.

"Otto Skorzeny," he clarified, a mixture of admiration and unease flickering in his eyes. "He's highly intelligent and cunning. I was recruited by him."

As Otto continued to share stories of his commando activities, Aafke listened intently, filing away every detail to pass on to the resistance. She was surprised at his joviality and passion. She should have been angry at him. He was the enemy, after all. But something about the way he saw the world was so different from anything she'd experienced. Over the dinner, she found she had to keep her mind on her task. There was revenge to extract here. This Otto was a friend of the head of the Gestapo in Eindhoven. Perhaps the best target she'd ever acquired. She wondered if she should try to take him back to the cottage. They might elicit valuable information from him before he was eliminated. But Maaike's death was too fresh, too raw. No, she wanted to drive a knife through his brain and watch the light go out of those piercing eyes.

As the last sips of wine lingered on Aafke's tongue, she glanced at the candle flickering on their table. Shadows danced along the walls of the restaurant, casting eerie patterns that seemed to mock her inner turmoil. She breathed in deeply, gathering courage, and then looked directly into Otto's eyes.

"Thank you for tonight, Otto. Would you like to come with me? There is a hotel nearby," she suggested, her voice steady despite the churning emotions within her. She was determined not to waver from her plan; Maaike's memory deserved no less.

Otto hesitated for a moment, his gaze holding hers. The silence between them stretched taut as he seemed to weigh the implications of her invitation. "Very well," Otto finally agreed, a hint of surprise in his voice, as if he had expected her to reject him outright. "I'll accompany you."

Aafke suppressed a shudder as they left the restaurant, walking side by side through the narrow cobblestone streets that led to the hotel. The resistance had a room rented permanently for opportunities like these. With each step, her resolve hardened, but so did the knot of dread tightening in her stomach. She wondered if Otto sensed her intentions. She looked at him. He was talking away as if they were on a garden stroll. She felt a little tug again, but she shoved it down. After all, he was just as willing to use her body as the others were. No, there was no difference. He was just another monster.

"This neighborhood is charming," he remarked as they climbed the stairs of the hotel. "It reminds me of my hometown."

"Really?" Aafke replied, feigning interest while her mind raced with details of her plan. "Where is that?"

"Munich," he said. "Have you been there?"

She shook her head.

"It's lovely. My mother still lives there. She's English. She married my father before the last war."

Aafke tried not to listen to his personal details. She didn't want to know him. She unlocked the door to the hotel room and stepped inside, beckoning Otto to follow. As she fumbled with the key, her thoughts took a darker turn. She imagined plunging the knife, feeling his blood pool around her fingers, hot and sticky. She shuddered at the thought but forced herself to remain composed.

"Please, have a seat," she said, gesturing to a small sofa near the window. "I'll make us some coffee."

"Thank you, Aafke," Otto replied, settling into a chair with a sigh. He took off his coat, revealing the crisp gray-green uniform that marked him as an enemy. The sight of it fueled her determination, reminding her of all the pain and suffering he represented.

As Aafke busied herself in the small kitchen, she listened for any sign of movement from Otto. She needed him to be close, to trust her completely, if her plan was to succeed. Her heart pounded in her chest, a mix of fear and anticipation coursing through her veins.

"Here," she said, returning to him with two steaming cups of coffee. She handed one to Otto, her fingers brushing against his as she did so. His touch surprised her. His hands were strong. He was such a big man, so powerful. She realized she might have taken on more than she could handle. She would have to strike from behind, and quickly, or he could easily overpower her.

"Ah, this smells wonderful," Otto said, inhaling deeply before taking a cautious sip. "You make excellent coffee, Aafke."

"Thank you," she murmured, clenching her free hand into a fist to steady her nerves.

They sipped their drinks in silence for several minutes, the tension between them growing heavier with each passing moment. Aafke clenched her jaw, trying to find the right words to lure him further into her trap.

"Would you like some more?" she asked. "Before we. . . ." She glanced over at the bed.

Otto's face blushed as if he were a schoolboy. "More coffee would be nice."

She put her own cup down and moved back into the kitchen. He was facing away from her, toward the bed. She placed the cup down and pulled open the drawer, removing a long, sharp kitchen knife. She would have to be careful. If she hit bone with the stab her fingers would slip up the handle and she would cut herself badly. Her heart was racing out of her chest. She hesitated again. He was bobbing his head back and forth as if listening to a song. There was something about this man. He had turned up a number of times looking for her, checking on her. Why? She'd told him to leave her alone, but he kept reappearing. It didn't matter. Maaike was dead. This man was friends of the chief Gestapo agent. She would exact her revenge. She stepped toward him, raising the knife. "Otto," she whispered, "I don't want to be alone tonight. Can you . . . stay with me?"

He didn't turn around. "I'm sorry, Aafke, but I cannot."

She lowered the knife. "What do you mean?"

"I'm a gentleman. And you are a lady. I am so thankful you had dinner with me. I'm hoping that you would consent for me to write to you. That I might come and see you again sometime. But I could not spend the night with you. I could not dishonor you. I'm sorry."

With that, Otto rose from the chair and put on his coat. Aafke hid the knife behind her back, her hands shaking. Otto looked at her for a moment with those piercing eyes. "Thank you for a wonderful evening. Did you enjoy yourself?"

She nodded, not sure what else to do. He smiled at that, like a schoolboy who's been granted an extra recess. "I don't know when I'll have leave again, but I'll take it here when I do." With that, Otto bowed slightly, stepped to the door, and departed.

Aafke collapsed to the floor, the knife clattering on the wood. She buried her head in her knees, a maelstrom of emotions tearing through her. He had walked away. He wasn't like the others. This man who had checked in on her multiple times, who seemingly was interested in her. She had rejected him again and again and yet he'd returned. And now, when she'd seemingly offered him everything, he'd politely declined to dishonor her.

"Stupid, stupid, stupid," Aafke berated herself, her voice barely audible. She should have killed him anyway. He was a Nazi after all. And they'd killed Maaike. Furious with herself, she unplugged the coffee pot and headed toward the door.

There was a bottle at her apartment. She still had somewhere to go.

As she reached the street, she noticed a familiar figure approaching the building: Arno. Her heart skipped a beat as she realized that he might have witnessed the entire encounter with Otto. Panic mixed with the anger and confusion already swirling inside her.

"Arno!" she called out, rushing to open the door just as he reached it.

"Hello, Aafke," he said, an unreadable expression on his face. "I saw you with Otto."

"Arno, please let me explain—" she began, but he cut her off.

"Explain what?" he demanded, his voice cold and sharp. "That you were trying to seduce him? Or worse, having an affair with him?"

"Neither!" Aafke shot back, her cheeks burning with indignation. "I was trying to execute him, for God's sake!"

"Execute him?" Arno scoffed. "Is that why he just strolled out of this hotel, whistling and smiling?"

"Arno, I swear to you, I wanted to kill him to avenge Maaike's death. But he refused to sleep with me."

"Refused?" Arno's voice was heavy with disbelief. "Otto Berg, an SS soldier, refused to be seduced?"

"Believe it or not, he did," Aafke said, her voice wavering slightly as she recalled Otto's actions.

"Then why the hell didn't you just stab him right there and be done with him?" Arno demanded, his anger palpable.

"Because I was taken off guard. I hesitated, all right? And now I'll never forgive myself for letting him go."

The two of them stood there, facing each other, their breaths coming in gasps from the intensity of their emotions. "Let's talk about this inside," he said sternly.

Aafke slammed the hotel room door shut behind her, the sound echoing through the small space and causing the few remaining knickknacks to tremble on their shelves. She turned to face Arno, her eyes blazing with anger and hurt.

"Explain yourself," he demanded, his voice sharp and cold like a winter wind cutting through the darkened room.

"Explain myself?" Aafke's voice rose in disbelief. "After what you just accused me of outside?"

"Otto Berg is a dangerous man, Aafke," Arno said, his eyes narrowing as he advanced toward her. "I saw you two talking, laughing even. And then you let him walk away."

"Laughing?" she spat. "Is that what you think I was doing? Laughing while Maaike lies dead because of me?"

"Then tell me," Arno challenged, his fists clenched at his sides. "Why did he walk free?"

"I just told you. He caught me off guard."

"Really?" Arno scoffed, his eyebrows raised in skepticism. "You expect me to believe that you had the opportunity to kill Otto Berg and didn't take it?"

"I hesitated," Aafke admitted, her voice cracking as tears threatened to spill down her cheek.

"Or is it that you couldn't bring yourself to do it because you're having an affair with him?" Arno shot back, his voice laced with venom.

"An affair? How dare you!" Aafke's hands balled into fists, her nails digging into her palms. "How could you even suggest something like that after everything we've been through? After Maaike?"

"Because I can't think of any other reason why you would let a man like Otto Berg walk away!" Arno yelled, his own emotions bubbling to the surface. Arno stared at her for a long moment, his chest heaving with each labored breath. Then, without another word, he turned and strode toward the door.

"Arno, please don't go," Aafke whispered, her voice barely audible above the pounding of her heart.

He stopped, his hand on the doorknob, but did not look back. "Why shouldn't I?"

"Because I love you," she said softly, her words heavy with the weight of their shared pain and loss.

The silence that followed seemed to stretch on forever, punctuated only by the distant sounds of the city outside. Finally, Arno let out a gasp and turned back to face her.

"Prove it," he said simply, his eyes searching hers for any hint of deceit.

Aafke hesitated only for a moment before crossing the room to stand in front of him. She reached up to cup his face in her hands, her fingers trembling as they traced the familiar lines of his features. And then, with a desperation born of fear and longing, she kissed him deeply, pouring every ounce of her love and regret into the embrace.

"Are you giving me what I want?" Arno asked.

She hesitated. Knowing what a refusal would mean. Finally, her eyes full of tears, she nodded her assent.

"You'll never tell me no again," he said, reaching down to kiss her roughly. "You owe me now."

Chapter 24

Instructie

Friday, September 15, 1944
5:45 p.m.
Amsterdam, Netherlands

The air was crisp and heavy with the scent of impending autumn, as leaves lazily drifted to the ground outside the small language school in the outskirts of Amsterdam. Inside, Otto Berg's brow furrowed in concentration as he repeated the American phrases his instructor dictated. The school had closed several hours before, but the German government persuaded the teacher to stay late every day for one-on-one time with Otto. He wondered just how the Nazis had persuaded this man. He certainly was eager to teach.

"Very good, Mr. Berg," the instructor said, nodding approvingly. "Your pronunciation is improving."

"Thank you, sir," Otto replied, his muscular frame tense as he tried to commit the strange inflections to his mind. He knew he needed to be able to pronounce them perfectly for the upcoming mission that Skorzeny had mapped out for him.

"All right, we've been at it for fourteen hours today," said the teacher. "Get some rest and we'll start up again on Monday." Otto hastily packed his books, eager to leave. As he stepped into the cool September air, he mounted his bicycle and pedaled toward the heart of Amsterdam. The streets were alive with people going about their daily business, yet an uneasy tension hung in the air as whispers of the war's progress reached the city's inhabitants. He found a little café on Prinsengracht and sat outside, sipping coffee and enjoying a meal while he watched the traffic on the bridges and the canal. He envied these people, despite their suffering. They had at least the semblance of peace.

An hour later, Otto arrived at the nondescript building that housed SS headquarters and carefully locked his bike to a post before entering. The stark interior was a sharp contrast to the vibrant world outside, and Otto felt the familiar chill run down his spine as he ascended the stairs to Skorzeny's temporary office.

"Ah, Sergeant Berg," the lieutenant colonel greeted him, leaning back in his chair. "How are your English lessons progressing?"

"Improving, sir," Otto answered.

"Good," Skorzeny replied, his eyes studying Otto intently. "We need you to be ready for what lies ahead."

Otto nodded. His commander hadn't shared exactly what this mission was. But he knew, as with all of Skorzeny's plans, success would be crucial.

"Is something troubling you, Sergeant?" Skorzeny asked, noting Otto's hesitation.

"Nothing, sir," Otto lied, forcing himself to meet Skorzeny's gaze. "I am prepared for whatever awaits me."

"Tell me, Berg," Skorzeny said, his voice low and measured, "what do you think of our current situation?"

"Sir, the invasion of France has taken its toll on our forces," Otto replied, carefully choosing his words. "The English and Americans are pressing forward, and it seems Holland may soon be under threat."

"Indeed." Skorzeny frowned, gaze fixed on the map occupying one wall of his office. Flags and markings denoted troop movements, the shifting tides of war. "Our enemies are closing in, and we must adapt if we are to survive."

"Yes, sir," Otto replied, swallowing hard. He was acutely aware of the weight of responsibility he had. As the German armies failed on all fronts and were pushed farther and farther back toward the Fatherland, their special operations were more critical than ever. And yet, amidst the turmoil of war, thoughts of Aafke still clouded his mind.

"Remember, Sergeant," Skorzeny continued, "your success could alter the course of this conflict. We cannot afford failure."

"*Jawohl.*"

"Sergeant," Skorzeny's voice cut through the tension in the room, "I'm granting you seventy-two hours of leave. Use this time wisely, and be back here on time, ready for our mission. We could be going any day now." His eyes bore into Otto, leaving no doubt as to the gravity of his words.

"Thank you, sir," Otto replied, his mind already racing with thoughts of what he might do with this unexpected reprieve.

As Otto left SS headquarters, he couldn't help but feel a growing sense of dread. The war was closing in around them. His beloved Germany was already in ruins, its cities crushed to rubble by allied bombers. But that would be nothing compared to the carnage that would come once their enemies reached the Fatherland, particularly the Russians.

Otto toyed with spending the three days in Amsterdam. He'd not had time to really see the city, but ultimately, he decided he would go check in on Aafke one more time. He also wanted to see Fritz, if his old friend would even talk to him, and try to patch up their relationship.

As Otto boarded the train bound for Eindhoven, he stared out the window, watching the landscape pass by in a blur of green fields and quaint villages. He recalled the last time he'd seen Aafke. Her words, her fragile features. Would she even talk to him? Her silence spoke volumes, but perhaps there was some other reason? He had to know.

Three days, he thought, mentally calculating the time he had left. *Three days to face my past, and to find some semblance of closure before I walk into the unknown.*

Otto felt the rhythmic vibrations of the train beneath him as it cut through the Dutch countryside toward Eindhoven. The sun was setting, casting warm amber hues across the landscape. He sat alone in his compartment, his thoughts consumed by Aafke and the short time he had to see her.

"Tickets, please," a conductor's voice called out as the door slid open, snapping Otto back to reality.

"Ah, yes." Otto fumbled in his pocket, retrieving the small, worn ticket and handing it over. The conductor examined it briefly before returning it with a nod.

"Enjoy your journey," he said, disappearing down the corridor.

"Thank you," Otto muttered, his gaze drifting back to the window. The fading light cast long shadows across the fields, giving them an eerie beauty that both entranced and haunted him.

As the train pulled into Eindhoven station, night had fallen on the city. Otto disembarked, feeling the mix of excitement and trepidation that came with entering unfamiliar territory. He took a deep breath, clenching his fists to steady himself before venturing into the darkness.

"Excuse me, sir," Otto said as he approached a man hunched

over a newspaper at a nearby bench. "Do you know of any hotels near the city center?"

"Sure," the man replied, not bothering to look up from his paper. "Head down this street and take a right after the church. There's a place called Het Rustige Herberg. Can't miss it."

"Thank you," Otto said, his heart racing at the thought of being one step closer to finding Aafke. Following the stranger's directions, he soon found himself standing before a modest brick building, its warm glow beckoning him inside.

"Good evening," Otto greeted the elderly woman behind the reception desk as he entered.

"Evening," she replied, eyeing him warily. "Need a room?"

"Yes, just for one night, please," Otto said.

"All right, then." She handed him a key with a weary smile. "Room twelve, up the stairs and to the left."

"Thank you," Otto replied, his mind already racing ahead to the next day and the possibility of seeing Aafke again. He headed upstairs and unlocked the door to his modest room. The scent of old wood and stale tobacco filled his nostrils as he entered, but it mattered little to him. This was merely a place to rest before the real challenge began.

Otto sat on the edge of the creaky bed, his hands clasped together, deep in thought. He'd thought of going to Aafke's apartment tonight, but the hour was too late. He was even having second thoughts. She'd never written him back after all. Perhaps he was lying to himself that she had any interest in him at all. Perhaps he should just straighten things out with Fritz and then head back. He laid his head on the pillow, exhausted from the day. He would wait until morning to determine a course of action.

The first light of day seeped through the cracks in the hotel room's curtains, casting a muted glow on Otto as he stood by the window. He had not slept much, his mind consumed with thoughts of Aafke and the task that lay ahead. Today, he would search for her.

"Let my instincts guide me," he whispered and left the hotel.

He wandered through the streets of Eindhoven, making his way to the neighborhood where Aafke lived. He hadn't been here in almost a year, and he found his memory was imperfect. He finally found the correct street and walked amidst the buildings, but he wasn't entirely sure which apartment structure she lived in. He could go back to the SS headquarters and ask for the address again, but he wasn't sure they would even admit him, and he had so little time. He kept looking, moving among the pedestrians as he peered at the buildings, trying to remember.

Finally, Otto approached an elderly woman tending to a small community garden, hoping she might have some information. "Excuse me," he said in Dutch. "Do you happen to know where Aafke Cruyssen lives?"

The woman's eyes narrowed suspiciously. "Why are you looking for her?"

"Because . . . I'm an old friend," Otto said, fumbling for words. "We lost touch, and I wanted to see how she's doing."

"Old friend, hm?" The woman didn't seem convinced, but she pointed down the road nonetheless. "It's the building in the middle of the street on the left, upstairs apartment. But don't expect a warm welcome."

"Thank you," Otto said, his heart racing at the prospect of finally finding Aafke. He headed in the direction indicated, his pulse quickening with each step.

He stepped into the building and started toward the stairs, checking his watch. It was early, not even eight. He realized he might be waking her up. With this hesitation, he felt the old fears. He barely knew this girl. She'd made no effort to contact him since he last saw her. Why did he keep coming back, both-

ering a woman who seemed to want nothing to do with him?
He felt panic rising, an emotion he'd almost never experienced.
Otto turned around and strode away, rounding the corner. He
decided he would spend the day in Eindhoven resting, then
look up Fritz on Sunday morning. He would try to work
things out with his old friend, and then head back to Amsterdam. He would let Aafke go.

Chapter 25
Nieuwe Crisis

Saturday, September 16, 1944
9:15 a.m.
Eindhoven, Netherlands

The sun glistened on the cobblestone streets as Aafke, her heart pounding against her chest, entered the doctor's office. The musty scent of old books and sterilized instruments filled her nostrils, and she shivered with a mix of cold and anxiety. Her hands trembled at her sides, fingers tapping nervously against the fabric of her coat.

"Miss Cruyssen," greeted the old doctor, wearing a pair of round spectacles that seemed too large for his thin face. "What brings you here today?"

"Doctor," Aafke began, her voice barely above a whisper, "I . . . I have been feeling unwell these past few weeks. Nauseous, tired, my stomach seems to grow, and I'm late, if you understand my meaning."

The doctor studied her with concern, his gray eyes scanning her face for any additional clues. "You suspect you may be pregnant?"

Aafke swallowed hard and nodded. She craved the confirmation, but also feared it. Her life was already in turmoil, and bringing a child into this war-torn world only added another layer of uncertainty.

"Let us perform a test, then," the doctor suggested, gesturing for Aafke to follow him to the examination room. As she lay down on the cold table, she couldn't help but think about Arno, the man whose love she cherished despite their many differences. Would he be pleased or angered by this news? The doctor examined her, running a series of tests. The process took the entire morning.

"Miss Cruyssen, I can confirm that you are indeed pregnant," the doctor announced after completing the examination, his voice neutral as he scribbled something in his leather-bound notebook. Aafke noticed he glanced down at her finger and frowned. So it had already begun . . .

Aafke's heart leaped into her throat, and her stomach twisted into knots. Pregnant. The word echoed in her mind like a jarring bell. She managed a weak smile, but her thoughts were a whirlwind of fear and uncertainty. How would she protect her unborn child from the dangers lurking just outside the door? And how would Arno react to this news?

"Thank you, Doctor," Aafke murmured, sitting up and buttoning her coat. She stared at her trembling hands, trying to quell the rising panic within her. "I must go now."

"I need to schedule additional appoints with you."

"I'm sorry, not now," she said, fighting the tears. "I'll come back next week."

"Very well. Take care, Miss Cruyssen," the doctor said softly, his eyes filled with a mix of empathy and sadness. "These are difficult times, but remember that life is a precious gift."

Aafke managed a nod and slipped out of the office, finding herself back on the streets. She walked briskly, clutching her coat around her swelling belly. Her mind raced with thoughts of Arno and how to break the news to him. But first, she needed to catch her breath and find a moment of solace amidst the chaos of her life.

As she pressed forward, Aafke's determination grew stronger. No matter what obstacles lay ahead, she would do everything in her power to protect her unborn child and those she loved. She was a survivor, and she would not let the harsh realities of this world break her spirit.

She arrived at the cottage headquarters of their resistance cell a half hour later. She opened the door and found Arno at the table with Joelle. She was horrified to see his hands holding hers, the two of them speaking in low voices.

"What's going on?" she demanded, fury tearing through her fear.

Arno looked up in surprise, snatching his hands away. Joelle watched her with an amused half smile. "A-Aafke," Arno stammered. "Nothing is going on."

"You were holding hands."

"Nonsense."

"I saw you."

Arno rose to his feet. "It was nothing of the kind. Joelle's upset about something, that's all."

"Yes," said Joelle, still wearing a crooked grin. "I was upset."

"You're lying to me!" shouted Aafke, the tears coming now. "What's going on with you two?"

"I told you, it's nothing," said Arno, his voice rising now. "Are you calling me a liar?"

"I saw what I saw."

"You saw me comforting a friend, nothing more." He took a step toward her, his hands clenched into fists. "You need to calm down, Aafke. You're hysterical and you're imagining things that aren't there. How long have we all known each other? I've given everything to you this last year, Aafke. I let you into this group when nobody wanted you. I stood up for you after your failures. And now you don't trust me. You don't believe me?"

"It's always the same with you," said Joelle, shaking her head. "You don't know what's good for you."

"Keep out of this!"

Arno took another step toward Aafke. "I'm not going to let you talk to her like that. She's a part of this group. She has been for a lot longer than you have. We've fought together. We've risked everything. And now you want to throw that all away over some imagined scene? Do you?"

Aafke hesitated. She didn't know what to say. Perhaps they were telling the truth after all. With what had happened today, anything was possible. She decided she would think about this later. "I need to talk to you," she said at last.

"Well, go ahead," said Arno, spreading his arms wide. "We're all here ready to hear your next grand observation."

"Alone."

"She wants to continue the conversation. She wants to blame me," said Joelle.

"No. There's something Arno and I must talk about. Please, Joelle, please. I'm upset about something else. Don't worry about what I just said. Just give us some time."

"You don't have to leave," Arno said to Joelle.

Joelle looked like she was about to say something but then she shrugged and rose to her feet. "I was leaving anyway," she said, walking past Aafke without another look. She turned back to Arno. "I'll see you later."

He nodded and then turned to Aafke as Joelle closed the door behind her. "So, what's so important?" he asked.

"Arno," she began, her hands instinctively moving to shield her still-flat belly. "There's something I need to tell you."

"Go on," he prompted, his eyes never leaving hers.

"I'm . . . I'm pregnant," she whispered, her voice barely carrying over the sound of the rain. "The doctor confirmed it today."

"Are you certain?" Arno asked, his face a mix of shock and confusion.

"Absolutely," she replied, moving toward him. "I know it's unexpected, but . . . I can't help but feel excited about it, Arno. I want you to be happy too."

Arno stared at her for a moment, his eyes searching hers for any hint of doubt or falsehood. "Aafke," he said, his voice trembling with emotion. "This is . . . this is incredible news. We were so careful, weren't we? We took every precaution."

Aafke's heart dropped, her breath catching in her throat. "Yes," she replied hesitantly. "We did everything we could."

"Then how did this happen?" he demanded. "You must've been careless!"

"Arno, I swear I wasn't . . ." Her words trailed off as she felt her world begin to shatter around her. She had expected him to be worried, but not like this—not accusing and cold.

"Or maybe," Arno continued, his voice laced with suspicion, "maybe it isn't mine at all. Have you ever considered that? Maybe it's Otto's child."

"Otto?" Aafke gasped, feeling as if the ground beneath her had given way. "How can you even suggest such a thing? Nothing happened between us. I told you. And I haven't seen him in a year."

"Really?" Arno shot back, his jaw clenched with jealousy. "I was told he was lurking around your neighborhood this morning. That's what Joelle came to tell me. I was comforting her because she was so upset by the news that you might be betraying me."

Aafke's chest tightened, her heart pounding in her ears. She clenched her fists and fought the urge to scream, to cry out against the injustice of his accusations. "I have no idea what you're talking about! I haven't seen Otto. If he's in the city, he didn't come and see me. And if he had, I would have sent him away! I would never betray you like that!"

"Wouldn't you?" he challenged, his eyes dark with suspicion. "You're resourceful, Aafke. You've had to be, to survive all this time. Who's to say you haven't been hiding secrets from me as well?"

"Arno, please . . ." She reached for his hand, but he pulled away, leaving her cold and alone.

"Yes, I'm sure it's Otto," said Arno, turning away from her to pour himself a drink.

"Otto?" Aafke spat the name out like a curse, her eyes blazing with indignation. "You think that I would choose some Nazi over you? That I would betray everything we've fought for together?"

Arno stared at her, his expression stony and unreadable. "I don't know, Aafke. Tell me, what am I supposed to think?"

"Think about the truth," she insisted, desperation edging her voice. "I hardly know Otto. I haven't seen him in a year, and the one time we went out together was to try and lure him to his death. He's the enemy, Arno, just like the rest of the SS who killed Maaike."

She took a step toward him, her hands trembling as she tried to make him understand. "This baby is ours, Arno. Our love, our hope for a better future. Please, don't let your fear destroy everything we have."

As the words hung heavy between them, the door tore open. Joelle was standing there, her eyes cold and calculating. She'd obviously been listening to everything that was said.

"Why would Otto be in your neighborhood, then?" she asked, her voice dripping with disdain. "What other lies are you telling us? How long have you been his lover? How long have you been working with the Germans?"

Aafke's heart plummeted, her breath catching in her throat. "I would never betray my country or all of you! How could you even say that to me? And as for Otto, I told you, I haven't seen him!"

"Are you calling me a liar?" Joelle demanded, her face contorted with anger. "I know what I saw, and I'm telling you, he was there!"

"Enough!" Aafke shouted, her frustration boiling over. "I don't care if he was there or not. It doesn't change anything. I didn't meet him, I didn't know he was there, and I don't know why he was in my neighborhood. And as for the rest, my loyalty has never wavered, and neither has my love for Arno. This is our child, and nothing you say can change that."

Joelle's eyes narrowed, and her voice lowered to a dangerous whisper. "You may be able to fool yourself, Aafke, but you can't fool the rest of us. You've always been attracted to Otto, ever since you first laid eyes on him. Maybe you don't want to admit it, but deep down, you know it's true."

"Stop this, Joelle," Arno warned, his voice strained as he tried to keep his emotions in check. "This isn't helping any of us."

"Maybe not," she replied, her gaze never leaving Aafke's face. "But sometimes the truth needs to be spoken, no matter how much it hurts."

Aafke felt her world spinning out of control, the ground beneath her feet slipping away. Her voice wavered as she fought back tears, trying desperately to hold onto what little certainty she had left. "You're wrong, Joelle, this is Arno's child. I've never been with another man.

"Arno, please," Aafke begged, her heart aching in her chest. "I swear to you, there's no one else. This child is yours."

"Is it?" Arno challenged, his eyes narrowing with suspicion. "Or are you just saying that because you're scared of losing me, of facing this alone? Tell me the truth!" He rushed forward and grabbed her arm, digging his nails into the flesh.

Aafke felt tears streaming down her cheeks as she stared into Arno's eyes, her voice shaking with emotion. "I'm telling you the truth, Arno. I would never lie to you about something like this. This child is ours—our future."

"Is it?" he repeated, his voice laced with doubt and bitterness. "Or is it just another lie you've convinced yourself to believe?"

"Arno, I—"

He shoved her and then lashed out, slapping her hard across the face. Aafke's words were cut off as she found herself reeling backward, her hand instinctively flying to her cheek. The pain seemed to echo through her body, a searing reminder of the fragile nature of trust and love.

"Hit the slut again!" Joelle cried out.

As Aafke stared at Arno, her vision blurred by tears, she couldn't help but think of all they had shared: the laughter, the passion, the moments of quiet peace amidst the chaos of war. And now, in the span of a single heartbeat, everything had changed—irrevocably and utterly.

"Please, Arno," she whispered, her voice barely audible above the sound of the rain. "Believe me when I say that I love you, and that I would never betray you."

"Love?" Arno scoffed, his eyes filled with hurt and disbelief. "Save your love for your German." He whipped the door open. "Now get out!"

"Arno, please—" Aafke began, only to be silenced by the icy fury in his gaze. Glancing at Joelle, who was smirking at her, she turned and fled into the woods.

Chapter 26
Verzoening

Sunday, September 17, 1944
9:00 a.m.
Eindhoven, Netherlands

Otto Berg stood in the hallway outside Fritz Geier's office, his heart pounding in his chest. The air was heavy with the smell of stale cigar smoke and damp woolen uniforms. He hesitated for a moment, remembering the harsh words they had exchanged the last time they'd spoken. Otto clenched his fists, took a deep breath, and knocked firmly on the door.

"Enter," came the gruff voice from within.

As Otto pushed the door open, he noticed that the room was smaller than he remembered, the walls lined with bookshelves filled to capacity with military tomes and maps of Europe. A single lamp cast a weak yellow glow over the desk cluttered with papers and photographs. Behind it sat Fritz Geier, now a lieutenant colonel in the SS, his once-youthful face hardened by years of brutal conflict.

"Sergeant Berg," Fritz said icily, barely looking up from the document he was reading. "What brings you here?"

"Hello, Lieutenant Colonel," Otto replied, trying to keep his voice steady. "I was just passing through and thought I'd pay you a visit."

"We have nothing to say to each other," said Fritz.

"There's always something to say."

Fritz stared at him for a moment. "Perhaps you are correct. However, I must warn you, if you plan to utter more seditious statements there will be no more quarter."

"Nothing like that," said Otto. "I want to see if there is any way to mend what's between us. My mother asked me to come."

His friend's features softened. He put down the papers he'd had in his hand and leaned back in his chair. "Your mother, aye? She was always kind to me. How is she doing?"

"Mother is well, thank you," Otto answered, surprised by the sudden warmth in Fritz's tone. "She sends her regards."

"The war has not destroyed her life?"

Otto shook his head. "We live far enough from downtown Munich. She's escaped the bombing. So far."

"Good, good," Fritz murmured, his gaze shifting to a photograph on his desk: a picture of the two of them in their soccer uniforms, taken before the war had twisted their lives into unrecognizable shapes.

Otto decided this was as good a time as any to broach the subject he'd come to discuss. "Fritz, tell me what's going on here."

"With what?"

"With the war."

Fritz sighed heavily, his dark eyes clouded with worry. "The Allies are on the verge of invading the Netherlands. We can't hold them off much longer."

There was a long pause as Otto absorbed this information. He had suspected as much but hearing it from Fritz—a man who had always been so confident in Germany's ultimate victory—sent a shiver down his spine.

"So you finally admit we are losing this war?" Otto asked, his voice barely above a whisper.

Fritz hesitated for a moment before admitting, "Yes, I believe we are."

"Then what does that mean for you, Fritz? For men like us?"

"Men like us?" Fritz scoffed, leaning forward in his chair. "Don't lump me in with you, Otto. You were just a soldier, following orders. I . . . I am Gestapo. If Germany loses, I will be hunted down like an animal."

Otto winced at the bitterness in Fritz's words but knew there was truth in them. The war had forced them all to do terrible things, but none more so than Fritz. His wartime activities as a member of the Gestapo had made him a prime target for retribution if the Nazis fell from power.

"Is there anything you can do to protect yourself?" Otto asked, genuinely concerned for his friend's safety.

"Protect myself?" Fritz laughed bitterly. "No, Otto. There is no escape for someone like me. No escape except at the end of a barrel, or a noose."

The room fell silent, the weight of their shared past pressing down upon them. Otto stared at the floor, wishing he could offer some form of comfort or solace to the man who had once been his closest friend.

Otto hesitated for a moment before daring to voice his thoughts. "Fritz, have you ever considered using your influence with your uncle? Perhaps you could . . . try to change the German policies about the Jews and other civilians? Surely if Himmler shifted his position, and you were responsible, that would have some kind of weight with the Allies."

Fritz shrugged. "You think I haven't tried? I raised this issue with my uncle Heinrich before, Otto, and all it earned me was a shouting match and threats of being sent to the Eastern Front."

"Then resign," Otto said firmly, his blue eyes locked on

Fritz's. "Refuse to be involved in any further Gestapo activities and go home. Maybe that's the best way to protect yourself."

The air in the room grew thick with tension as Fritz weighed Otto's words. He stared at his old friend, his face unreadable. Finally, he let out a heavy sigh. "I was going to accuse you of treason again, but what is the point? No, you're right, Otto, and I've been wrong. The war is over. And resign? It wouldn't make any difference—at the end of the day, I will have to pay the piper."

"If there is anything I can do for you my friend, you have only to ask," Otto murmured.

"I appreciate the sentiment, Otto. But enough about me," Fritz said, leaning back in his chair and changing the subject. "Tell me about yourself. For one, I know I'm not the real reason you're in Eindhoven. You're here to visit that Dutch girl you can't seem to get out of your head. Aafke, wasn't it?"

Otto felt a pang in his chest at her name, and he looked away, unable to meet Fritz's gaze. "I was on my way to see her before I came here, but . . . I couldn't work up the courage."

"Courage?" Fritz scoffed, shaking his head. "You stormed positions and faced enemy fire without flinching, and yet you're afraid to visit a girl?"

"Romance is a different kind of battlefield," Otto replied quietly, remembering Aafke's haunting blue eyes.

"Don't be absurd. Go see her," Fritz urged, his tone unexpectedly gentle. "The war is almost over, Otto. What do you have to lose?"

Otto's heart raced at the thought, but fear held him back. Aafke had every reason to hate him, a German soldier who had brought nothing but pain and suffering to her homeland. And yet he couldn't shake the feeling that there was something between them, a connection that transcended the horrors of war.

"Maybe you're right," Otto conceded, his voice barely audible. "I should go to her."

"Good," Fritz said, nodding firmly. "Now, get out of here. I have work to do. I must keep the pieces together until my jailers come. And Otto. Be careful out there. Not with Aafke, with combat. The war is coming to a close. No need to get yourself killed."

Otto smiled faintly, grateful for Fritz's support despite the rift that had grown between them. He stood up and extended a hand to his old friend. "Thank you, Fritz. Take care of yourself."

"Same to you, Otto," Fritz replied, clasping Otto's hand tightly. "And let me know how it goes with Aafke."

"I will," Otto promised, before turning to leave the room. His heart pounded against his chest, both fearful and hopeful as he prepared himself to face the woman who had haunted his thoughts for so long.

As he turned to leave, the phone on Fritz's desk rang. He answered and Otto saw his friend's forehead crease in concern. He hung up the phone after a few moments.

"What is it?" asked Otto.

"Probably nothing," said Fritz after a moment. "Rumors of some fighting going on up north. Paratroopers reportedly. It's probably nonsense. We get a half dozen of these reports a day now that the allies are getting so close." Fritz smiled. "I'm glad you came, my friend. Now run along and chase after that girl you can't get your mind off for *Gott* knows what reason!"

With Fritz's encouragement still echoing in his ears, Otto found himself marching toward Aafke's apartment building, nerves writhing like snakes in his stomach. Trying to summon the courage to go inside and up to her apartment, he stood there for a moment. He had to do it. The war would soon be over, and this might be his last chance to see her. Taking a deep breath, he strode forward.

As he rounded the corner near her apartment building, Otto

was shocked to find Aafke on the street, her golden hair glinting in the weak sunlight that filtered through the clouds. He hesitated for a moment, drinking in her beauty, before he noticed the dark bruise surrounding her left eye. Anger surged through him, eclipsing his fear.

"Aafke," he called out, unable to keep the rage from his voice. She turned toward him, surprise flickering across her face before she quickly looked away, her eyes darting up and down the street.

"Otto," she said softly, her voice trembling. "What are you doing here?"

"Never mind that," he replied, taking a step closer. "What happened to your eye? Who did this to you?"

Aafke hesitated, "My father . . . he was angry with me."

"Your father?" Otto seethed, his hands balling into tight fists at his sides. "I'll confront him right now. This is unacceptable!"

"No, Otto, please!" Aafke pleaded, tears welling up in her eyes. "Leave my father alone. Just leave me alone. You need to get out of here right now."

"But Aafke—" he protested.

"Please," she sobbed, pulling away from his grasp. "I can't handle any more trouble, not now."

"Tell me what's going on," Otto said gently, his anger dissolving into concern. "Why are you so upset? I want to help you."

Aafke hesitated, her gaze darting around the street as if searching for an escape. Finally, she sighed and admitted, "I'm pregnant, Otto. And I don't know what to do."

"Who's the father?" Otto asked, his mind racing.

"Arno," Aafke whispered, her cheeks flushing with shame. "You've met him before. He accused me of having the child with . . . with you."

Otto shook his head, incredulous at the suggestion that he could be the father of Aafke's unborn child. "That's absurd," he scoffed. "We've never even kissed, let alone been together in that way." He looked into her eyes, searching for some glimmer of understanding.

"I know, Otto," she whispered, her voice barely audible. "But right now you can't fix things. I just need you to leave me alone. Please."

"Leave you alone?" Otto asked, his frustration mounting. "Aafke, I can't just walk away from you when you're in this situation. Let me help you. Tell me what I can do."

"Nothing, Otto," Aafke replied, her eyes welling up with tears. "There's nothing you can do."

As they argued, the distant hum of aircraft engines caught Otto's attention. He looked skyward and saw the silhouettes of dozens of Allied planes streaking across the sky. His heart raced as realization set in: the rumors were true. They were on the verge of an invasion.

"Look!" he shouted, pointing to the sky. "Paratroopers! The Allies are here!"

Aafke's tearful gaze followed his outstretched arm, and her own fear became palpable. Panic spread through the streets as people began to run for cover, desperately seeking shelter from the impending chaos.

"Stay safe, Aafke," Otto pleaded, grasping her shoulders. "Take care of yourself and your baby. I have to go."

Before she could respond, he sprinted away, weaving through the growing throngs of panicked citizens. The sound of gunfire echoed through the air, punctuating the urgency of his flight. As he ran, Otto's mind raced with conflicting thoughts. His loyalty lay with his fellow soldiers, but he couldn't shake his concern for Aafke, alone and vulnerable in the midst of a war zone.

"Damn it," he muttered under his breath. "I have to make sure she's safe."

He tried to circle back to where he'd left Aafke, but the disarray of the city made it impossible to retrace his steps. The streets were filled with chaos, and American paratroopers seemed to be everywhere, descending from the sky like ominous specters. Otto knew that if he were caught by the invading forces, his status as a Waffen-SS sergeant would place him in grave danger. With a heavy heart, he decided that his best chance at protecting Aafke was to flee Eindhoven and regroup with his comrades.

"Stay safe," he whispered to the wind, praying that his words would somehow find her amid the turmoil. And then, with one final look in Aafke's direction, he plunged into the chaos, determined to survive and return when the dust settled.

As Otto fled, he thought about Fritz. If his friend were captured, he would be in terrible danger. He set out for SS headquarters, moving from block to block. As he passed Dutch civilians there were threats and profanities. One woman even upended a bowl of slop on him from an upstairs window. But he kept moving, intent on reaching his friend. He finally made it back. The front doors of the headquarters were guarded by several privates, machine guns at the ready. Otto raised his hands as he approached. The men recognized his uniform and waved him inside.

"Otto!" a familiar voice called out amid the pandemonium, and he recognized Fritz Geier's angular face as it emerged from behind a clustered group of men in the lobby.

"The Americans are here!"

"I know it," said Fritz.

"I have to get you out of here!"

Fritz looked at his men. "I've made my own arrangements. We have a car outside."

"A car will never make it. They'll be expecting that. You'll be shot to pieces."

Fritz looked back at the men, then over at Otto. "You're right," he said at last. "You're the expert. Can you get us out of here?"

"You. Only you. Send the others out in small groups, each in a different direction. It's the best chance some of us will make it out alive."

"All right," Fritz said, turning to give some orders to the men. He turned back to Otto. "Let's go."

As they navigated the besieged city, Otto's mind raced with a torrent of conflicting emotions. He wanted nothing more than to stay by Aafke's side, to protect her from the horrors of war that were now quite literally raining down upon them. But he also understood that doing so would only place her in greater danger, for she would become a target by association.

They made their way through street after street, a constant focus of the crowd. A man rushed at them, a heavy round club in his hand. Otto dropped his shoulder and crashed into him, knocking him to the ground. "Keep moving!" he shouted to Fritz, as they sprinted to the next intersection.

"God help us," Fritz breathed as they rounded a corner and found themselves face-to-face with a squad of American soldiers. For a heartbeat, time seemed to stand still as both groups regarded each other in shocked silence.

"Run!" Otto shouted, his voice cracking with the strain of terror. He shoved Fritz forward, propelling them both into a desperate sprint as gunfire erupted behind them.

"Fritz, this way!" Otto cried, yanking him down another narrow passage. They could hear the Americans closing in, their boots pounding against the cobblestones like the drums of doom.

"Almost there," Otto panted, his breath coming in gasps as he willed his legs to keep moving. It felt as though the very ground beneath him was conspiring to slow his progress, every step an agonizing battle against exhaustion and despair. They scrambled down a narrow alley, for the moment deserted.

"Here!" Fritz exclaimed, pulling open the door to a cellar and motioning for Otto to follow him inside. With a final surge of adrenaline, Otto leapt into the darkness, the door slamming shut behind him. There was a pounding of footsteps as the soldiers passed.

"Close call," Fritz whispered, his voice trembling with relief. "Where are we?"

Otto looked around, his eyes slowly adjusting to the dim light that filtered in through the cracks in the wooden door.

"An old wine cellar," he said. "We should be safe here for now."

"Thank you," Fritz murmured, slumping to the floor as he battled to catch his breath.

"Of course," Otto said softly. "You're my brother. I'll always have your back."

As they huddled together in the musty shadows, Otto found himself thinking of Aafke. He knew she should be safe with the Americans arriving. Perhaps safer than she ever would be with his protection. But he had a feeling that this wasn't true. There was something going on with this Arno. How could the man believe there was something between him and Aafke? Why wouldn't he believe her words to the contrary? He couldn't shake the feeling in his stomach that if he didn't act, didn't risk everything to find her, that something terrible would happen to her. But for now, there was nothing he could do.

Chapter 27
Verrader

Sunday, September 17, 1944
Noon
Eindhoven, Netherlands

Aafke stood amidst the wild crowd lining the streets of Eindhoven, awash in makeshift orange flags. She tried to be happy. This was the moment she'd waited for since the war began. Liberation. The American paratroopers with the eagles on their shoulders walked through the town, rifles at the ready. But they could hardly keep their military composure as they were swarmed by celebrating citizens, hugging and kissing them. The GIs handed out cigarettes and candy bars. Some people, stunned to see chocolate again after all this time and half starved, ripped open the containers right then and there and wolfed down the delicacies. The Americans seemed to appreciate the attention, especially the kisses from the pretty young Dutch girls.

Someone shoved a flag into Aafke's hand. She held it listlessly at her side, her face still blank. How did this happen to her? She'd fought hard for her country, risking her life and doing everything she could to do her part. She'd found a man whom she'd grown to love, and whom she thought loved her as well. It wasn't always perfect. At times they seemed to be so different in the way they saw the world. And they'd experienced pain. They'd lost Maaike, and she still didn't know where her brother was. But this was war. Loss was bound to happen. Her little group had taken out a dozen key Nazis in the city, and conducted acts of sabotage that slowed down their enemy and robbed them of vital war supplies.

Then in the space of a day everything had fallen apart. Her fears of pregnancy had been confirmed. Finding Arno, she'd witnessed what she was sure, despite his protests, was a romantic moment with Joelle. He'd denied it, but worse, when confronted with the news of their pregnancy, he'd accused her of having the child with Otto. It was preposterous! He had to know she had nothing to do with the German. They'd had that one dinner together, a spontaneous event where she had plotted to kill him. *She should have killed him!* That thought plagued her again. If she had, she wouldn't have any of these problems. Instead, caught off guard by his integrity, she'd let him go, and plunged herself into a world of trouble. If she could just explain things to Arno, she was sure she could make things clear. She just needed a little time with him.

And, as if summoned by her thoughts, Arno materialized out of the crowd, pushing and shoving his way through as he headed directly toward her. She waved at him, smiling, relieved, but her happiness fell when she saw the angry scowl he wore. He reached her and grabbed her arm hard. "We need to talk!" he shouted over the crowd.

"Arno, you're hurting me!" she protested. He lessened his grip but still held on to her, pulling her back away from the celebration and down a nearby alley. She followed, trying to bring her emotions under control. She had to convince him, make him believe. "I'm so glad you came," she said.

"Why is that?" he asked, spitting the words at her.

"Arno, look at me. You know it can't be true. I've never been with Otto. I told you, I hardly know the man. I've only been with you. This is your child."

"I don't believe you."

"Why? I don't understand this! We've been together practically every moment for the past year. Do you really think I've been secretly dating a German soldier behind your back? Think about it, Arno. He's on active duty. He's not stationed in Eindhoven. How would I possibly have time to see him, even if I wanted to? Which I certainly don't. I have to wonder if something has changed. If you want out and that's why you're doing this. Does this have something to do with Joelle?"

His eyes flared. "I told you, there's nothing going on between us. You're trying to put this on her. On me. How did you manage to get pregnant in the first place? You were careless!"

"*We* were careless!" she said, taking his arm. "Arno, this is our child. You were the one that pushed me to be with you. How can you do this to me?"

"A pregnancy is a woman's problem," he said coldly, removing his arm. "I don't want a child. I never have. I'm a socialist, Aafke, you know that. When this war is over, the people will rise up and take the government from that bitch queen hiding in England. When they do, I'll be a part of things. I've made my mark in the resistance. There will be a spot for me in things to come." He looked at her, his lip curling up in disdain. "I don't need a child, and I don't need you. This was fun while it lasted, but take your bastard German child and stay away from me."

He ripped his arm away from her and started back into the crowd. Aafke followed him, trying to stop him, but he shoved her back. "Arno!" she cried, trying to push through the people to reach him.

He turned and glared at her, his eyes wild. Pointing, he

began screaming. "Collaborator!" he shouted. "Collaborator! She carries a bastard German child in her belly."

Nearby people began staring at Aafke, their faces twisted in anger. "Traitor!" one of the men yelled at her. "Get her!" yelled another.

Aafke was seized by her arms as the chant was taken up by the crowd. "I'm innocent!" she pleaded. "I've never been with a German!"

"Liar!" a woman screamed, spitting in her face. Aafke was pulled into the street, a growing crowd pressing against her. They pulled her along as she shouted her innocence, but nobody was listening. The mass surged down the road, dragging her with them. A man ran into the street with clippers in his hands. Holding them over his head, he screamed to the crowd, "Cut the whore's hair!" The people shrieked and shouted their approval. The man wove through the crowd. "Hold her!" he ordered.

Aafke was crying now, the tears streaming down her face. The man seized her and began running the hand clippers through her hair. His movements were violent and she felt the searing tear of her roots as he ripped the hair out of her head. Aafke closed her eyes, dizzy, as the screaming and threats continued around her, the clippers pulling and biting.

"A sign!" someone shouted. "We need a sign!" Minutes passed as the barber finished his work. Aafke felt rope harshly shoved against the back of her neck and then the weight of something hanging on her chest. She looked down. There was a crudely crafted sign made of wood, attached at the rope around her neck. The sign said *verrader*: traitor.

"Let's parade her!" the barber shouted. Aafke was lifted up onto the shoulders of a couple men and held in place by the crowd. They moved forward, calling out "traitor" over and over. Aafke was pelted with rotten fruit and garbage. She felt blood trickling down her head from the harsh cuts of the clippers.

"Arno, save me," she whispered. But he didn't come. She didn't know if he was even there, in the crowd, or if he'd gone back to the cottage in the woods. But he had left her to this torture, and he didn't seem to care.

After what seemed like hours, the barber ordered her down and then shoved her harshly to the pavement. "Get out of Eindhoven!" he ordered. "Or we'll take more than your hair!"

Aafke didn't try to protest. The people didn't care. After years of occupation, they were free, and all their pent-up anger and lust for revenge was being released. It didn't matter if she was a collaborator or not. She'd been named one. She was easy vengeance, within reach. She lay on the pavement for long minutes, unable to move. Finally, she managed to reach up and pull the sign over her head. Breathing heavily and still under shouts from spectators, she crawled slowly to her feet and stumbled past the people, refusing to look in their eyes. She managed to reach the corner and took a few steps down a street, away from the parade, before collapsing again to the sidewalk.

"Aafke." The whispered words surprised her. At first she couldn't raise her head, or open her eyes to see who was speaking to her. She felt strong hands on her and she was lifted into the air. She screamed, trying to claw and fight this new threat. "Stop it!" a man's voice commanded. "I'm carrying you to safety."

She looked up in shock to find herself in Otto's arms. He was dressed in a civilian suit and he was marching away from the chaos in long measured strides.

"Leave me alone," Aafke managed to whisper, her voice hoarse and cracking. "Please, just leave me alone."

But Otto ignored her. They were already several blocks away from the celebrations. Finding an alley, he turned to the right, stepping swiftly down the passage. Pausing about halfway, he set Aafke gently down on the pavement and removed his jacket, covering her. She was shivering now, her teeth chattering so violently she bit her tongue. He stared down at her, his face a set mask of concern and anger. "Who did this to you?" he asked.

"Nobody . . . it doesn't matter." She looked up at him. "You need to leave me, Otto. Right now! You're putting my life in danger."

"Not yet," he said. He looked in both directions, making sure they were alone. "Stay here," he commanded. He took off at a run and was soon out of sight.

Aafke lay with her head against the wall. If she'd had the strength, she would have tried to get away. If Arno caught her with Otto now that would be the end of things. She might be shot on the spot. She was exhausted, freezing, her head and her body aching from dozens of cuts and scrapes. In some ways, she might have welcomed a bullet. Her life was over. She was an outcast with her people now. Unless somehow she could make Arno understand. Make him believe.

What would her father say? She hadn't had the courage to tell him last night what had happened. She wanted to sort things out with Arno first. She'd never imagined that he would react the way he had today. That he would still refuse to believe her.

And was that even true? At the end, he seemed to be saying he didn't care. He didn't want a child. Didn't want her anymore. He had some crazy future planned for himself that didn't include her. Had everything they'd gone through, everything between them, been a fantasy? She couldn't believe that was true. That her entire relationship with Arno was a lie. It couldn't be true. There had to be something she could say to him, something that would make him believe.

She saw movement out of the corner of her eye. Otto was back. He had a bucket and some cloth. He hurried to her, leaned down and dipped the fabric into the water, beginning to wash her head. "Otto, please, I told you, I need you to leave me."

"It's that boyfriend of yours, isn't it?" he said, ignoring her pleas. "That Arno. He did this to you."

She wanted to lie to him, to tell him he was wrong. But she

couldn't. Aafke closed her eyes, letting him tend to her wounds. She felt the tears pouring down her cheeks as her body was racked in sobs. All of the pain and fear of the past twenty-four hours exploded out of her.

She felt his hand on her back, gently patting her. "Everything will be all right, Aafke. I know it will. I won't let him do anything to you again. I won't let anyone do anything to you."

She pulled away. "You don't even know me."

"I know enough. I see you. You have a good heart. You don't deserve this," he said, pointing at the bruise on her face. "You don't deserve any of this. The war is almost over. When it is, I'll be back."

His words confused her. She looked around, but fortunately the alley was still vacant. What did he mean he would be back? For her? If she was able to work things out with Arno, that would be a disaster. But Arno had hit her. He'd denied their child. And what about what she'd seen when she'd walked in on Joelle and Arno?

"Will you let me come back to see you?" he asked.

She closed her eyes and turned her head away. "I'm all right now," she said. "Can you please go, Otto? I'm sorry, I just need to go home."

"I understand. I'll go, but take this," he said, placing a roll of money in her hand. "This will help while I'm gone. Stay away from Arno. Keep your head down. The war will be over soon. Then I'll be back. Back for you."

He rose and started to move away.

"Otto?" she found herself saying.

He turned. "Yes?"

"Thank you."

He nodded. "You must be careful. Take care of yourself. I'll be back."

She watched him stride off and round the corner. She rested her head against the wall, her emotions swirling. What was she going to do? She realized Otto had left his coat behind and she pulled it back on, covering herself as she rested against the wall. She sat that way for another hour, until darkness started to fall and it was too cold to remain where she was. Finding enough strength, she pulled herself up and limped toward her apartment, steeling herself for the conversation ahead of her.

She arrived home a few minutes later. How ironic that all this suffering happened so close to her flat. Of course, her home had always been a place of suffering. She dragged herself up the stairs and fiddled with her keys, opening the door and closing it behind her. Her father was at the table, his face a mottled red and his eyes half closed. He'd been celebrating, it appeared. A fair amount. This would be even harder.

"Father, I'm home," she said.

He grunted in response. "What's for dinner, girl? It's late and I've sat here with nothing to eat."

"I was down at the parade. I . . . I got caught up in things."

He looked up at her and his eyes widened. "Sweet Joseph!" he exclaimed. "What have you gone and done with your hair?"

"Something terrible has happened, Father."

He took a deep drink from his mug. "What is it now, Aafke? You're always in the middle of some woe or another."

"I'm with child."

"What in heaven are you talking about?" he asked, his face a burning scarlet now.

"I'm having a baby. It's Arno's, although he denies it."

"Why does he deny it? Have you been whoring around town?"

"No, Father. Of course not. It was just the two of us. But he accused me of being with a German. That Otto who came to our apartment that one time."

"Don't tell me you've been laying with a Nazi. Oh Lord! What's to come of us? You've brought the final bit of shame down on top of us. And pregnant to boot! I'll never be able to show my face in the parish again."

"I told you, I was never with a German! But Arno accused

me of it, and then he told the crowd I was a collaborator. They did this to my head."

"And the bruise on your face?"

"Arno struck me."

Maarten nodded. "And well he should have. To think my own daughter slept with a German."

"Why would you even believe Arno?" she asked. "You've never liked him."

"I'd believe him any day over a girl sleeping about town, and getting herself in the wrong way with a Nazi. What am I going to do? What will the neighbors think of me?"

"It's not about you!" Aafke shouted, the tears coming again. "I'm in trouble here, Father, and I'm telling you the truth! What's going to become of *you*? How about what's going to become of *me*?"

"Now, now," he said, waving her off and taking another sip of his whiskey. "Don't go raising your voice to me or I'll give a matching shine to the one you already have. You're the one who's found yourself with a baby. Don't go blaming me for your troubles. Oh, that Christiaan were here to save me! Well, he's not. And, as usual, I'm going to have to rescue us from your mess. Here's what you're going to do. You're going to go to Arno tomorrow and apologize. You're going to listen to whatever he tells you to do. When you're further along, we'll send you out to the country. That should be easy to manage with the Americans here now. You can have the baby. There's places for that. Then you give the child up and come back to live with me. You'll never marry now, and that's a fact. But who would have wanted you in the first place? I mean, besides a communist and a German. But don't you worry. I'll take you back. If you mind yourself, you can stay with me."

"So I have to admit to something I didn't do? Is that right? And then I have to give up my child? Arno's child and mine? Then you want me to come back here and take care of you?"

"Mind your mouth, or I'll change my mind."

"To hell with you!"

"What did you say?"

"I said to hell with you. I've taken care of you all of my life. For the last four years, you've sat back and done nothing but drink and complain."

"Now here—"

"I'm not done! You haven't worked. You've drunk when we've needed the money for food. I've worked twelve-hour days, six days a week to buy you your cheap brandy and all you've done in return is run me down."

"Your brother—"

"My brother is a good young man. But he's been gone a long time now and I've been left to pick up the pieces. Well, I'm not going to do it anymore. I'm not going anywhere, Father, and I'm not giving up this child! If you want me to stay a minute longer, you're going to start pulling your own weight. You're going back to work. And together we'll pay for our food and rent. If you refuse, I'll move out. I'm not without friends, no matter what has happened. One of the girls from the factory will take me in. And you can stay here and rot—at least until they throw you out!"

There was a knock at the door. Her father was about to answer her, but instead he rose. "What is it?" he asked.

"A message for Maarten Cruyssen."

Her father stepped to the door and opened it. There was a young Dutch man wearing a postal uniform at the door. "Sign here," he said, handing over a clipboard.

Maarten signed and then took the letter, closing the door without another word. He looked back at Aafke. "I'll attend to you in a moment." He ripped open the envelope and read the message. His face turned white and he collapsed against the door. "My boy. They killed my boy." He slumped to the ground, burying his face in his knees.

Aafke rushed to the letter, skimming the contents. It was from a German interior department, announcing that Christiaan Cruyssen had contracted typhoid fever at a work camp and died on August 27. There wasn't even a condolence. Aafke screamed, falling to the ground next to her father. She put her head against his shoulder, wailing uncontrollably.

After a time her father looked up. "It should have been you."

Chapter 28

Operatie Griffen

Sunday, December 17, 1944
10:45 p.m.
Cobru, Belgium

Otto Berg moved silently through the dark forest on a moon-less night. He was acutely aware of his surroundings as he crept toward his target, his feet crunching through the snow. He was moving toward a vital fuel depot behind enemy lines in Belgium. Otto had been handpicked by Skorzeny for this danger-ous mission, not only for his athletic prowess but also for his unique upbringing. Otto and a handful of other men had trained for months in preparation for the operation, including the hours of instruction in Amsterdam. They were to operate alone or in small groups, attacking depots and supply lines. He was already miles behind enemy lines, marching through the woods of Belgium.

Hitler had launched this massive counterattack against the Allies in the Ardennes forest. The purpose was to drive the enemy back and recapture Antwerp, perhaps even break through and cut off the northern forces against the sea the same way they had the English and French in 1940. Otto and the other men in his special unit were operating behind enemy lines. He'd trained for this mission for months—not just the language training but also special weapons, explosives, the use of American equipment. He'd studied maps, topography, and escape routes.

"Focus," Otto muttered under his breath. There was no time to think about his training, or the danger he was in. He had to think of his mission.

He felt the weight of his backpack on his shoulders, its contents meticulously arranged for maximum efficiency. Inside were three types of explosives: four sticks of dynamite with timed fuses, two magnetic limpet mines designed to attach to metal surfaces, and six pineapple-shaped grenades with pull pins. These deadly tools were accompanied by a coil of detonation cord, a pair of wire cutters, a waterproof map, and a small compass.

The American uniform felt strange and ill fitting. Still, he felt excitement coursing through him. It was the old familiar feeling of combat, heightened by the nature of this operation. It was like he was back on the pitch in Munich, stealing the ball and passing up to Fritz for a goal.

Fritz. He wondered if his friend had made it out of Eindhoven alive. He'd made inquiries after but nobody seemed to know where he was. He hoped he had survived, that he was safe somewhere. If not, he prayed the end had come quickly. Otto stopped and knelt down behind a tree. Making sure nobody was nearby, he retrieved a map from his coat and studied the contents under this coat with his flashlight.

The fuel depot, Otto knew, was heavily guarded and fortified. The enemy would not make it easy for him, but he had a job to do, and he would not let anything stand in his way. He walked the miles along the map with his fingers, calculating the distance. He wasn't much farther than two miles now from his target. When he arrived, he would hunker down an hour or so before dawn, when sentries tended to be their most exhausted and least vigilant. He would sneak in and set his explosives, then clear the area and detonate the dynamite. The fuel would do the rest. If he was successful, the American tanks, already pressed to the limit by the surprise onslaught, would be bereft of fuel. As he drew nearer, Otto's senses heightened, his muscles tensed beneath his uniform, ready to spring into action at a moment's notice. He gripped his pistol tightly in one hand and clutched a grenade in the other, prepared for whatever challenges lay ahead.

"Time to go to work," he murmured, taking a deep breath and moving into the forest, his eyes scanning the tree line for any sign of movement.

The dense foliage of the Belgian forest seemed to close in around Otto, its branches clawing at his uniform with every step. The snow beneath him was frozen, causing his boots to slide as he struggled to maintain his balance. He could feel the weight of his mission bearing down on him while fear gnawed at the edges of his mind.

Otto noticed a sudden rustling in the undergrowth, followed by the unmistakable sound of footsteps approaching, crunching in the snow. His heart thudded wildly in his chest, adrenaline tearing through his veins as he prepared for a confrontation. Within seconds, twelve soldiers emerged from the trees, wearing American uniforms and carrying rifles and pistols. They blocked Otto's path, their faces grim and determined.

"Identify yourself!" barked the sergeant in charge, leveling his rifle at Otto's chest.

"Um . . . John Miller," Otto replied, focusing on the American accent he'd worked on for months. "I'm just out scouting the area, sir."

"What unit are you with?" the sergeant demanded, suspicion etched across his features.

Otto hesitated for only a moment before he repeated the unit designation he had memorized again and again.

The sergeant scrutinized Otto's face, looking for something in it. "What's your mission, Private?" he asked, his voice laced with skepticism.

"I'm, uh . . . supposed to locate and report on enemy movements in the region," Otto answered, his palms sweating as he tried to maintain eye contact with the stern-faced American.

"Is that so?" the sergeant replied, his eyes narrowing as he considered Otto's response. "And you're out here all by yourself? That's an unusual patrol, wouldn't you say, Miller?"

"Sir," Otto began, his voice wavering slightly, "I assure you, I'm just doing my job."

"Your job, huh?" The sergeant snorted, glancing at the other soldiers around him. "Well, your story seems a bit shaky, Private. How do we know you're not one of those damn Nazi spies we've been hearing about? Running around behind enemy lines in our uniforms?"

"Because," Otto said, trying to sound confident despite the fear that threatened to consume him, "I'm here to help, not hurt. I just want to get home to my girl, sir. Like everyone else."

"And where are you from?"

"Hoboken, New Jersey."

"All right," the sergeant said, narrowing his eyes at Otto. "Let's see just how 'American' you really are, Private." He leaned in closer, a smirk tugging at the corner of his mouth. "Tell me, who played Rhett Butler in *Gone With the Wind*?"

Otto's heart raced. He had heard of the film, of course, but the name of the actor escaped him. He swallowed hard and tried to recall any scrap of information that might help. His instructor had mentioned it once. But what was the actor's name?

"Uh, Clark Gable, sir," he stammered, relief flooding through him as the memory surfaced.

"Good." The sergeant nodded. "And who won the 1943 World Series?"

"Yankees," Otto replied quickly. They'd practiced sports team information over and over, for just this situation.

"All right," the sergeant said, still not entirely convinced. He gestured to Otto's backpack. "You've got quite a load there, soldier. What happened?"

"Sir," Otto replied hesitantly, sensing the trap, "our vehicle ran out of petrol a few miles back."

"Petrol?" the sergeant repeated, his suspicion flaring. "Interesting choice of words, Private. We say 'gasoline' in the good ol' US of A." The sergeant raised his rifle at Otto's chest. "You're under arrest for questioning. Drop your weapon."

"I would prefer that you let me go."

"Did you hear me? Hand it over!"

Otto raised his right hand slowly to turn his pistol over to the sergeant, but that was a feint. He dropped to one knee in the snow and fired two quick shots, hitting the sergeant and the man next to him both in the chest. He rolled forward, landing in a crouch. The Americans were starting to react, raising their weapons to stop him. Otto flipped the pin off the grenade in his left hand and tossed it at a GI while simultaneously firing his pistol at another, dropping the man. Rolling away, he saw a flash and heard the thunderous explosion of the grenade. The shock wave from the detonation threw him away to his right and he hit the ground hard. He felt a burning fire in his leg and a piercing stab in his eye, but he didn't have time to deal with any wounds. There were still four Americans preparing to fire.

Otto rose and fired another round wildly at the remaining Americans, missing. Ignoring the searing pain, he started off into the woods, half running, half limping, with bullets ricocheting around him in the dirt and hitting the trees. He was hit twice in the back and he tumbled forward, landing hard on the ground. He lay there, not moving, playing dead, knowing his only chance was to let the Americans get close. He didn't have to wait long. He heard their voices as they approached.

"Looks like we got him."

"The bastard. He killed eight of us!"

"Make sure he's dead."

Otto heard the sound of a soldier shoving a new clip into his M1 Garand. Another stepped forward and kicked him hard in the side. It took everything in his being to remain still, not reacting to the blow.

"Hell, he's a goner."

"Make sure of it."

"I've got this."

Otto flipped to his side, raising his pistol at the GI approaching him with rifle raised. He fired a shot, hitting the soldier in the face. Otto rotated and fired again, taking another American in the chest. He turned and aimed at the third soldier, who was staring wide eyed with his mouth open. He shot the man in the neck, his head snapping back as he crumpled to the ground. The last soldier was already beginning to run. Otto rolled onto his chest and took aim. He fired, hitting the man in the shoulder, but to his surprise the American kept running, stumbling on through the woods.

Otto could not let the soldier get away. Pulling himself to his feet, he started after the man. The pain in his leg was excruciating and he could only manage a limping walk. His vision was blurry and he felt the hot blood running down his cheek from his head wound. Keeping an eye on the snow, he was able to spot a blood trail and he kept moving after the last American. He had to stop the man or his mission would be a failure. Fortunately, the GI seemed to be moving in the same direction as his ultimate objective. This allowed Otto to close in on his target, although if the man reached the depot before he could catch him, he would blow the operation.

As Otto trudged on, he struggled. He was growing dizzy and weak. His mind wandered and he thought of Aafke. The image of her face burned clear in his mind, as if she was standing in front of him. He hadn't been able to contact her since he'd fled Eindhoven. Although the American and British operation to surge through Holland and into Germany had been a colossal failure, the Allies had held on to parts of Holland, including her hometown. There was no way to get a letter to her. He'd worried about her until the training for his mission became so intense he had little time for anything else. Now, out here in the cold, badly wounded, his mind wandering, she came forcefully to his mind. He tried to focus on her image as he stumbled forward, wobbling between trees as he followed the patches of blood, stalking his target.

He was moving slower now. The blood ran down the front of his coat. His leg was dragging. Otto had to keep going. He had a mission to complete. His mind was a fog. The pack he was carrying was so heavy. He reached up and pulled the straps off, dumping it into the snow behind him. Stumbling on, he moved past one tree, then another. He stumbled and fell to the snow. His breath was labored now and he lay there for long minutes, unable to move. Finally, he struggled to his knees and started moving forward again, crawling through the snow. He edged forward inch by inch. It was growing dark out now. He tried to hurry his pace. It was time to complete his mission.

Otto collapsed in the snow, unable to move again. In his mind, he was still marching forward, taking out the last American squad member before he completed his mission and destroyed the fuel depot. But another part of his brain told him this wasn't true. That he was lying in the snow, bleeding out. He thought of Aafke again, smiling. He could see her as she had sat there in the alleyway, head shaved, bruised, more beautiful than ever. She smiled back at him, even as the darkness fell and he knew no more.

Chapter 29
Gewond

Tuesday, January 2, 1945
5:50 p.m.
Bastogne, Belgium

Otto awoke to the sharp smell of antiseptic, his vision blurred and hazy. A choir of moans and cries surrounded him like a grim symphony, echoing through the vast canvas tent. He tried to raise his hand to his face, but pain shot through it like electricity, forcing him to abandon the attempt.

He blinked hard, trying to clear away the fog that clouded his vision. His left eye was useless, the darkness absolute; a sinister void that consumed all light. The right eye, however, revealed the harsh reality he found himself in: an American field hospital, filled with soldiers whose bodies bore the brutal marks of war.

"Take it easy there, Private," said a voice next to him. A wounded soldier, his arm in a sling, offered a weak smile. "You've been out for a long time."

"A long time?" Otto echoed, his voice barely more than a

whisper. He remembered at the last moment that he was supposed to be an American, and thankfully answered in English. The memory of the confrontation with the American squad played in his mind, culminating in the wounds that had taken him out of the operation. He glanced down at his own body, taking stock of the injuries he had sustained.

His chest was wrapped in layers of white gauze, stained crimson in places where blood had seeped through. Beneath the bandages, the pain pulsed in time with his heartbeat: a steady reminder of the bullet wounds he had suffered in the back and clean through his chest. Each breath was an agony, a thousand tiny knives dancing across his rib cage. His leg burned as well.

"Your eye, though . . . that's the worst of it," the soldier continued, nodding sympathetically toward Otto's left side. "Doctors say there's no hope of saving it. I'm sorry." Otto remembered the pain in his eye, the blood trickling down his check from the grenade wound. So he'd lost his eye? How would he fight now? What use would he be to his unit? To Germany?

Otto swallowed hard, trying to suppress the rising tide of panic. The loss of his eye was not only a physical handicap, but a symbol of his failure. He had been spared by the enemy, only to be trapped within their care.

"Thank you," he murmured, turning away from the sympathetic gaze of his fellow patient. Otto focused on the uneven stitches that held the canvas walls together, desperately trying to piece together a plan of escape. He attempted to rise and fell back immediately. He steeled himself. There was no way he could move now. He would have to gather his strength.

The wounded soldiers around him stirred restlessly, caught in the throes of their own private battles. In this sea of pain and despair, Otto was just another broken man, cast adrift and clinging to the wreckage of his former life.

As the shadows of the field hospital lengthened, a figure in white materialized beside Otto's cot. A nurse, with blond hair pulled back into an efficient bun, leaned over him and examined his bandaged eye with a clinical detachment that belied the kindness in her gaze.

"You're awake, I can't believe it," she said.

"Where am I?"

"You're in a field hospital in Belgium," she said. "You've been out a long time. I didn't think you were going to make it."

"How long?" he asked.

"Two weeks."

He was shocked by the news. Two weeks. It seemed like it had been an instant since he'd lost consciousness. What could have happened in that time? He wondered about the war, about Aafke. And how was he going to get out of this situation? He was shocked he hadn't betrayed himself yet.

"I'm Shelle Singer, by the way," she said, giving him another smile. "Let me take a look at your dressings." With deft fingers, she gently peeled back the layers of gauze that swathed his chest. Otto winced as she probed the raw edges of his wounds, the pain a keen reminder of his vulnerability.

"Sorry, I know it hurts," she murmured, eyes softening. "You're healing well, given the circumstances." Straightening up, she uncapped a canteen and held it to his parched lips. "Here, drink."

Otto gulped down the cool water gratefully, each swallow a balm for his throat, parched from disuse and fear. As the water trickled down his throat, he ventured a question, desperate to maintain some semblance of control.

"Tell me about yourself, Nurse Singer. Where do you come from?"

Shelle hesitated, as if weighing the merits of divulging personal information. But something in Otto's gaze seemed to sway her. She settled on the edge of his cot, the faintest hint of a smile playing at the corner of her mouth.

"Alabama," she replied, her accent betraying a trace of Southern warmth. "A small town called Selma. It's nothing special, really—just a quiet place where everyone knows their neighbors."

"Sounds peaceful," Otto mused, imagining the sun-drenched streets of a world far removed from the blood and chaos of war. "And your family? What are they like?"

"My father's a preacher, and my mother . . . well, she's the glue that holds our family together. I've got two younger brothers—one's in the Navy, and the other works at our local grocery store. He has a bad leg, so he couldn't enlist."

"Must be hard for them," Otto ventured, thinking of his own family, scattered by the ravages of war. "You being here, I mean."

"Of course it is," Shelle said, her voice momentarily tinged with sorrow. "But they're proud of me too. We all do what we can to help the cause."

"Indeed." Otto hesitated, unsure whether to pursue this line of inquiry further. But something gnawed at him, an insatiable curiosity that demanded satisfaction. "And when you're not tending to the wounded, what do you like to do?"

"Before the war, I used to spend my days off exploring the woods behind our house," she confided, her eyes shining with the memory. "I'd pick wildflowers, or just sit and listen to the birds sing. It was my way of escaping the world, I suppose."

"Sounds lovely," Otto said, his heart aching for such simple pleasures, now lost to him forever.

"Yes . . ." Shelle sighed, then glanced away, as if sensing the weight of his thoughts. She stood up, her hands moving automatically to straighten her uniform. "I should go tend to the others now. You get some rest. You'll need your strength."

"Thank you," Otto whispered, watching her move through the dimly lit room, a ray of light amidst the shadows. As she disappeared from sight, he clenched his fists, vowing to himself that he would find a way to survive, no matter the cost.

* * *

The following morning, the first rays of sunlight began to filter through the windows of the field hospital, casting a warm glow on the wounded soldiers lying in their beds. Otto stirred awake, his body protesting each movement as he shifted in the narrow cot.

"Good morning, Private," Nurse Singer greeted him with a warm smile as she checked his bandages. Her steady hands moved with practiced efficiency, and Otto marveled at her ability to remain so composed amidst the chaos of war.

"Good morning, Nurse Singer," he replied, wincing as she applied fresh dressings to his chest wound. "Any war news?"

Her face grew somber, and she paused in her ministrations to look out the window. "Well, it's hard to say for certain. We've heard rumors that the Allies are making progress, but the Germans still have a strong presence in many areas. It's a deadly game of cat and mouse, really."

Otto swallowed hard, his heart pounding in his chest as he considered the implications of her words. He knew all too well the dangers posed by the German forces—after all, he was one of them. But he had no choice now but to play the part of the American soldier, lest his true identity be revealed.

"Hope springs eternal, doesn't it?" Nurse Singer continued, her tone cautious but laced with optimism. "We just have to keep pushing forward, believing that we can make a difference."

"Indeed," Otto murmured, forcing himself to meet her gaze.

"Speaking of which, you talk in your sleep, Private." She held his gaze pointedly, and Otto felt the blood drain from his face. Had he betrayed himself? Did she know he was German?

"Really?" he managed to choke out, his mind racing with panic. "What did I say?"

"Mostly just random words and phrases," she replied, her

expression unreadable. "But don't worry, I've seen enough sol-diers come through here to know that the mind can play tricks on us during sleep. It's nothing to be ashamed of." She looked at him again. "Just be careful."

"Thank you," Otto whispered, relief washing over him as he realized she was still treating him kindly. Perhaps she didn't suspect his true origins after all. But what did she mean by *be careful*?

"Get some rest, Private," Nurse Singer advised, patting his arm gently before moving on to tend to another patient. "You'll need your strength for the days ahead. I'll be leaving about noon, but my replacement will be here soon."

Otto nodded, his heart still pounding in his ears as he lay back against the pillows. He couldn't afford to let his guard down, not even for a moment. For now, though, he would focus on healing, on regaining his strength. And when the time came, he would face whatever challenges lay ahead, no matter how daunting they might be.

Several weeks passed that way. Otto gradually healed and in-creased in strength. He was tended by Nurse Singer, who seemed to have made him a personal favorite. Perhaps it was just how long he had been there. Other men came and went, some living, some dying. Soon he had been there longer than any other patient, at least according to the nurses.

Otto was in constant fear of being discovered—what he might be muttering in his sleep. But there was nothing he could do. He still felt too weak to try to escape. He stared at the ceil-ing, tracing the lines where plaster met wood and focusing on the rhythmic ticking of a distant clock.

"Private!" Nurse Singer's voice broke through his reverie as she approached his bedside, balancing a tray laden with medical supplies. "I've some news I think you should know."

"News?" Otto replied hesitantly, his one good eye locked onto hers. The bandages covering his lost eye felt heavy, a constant reminder of his vulnerability.

"Word has it we are hunting down a Nazi spy," Nurse Singer began, her voice low and cautious. "Apparently, this infiltrator killed an entire squad of our boys. But one man escaped, and said the Nazi was badly wounded. They are looking for him in the hospitals."

Otto's heart stuttered in his chest, a cold sweat breaking out across his brow. He knew all too well that the spy she spoke of was him. "Is that so?" he managed to say, feigning surprise.

"Indeed," Nurse Singer confirmed, furrowing her brow as she assessed his reaction. "It's a terrible thing."

"Of course," Otto agreed, swallowing hard and fighting the urge to glance around the ward in fear. "We cannot let such a man go unpunished."

"Agreed," she murmured, her eyes never leaving his face. "Now, let me change those bandages of yours."

As she tended to his wounds, Otto couldn't help but notice the subtle differences in her demeanor: the lingering glances, the almost imperceptible tightening of her lips when he spoke. She seemed to scrutinize his every word, her eyes searching for something hidden beneath the surface.

"Are you feeling all right?" she asked, her voice soft and measured. "You seem a bit . . . on edge."

"Ah, it's just the pain, ma'am," Otto lied, wincing as she removed the bandage from his chest. "It comes and goes."

"Of course," she said sympathetically, yet her eyes remained watchful as she continued to treat him. "I'll see if I can get you something stronger for the pain later."

"Thank you," Otto whispered, his heart pounding in his ears as realization washed over him. Nurse Singer knew—or at least suspected—that he was the German spy. Her gestures and hints were too deliberate, too pointed to be mere coincidence.

He couldn't shake the feeling that he was walking on a tight-rope, one misstep away from plummeting into the abyss. But so long as Nurse Singer held her tongue, Otto still had a chance to escape this place and evade capture. And though he feared what her silence might cost her, he could only hope that her kindness would continue to shield him from discovery.

"Rest now," she urged gently, smoothing the fresh bandages across his chest. "You need to regain your strength."

"Thank you," Otto repeated, closing his eyes and praying silently that his precarious situation wouldn't unravel before he had the chance to make his move.

The full moon peeked through the window, casting a silvery glow on the cold linoleum floor of the hospital ward. Otto's sleep was restless and plagued by nightmares, his guilt manifesting in feverish visions of his comrades and the soldiers he had killed.

"John," a soft voice whispered urgently, rousing him from his fitful slumber. It was Nurse Singer, using the name on his dog tags, her eyes wide with fear and concern. "You need to wake up. The MPs are coming—they're searching the hospital."

His heart leapt into his throat as adrenaline coursed through his veins. He'd spent the past few days dreading this very moment, knowing that his time was running out. With a weak nod, he murmured, "Thank you for the warning, Shelle. But why are you helping me?"

"Here, take this," she said, ignoring the questions. She pressed a small parcel into his hands. "It's some food, water, and painkillers. You'll need it."

"Why are you helping me?"

"I've got to know you these past few weeks," she said. "I can tell you are a kind soul. A caring soul. Besides, we all have secrets."

"What kind of secrets?"

"I have someone back home. Someone I'm not supposed to have. A woman. Her name is Elizabeth. If they knew, I would be drummed out of the army. So you see, John, we all have things we need to hide." She looked down at him. "Just tell me the truth. Tell me you didn't murder those American boys."

Otto relayed to her the whole story of his confrontation with the squad.

"So you tried to get away from them. It was just combat. Just normal war?"

Otto nodded.

Shelle stared down at him for long moments. "That's all right, then. But please, tell me your real name."

"It's Otto. Otto Berg."

She took his hand and squeezed it. "You have to go, Otto," she whispered. Reaching down, she kissed his cheek.

"Thank you," he whispered, his voice choked with gratitude and the weight of their shared secret.

She paused, her silhouette framed by the moonlight. "Just go, Otto. And be careful."

With that, she disappeared down the hallway, leaving him alone in the shadows. Gulping down his fear, Otto swung his legs over the side of the bed, taking a deep breath to steady himself. His military training kicked in, his mind rapidly assessing the situation and formulating an escape plan.

He knew the layout of the hospital intimately, having memorized it during his stay, and silently thanked his former commanders for drilling the importance of situational awareness into him. He would have to move quickly but cautiously, avoiding the MPs and the staff while navigating the labyrinthine hallways.

Otto clenched his jaw as pain lanced through his chest, the wound protesting his sudden movement. But he couldn't afford to waste any more time. He gritted his teeth and pushed through the agony, limping toward the door.

As he peered around the corner, the sound of heavy boots echoed in the distance. The MPs were drawing nearer, their presence a looming threat that sent shivers down his spine. He retreated into the shadows, waiting for the opportune moment to slip away unnoticed.

Please, God, let me make it out of here, he prayed silently, his heart hammering against his ribs.

When the coast was clear, Otto made his move, hobbling from one shadowy alcove to the next. He could sense the danger lurking around every corner, the tension in the air coiling tighter with each step he took.

An icy gust of wind tore through the empty hallway, making Otto shiver involuntarily as he pressed himself against the cold brick wall. The flickering light overhead cast eerie shadows on the floor, making the corridor feel like a haunted maze. He strained his ears to catch any sound that would betray the presence of MPs or hospital staff.

"Keep moving," Otto whispered, pushing off the wall and forcing his legs to carry him farther down the corridor. The sound of his footsteps echoed ominously, making his heart race even faster. He couldn't afford to be caught now, not when the stakes were so high.

"Did you hear something?" a distant voice asked suddenly, making Otto's blood run cold.

"Probably just the wind," another voice replied, but there was a note of uncertainty in the speaker's tone. "Let's check it out, just to be safe."

Otto cursed inwardly as he heard the unmistakable sound of approaching footsteps. With no other option, he slipped into a darkened room nearby, praying that it wouldn't be discovered.

"This way," one of the voices murmured, growing closer. "We need to find him before he gets far."

"Right, we'll search every room if we have to," the other agreed, determination lacing his words.

Otto held his breath, hoping against hope that they'd pass by without checking this particular room. As he listened to their footsteps draw nearer, he couldn't help but think of Shelle, the kind nurse who had treated him with such compassion, despite knowing his true identity. She had risked everything to warn him, and he couldn't let her sacrifice be in vain.

"Nothing here," one of them muttered after a cursory glance inside the room, and Otto breathed a silent sigh of relief as they continued down the hall.

"Thank you, Shelle," he whispered, his chest aching from the tension that had seized him moments before. He knew he needed to keep moving and make it outside, where the darkness would provide some cover for his escape.

As Otto neared the exit, he could hear the faint rumble of engines in the distance. His heart sank—the MPs were already here, searching for him. He peered out through the cracked door, trying to gauge the situation. A number of vehicles had pulled up, their headlights illuminating the grim faces of the armed soldiers as they piled out, ready to hunt down their quarry.

"All right, let's sweep the area," one of them barked, his voice hard and unyielding. "He couldn't have gotten far."

Otto knew he had to act now or risk being caught. Taking a deep breath, he mustered every ounce of strength he had left and forced himself through the door, desperately hoping that the shadows would conceal him from the watchful eyes of the MPs.

"Keep moving, Otto," he muttered under his breath, the cold wind biting at his face as he limped forward. "You can't stop now."

His chest tightened with every breath, and the pain radiating from his wounds threatened to overwhelm him. But he couldn't think about that now, not when his freedom—and his life—hung in the balance.

"Did you hear something?" a voice called out nearby, cutting through the silence like a knife. Otto's heart skipped a beat, and he instinctively ducked behind the nearest tree trunk, praying that the darkness would shield him from their prying eyes.

"I think it was just the wind," another voice replied, but the uncertainty in his tone made it clear that he wasn't convinced. "But we should check it out anyway, just to be safe."

"Right, fan out and search the area," the first voice ordered, and the sound of boots crunching on the frozen ground filled the air.

Please, God, don't let them find me, Otto thought, his muscles tensing as he prepared to bolt if necessary. He knew that capture would mean certain death, and he had come too far—and sacrificed too much—to surrender now.

"Clear over here!" one of the MPs called out after a tense few moments, and Otto exhaled in relief as they moved on. He took the opportunity to continue his escape, his mind racing with plans and contingencies.

Where will I go? he wondered, his thoughts shifting between memories of Aafke and the stern countenance of Skorzeny. *Will they ever stop hunting me?*

He couldn't answer those questions, not yet. All he knew was that he had to keep pushing forward, one painful step at a time. Sirens wailed in the distance, a chilling reminder of the dangers that lay just behind him.

Otto pressed onward, leaving the hospital—and his old life—farther behind with each labored stride. The searchlights cut through the night sky like vengeful ghosts, their piercing gaze sweeping across the barren landscape as if daring him to make one false move.

As the sirens grew fainter and the searchlights began to fade into the distance, Otto realized that he could no longer afford to dwell on such questions. He was a man on the run, with nothing but an uncertain future ahead of him.

But as long as he kept moving, as long as he clung to the memories of those he had loved and lost along the way, Otto knew that he still had a chance—however slim—at redemption. And that was enough to keep him going, despite the odds stacked against him.

Chapter 30

Banneling

Aafke's fingers trembled as she adjusted the fabric on her sewing machine, the incessant hum of needles piercing the air. Four months had passed, and her once-flat belly now swelled with life, making it increasingly difficult for her to maneuver around the cramped seamstress factory. The other women in the workshop cast sidelong glances at her but refused to speak; their silence weighed heavily on Aafke, a constant reminder of her status as a collaborator. She thought about the factory. How ironic that it was still in operation. The management had changed and the German foreman was gone, but besides that, the work remained the same, day after day. There were fewer hours she was required to work. A little more pay. A little more food available. Still, they were far better off under Allied occupation. They were free. There was no Gestapo, no arrests, no murders in the middle of the night.

The sun dipped low in the sky as Aafke made her way home, her swollen feet throbbing with each step. She tried to ignore the whispers and stares that followed her through the streets of Eindhoven, focusing instead on the delicate life within her—a life that deserved better than this.

Home. She dreaded heading there. She'd wanted to leave so badly that night and never come back. But with the news of Christiaan's death, her father had fallen into a deep depression. She was sure he would die without her, and so she had decided to stay, to not push the issue of him getting a job. She had kept up her labors at the factory, kept supporting both of them while trying to ignore the stares and the comments from coworkers and neighbors. She didn't know what else to do.

She thought of Otto. She hadn't heard from him since he'd left. He'd been so kind to her that day. So different from what Arno had done to her. But really, she hardly knew him and would likely never see him again. He was a wisp of compassion, a flicker of light that passed away in the darkness.

As she opened the door to her apartment, the stench of stale alcohol assaulted her nostrils. Her father slumped in his armchair, eyes glazed and unfocused, an empty bottle clutched in his hand and a framed picture of Christiaan in his lap. When he caught sight of Aafke, he gave her the slightest nod, then returned to staring at the wall.

"Look at you," he snarled, his words slurred by drink. "That belly sticking out bold as brass. The shame of it on this house."

Aafke drew in her breath. They'd been through this a hundred times. Some nights Maarten wouldn't bring it up at all. He would just sit there with his brandy and the picture of Christiaan, talking about his son and how their future would have been if he had survived the war. How Christiaan would have gotten the store back and saved them all. She let him rant like that, feeling her own guilt and pain at surviving while her brother was gone forever. Christiaan would never grow old, never get married or have his own chance to bring new life into the world. Because of him, she stayed. Because of her brother, she kept working, ignored her father's jabs and his failure to contribute. Besides, where would she go? She'd threatened to leave that first night, before the news of Christiaan's death, but it was an idle gesture. In truth, nobody would take in a collaborator. So now she tried to have patience with her father, knowing what he'd lost, what she'd lost.

"I don't know how many times I've told you, I didn't sleep with a German. I—" Aafke began, her voice wavering, but her father cut her off with a dismissive wave.

"Save your lies for someone who cares!" he spat. "I've been left here, alone, while you parade that bastard for all to see."

The room fell silent, save for the heavy breathing of her father and the pounding of Aafke's heart. She knew she couldn't change his mind, but she refused to accept his scorn as her own.

"Otto never touched me," she whispered, tears prickling at the corners of her eyes. "But it doesn't matter what I say. You've falsely condemned me."

Aafke's father sneered, his bloodshot eyes narrowing as he swayed precariously on his unsteady feet. "If you didn't sleep with that damned German, and this baby is Arno's, then why did he call you a collaborator? Why hasn't he come to see you all these months?"

Aafke clenched her fists, the anger and hurt welling up inside her like a storm. She wanted to scream, to deny everything, but she knew it would only fuel her father's rage. Instead, she took a deep breath and tried to steady her voice.

"Arno was wrong," she whispered, her voice barely audible. "He misunderstood, and I've been paying for it ever since."

Her father snorted derisively, his gaze flicking away from her face and down to her swollen belly. The contempt in his eyes was unmistakable, and Aafke felt the familiar sting of tears threatening to spill over.

"Wrong or not, he's left you here to deal with your shame alone," he spat, turning away from her.

As they argued, there was a knock at the door. Aafke's heart skipped a beat.

"Get the door, girl!" her father growled, sinking into the chair and reaching for a bottle on the floor beside him.

Trepidation gripped Aafke as she approached, her fingers shaking as she grasped the handle. When she pulled it open, there stood Arno, his thin frame casting a spindly shadow across the threshold.

"Arno," she said, stunned. Her voice was laced with disbelief and a hint of bitterness. Now that he was here, she didn't know how to react, what to say. "What are you doing here?"

"May I come in?" he asked, his eyes flicking nervously past her into the room.

"Of course," Aafke replied, stepping aside to let him enter. As he crossed the threshold, she felt the swirling emotions whipping through her. She wanted to hate him, for everything he'd done to her. But he was the father of this child.

"How are you doing?" Arno inquired, his gaze darting between Aafke and her visibly intoxicated father.

"Surviving," she answered, her voice strained as she fought to contain her emotions.

"Still working at the factory?"

"Yes."

He glanced down at her stomach and she saw the anger in his eyes. "I see you kept that thing of Otto's."

"It's not a 'thing,' Arno. And it's *your* child."

Arno looked at her for a long moment, his face a mix of bitterness and something else she couldn't quite identify. Then, taking a deep breath, he opened his mouth to speak.

Aafke's heart pounded in her chest as she held onto the hope that perhaps Arno had come to apologize, to accept their child and be a family once more. Instead, his expression darkened, and he shook his head slowly.

"Aafke, that's not why I'm here," he said, his voice heavy. Her stomach dropped, the flicker of hope snuffed out like a candle in the wind.

"Then why?" she demanded, her voice cracking. "Why are you here, after all this time?"

Arno glanced at her father, who slumped in a corner, his eyes glazed over from drink. "The resistance . . . they've made a decision about you, Aafke." He hesitated, swallowing hard before continuing. "You can no longer stay in Eindhoven."

"Why not?" Aafke's heart lodged in her throat, her hands instinctively moving to cradle her swollen belly protectively. "I haven't done anything wrong! I never helped the Germans!"

"Listen to me, Aafke," Arno implored, desperation creeping into his voice. "You have seven days to pass through the German lines and back into occupied territory. Maybe Amsterdam. It's your best chance for safety."

"Seven days?" Aafke felt sick, her world crumbling around her. "How am I supposed to do that? I'm four months pregnant, Arno! Don't you care about our child?"

"It's not my child!" Arno snapped, his face contorted with anger. "I've warned you. If you're found in Eindhoven after those seven days . . . I can't guarantee your safety."

"You don't even have any power anymore!" she snapped. "The Germans are gone. What do you think you're 'resisting' now?"

"Don't think the Allies will help you. They still have a war to win. They rely heavily on us to keep order. Trust me, Aafke, if you disappear, nobody is going to come looking for you."

"And you would order that?" she asked. "You'd let them kill me? After everything we've been through. I loved you, Arno. And you loved me."

She could see her words affected him. He flinched slightly

and his face grew pale. But then he stiffened and drew himself up, as if he was completing a speech he'd prepared. "That was then and this is now. You betrayed me with that German. Joelle says—"

"Oh, is it Joelle now? Is that it? I saw you holding her hand that day. Is that what this is really about, Arno? That you'd moved on already when I told you about the baby? That you were just looking for a way out?"

"There's no end to your lies," he said. "Look to your own actions. Joelle and I are together, that's true. But it was only after you betrayed me, betrayed our group, that it happened."

The words stunned her. So he was with Joelle after all. Why did she even care, after what he'd done to her? But this information stung more than the eviction, more than what he'd done to her on liberation day. Now she knew the truth about Arno, that he had been involved with Joelle. That he'd looked for an easy excuse to get out of the relationship. That he was willing to destroy her life, and the future of his own child, because he'd found a shiny new toy to play with.

"Well, at least I finally know what happened," she said.

"I told you. You don't know a thing."

"If you're with Joelle, fine. Why can't you just leave me alone? Look at my father. He's got nobody, nothing. He won't be able to make it without me."

"Bah," said Maarten, speaking for the first time since Arno arrived. "I'll be just fine without you. I've taken care of myself since this thing started. You've just thrown obstacles in my way. Get you gone. I'll be better off without the stigma of having a traitor and a German bastard in the house."

"See, even your father doesn't want you here. Do us all a favor, Aafke. You're a burden on this community. A reminder of the past. And your child will be more than that—a German child is spitting in everyone's face." He shook his head. "No, you must do what the resistance has ordered, and leave."

"Did you ever love me?" she asked, pain rattling through her voice.

He looked at her for long moments. "It doesn't matter what I might have felt about you. You proved who you are. Joelle understands me. She's a socialist too. Right now we're stuck with these British and Americans, but when they defeat the Germans they'll soon lose interest in us. This country is in tatters—industry broken, the monarchy fled. The people will rise and take what is theirs. I'm going to be a part of that, with Joelle at my side. And if we have a child together, it will be a child of the people, a socialist child."

"I always told you he was a communist nitwit," mumbled Maarten into his cup.

"And how am I supposed to get to Amsterdam?" she asked. "I've got no money, no way to get through the lines. I'm four months pregnant."

He looked down at her stomach again. "That's not my problem, or the people's problem. You're an enemy of the state, Aafke. You better get out of here and go try to find that shiny blond soldier you fancied so much. Maybe he will take care of you, although with the way the Germans are collapsing, I'm not sure there will be much left of it. Still, that's your problem, not mine. I've got a new nation to build, and you need to go hide with the rest of the rats and await your punishment."

She spit in his face. She couldn't stop herself. She thought she'd known this man, that he was her protector, that he loved her. But now she realized he'd always been there for himself. She was no more to him than a passing dalliance, something to keep him warm at night and distract him while he planned this broken future of his.

He slapped her hard across the face, without hesitation. She spun around, nearly falling.

"Now, now," mumbled Maarten. "Only a father has that right. Or a husband. Be on your way now."

Arno turned back to Aafke. It looked like he was going to say something else.

"Get out," said Aafke. "Get out and don't come back."

"Just make sure you're not here in seven days. I'll send my people to check."

"You'll never lay another hand on me. I promise you that."

"Just go, Aafke." With that, he turned and slammed the door behind him.

"Well, we're in a fine pickle now, girly," said Maarten. "What are we going to do?"

"We? You just told him you don't need me, that you're better off without me."

"Bah, you can't listen to everything I say. I was mad at the boy, and trying to speak up for you."

"You did nothing of the kind!" Aafke could feel the fury burning through her. "You took his side as you take everyone's side against me. So you can take care of yourself just fine, is it? We shall see. I'm not waiting seven days, Father. I'm leaving tonight."

"Now, now, don't get yourself in a fuss. We've got to think this through. That communist can't boss you around. Go to the Allies tomorrow and tell them what's happening," he said. "That's the ticket. They'll tell the resistance to back off. Then all will be right and well. And when you go to them, pick up another bottle won't you, my little broomstick? I'm running low."

"You're not listening to me. I'm not going to go fix everything just so you can be taken care of. I'm done with Arno and I'm done with you. You've insulted me my entire life. You hit me, you did nothing to help us, leaving me with every burden. I tried to leave before but Christiaan's death stopped me. I realize now that was a mistake. I'm leaving, Father. Goodbye."

"What are you saying, you crazy girl? Now don't make me angry, you're in enough trouble already." She had his attention now and she could see a touch of fear in his eyes. She felt sympathy for him, but she shoved it down.

"I'm not in any trouble. Not from you. Not anymore. I've had enough, and whatever is out there, it's better than what I've faced here." She turned and went into her bedroom, shoving a few possessions into a small suitcase. Her father stood at the door, watching her silently, not saying a thing. She dug around in a particular drawer until she found the roll of Reichsmarks Otto had given her. Useless in Allied territory, but perhaps helpful for her now. She stuffed it into the case and closed the latch. Her father was blocking the door.

"Move, Father."

"I'm not letting you go."

"Yes, you are. I told you, I'm leaving!"

"And I'm telling you that you'll stay and do as I say."

She started to move toward him again and he raised his hand.

Aafke sprinted forward, hitting her father with both fists in the chest like a battering ram. They crashed to the floor together. She pinned his arms to the ground with her knees and struck him in the face, first one time, then another, hitting him over and over. "You beat me!" she screamed. "You ran me down! I'm done with you! I'm done with you!"

"Aafke," he mumbled. "You'll get the beating of a lifetime when I get ahold of you."

She kept hitting him, her anger burning through her. Blow after blow. He tried to resist, to break free, but she kept his arms pinned to the ground and his body still.

Her father's nose was bloody and his eyes and cheeks were already swelling. "Stop it," he managed to mumble through thick lips. She had never felt more fury. If she'd had a knife or a gun in her hand, she knew she'd have used it. There was no sympathy now. Only her anger and a triumphant feeling she'd never experienced in her entire life.

Aafke pulled herself to her feet. Her hands were bloody and throbbing, but she didn't care. Ignoring the pain, she picked up her suitcase and started toward the door, looking down at her father again as she did so. Turning, she started toward the entrance.

"Aafke," she heard the words behind her. "Aafke. Please don't leave. You're all I've got left."

She turned at the door.

"Please don't go. What am I going to do without you?"

She stared at him for a moment.

"To hell with you," she said. Turning away, she walked through the door and out of the apartment, slamming the door behind her.

Chapter 31

Reünie

Tuesday, January 23, 1945
11:01 a.m.
Near Sint-Truiden, Belgium

The frigid wind whipped at Otto Berg's face, stinging his cheeks like a thousand needles. Pain radiated through his body, every step feeling as if it would be his last. The once-muscular former soccer star was now a shadow of his former self, weakened by hunger and exhaustion. Yet he forced himself to keep moving, knowing that the German lines were just a few miles away.

"Must . . . keep . . . going," he whispered, pressing on despite the throbbing pain in his leg from his infected wound.

As he trudged through the snow-laden forest, thoughts raced through his mind. For years, Otto had been a loyal soldier in the Waffen-SS, a believer in Germany's cause. But as the war raged on, he found himself questioning everything he held dear.

Was this really the right path? Otto asked himself, remembering the camaraderie he shared with his fellow soldiers. *Have I been fighting for the wrong cause?*

His memories took him back to his younger days when he first joined the Nazi party, swept up by their promises of a stronger Germany. But as the atrocities of war unfolded before his eyes, Otto's faith wavered.

Did we really have to go this far? Otto wondered, feeling the weight of disillusionment bearing down on him.

Despite his internal turmoil, Otto remained committed to his comrades, the bonds forged between them thicker than blood. They were his brothers-in-arms, and that loyalty was something he couldn't easily shake off.

As he pondered the dilemma that plagued his mind, Otto recalled the words of Otto Skorzeny, the charismatic and ambitious SS officer who had recruited him for increasingly dangerous missions.

Remember, Berg, Skorzeny had said, his scarred face etched with determination, *we are fighting not only for Germany, but for all of Europe. We must stand together as one.*

But Europe didn't want them, he realized. And for those who had, like the Ukrainians thrilled with their deliverance from the Soviet regime, they'd destroyed the good will with harshness and atrocity.

With each labored breath, he pushed onward, driven by both his loyalty to his comrades and the gnawing questions that haunted him. As the first light of dawn broke through the treetops, he had come upon American troops, dug in, facing the opposite direction. Working his way carefully along the tree line, he had found a gap between two companies. He would wait until nightfall, then thread the needle, eventually reaching German lines. He would have to be careful, with his American uniform. He could be killed by his own countrymen.

"Almost . . . there," he gasped, pain and exhaustion threatening to overwhelm him.

But even as he reached the edge of safety, Otto couldn't shake off the doubts that clouded his mind. Was his loyalty misplaced? Were they really fighting for the greater good?

"God help me," he whispered, gritting his teeth as he took another step forward, his body trembling from both cold and fear. "What have we become?"

Otto's thoughts shifted to Aafke, her image enveloping him like a warm embrace. He recalled the first time he had seen her, her golden hair cascading down her back, her blue eyes wide and filled with an inner fire. He remembered her resolute spirit, even in the face of adversity. He wondered where she was now. He'd had no contact with her for months. No way to know what had become of her.

"What if I don't go back?" he mused out loud. "Could I leave it all behind, for her?" Otto asked himself, feeling his resolve falter as he considered the consequences of such a choice. "To abandon my comrades, my country?" And if he did, would it even matter? Would she welcome him, or turn him over to the authorities?

Otto laughed, reaching up to touch the bandage over his eye. He was kidding himself. He'd never serve in the military again. His war was over. His choice now was to go back to Germany, and face the final collapse of his nation, or to go back for Aafke, who probably wanted nothing to do with him.

With a deep breath, Otto stepped off the beaten path, veering away from the German lines and toward Eindhoven. His heart raced as he crept through the dense forest, ducking behind trees and concealing himself in the underbrush to avoid detection by enemy patrols.

"Please, just let me get there safely," he prayed, his every step fraught with danger and uncertainty.

As he journeyed deeper into the heart of enemy territory, Otto found himself begging for food from wary farmers. Each morsel of bread, each sip of water, was a small victory—one that brought him closer to Aafke and farther from the life he had known.

"Is this madness?" he asked himself as he huddled in the shadows of an abandoned barn, the wind howling around him like a chorus of lost souls.

His body ached with exhaustion, but Otto refused to yield. He pressed on through the darkness, driven by the singular goal of seeing her again. Germany had failed him. At least Hitler had. All he had left were his comrades in arms, his mother, and this woman he hardly knew in Eindhoven.

As the days passed, the distance between Otto and Eindhoven shrank, while the specter of danger loomed ever larger. His once-robust frame was now gaunt and hollow, his eye sunken with fatigue, yet still, he pushed forward, his will refusing to waver.

In the frozen forest, Otto held his breath as a patrol of soldiers passed nearby. He was crouched behind a thick bush, his heartbeat threatening to give away his position. Every muscle in his body tensed, ready to flee at the slightest indication that he had been discovered. He closed his eyes and pictured Aafke's face, her gentle smile, and the softness of her touch.

Once the soldiers were gone, Otto moved cautiously through the woods. His progress was slow and arduous, but he knew that any misstep could be fatal. He scavenged for food, stealing what little he could from farms along the way, always careful never to linger too long.

Eventually, Otto found himself on the outskirts of Eindhoven. He looked down at his uniform. It was a bloodstained, tattered mess. If he entered the city like this, the first soldier who spotted him would detain him for questioning. He looked at the sun. It was still some hours before darkness. Despite his impatience, he decided to wait until nightfall before trying to enter the city.

While he waited, he peered into Eindhoven, gathering as much information as he could. There was a jeep at one intersection with a couple of soldiers. They were just sitting there, watching the traffic go by. There didn't seem to be any checkpoints. He did notice there was much more motor traffic than when the Germans had occupied the place. The people were being restored their freedoms. *So much for a united Europe under Germany*, he thought. The time ticked by. He was freezing, so he stomped his boots in the snow occasionally and slammed his hands together, trying to keep the circulation going. He had no food, but he slaked his thirst by consuming handfuls of snow now and again. Time seemed to be as frozen as he was, but eventually the sun set beyond the horizon and the sky dimmed.

When Otto judged it dark enough to escape attention, he shuffled forward. He was weak and his limbs were stiff, but he felt renewed energy as his goal was in reach. He passed into the city without incident and traced the streets from memory until he finally found himself standing outside Aafke's apartment building. Steeling himself, he entered and climbed the stairs, pausing for a moment at her front door before he knocked.

As the door creaked open, Otto's heart leaped into his throat. Aafke's father stood in the doorway, eyeing Otto with a mix of surprise and suspicion.

"Who are you?" he demanded, his voice slurred by alcohol.

"Um, my name is Otto Berg," he replied hesitantly, deciding to give his real name. "I met your daughter some time ago, before—" He paused, unsure of how much to reveal. "Before all this. I need to speak with her. It's important."

Aafke's father narrowed his eyes as he studied Otto. "I know you, and you're no American. What are you doing in that uniform, and what's your business here?"

"Sir, may I come in for a moment?" Otto asked.

Maarten hesitated, then opened the door further. Otto limped into the apartment. He was shocked by the condition inside. There were clothes everywhere. Plates filled the sink and the stale smell of tobacco and alcohol inundated the place. Otto stumbled over to one of the chairs and slumped down into it. He felt dizzy and had to steady himself with his hands on the table.

"Please, sir," Otto implored, desperation creeping into his voice. "I've come a very long way just to see Aafke. Is she here?"

"I asked you once. What's a German doing in an American uniform? And behind enemy lines? A pretty fix you've got yourself into! Don't tell me it's all on account of my little Aafke. Your wounds must have jarred your thinking."

Otto was having a difficult time keeping his balance. He'd drawn every last bit of his energy to get here. He'd gone without food for days. His wounds, particularly his leg, were burning. He worried he was losing consciousness. "Please, sir. If you can just bring Aafke to me."

Her father slumped down in a table across from him. "And why would I do that for you? What's in it for me? Do you have food? Money?"

Otto shook his head. "I haven't eaten in days."

"Bah!" Maarten exclaimed. "What use are you to me, then? Look around at this mess! This filth! We've no coal to heat the place. Hardly any food. Little to drink. And all your fault, you Germans. You took my boy from me too. You took Christiaan away forever. I ought to turn you into the police and be done with you!" He looked at Otto shrewdly. "Surely you've got something you could give me? A little something for the trouble."

Otto couldn't think of anything, and then it hit him. His father's watch. He looked down at it, the pain searing through his mind. It was the one thing of his father's that he had. He'd carried it since his mother gave it to him, kept it miraculously safe from harm through gunfire, explosions, cold and heat. But he wanted to see Aafke. He'd come this far. He carefully undid the clasp. "Here," he said. "I have this."

Maarten took the watch and looked it over, rotating it in the dim light. He whistled. "That's a fine piece," he said at last. "That should fetch a pretty price." He laughed. "And to think someone would turn this over just to see my little drowned rat. Oh you're a peculiar one, that's for sure."

"Will you bring her to me?" Otto asked.

"For this, certainly. But she's not close. Not close. In hiding she is. She's staying with someone else. But I know where. She doesn't think I know, but I know! Yes, give me a half hour, and I'll bring you to her. Great with that baby in her belly, but I suppose you know all about that," said Maarten, chuckling.

"What are you talking about? I know she's pregnant, yes, but so what?"

"Pregnant with your baby, isn't it?" asked Maarten with a wink.

"The baby isn't mine," said Otto. "I've never touched her."

"Hah! You're as bad as she is with your lies. Well, no matter, I'll be off, and I'll bring her back to you in just a little bit. Make yourself at home while I'm gone." He looked Otto over again. "A fine pair you two will be." With that, he turned and disappeared down the hallway, leaving Otto alone with his thoughts.

As he waited, Otto reached out a shaking hand and jiggled one of the bottles on the table. There was a little liquid in the bottom. Not even bothering to locate a glass, he lifted the bottle and drank the stuff down, coughing from the harsh burn in his throat. He wondered if he was doing more harm than good, but in a few moments the alcohol had an effect. He felt a little warmth creeping up his arms and down his legs. His vision cleared a little and the dizziness faded. Now he felt well enough to face Aafke.

What if she refused to see him? What if she had already

moved on and forgotten all about him? His stomach clenched with anxiety, and he found it difficult to breathe. He tried to focus on the sound of his own heartbeat, steady and strong despite the fear that threatened to consume him.

The door creaked open, and Maarten returned, followed swiftly by three more men. Otto was shocked to see Arno, followed by two others he didn't know. The thin man's eyes narrowed behind his glasses, and a scowl darkened his features. "You!" Arno shouted, drawing a pistol. His men did the same, each moving around the outside of the room until Otto was surrounded. "What the hell are you doing here?"

Otto looked at Maarten, who was smirking at him. He'd been set up, he realized. "So you don't know where she is after all?" he said.

"Oh we know where she is," said Arno, grinning. "We sent her back to the German bastards she's collaborated with. Weeks ago. She's probably up in Amsterdam, drunk at a bar, taking a German home a night as she used to do. Don't think for a second you're the only kraut she's been with."

"We were never together," said Otto. His mind reeled from what Arno was saying. Aafke was not here? Worse yet, she'd been sleeping with many German men during the war? How could that even be true when she'd told him she was with Arno? "I think you're lying," he said at last.

"I'm afraid that's the full truth, my German friend. She's had many of your comrades in her arms. But they're all gone now. More's the pity. Then who should fall into my hands at this late date but the biggest kraut of them all? The one who's been pining after her all this time? Back again, and in an American uniform as well." Arno whistled. "Our Allies wouldn't like that. They'd line you up against a wall for that action. But don't you worry, Otto. I won't let them have you. I have different plans for you."

"Where's Aafke?"

"You still want to know? Even after what I just told you? Well, it's all true. We sent her through the German lines a week ago. Maarten here will confirm it. She headed north. Probably to Amsterdam. You'd find her there in a bar. Pregnant as can be, pining after some SS officer or another. That is, if she didn't get rid of the baby."

"As she should have," said Maarten.

Otto started to rise but one of the men stepped forward, shoving him down.

"Where do you think you're going?" asked Arno.

"I'm going to Amsterdam."

Arno laughed. "I see what she liked in you," he said. "Your sense of humor. You're not going anywhere, my friend. I have plans for you."

"What plans?"

"Well, we're going to march you right out of town in a few hours, once it's late enough that we won't have any problems with our new soldier friends out there. I have a little cottage out there. Aafke knew it well. We spent plenty of time together in bed out there, before she developed a taste for Germans. I'm going to tie you to that very same bed, Otto. And then I'm going to start cutting little pieces off of you." Arno reached down with his empty hand and removed a knife. "This is my cutting knife," he said. "I've used it on a number of your friends, and now I'm going to use it on you."

Arno's face changed and he cocked his head. "You know what, Otto? I just realized something. I said *friends* a moment ago but in your case, it's really true. The last German I got ahold of was on liberation day. We pulled a car over at a road-block and pulled a little sniveling colonel out. Imagine my surprise to have captured Fritz Geier, head of the Gestapo for Eindhoven. Aafke told me you and he were friends. He's the last German I got to use my knife on. He lasted the whole night, Otto. But I bet I can make you last even longer, although

310 James D. Shipman

you're half finished off already. Don't worry, I'll take my time and make sure you get to relish every minute. Just so I have something to think about while we wait, would you like me to start with your fingers or your toes?"

"Arno, this is too much," said one of the men. "We should just turn him over to the authorities."

"Quiet, Peter. You know what they would do with him. A quick bullet. Hell, they might even let him talk his way out of it. This Otto is supposed to be some sort of commando. Not that he looks like much now. They might even keep him for his knowledge. No, I'm not letting him get off that easy. We've got unfinished business together, don't we, my boy?"

Otto upended the table in one motion, rising to his feet and rushing Arno. He slammed him into the wall, knocking him so hard against the wood that it cracked. He grabbed Arno by the throat with one hand and lifted him off the ground.

"Where is Aafke?"

Otto felt a thunderous explosion against the side of his head. He turned to see one of the men, pistol turned upside down and raised in the air. The man brought the pistol butt down again, smashing against his mouth. Otto collapsed backward, staggering. Warm metallic liquid filled his mouth. He reached out and grabbed the man by the chest, slamming him against Arno. Both of them tumbled onto the ground. He turned to the last man, Peter, whose pistol was still trained on him.

"Drop it!" commanded Otto.

Peter hesitated, then lowered his weapon.

Otto turned back toward Arno but out of the corner of his eye he saw Maarten rushing toward him. The man struck him hard on the head with a bottle. The glass shattered with the blow and Otto fell to his knees. Maarten picked up a chair and brought it down on Otto's head, knocking him to the ground. He blinked, staring up at the ceiling, the room spinning, then he passed out.

* * *

Otto opened his eyes in what seemed a moment later. He was lying on a bed. He tried to move but he realized his hands and feet were tied. His mouth was tightly gagged. Arno was standing over him, a knife in his hand. He had an ugly red welt on his cheek and his left eye was black.

"Good, you're awake," he said. "You're quite a customer to handle, my friend. After we knocked you out, I wanted to transport you to our little cottage in the woods but, my Lord, if you're not a mountain to move. So I decided we would just keep you here and take care of business. You'll be happy to know you're lying on Aafke's bed. That should be some comfort to you for what's to come. I have to say, I thought you were going to get the best of all of us there for a minute. And who would have thought that Maarten would come to my rescue?" Arno laughed. "It's always the little fellows you have to look out for. And the big ones, of course. But now back to business. You never answered me: Do you want me to start with the little fingers or the little toes?"

Otto closed his eyes, not answering. His mouth was on fire as was his leg. He steeled himself for what was to come. He tested the ropes on his hands and feet. There were tight and he couldn't feel any give. He was too weak in any event to break free. He'd used the last reserves of his energy to go after Arno. Whatever was about to happen, there was no stopping it. He thought of poor Fritz. He'd met his end in Eindhoven after all. And at the hands of this bastard. He thought of his comrades and his mother, whom he'd never see again.

Finally he thought of Aafke. He wondered where she was, if she was safe. How could she have ever been involved with this monster? As to the other things Arno had told him, he wouldn't think about those. She was a woman and had her right to her own choices—whatever the truth. Now he would never get the chance to ask her about it. He hoped she would be safe, that her baby would be born and bring her some happiness. He prayed she would never have to suffer another moment of tyranny from Arno, and that she would somehow, someday, have her revenge on him. The pain from his wounds was overwhelming him again. He was losing consciousness. He wondered if he would even awaken when Arno began . . .

Chapter 32

Verbergen

Wednesday, January 31, 1945
1:10 p.m.
Eindhoven, Netherlands

Aafke crouched in the darkness of the small, musty closet, her tense muscles aching from remaining motionless for hours. She could barely breathe as she strained to listen for footsteps approaching the house. The only light in the confined space came through the thin crack between the closet doors, casting eerie shadows on the wall. Aafke knew that she had to remain silent and still, no matter how much her limbs protested. One wrong move, one careless sound, and everything would come crashing down.

Remember, Aafke, Mrs. Smit had whispered to her when they first hid her away, *not a word, not a sound. They cannot find you here.* The fear in the older woman's eyes was enough to make Aafke's heart race, but she nodded solemnly, understanding the gravity of the situation.

Aafke had been hiding with Mrs. Smit ever since Arno had

ordered her out of Eindhoven. He had warned her that it was too dangerous to stay; she had to go to Amsterdam, which was still under the oppressive grip of German occupation. But even in that city, there was no guarantee of safety. Aafke was labeled a collaborator now, and her former ties to the resistance had made her even more of a target, because the resistance leaders feared one of their members telling everything they knew to the Germans.

Aafke had left the very night that Arno gave her notice. She had walked the streets of Eindhoven, gathering her thoughts. She had been trying to figure out how she would even get to Amsterdam, how she would cross enemy lines, when she'd run across Mrs. Smit on the street. She'd never liked the woman, and when the old shrew had inquired about what she was doing in the old neighborhood, Aafke had surprised herself by telling the whole story. She was even more surprised when Mrs. Smit offered to hide her in Eindhoven. *I never liked that Arno*, she had said. *Never trusted him a bit. And the less said about your father the better.* She'd gone home with her new benefactor, and they'd carved out a hiding place for her that very night. Aafke was sure that this was some kind of joke. That the resistance would show up immediately and escort her to the border. But nothing had happened. Not that life was pleasant as she had little food and was forced to spend the entire day and most of the night in the cramped closet.

Why was she staying? She didn't even know. Her father had turned on her and so had the man she thought would be her husband. Worse, her entire people had turned against her. Still, she was Dutch, and this was her home. And she hated the Germans. She could never flee from the Allies and back into their hands, no matter what everyone thought of her. She hated all of them except Otto. Her thoughts turned to the giant again. Where was he? Was he still alive? Was she thinking of him? She shook her head. Why bother even considering him? She'd spent a few hours with him. She knew nothing about him. But that wasn't quite true either. He'd gallantly refused to go to her bed. And when she'd been beaten and abused as an alleged collaborator, he'd come to her rescue. No, she knew a lot about Otto, in fact. He was just the kind of man she'd always dreamed of. The kind of man she thought that Arno was.

Arno. She couldn't help but think about him. What had happened in their relationship? He'd sought her out for so long, even before the war. She'd always ignored him. What interest would she have in a frumpy little socialist ten years her senior? But he'd protected her, helped her, when her father had abandoned reason and turned to the bottle. He'd fought for her future, for the store. He'd led her on her first grand adventure out in the farmlands to seek black-market goods. When he'd returned from captivity, after three years, he'd sought her out and brought her into the resistance, giving her a chance to fight back, to do something for her country.

But then he'd changed. He'd pushed her to be intimate against her dearly held beliefs. When she'd given into that, instead of becoming closer, kinder, he'd become distant, quick to anger. She began to notice his wandering eye, first with strangers, and then with Joelle. Then, worst of all, he'd repeated the sins of her father, striking her, abusing her. Finally, when she'd become pregnant with his child, he'd denied her, and worst of all, labeled her an enemy of her own people.

Now, as she sat in the darkness, she realized that Arno hadn't changed. He was always the same person. She'd been nothing but prey for him. A shiny object he desired that seemed out of reach. He'd pursued her until she was his, and then slowly, over time, he'd lost interest and began looking for a new adventure. He'd found new comfort in Joelle's arms, at least for the time being, until he would likely grow tired of her as well.

She heard something. Aafke's heart pounded in her chest as she strained to listen for any sounds outside the closet. The air was stale and heavy, making it difficult to breathe. She could feel the rough texture of the wooden floor beneath her, the cold seeping through her thin dress. Every creak of the floorboards sent a jolt of fear through her. But the minutes passed and there were no more noises. She had imagined whatever it was.

As time dragged on, Aafke found herself succumbing to the weight of her own thoughts. Hours dragged by. It was in that moment of vulnerability that she heard footsteps approaching. These were real noises, not something her mind created, and they were coming rapidly toward her. Panic seized her as she held her breath, feeling the walls of the closet close in around her.

The door swung open, revealing Joelle. Aafke was shocked. What was she doing here? Her black hair was disheveled, framing an expression that was both determined and resentful. In her hand, she gripped a pistol, its barrel gleaming ominously in the dim light.

"Get up," Joelle snarled, gesturing with the gun. "Arno wants to see you."

"Joelle, what are you doing?" Aafke asked, her voice trembling as she slowly rose to her feet. The betrayal in Joelle's eyes was unmistakable, and so was the anger that fueled it.

"Did you think we didn't know where you were?" Joelle spat. "You were followed the very night you left. Arno's known all along exactly where you were. He was biding his time to decide what to do with you. But something came up tonight. Something too good to be true. He's got Otto, and he ordered me to come get you."

"Get me for what?"

"To watch."

"Joelle, please," Aafke whispered, desperation creeping into her voice. "You don't have to do this. We're on the same side."

"Are we?" Joelle's eyes narrowed, the bitterness in her voice unmistakable. "You were always Arno's favorite, weren't you?

I put up with that for years. But that's over now. Now it's my turn to be in his favor. My turn to have what's coming to me."

"Joelle, listen to me," Aafke pleaded, searching for a shred of empathy in her former comrade's gaze. "Arno is not who you think he is. He's using you, just like he used me."

"Shut up!" Joelle hissed, her finger tightening on the trigger. "You don't know anything about him or what he's been through. You just want to save yourself."

Aafke knew that she had to make a choice. She could either submit to Joelle and face the torture that awaited her, or fight back and seize control of her own destiny. As the weight of her decision loomed, she could feel the fire of determination ignite within her.

"Fine," Aafke said, raising her hands in surrender. "Take me to Arno. But remember this, Joelle: the truth will come out eventually. And when it does, you'll have to live with the consequences."

Joelle's eyes flashed with uncertainty for a moment before she hardened her resolve. Gripping the pistol firmly, she led Aafke out of the closet and into the unknown.

Aafke's heart pounded in her chest as she scanned the room for anything that could be used to her advantage.

Joelle, with her pistol still trained on Aafke, moved closer, and Aafke knew she had only one chance to save herself and Otto. She couldn't let Joelle take her to Arno; the consequences would be too severe.

"Joelle, think about what you're doing," Aafke said, trying to buy herself a few more seconds to formulate a plan. "You don't have to do this."

"Shut up, Aafke!" Joelle snapped, her eyes cold and unyielding. "It's too late for that. Now move!"

As they approached the door, Aafke noticed a wooden coat-rack standing by the entrance. She remembered how Arno had taught her to use everyday objects as weapons during their time together. It was a long shot, but it was her only chance.

"Please, Joelle," Aafke pleaded once more, forcing her voice to tremble with fear. "Don't do this."

"Enough!" Joelle growled, pushing Aafke forward. "I've made up my mind."

Aafke stumbled toward the door, feigning weakness. Her hand brushed against the coatrack, and she grabbed hold of it, swinging it toward Joelle with all her strength. The improvised weapon connected with Joelle's wrist, causing her to cry out in pain and drop the pistol.

"Damn you, Aafke!" Joelle hissed, clutching her injured arm. But she didn't relent, lunging at Aafke with surprising speed.

Aafke sidestepped, narrowly avoiding Joelle's grasp and using her own momentum against her. Joelle crashed into the wall, momentarily disoriented. Aafke seized the opportunity, scooping up the pistol from the floor and pointing it at Joelle.

"Stay back," Aafke warned, her voice steady despite the adrenaline coursing through her veins.

"Or what?" Joelle sneered, slowly rising to her feet. "You won't shoot me, Aafke. You don't have it in you."

Aafke's finger hovered over the trigger, but she hesitated; she didn't want to kill Joelle, even after everything that had happened. Instead, she focused on the bigger picture: saving Otto and escaping Eindhoven. With a deep breath, she made her decision.

"Maybe I won't," Aafke said, lowering the pistol. "But I will do whatever it takes to protect the people I care about. And if that means fighting against you, then so be it."

Joelle stared at her for a long moment before finally nodding, her expression a mix of rage and resignation. Aafke led Joelle to a chair at the kitchen table and sat her down. Finding some nearby linens, and keeping her pistol nearby, she tore the fabric into long strips. Using the makeshift rope, she tied Joelle's hands to the back of the chair. She was pulling up Joelle's sleeve when she came across a series of bruises up and down her arms, the clear sign of fingers that had grasped too tightly.

"So he's started on you also, hasn't he?"

Joelle stiffened. "I don't know what you mean."

"Yes, you do. Arno's been violent with you."

"It was only once. He was drunk. I was mouthing off."

"There's always an excuse but it will never be once. Joelle, look at me." Her former resistance comrade looked up at her, her face a mix of anger and humiliation. "He's never going to stop. You don't deserve it. Why don't you go with me and help me? Arno wants to kill an innocent man."

"Innocent!" spat Joelle. "You truly are a collaborator. The man's a Nazi, Aafke, a member of the SS. He was friends with Fritz Geier, the monster responsible for killing Maaike and so many of our other friends. They single-handedly took all the Jews out of Eindhoven for no reason at all. These weren't criminals, Aafke, they were just people. Store owners, factory workers, friends. They'd done nothing other than to be part of another race, another religion. And they're gone, Aafke. They're all gone. Your friend Otto is part of that organization. And there's nothing you can ever do to change that. Nor can he. He's a long way from innocent. I don't know how you became so twisted. We're the victims here."

"You're a victim, all right," said Aafke, touching the bruises on her arm again. "But not of Otto. Listen to me, Joelle, and listen closely. I never slept with Otto. I never helped the Germans. Not one time. I was devoted to the resistance, to our cause, as you were. Arno used all of this, including your suspicions, to get me out of the way. Joelle, this child is Arno's, but he didn't want it. Didn't even want the inconvenience of dealing with me any longer. So he took the opportunity you presented him to blame Otto and label me a traitor. He'd grown tired of me. He didn't want me anymore. He's going to do the same thing to you someday. Perhaps someday soon. Don't let him! Stand up to him now. Today! Go with me and help me free Otto. After that, I don't care what happens. But I can't be responsible for that man's death. Not at the hands of Arno."

"You're deluded," Joelle said, although without much conviction. "You might as well shoot me. Because if you don't, I'll get free of these and then I'm coming after you. Me and Arno."

"I won't kill you, Joelle. I know that's what you expect of me, but you are wrong. You've always been wrong. I was never your enemy. You wanted to make it so from the day I met you, I guess because you were harboring feelings for Arno, even then. But for my part, I never was against you. You'll get out of this just fine. You'll escape yourself or Mrs. Smit will return from wherever she's gone and release you. When that happens, I wish you the best. For happiness. And I pray you get away from Arno before it's too late. Before he destroys your life as he has ruined mine."

Aafke poured a cup of water from the sink and placed it in front of Joelle. She took a half loaf of bread and placed it on a plate next to the water. "There you go," she said. "You won't starve or die of thirst while you wait. Sorry I can't release your hands, but you'll manage. Truly, Joelle, I wish you the best. Think about what I said about Arno. His hitting got worse and worse with me, until I thought he might kill me someday. He's going to do the same to you, and there's nothing you can say, or do, or apologize for, to stop him. He's the monster, Joelle, not Otto." Aafke turned and walked out of the apartment, closing the door behind her.

Aafke stepped into the hallway, her heart pounding in her chest. The wallpapered walls felt as if they were closing in on her, and the silence that enveloped the house seemed to mock her desperate situation. She knew she had little time to act;

every second passing could be the last that Otto would have on this earth.

"Think, Aafke," she whispered, gripping the pistol tightly. Aafke silently crept down the stairs, her senses heightened by fear and adrenaline. Each creak of the floorboards sent a shiver down her spine, and she found herself holding her breath, straining to hear any sign of danger. She knew that Eindhoven was teeming with resistance members who might be on the lookout for her. She couldn't afford to make a mistake.

She considered her options carefully, knowing that the wrong choice could be fatal. She would make her way to her apartment building, taking backstreets and alleyways to avoid detection. Once there, she would use the pistol to force her way inside, relying on the element of surprise to overcome any resistance. She would free Otto, and together, they would flee Eindhoven, using the chaos of their escape as a cover.

"All right," Aafke whispered, steeling herself for the perilous journey ahead. "Let's do this."

Aafke stepped into the chilly night air. The darkness wrapped around her like a cloak, both concealing and threatening her. She knew that every step she took brought her closer to danger, but she refused to be deterred. Otto's life—and her own—hung in the balance, and she would not let fear dictate her actions. "Stay focused," Aafke told herself, navigating the shadowy streets with unwavering resolve. "One step at a time."

The streets of Eindhoven, though dark and deserted, still teemed with danger. "Keep moving," Aafke whispered, her breath frosting in the cold air. "Stay low. Stay quiet." As she moved closer to her building, Aafke went over her plan again and again in her mind, refining it, searching for any flaws. She knew that the slightest misstep could lead to disaster, but she refused to be paralyzed by fear. Instead, she focused on her determination to save Otto—and herself—from the clutches of Arno.

Aafke paused in a shadowy alley, her heart pounding in her chest as she caught sight of the building. It loomed before her like an ominous fortress, its dark windows watching her every move. Might Arno have posted sentries to keep an eye out for her and Joelle? She had to trust her luck and hope she could slip into the building unseen by any of his men. She took a deep breath, steeling herself for what lay ahead, and made her decision.

"All right, Otto," she murmured, her voice barely audible. "I'm coming for you."

Chapter 33
Confrontatie

Wednesday, January 31, 1945
5:31 p.m.
Eindhoven, Netherlands

Aafke's heart pounded in her chest as she approached her apartment, the glow of a single streetlamp casting eerie shadows on the cobblestone pathway. The air was thick with tension, and she could sense danger lurking just beneath the surface. She steeled herself for what lay ahead.

As she turned the corner at the top of the interior steps, she spotted a man standing directly in front of her door. It was Mikel, a lumbering brute of a man who Arno occasionally used for operations he thought might turn violent. Without pausing to think, she sprinted toward him, closing the distance even as his head started to turn toward her. She struck him hard in the head with the butt of her pistol, sending him crashing to the ground, unconscious. The thrill of adrenaline coursed through her veins, but there was no time to revel in her victory.

"Sorry, Mikel," she whispered, stepping over his prone form

and slipping into the apartment. "But I've got more important matters to attend to."

Reaching into her coat, she removed a key and fit it into the hole. Turning the handle slowly, she unlocked the door and pushed as gently as she could, until she could just see inside. The room was shrouded in darkness, but Aafke's keen senses quickly adjusted to her surroundings. The first thing she saw was her father slumped over the kitchen table, his drunken snores providing a macabre soundtrack to the scene. A wave of disgust washed over her, but she pushed it aside—for more pressing concerns.

She heard voices coming out of her bedroom. "Arno, we can't do this!" Peter's voice carried from down the hallway, hoarse and desperate. "We can't allow ourselves to become like them. I told you this last time and I'm telling you again: We should turn him in to the authorities. They will know what to do."

"Are you mad?" Arno's response was ice cold, dripping with disdain. "That Nazi scum deserves every ounce of pain we can inflict upon him. I'll see to that myself, just like I took care of Geier. But this time, I'm going to enjoy it."

Aafke's stomach churned at the thought of Otto being subjected to Arno's twisted idea of justice. And she knew this was her fault, that Otto was here because he had gone out of his way to help her, to make sure she was all right.

With her heart pounding, Aafke burst into her bedroom, the door slamming against the wall. The scene that greeted her was straight out of a nightmare: Arno and Peter loomed over Otto, who lay unconscious on the bed, his wrists and ankles bound tightly to the wooden frame. There was blood all over his mouth. Sweat glistened on his pale forehead, each shallow breath a testament to his pain.

"Get away from him!" Aafke shouted, leveling her pistol at Arno. He glanced at her, startled, his fingers tightening around the hilt of the knife in his hand.

"Whoa, Aafke, what are you doing?" Peter asked, raising his hands in surrender.

"Let him go, Arno," she demanded, her voice shaking slightly. She couldn't let them see her fear—not now when Otto's life hung in the balance.

"Are you insane?" Arno spat, his eyes narrowing behind his glasses. "This is the enemy! We can't just—"

"Untie him, or I swear I'll shoot you," Aafke interrupted, her finger twitching on the trigger. In that moment, she truly meant it—for Otto. She owed him this much.

"You've lost your mind, Aafke," Arno said, his voice dripping with scorn as he eyed the gun she held steadily in her hand. The rage in his eyes was palpable, and it sent a shiver down her spine.

"Arno, I know what I'm doing," she replied, trying to keep her voice steady despite her racing heart. Her knuckles were white on the grip of the revolver, but she refused to let her resolve waver.

"Clearly not! This man is a Nazi, our enemy!" Arno gestured toward Otto's unconscious form. "He would have killed any one of us without a second thought!"

"War isn't that simple, Arno," Aafke retorted, her blue eyes flashing with determination. "He's just another soldier, caught up in something bigger than all of us."

"Really? And how do you know that?"

"Because I've seen it in him," she answered, her voice barely more than a whisper. "I've seen the conflict in his eyes, the way he questions his orders—the choices he's made. The way he went out of his way to make sure I was okay. Even when you stopped caring. When you abandoned me."

"Even if that's true," Arno said, his face contorting with anger, "he's still on their side. He'll always be a part of the machine that has destroyed so many lives."

A heavy silence hung over the room like a thick fog, broken only by the creaking of floorboards under Arno's shifting weight. His eyes scanned the scene before him—Otto's battered body, Aafke's determined stance—and then narrowed suspiciously.

"Where's Joelle?" he asked, his voice low and venomous.

Aafke hesitated for a moment, her grip tightening on the gun. "I tied her up at Mrs. Smit's apartment," she admitted, her voice wavering slightly. "She wanted to bring me to you, but I couldn't let her do that."

"Of course," Arno sneered, his disdain dripping from every syllable. "Joelle's too weak and sentimental to be of any use. Women are useless. But think! You wanted me to believe that Otto wasn't with you? Now is your chance! We have this bastard in our hands. Leave me to it and I'll let you walk out of here. I'll get the word out that we were wrong about you. That you're not a collaborator. You can stay in Eindhoven. You can have that baby here. Who knows, if you give the thing up after you have it, perhaps we could even be together again someday."

The hurt in Aafke's eyes was eclipsed by anger as she glared at Arno. "You must be mad, Arno! I'm done with you. I loved you. I wanted to marry you, despite what you'd done to me. I wanted to bring your child into this world, for us together. Instead, you denied me out of convenience. You destroyed my life, simply because you were bored with me. I'll never come back to you."

"So be it," said Arno, stepping closer to Aafke. The shadows cast by the flickering candlelight danced across his face, turning his features into a twisted mask of rage. "You really are a fool, aren't you?"

"Get away from me," Aafke warned, her voice shaking with fear as well as fury.

"Or what?" Arno taunted, inches from her face now. "You'll shoot me? Go ahead, then. Prove just how far you're willing to go for some Nazi who has done nothing but bring pain and suffering to our people. With every moment you prove more and more that he is the father—that you betrayed us all."

Aafke's finger twitched on the trigger, her heart pounding like a drum inside her chest. She knew that Arno was trying to provoke her, to push her over the edge and make her question her own morality. But as she stared into his cold, unfeeling eyes, she couldn't help but wonder if he was right—if saving Otto was truly worth all of this.

"Enough!" Arno roared, lunging forward with surprising speed. Aafke's heart skipped a beat as his hand closed around her wrist, wrenching the gun from her grasp. It clattered to the floor, echoing through the room. He crashed down on top of her. His weight was heavy on her, as he scrambled to retrieve the pistol and held it to her head.

"Well," he said. "It's been a long time since we've been like this, hasn't it? Too bad you have that bastard in your belly, or I might let you have one last thrill."

"Arno, leave her alone!" demanded Peter. His face was pale, but his voice held a note of determination. "You're letting your anger cloud your judgment. This isn't the way."

"Stay out of this, Peter," Arno snarled. "Get out of here for a minute."

"Please, Arno," Peter implored. "Don't do something you'll regret!" He reached down and grabbed Arno's arm, starting to pull him off of Aafke.

"Too late for that," Arno growled, and without another word, he pulled the trigger.

The gunshot rang out like a thunderclap, reverberating through the room. Peter staggered backward, blood blossoming across his chest as shock painted his face. Aafke's heart seemed to stop entirely as she watched him crumple to the floor, her mind unable to process the horror unfolding before her.

"Peter!" she screamed, her voice choked with disbelief and anguish. "No!"

"His blood is on your hands, Aafke," Arno sneered, his tone devoid of remorse. "You chose this path—now live with the consequences."

The acrid scent of gunfire hung heavy in the air, mingling with the metallic tang of blood as Aafke lay unable to move, her gaze locked on Peter's lifeless body. The cold, unforgiving steel of Arno's gun pressed against her temple, a chilling reminder of the danger she still faced.

"Well, my dear, that shot is going to bring too much attention from your neighbors, I'm afraid. It looks like I'm not going to have time to give your lover a proper send-off. I'm going to have to expedite things. But first, I'll take care of you." He pressed the barrel harder against her temple.

Aafke squeezed her eyes shut, preparing for the inevitable, when the sound of splintering wood echoed through the room. She opened her eyes to see Joelle burst through the doorway, her face flushed with anger and determination. In her hand, a gun glinted menacingly.

"Get away from her!" Joelle bellowed, leveling her weapon at Arno. He faltered, turning toward the unexpected threat.

"Joelle?" Arno's voice wavered with disbelief. "What are you doing? We've got her. Let's finish this!"

"I heard what you said about me a moment ago, you bastard. So, I'm weak, am I? Aafke told me I was just another plaything for you. I didn't want to believe it, but after what I just heard . . ."

"Joelle, please," Arno begged, his eyes darting between the two women. "We can talk about this—"

"Talk? Like you talked with Peter?" Joelle's voice trembled with rage. "No more talking."

Aafke grabbed the barrel of Arno's gun and shoved it away. A shot rang by her head; her ears exploded from the pain but she kept her hold on the steel. She lashed out with her legs, kneeing Arno in the back. He fell off-balance and she rolled with him, both of them hitting the floor on their sides. Aafke slammed the pistol hard on the ground and pulled it away from him. She grasped the trigger and aimed.

The gunshot rang out like a death knell, echoing through the small room. Arno crumpled to the floor, his lifeless eyes staring up at the ceiling, accusation etched on his face even in death as his arms and legs kicked spasmodically in their death throes.

"Aafke," Joelle whispered, her voice barely audible, "What have you done?"

"Survived," Aafke replied, as she turned toward Otto, still unconscious and bound to the bed. "But we need to move quickly." The weight of their actions pressed down upon her like a leaden shroud. She forced herself to focus on the task at hand, her hands shaking as she untied the knots binding Otto's wrists. "Damn it," she muttered under her breath, struggling with the tight restraints. "These knots are too tight."

"Here," Joelle said, handing her a small knife. "Cut them. But hurry. The authorities must be on their way!"

As Aafke sliced through the ropes, Joelle kept watch at the doorway, her grip on the gun firm and steady. Her eyes scanned the hallway outside, alert for any signs of danger.

"Got it," Aafke announced, finally freeing Otto from his bonds. His chest rose and fell weakly, his bruised face a testament to the pain he had endured.

"Good," Joelle said tersely. "Now let's get out of here before anyone else shows up."

Together, they attempted to carry the unconscious Otto between them, their movements fueled by urgency and desperation. The echoes of gunfire still rang in their ears. They managed to drag him into the kitchen before they were forced to lay him down, their breath coming in gasps. Aafke looked up and saw her father was still passed out at the table, having slept through the whole thing.

"What are we going to do?" asked Joelle. "We'll never get him out of here in time."

"I don't know," said Aafke. "Give me a moment to think and catch my breath."

Otto's eyelids fluttered open, and he locked gazes with Aafke. "Thank God," Otto rasped, his voice barely above a whisper. "Aafke . . . you're alive."

"Of course I am," Aafke replied, her voice trembling but determined. "I couldn't leave you here."

Otto tried to sit up but winced, his muscles protesting the movement. Aafke placed a steadying hand on his chest, urging him to remain still.

"Listen to me, Otto," Aafke said urgently. "We're in danger. We have to leave now."

"Can you walk?" Joelle asked, her voice echoing Aafke's urgency.

Otto gritted his teeth and pushed himself into a sitting position. "Yes," he managed, his voice strained. "I'll walk." It took him several attempts, but eventually with Aafke's and Joelle's arms under him, he fumbled to his feet. As they hobbled toward the door, the apartment seemed to close in around them—a suffocating reminder of the horrors they'd endured.

"Where are we going?" Otto asked as they shuffled toward the door.

"Somewhere safe," Aafke answered, her voice determined. "We'll figure it out as we go."

"Be careful," Joelle warned, peering down the hallway as they emerged from the apartment. "There could be more of them."

"More?" asked Otto.

"Arno had friends," Aafke explained, her words laced with bitterness. "More members of the resistance. They could be out there somewhere, waiting, or they could be on their way."

"Keep moving," Joelle urged, her eyes scanning their surroundings for any sign of danger. "Time is running out."

As they stumbled through the corridor, their footsteps echoing ominously in the silence, Aafke couldn't help but wonder if they'd ever truly escape the shadows that haunted them. But with Joelle and Otto by her side, she found the strength to keep moving—one step at a time, toward whatever uncertain future awaited them.

The sound of sirens pierced the air, shattering the silence that had cloaked Aafke, Otto, and Joelle as they made their way through the corridor. The wail grew louder with each passing second, sending a chill down Aafke's spine as she realized the police were closing in on them.

"Damn it," Joelle cursed under her breath, her eyes wide with fear. "We need to move faster."

"Otto, can you?" Aafke asked, her voice laced with concern as she glanced at the injured man beside her.

"*Ja*, I can manage," he replied, gritting his teeth against the pain.

"Good. We don't have much time," she whispered, her heart pounding in her chest like a drum. She knew they needed to find a way out—and fast.

As they hurried along, the sirens seemed to grow closer and closer, bearing down on them like a pack of wolves. Aafke could almost feel the police cars screeching to a halt outside the building, officers pouring out with weapons drawn, ready to hunt them down.

"Where do we go?" Otto gasped, his face pale from exhaustion and pain.

"Think, Aafke, think," she muttered to herself, her mind racing for a solution. She knew the city well, but escape routes were limited, especially with the police on their tail. It was as if the walls were closing in, suffocating them in an inescapable trap.

"I can get us away from the police, but we've got to get out of this damned building first. Keep moving," Joelle urged, her voice barely audible over the sound of rushing water. "We're not safe until we're out of here."

They passed into the hallway and stumbled past Mikel, who

was still knocked out on the floor. They eventually reached the stairwell and started moving down it. But if the hallway was difficult, the stairs were impossible. Otto made it down the first couple of steps and then collapsed, falling hard on this back.

"I need a moment," he said.

Aafke could hear the sirens growing ever closer. "Otto, we have to go."

He looked up at her and smiled. "You go," he said.

"What do you mean?"

"You've already saved me, Aafke. Let the police take me to the Americans."

"But you're in an American uniform. They'll kill you for it."

"So be it. But I don't think so." He laughed, coughing up a little blood. "They aren't the Gestapo. And they'll get me the medical treatment I need. I've done what I came here to do. I made sure you're safe. Now you need to go before you're accused of these murders."

"He's right," said Joelle. "Listen to him, Aafke. We did what we came here to do: We saved him from Arno. And I paid my debt to you. You were right, by the way. Right about him. A few hours ago I was still struggling with the truth. But when I was stuck there, tied up with nothing to occupy my time, I couldn't get your words out of my mind. I kept staring down at those bruises and thinking about everything he'd done to me. Well, he won't do that to another woman again."

"Thank you for coming for me," said Aafke.

"We saved each other. And we saved this big oaf as well. But we can't help him any further."

"She's right, Aafke. Just go. If I survive somehow, I'll come and find you, if you want me to."

Tears were running down Aafke's face. "I don't want to leave you," she said.

"But you must."

"Let's go!" shouted Joelle, her head cocked to listen to the sirens. "They're almost here."

Aafke took Otto's hands in hers and gave them a squeeze. "Survive, Otto. Tell them anything they want, but you survive." With that she rose and followed Joelle down the stairs, moving as fast as they could. They reached the door in a few moments and Joelle peeked her head out the front door.

"It's clear still!" she shouted. "Let's go!"

But Aafke couldn't. Otto had come back to Eindhoven to find her. She thought back on all the times he had checked on her. A woman he knew nothing about. Even during the liberation when her hair was shorn, and she was beaten and bruised, pregnant with another man's child, he had been there for her.

"I'm going back," she said at last.

"Are you mad?"

"No. I'm seeing clearer than I ever have."

Joelle stared at her for a moment. "Well, I'm leaving."

"You should. Get out of here before the police arrive."

She threw her arms around Aafke, giving her a squeeze. "Fair travels," she said. "Wherever you're going."

"You too, Joelle. I wish we could have been friends."

"We are."

As Joelle ran outside and down the street, Aafke returned to the building and moved up the stairs to Otto. When she reached him, his eyes were closed and he was snoring loudly. How could he sleep at a time like this? She nudged him and he opened his eyes.

"Aafke. You're supposed to have made your escape!"

"I couldn't leave you."

"You should have. The police will be here soon. I can handle this."

"There are two dead Dutchmen upstairs, a knocked-out one, and you're wearing an enemy uniform. You're a member of the SS. I'm not sure you *can* handle this."

"We'll see." He took her hand and closed his eyes again. "You know," he said, smiling, "I've wanted to hold your hand for five years now."

Her eyes welled up again. Who was this man? "Otto, you're so kind. But you don't want me. I'm pregnant with another man's child. I've lured Germans, men like you, to their death for the resistance. We are enemies."

He shook his head. "War is war," he said. "You must do what it takes to survive."

"But the baby—"

"*Our* baby. If I survive this, it's our baby from now on."

"But where will we go? What will we do?"

"I'll stay with you here. In Eindhoven. I'll help you take care of your father."

She thought about that for a moment. "No," she said. "There's nothing for me here now." She heard shouting below and rapid feet moving toward the stairs. "They're coming."

Otto closed his eyes. "Let them come. I'm ready to tell my story." He held her hand tightly and closed his eyes again. "Let them come."

Chapter 34

Toekomst

Wednesday, February 7, 1945
2:07 p.m.
Near Liege, Belgium

The biting cold was the first thing Otto noticed as he and Aafke were marched through the snow-covered grounds of the American army compound. The wind sliced through his tattered clothes, chilling him to the bone. He could only imagine how Aafke felt, shivering beside him, her blond hair whipping around her face like a banner of defiance.

They'd spent a week in an Eindhoven jail, segregated and without the chance to talk to each other. Otto had received medical treatment for his wounds. There was a point where the visiting doctor had considered transferring him to a hospital, and perhaps even surgery. But the infections had passed and ultimately those actions were unnecessary. At the end of the week, an American unit had come and transported both of them in the back of a truck. They'd been allowed to sit next to each other, but they couldn't talk. Otto was just grateful for the time to hold Aafke's hand and sit with her. The trip took several hours, and there was a peace about their time together that he'd never felt during the war. He wondered if it was truly going to be the beginning of peace for both of them, or if they were merely in the eye of the storm. After a long and jostling trip, they arrived at an American army base built in an open field. There were several tanks placed strategically at the entrance, and within the compound a number of tents spread out near some buildings that looked like they might have been former barracks for the Dutch military. They were led out of the truck and into the compound. Otto paused as they were walking, taking in the scene around him.

"Keep moving!" barked one of the American soldiers, prodding Otto in the back with the barrel of his rifle.

Otto swallowed hard and focused on putting one foot in front of the other. He couldn't afford to let any apprehension show; he had to be strong for Aafke. She needed him now more than ever.

"Where are you taking us?" Aafke asked in English, her voice trembling slightly. She glanced at Otto, her blue eyes filled with concern, before turning back to the soldier.

"Separate interrogation rooms," the soldier replied gruffly. "No talking."

"Please," Otto said, struggling to keep his own voice steady. "Let Aafke stay with me. She doesn't know anything."

"Silence!" The soldier shoved Otto forward, causing him to stumble and nearly fall on the icy ground. Aafke reached out to steady him, but the soldier pulled her back, separating them by force.

"Otto, please," Aafke whispered, her eyes pleading. "Don't let them take me away from you."

"I won't let anything happen to you," Otto promised, his heart breaking at the desperation in her voice. "I swear it, Aafke."

They reached one of the buildings, a brick structure, one

story with a single, long corridor down the middle. Their captors forced them apart, marching Otto inside while Aafke was being moved to another of the buildings. The interrogation room was small and dimly lit, the only source of light coming from a single, flickering bulb hanging overhead. A table and two chairs sat in the center.

"Sit down," ordered the soldier who had brought Otto in.

Otto obeyed, lowering himself into the uncomfortable metal chair, feeling its coldness seeping through the thin fabric of his clothes. His heart pounded in his chest as he stared at the barren walls, trying to quell the rising panic within him.

He wondered how Aafke was faring in her own interrogation room, praying that she was as strong and resourceful as he knew her to be. He wished he could be with her, holding her hand and reassuring her that everything would be all right. But for now, he had to face this trial alone.

The door to the room swung open, and a man in a crisp American Army uniform stepped inside. He was a tall, imposing figure with a chiseled jawline and steely gray eyes that seemed to pierce straight into Otto's soul. He carried a folder under one arm, which he placed on the table before taking a seat opposite Otto.

"Mr. Berg," he began, his voice stern and unyielding. "I'm Captain Nicholas Varberg with OSS—the Office of Strategic Services. I've been sent here to question you. I'm sure you understand the gravity of your situation."

Otto clenched his fists beneath the table, fighting the urge to demand information about Aafke. Instead, he remained silent, fixing his gaze on Captain Varberg and waiting for him to continue.

"Let me be clear," Varberg said, leaning forward slightly. "You were caught wearing an American uniform—a crime which carries severe consequences, including the possibility of being shot."

Otto felt a shiver run down his spine at those words, but

held his ground, refusing to let fear overtake him. *What happens to me is secondary*, he thought, his mind racing with concern for Aafke. *She must be protected at all costs.*

Varberg opened the folder, reviewing its contents. "You also are wanted by the Dutch government for the murder of two prominent resistance leaders."

"There's a lot more to that story, if you'll let me explain."

"You'll have a chance to respond. But I'm not finished. Lastly," he said, flipping another page, "we believe you are The Demon."

"The Demon?"

"The member of Skorzeny's commando group who murdered a squad of Americans during the Battle of the Bulge. You fit the description given to us by the only surviving member." Varberg looked down, moving his finger along the page. "Here it is: 'A mountain of a man, blond, pale skin. He was wounded in the eye, the leg, and shot twice in the back, but he kept on coming like some sort of machine.'"

Otto didn't answer, but looked at the table, wondering what he was going to do.

"And this description from a doctor at one of our field hospitals: 'The German spy was posing as a wounded American prisoner. He was a massive specimen, well over six feet tall, with wounds to his eye, his left leg, and shot twice through the back, with the wounds exiting out of his chest. He escaped out of our hospital just as American MPs arrived to apprehend him, potentially assisted by Nurse Shelle Singer, who is under questioning as well.'"

"I don't understand the reference to The Demon."

"That's the nickname that developed after the battle for this ghost of a man. This monster who can kill a dozen men, but who can't be killed himself." Varberg looked him up and down. "In other words, for you. So, what do you have to say for yourself, Sergeant Berg of Skorzeny's commando group?"

Otto knew there was no point in lying. "It's all true," he said. "I was responsible for the killing of those two Dutchmen. But Aafke had nothing to do with that," he said. "She was a member of the resistance group, an innocent."

"Yes, we know. But she was carrying your son by all accounts."

"That's a lie. The child was Arno's."

"Explain what that means."

Otto told the whole story about Arno's relationship with Aafke, the pregnancy, everything he knew. "She told me that she was luring Nazis to their death. But you will have to ask her more about that. She's a hero for your side. She has done nothing wrong."

"Then why is she here with you?"

Otto explained that too.

"I see. Fascinating, if it isn't made up lock, stock, and barrel. And what about this American squad?"

"They came on me in the forest. I asked them to leave me alone, but they refused, so I shot them."

"You shot them?"

"*Ja*, with a pistol."

"You shot twelve men with a pistol?"

"And one grenade. But I didn't do anything wrong. They were the enemy. It was war."

"In a battle where you wore the uniform of an American. An offense, let me remind you, that is punishable by death. They've already shot a number of your comrades who were caught, by the way."

Otto hadn't known that. He nodded. "That's too bad. They were good men, good comrades."

Varberg rose, checking his watch. "I'm going to take a break. It's been three hours. I'll have some dinner brought your way." He looked back at Otto as he left. "I still don't know what I'm going to do with you, Otto. Do you need anything else?"

Otto shook his head. The captain left and an orderly arrived a few minutes later, bringing a tray of hot food. Otto dug in immediately. He hadn't eaten in nearly twenty-four hours. The Dutch police hadn't starved them, but they'd given them barely enough to get by on. He finished his meal and then stood, limping around the small room to try to get his circulation going again.

Captain Varberg returned an hour later. He brought two cups of coffee, one for him and one for Otto. He also offered Otto a cigarette, which was gratefully received. "I spoke with my fellow interrogator and your story matches perfectly with the one we obtained from Aafke. I also learned a lot more about her operations in Eindhoven and about Arno. I've radioed into the police to pull in Joelle. If her story matches yours, then Aafke will be in the clear. Although I don't know if she'll ever be able to convince the people of Eindhoven of the same. Arno is a hero of the resistance there, and Aafke a well-known collaborator."

"That's not true."

"You might be right, Otto. But truth and the perception of reality don't always match. And people cling to easy explanations. Nobody wants to know that a Dutch woman who fell in love with a Nazi is the hero of the story, and their beloved resistance leader is the villain. My opinion is she can never go back to Eindhoven."

Otto nodded. "I agree."

"Then where does she go?"

"That depends."

"On what?"

"On whether I leave here in a car or a coffin."

Varberg nodded. "Fair enough. I'm trying to decide that myself. I'm having a cot brought in for you. There are some more things I want to check out before I can give you a decision. Try to get some sleep." With that, the captain rose and left the room again.

Otto spent that night tossing and turning on the cot. He wasn't so concerned about what was going to happen to him. He suspected they would kill him in the end. But he was terribly worried for Aafke. If he were executed, where would she go? What could she do? Perhaps they would let him get a letter to his mother. He knew she would take care of Aafke, would welcome her and her future child into her home. But would Aafke want to live in Germany by herself, without him? He wasn't sure. Perhaps she could find another place in the Netherlands to live. No, he realized. No matter where she went, her past would eventually catch up with her. It was his fault, he realized. By caring for her, by checking on her, he had made her a pariah to her people. Otto prayed that some miracle would happen, that there would be a way out for her.

Varberg returned the next morning with a thicker file. He sat down across the table from Otto and stared at him for long moments. Finally he opened the file and scanned the contents.

"What is that?" Otto asked.

"Some interesting information we retrieved from SS headquarters in Eindhoven. This is a file related to you. Impressive war record, top medals, but surprise, surprise, you were tried by court-martial for disobeying orders and nearly shot. Tried because you questioned the shooting of English prisoners of war. And later, a Lieutenant Colonel Fritz Geier, the head of the Eindhoven Gestapo, who you apparently knew, tried to recruit you to serve with him. He reports that you refused, and called into question the conduct of the war, and the treatment of Jews and civilians." Varberg raised an eyebrow. "This hardly seems the conduct of someone who would go around murdering squads of Americans for fun."

"I served with my comrades. I did my duty."

"You did. But you also did something almost nobody else under Hitler did: You questioned what was going on. You refused orders. You put your life on the line for your beliefs."

Captain Varberg leaned forward and scrutinized Otto's face

for a moment, as if searching for any hint of deception. Finally, he spoke again. "Your connections within the commando community could be valuable to us," he said slowly, a calculating expression on his face.

"What do you mean?"

"I mean, Sergeant Berg, that I would like to hire you."

Otto shook his head. "I can't fight against Germany, against Germans."

"Of course not. At least not *all* Germans."

"What do you mean?"

"I propose that I set you and Aafke free. I'll get you a proper uniform and you can return to Munich. To your home."

"I'll be fighting you again in a week," said Otto. "The SS—"

"Won't have a use for a one-eyed, badly wounded soldier," said Varberg. "Besides, you probably don't know but the war is practically over. We're at the Rhine and the Russians are closing in on Berlin. Hitler's regime is measured in weeks, perhaps a few months at the most."

"Then what would you want from me?" asked Otto. "Why can't I just go home and you leave me alone?"

"Because there's hell to pay for that squad," said Varberg. "I can't let you off for free, even if I wanted to. If I turned you over to the regular army they'd have you up against a wall before you could snap your fingers. But on the other hand, if you're hired by the US government, you'll be untouchable."

"For what?"

"I'm not sure of everything yet. But I have some ideas. When the war is over, we are going to have to occupy Germany. You have contacts in the Munich area, and in the SS. You can keep an eye on things and pass on anything relevant. Anything about guerilla units or such."

"I won't fight Germans."

"I won't expect you to. Again, like I said, at least not the average man. But Otto, what about the killers? What about the men who orchestrated the mass murder of Jews? The ones who shot American and English prisoners of war? We will want those men for justice. And they are not your countrymen, they are villains, just like Arno."

Otto thought for long moments and finally nodded. "*Ja*, I can help with that."

"You won't tell anyone you work with the government. I want you to reconnect with your comrades from Skorzeny's unit. The local ones. We will purchase some property and you can suggest building a group of homes for your friends. I don't want you to spy on them. I know how you feel about comrades. But that will give you even more legitimacy in the postwar community. From there, we will contact you as needed for any special things we want handled. Do you know how to use a sniper rifle?"

Otto thought back to his training with long-distance shooting, and to several operations he'd been involved in. "*Ja*, I can operate that rifle."

"Good. There won't be any work for months." Varberg pulled out an envelope. "Here is ten thousand dollars in cash— a little in Reichsmarks and the rest in dollars. Use this to get by for a few months, then when the war is over and the dust settles, use the dollars to purchase the property. There will be more money here and there as needed, for operational expenses and payment for services rendered. I don't want you to get a regular job. We'll need you ready at a moment's notice."

"Can I bring my mother?"

Varberg's eyes widened. "On operations?"

Otto smiled. "No, to the new house?"

"Of course. Your mother, Aafke, the child. We want you to have a legitimate family, a legitimate future."

"Agreed. I'll do it. But two more conditions."

"Yes?"

"I want any investigation of Nurse Singer to stop immediately."

"So, you're saying she did help you?"

"Immediately."

Varberg hesitated. "Done. And?"

"And I want Aafke brought to me here and now."

Varberg laughed. "That's much easier to swallow. Done and done." He stood and extended his hand. Otto took it. "You'll be doing great work for us," he said. "And believe it or not, for Germany. We don't want an end to your nation, Otto, we just want Hitler gone. We'll need a strong Germany soon enough."

"The Russians?"

"Yes, the Russians."

"I've got experience there as well."

"We know. Another factor in our calculations. I'll be in contact soon, Otto. For now, I'll leave you to some time with Aafke. I wish there was a proper bedroom we could give you."

"We don't sleep together."

"What?"

"We're not married."

Varberg nodded. "My kind of man, Otto. We'll work well together. So, I guess it's a car instead of a coffin. Is that correct?"

"That's correct."

"I wish you had served with me as a soldier, Otto. I could have used more men like you."

"We'll get our chance."

"I won't order you to do anything your conscience objects to."

Otto nodded. "If you do, I won't do it."

Varberg laughed. "Your file seems to validate that. That's fine. You get settled in Munich and take care of business with Aafke and the baby. We'll wrap things up in the next month or so with the war and then when we are all done, I'll come looking for you. I think it will be at least six months. So for now, forget me, forget the war. But don't forget forever. And don't take off on me. That would go very poorly for you."

"You'd never find me," said Otto. "I'm invisible."

Varberg looked at the huge man and laughed. "You are

many things, Otto, but I don't think invisible is one of them."
He took Otto's hand again and shook it firmly. He motioned
behind him and a sergeant stepped into the room, he was mid-
sized and dark complexioned, looking to be a Pacific Islander—
Hawaiian or Samoan perhaps.

"This is Sergeant de Soto," said Varberg. "He's been a tank
commander, but we've recruited him for special operations.
When you're ready, he'll take you and Aafke wherever you
want to go. Within our lines, of course."

Otto nodded. "Nice to meet you. Where are you from?"

"Samoa, but I was adopted as a baby. I grew up north of
Seattle with my folks and my sister and brother."

"How did you end up in tanks?"

"I've always loved tanks. Since I was a boy. Do you have any
experience with your panzer tank?"

Otto grunted. "A little. I've ridden on one into an operation."

"It's the best tank out there."

"They all go boom. Nice to meet you, Sergeant."

"You too. I'm excited to talk to you about your German
tanks. My favorite subject." The sergeant beamed. "When you're
ready, I'll be waiting for you."

A few minutes later, the door opened again and Aafke was
there. She flew into his arms, holding him tight. Otto had never
held her before, and he felt an electric thrill coursing through
his body. "Are you all right?" he asked. "Did they treat you
well?"

"Very well," she said. "At first, they were pretty aggressive
with their questions but after I got my story out, and they compared notes, their whole demeanor changed. They also took me
to the doctor and checked everything out."

"Is the baby all right?"

"Everything is perfect. And they gave me vitamins too. Something I couldn't get in Eindhoven."

"That's such a relief."

"Captain Varberg's assistant, Ann McNeil, just came and saw me. She said he'd worked out a deal with you and they are going to let us go to your home to Germany? Is that correct?"

Otto nodded.

"She was very nice. She told me a little about herself. She lives in the west coast of the US, up near Canada. She's married to a fighter pilot named Blaine, who's some kind of hotshot. And she's a teacher. But she wanted to be closer to her husband. He's stationed nearby, so she volunteered to serve and was assigned to Captain Varberg."

Otto grunted. "That's nice. Nice to know people still have normal lives. Maybe with the deal I made, we can too."

"I hope you're not doing something just for me?"

"No. But it is also for you. Captain Varberg didn't ask of me more than I could give. I'm going to help him, but I won't have to betray my beliefs, or my close comrades. But what about you, Aafke? You've been swept up in this. You have the right to go anywhere you want. Even to America, I'm sure. I could make that part of the deal. You could start a new life in a new place."

"What do you mean?" she asked.

"I don't want you to feel forced to go with me, just because of the war, or what's happened."

She put her arms around him again and rested her head against his chest. "I'm not going anywhere except with you."

"What about your father?"

"He can rot in Eindhoven. I'm leaving the past behind. I don't want my child to know him."

"And we'll be married?"

She looked up at him. "And we'll be married."

"Today?"

She took both his hands in hers. "Today."

"*Gut.*"

"Oh, Otto, I don't know what I would do without you!"

"And me without you. And we have our child to raise."

"Can you truly see this child as yours, Otto?"

He nodded. "We'll never speak of another story again. This is our child, and the past is forgotten."

"I'll bring you more children, Otto, I promise."

"We shall see, but this one is mine from now on, no matter what."

She pulled him down to her and kissed him on the lips. He held her against him for long minutes, tears falling down his cheeks. They moved to the cot and sat there together, sharing a blanket for warmth, talking about their past, their childhoods, everything. And when dawn came, the door opened, and they started their future together, a future that would last to the end of their lives.

Author's Notes on Historical Figures/Events

The Netherlands During World War II

The Netherlands suffered terribly during the war. During the previous war (World War I), the nation was circumvented by the Germans and the Netherlands was neutral. The government and people clung to the same hope in May 1940, but such was not to be the case. The Germans stormed through on May 10, defeating the meager Dutch army in a few days. The first mass bombing of a city occurred on May 14 in the city of Rotterdam, resulting in mass casualties. The Dutch government surrendered shortly thereafter and the queen fled to England, a move that was resented by many Dutch citizens.

Thus began almost five years of occupation by the Germans. Conditions were difficult from the first, because much of the food produced in the Netherlands and other occupied countries was transported to Germany so that the Führer's people wouldn't suffer privations. Large numbers of prisoners of war were also moved to Germany to perform slave labor.

Creating additional problems for the citizens was a robust fascist movement. Never by any means in the majority, there was a segment of the Dutch population that supported Hitler, even before the invasion, and served the German government during the occupation. This created dissension in what would have otherwise been a unified opposition.

The resistance in the Netherlands was significant throughout the war. The individual groups were constantly hunted by the Gestapo, and many were betrayed by spies and informants, but they carried out important work including the assassinations of prominent Nazis, hiding Jews, blowing up supplies and operational centers, and hiding Allied pilots shot down over the Netherlands. It is very important to note that within this book, Arno, a fictional character and resistance leader, is portrayed as a scheming narcissist. While bad actors exist in every country, and every situation, this is not to any way impinge on the heroic Dutch Resistance during World War II, which deserves nothing but praise and honor.

The Jews of the Netherlands suffered an even worse fate than the average Dutch citizen. There were approximately 150,000 Jews living in the Netherlands at the time of the German invasion. By the end of the war, there were only 35,000 alive. Over a hundred thousand had been shot outright, starved or died of disease in local camps, or were transported into death camps like Auschwitz in the East and murdered. In Eindhoven, there were 866 Jews in 1941; 332 of them were killed by the Nazis during the war.

The Eindhoven Dating Club

Although the characters in this book are fictional, the Eindhoven Dating Club is inspired by the true story of Hannie Schaft and sisters Truus and Freddie Oversteegen, who lured Nazis under the pretense of seduction to secure locations where they could be interrogated or assassinated.

The true story is a fascinating read, and an excellent book about this event is *Three Ordinary Girls* by Tim Brady.

Heinrich Himmler and the SS

The Schutzstaffel or "Protection Squad" was a private organization within Germany headed by the Reichsführer, Heinrich Himmler. It began as a group of volunteers that provided security for meeting. Over time, the unit took over protection for Adolf Hitler, and became his private group of elite men who could be counted on above all others.

The SS grew with Hitler's powers, infiltrating every part of German life. There was a police branch, the Gestapo; a military branch, the Waffen-SS; a foreign-service branch, intelligence branch; and other shadow departments that mirrored just about every branch of the German government.

The SS is best known for two insidious elements. The first is the Gestapo, the secret police of the Nazi regime. They were not only involved in investigating "undesirables" within Germany but the unit also wielded vast powers in the occupied territories as the war went on. The Gestapo was heavily involved in the rounding up of the Jewish populations throughout Europe, and facilitated their transport east and eventual liquidation.

The most infamous branch of the SS consisted of the units running the concentration camps. The SS essentially organized and implemented Hitler's Final Solution of the European Jews. The SS constructed dozens of camps throughout Central and Eastern Europe, the most famous of which was Auschwitz-Birkenau. These camps were designed for labor, but ultimately to liquidate the Jewish population and others within Europe including Jehovah's Witnesses, homosexuals, Roma people, and Russian prisoners of war.

The Waffen-SS, the military branch of the SS, was more of a traditional fighting unit. This was the unit that Otto belonged to. They were known for their training, their loyalty to Hitler, and their ferocity in battle. That said, there were notable instances of atrocities committed by the Waffen-SS, including the outright shooting of prisoners such as was illustrated here.

Otto, as a member of the Waffen-SS, faced these very issues. Very few members reacted as he did. Most finished the war still as strongly devoted to Hitler as they were at the outset, regretting only that Germany lost the war. The SS officers created a secret society, Odessa, which assisted in hiding notable SS members and in many cases secreting them to other countries, primarily in South America. The US government was not only aware of Odessa, but at times interacted with their members for intelligence and other reasons, as the focus at the end of the war quickly turned away from Germany and toward the cold war with Russia.

Operation Market Garden

Operation Market Garden was an invasion of the Netherlands engineered by Field Marshal Montgomery from September 17 to September 27, 1944. The purpose of the plan was to use the flat spaces of Holland to attack by air and on land and to achieve a dramatic breakthrough that would serve as a gateway to Germany.

The Market portion of the plan was designed to seize nine bridges over various rivers that would lead to the Lower Rhine River and give the allies access to Germany. The Garden portion of the plan was designed to rush British land forces over those bridges and across Holland as quickly as possible.

Forty-one thousand paratroopers from the US and Britain landed in the Netherlands on Sunday, September 17. The operation went smoothly and they quickly seized bridges and towns, including Eindhoven. However, the operation failed to capture the bridge over the Rhine at Arnhem. The Germans then began a significant counteroffensive that cost the Allies thousands of casualties (killed, wounded, and captured), along with the loss of equipment.

The operation, if successful, might have ended the war in 1944. Instead, the Allies would fight on into 1945, and suffer significant additional casualties, especially at the German counteroffensive in the Battle of the Bulge.

That said, the Allies did hold on to one-fifth of the Netherlands, including Eindhoven. The rest of the country would not be liberated until the end of the war, in May 1945.

Otto Skorzeny and His Commandos

Otto Berg is a fictional character, but his commando group is not. Otto Skorzeny was one of the most colorful people in World War II. He served in the military branch of the SS, the Waffen-SS, and was involved in a number of significant special operations during World War II.

Skorzeny and his forces rescued the Italian dictator Benito Mussolini in 1943, after he was deposed and held by Italian partisans. Skorzeny executed a daring airborne raid with gliders that landed in a tight area in the mountains.

Perhaps his most famous—or infamous—action was Operation Greif during the Battle of the Bulge in December 1944. Otto participates in this action in the book. Skorzeny sent a group of English-speaking soldiers in American uniforms to infiltrate the Allied lines during the German offensive and sow chaos. Although only a few dozen men were involved, the operation had the intended effect, with rumors flying about their intentions, and men and supplies held up at checkpoints where nervous soldiers would quiz men about Hollywood stars and sporting events, trying to ferret out the Germans.

Twenty-three of his men were captured, and eighteen of them were shot as spies. Skorzeny was tried as a war criminal for Operation Greif and spent several years in prison. He escaped from a US camp in Darmstadt and hid for a while with the assistance of other former Nazis.

Skorzeny later assisted the military in Egypt and allegedly

354 *Author's Notes*

advised President Juan Perón in Argentina. He may also have worked for the Israeli secret service, Mossad. Szorzeny's life after World War II is illustrative of the complex web of alliances and approaches after the war, where he was first tried, then escaped, then lived first in hiding and then essentially in the open. After that, he served as an advisor for a number of countries, some of whom were enemies of each other.

Aafke Cruyssen

Aafke Cruyssen is a fictional character but representative of a common experience in Occupied Europe during World War II. She had to decide whether she would support the Nazis, live as a passive witness trying to survive, or to resist. She chose resistance, and risked her life in numerous operations.

But her experience had a twist, because she was faced with the reality that is so true of the world that we live in, that not every person on the good side is "good" and not everyone on the bad side is "bad."

Aafke and her friends, Maaike and Joelle, also suffered gender prejudice, having to fight doubly hard to earn a place in the resistance movement. And Aafke's pregnancy, Arno's reaction, and the ease with which the people turned on her illustrates the layers of additional problems present for women of the time, and that still exist, perhaps to a lesser degree, today.

Otto Berg

Otto Berg, also a fictional character, represents many in Germany who questioned the actions and policies of Adolf Hitler. He went beyond this, however, when few others did. He revolted. He refused to follow orders and ultimately deserted, choosing to work with the Americans at the end of the war and after. There were others, real people. The members of the White Rose Resistance. Pastor and theologian Dietrich Bonhoeffer. The military generals who revolted in 1944 and attempted to